THE ZOMBIE PRINCIPLE

BY

David R. Vosburgh and Daniel J. Pinkham

All rights reserved
Copyright 2013
Number Five Publishing LLC
146 Pedersen Ridge Rd
Milford, Pa 18337

ISBN: 978-0-9913393-2-7

PROLOGUE

The old proverb states that, "the road to hell is paved with good intentions." If only humanity would have learned to heed that warning, things may have gone differently. In early 2021 an elaborate cave system was discovered in the depths of the Amazon River rainforest. Located near the famed Jumandi caves near the town of Tena in the Napo Province of Ecuador, it had remained undiscovered by humans, until now. It appeared to have been created by an underwater river system similar to the one discovered in Brazil in 2011. It was in this cave that scientists made a startling discovery; an ancient bacterium unlike anything modern science had ever encountered.

A small collection laboratory was quickly built near the discovery site. Samples were collected, labeled, and categorized based on where they were unearthed in the cave.

The samples were then transported to a secret research facility in Southern Florida. A group of top scientists from around the globe, each with a particular specialization, were called in to study and document the amazing find. At the insistence of the donors funding the project, it was decided that secrecy was best for the safety and security of everyone involved. The scientists really had no idea what they were dealing with, so the strain was simply referred to by the code name: The Principle. Unsure how to proceed; each scientist was given time to study the bacteria and present their findings. A few became frustrated and left. Others presented their ideas with all the conviction of a bad poker player. After several years of trial and error which yielded underwhelming results, an interesting discovery was made.

Dr. Lemuel Sanderson, a noted neurologist specializing in neurodegeneration diseases (Alzheimer's, Parkinson's, and ALS) and severe brain trauma, noticed a slight similarity to Levodopa, a drug commonly used to treat Parkinson's disease. Under his supervision, the few remaining scientists and research assistants began conducting tests with lab rats as subjects. Initial results were disappointing. The rodents seemed unaffected by the bacteria. Different doses and combinations were tried. Finally in the delta test group a breakthrough was achieved, several subjects seemed to have improved cognitive ability. They were able to solve simple problems or obstacles put before them by the researchers.

Through his connections with the Brain Research Centre in Vancouver, British Columbia, Dr. Sanderson was able to obtain volunteers for the experimental procedures he was planning next. These were unfortunate individuals suffering from late stage dementia, advanced Alzheimer's, ALS, and several patients with traumatic brain injuries. With little to lose, these patients and their families were willing to try anything to get better.

The patients were given individual doses of varying amounts. At first, nothing happened. Then in the echo test group, subject number five awoke from a long slumber and not only could remember his name but knew the names of the research staff, the particular day of the week and the name of his second grade teacher. Photos were shown to him of his family members whom he recognized immediately. The results were astonishing.

Soon after, others were starting to show similar results, all except those suffering from ALS. The bacteria seemed to have little to no effect on them. These ALS patients were soon returned to the care of their former physicians. Those suffering from Alzheimer's disease and dementia, however, made amazing strides. It was as if something had awakened from deep inside them, something with great patience; something willing to wait in a dark cave for a millennium to be discovered.

Largely forgotten by a fickle populous, the small research team now operated in anonymity. What was once front page news was now merely an interesting footnote in history. The lack of progress had bored the general public. They couldn't care less what was happening in that laboratory in the Florida Everglades. That, however, was about to change.

Chapter 1
Numbcr 5

Test subject Number 5 had arrived eight months earlier, the victim of a horrific auto accident which left him in a deep coma. Number 5 was completely unresponsive and showed very little sign of brain activity. Three months after introducing the bacteria into Number 5's brain stem, the first sign of improvement was observed. As the weeks progressed and the dosages increased the brain became more active. Three weeks ago Number 5's brain had been repaired to a point where he awoke from the coma. Beyond just waking, Number 5 had regained his full memory and had regained full use of his body. Surprisingly there was no muscle atrophy as would normally be the case in a person waking from a lengthy coma. As Number 5 was observed and put through tests, the scientists discovered that the bacteria was no longer confined just to the brain; but had traveled down the spinal column and into the nervous system, slowly spreading throughout the entire body. Outwardly Number 5 looked and acted normal but inside his body, he was undergoing something that none of the scientists could explain.

As the automatic glass door slid shut and sealed behind Dr. Sanderson he could not help but turn his nose up at the smell. He had been a doctor for 25 years and would never get accustomed to the sterile smell of a medical lab. It was a long, fairly narrow room with a rectangular table, or work bench, in the center of the room. Smaller benches were located on either side. In the near corner was a refrigerator with cabinets above it containing supplies, most notably, test tubes. An incubator was located in the far corner and scattered throughout the room you could see a scanning electron microscope, cell counters, centrifuges, and micro-plate readers. At the far end of the lab, a Plexiglas window looked into a medical ward. A keypad secured door separating the ward from the lab was next to the window.

Seeing his young lab assistant, Keith, in the corner sitting on one of the many stools in the lab and working with the light florescent microscope, Dr. Sanderson cleared his throat.

"Any new developments with test subject Number 5?" he asked picking up a nearby chart.

Given a small start, the young assistant adjusted his glasses and replied, "Just more of the same boss, and it's starting to creep me out. It's just not normal."

"What about any of this is normal? It is not every day you find an ancient bacteria that has been lying dormant in an unexplored cave, that just happens to have miraculous healing powers in the human brain," replied Dr. Sanderson with a smile.

"That's not what I'm talking about boss. It's just the way they look at you sometimes. It's like looking into the eyes of something that's not really there, something dead … like a zombie."

"Come on Keith, that's ridiculous, you used to work for the CDC, so you know there is no bacteria or virus that can reanimate dead tissue. I simply think the patients sometimes get lost in all the memories they can finally remember. There has got to be a lot going on in their minds that we don't even know about."

"You're probably right Doc, but it still gives me the creeps," Keith said rolling his chair over to the computer.

Keith was short, with wide brimmed glasses, and an overactive imagination. He had come highly recommend to Dr. Sanderson from the CDC for his work with clinical trials. He was now Dr. Sanderson's go to guy for test results and observation records.

As Keith cycled through the camera feeds on the monitor he said, "Number 5 is the oddest of all. Ever since he woke up something seems different with them all. It's probably just me though; I haven't been above ground in 4 months now. I think it's time for a vacation, boss."

"You'll get your vacation after we present our findings to the World Health Organization, unless we need you to clean this place up once we are done with the tests," Dr. Sanderson said with a chuckle. "By the way where is John? I thought you two were on the night shift?"

"Where do you think he is boss? He says he's sick again but I'm telling you he snuck out to the local watering hole and he's just hung over again."

"You sound jealous Keith."

"Laugh all you want, but look who showed up for work."

"And that's why you're in charge."

"Whatever you say, boss, how about you keep me company tonight?"

"Yeah, that's not gonna happen. I've got a conference call with our benefactor, and then I need some sleep. Tell you what I'll do, on the way back to my quarters, I'll stop by John's room and see if he's really sick. Maybe I can persuade him to come down and keep you company. If not, you'll be fine on your own. But if you run into trouble you can give me a call. I might be able to drag myself down here and give you a hand."

Dr. Sanderson gave one more look to the computer monitor and put the chart back, then turned to leave. "Night Keith, I'll see you in the morning."

"Yeah, see you in the morning," Keith said as the automatic glass door slid shut behind the Doctor.

After he was sure the Doctor was gone, Keith rolled over to the mini fridge across the room and pulled out a soda and a microwave pizza. Opening the small microwave he put in the pizza and turned it on. Putting his feet up on the computer desk he pulled out his book reader and turned it on.

"I don't even know why we have to have a night shift. All the test subjects do is sleep, they don't even look like they dream, they just lay there," Keith mumbled to himself. He did not need to check up on the subjects for another hour so for now he would engage in his favorite activity at work, getting paid to read sci-fi books.

Keith's head jerked back and he almost fell out of his chair. His book reader lay on the floor alongside his empty soda can. Franticly looking at the clock Keith realized, to his horror, that he had fallen asleep for the better part of four hours. Quickly waking his computer, he began to switch through the test subjects video feeds. To his dismay every image he brought up was the same. The test subjects lay just as they had every night before, however, the vitals that accompanied the image showed that every test subject had flat lined. He typed away furiously on his computer bringing up the full real-time vitals of each test subject. It was all the same, each test subject was clinically dead.

"The one night I actually fall asleep at this job and everything goes wrong," he thought.

Picking up the nearby phone Keith dialed Dr. Sanderson's number. Nine agonizingly long rings later a very groggy Dr. Sanderson answered the phone, "…um ... hello ..."

"I'm sorry boss, I didn't mean to fall asleep, I really didn't. I was just reading and nothing ever goes wrong and -"

"Whoa, slow down Keith, what time is it?"

"I … I ... don't know, it's almost 2 in the morning. You've got to get down here boss."

"Alright, alright, Keith take it easy. Let me just wake up. What happened?"

In a rush of words Keith explained what he had discovered. By the time he finished talking Dr. Sanderson was fully awake and in a small state of panic.

"OK Keith, let me get dressed and I'll be right down. Have you run a diagnostics test on the computers?"

"Of course, the computers are working fine. They are all dead. I'll go in and physically check them myself."

"Alright, I'll be there in about 20 minutes. It's going to be OK."

Keith hung up the phone and rushed to the door separating the lab from the test subject's quarters. Hurriedly, he punched in the combination into the keypad. With a hiss the door slid open. Grabbing the crash cart next to the door Keith wheeled it into the medical ward where the test subjects lay, apparently dead. Going from bed to bed Keith checked the monitors only to discover there were no errors, everything was functioning properly.

Keith checked his watch anxiously counting the minutes before Dr. Sanderson would arrive. *"He'll know what to do, he always knows what to do,"* he thought frantically.

Moving from bed to bed Keith checked for signs of breathing or a pulse from the test subjects, each of which remained unresponsive. Rushing back into the lab he grabbed the medical kit and brought it back into the ward. Setting it down on the crash cart Keith opened it and then stopped realizing there was nothing he could do.

Sinking to the floor with his head in hands Keith thought, *"There's nothing I can do. I cannot just bring the dead back to life. It's all my fault, I fell asleep and they died. It's as simple as that."*

Keith was startled out of his thoughts by what sounded like a cough. Looking toward the lab, it did not appear that Dr. Sanderson had arrived yet. Slowly standing, Keith looked down the line of patients, his eyes settling on Test Subject Number 5 who again let out a strangled cough. Rushing to his side Keith checked for a pulse but strangely felt nothing. None of the monitors showed any signs of life. In fact, Keith could not detect any respiratory activity from Number 5. As he began to check the machines again Number 5 let out another ragged cough, but this time his eyes sprung open.

Before Keith had a chance to process this development, he heard the same guttural coughs coming from the other nine test subjects around him. Making the rounds again to each bed he could detect no signs of life from any of the subjects. Somehow they all continued to cough and one by one their eyes opened. Unnerved and completely confused, Keith made his way to the far end of the room to hit the reset button for all the diagnostic machines. The lights dimmed as all the machines turned off and then back on again.

When Keith turned back around he was surprised to see Number 5 standing next to his bed staring at him. It was the same stare that Dr. Sanderson attributed to the subjects being lost in thought, the same one that gave him the creeps. In fact, by this time, each of the other nine test subjects had begun to get up and stand beside their beds. Each turned to stare at Keith with vacant eyes.

"Hey … are … are you guys ok? What's … ah … going on?" Keith stammered.

As if in response, Number 5 made a sound like a moan and cough combined. Then all 10 test subjects started stiffly moving towards Keith.

Putting his hands up Keith managed to say "Whoa hold up there. What are you guys doing? Dr. Sanderson will be here any minute."

His confusion quickly turned into fear as the patients drew closer. "Hey, wait don't touch me, what are you doing?"

Pressing his back to the wall, Keith tried to keep the test subjects at bay but they cornered him and were now grabbing for him. With the path to the door blocked, Keith tried to fight back but there were too many of them, each one grabbing at his arms, chest, and face.

"Stop it, I said stop it! Help, somebody help me! Somebody hel … mprhhh … mprhhh," Keith screamed in vain as Number 5 slowly and deliberately put a big cold hand over his mouth.

Keith let out another muffled cry as one of the patients bit into his arm and another into his leg. With one last adrenaline fuelled effort Keith pushed off from the wall toppling to the ground onto two of the test subjects, the others quickly piling on top of him. They began to claw and bite at Keith's clothes and body. The last thing Keith McFadden noticed before losing consciousness, as the test subjects began to tear into his flesh with their teeth, was that he had left the door to the lab open.

Chapter 2
The Students

"Another beautiful day in paradise," thought Stephen Russo sarcastically as he looked out his second floor bedroom window. *"The weather around here never changes; quite boring really."* It is said the easiest job in America is a weatherman in Southern California. *"It's another gorgeous day out there today ... over to you Tim with sports."* Stephen was hoping his upcoming trip to Six Flags amusement park would be a little less boring. Having just finished packing for the trip, he was antsy and ready to go.

His father traveled quite a bit for business when he was younger, before settling here in Anaheim. They would move every few years, requiring a new school, new friends, and a new house. On family vacations they would go to the nearest (or in some cases not so near) Six Flags park. Most likely born out of guilt for moving his family around so much, his father would ask him where he would like to go on vacation and little Stephen would scream "Six Flags!" So off they would go. They always had a great time and it became something of a family tradition. The family had, as a matter of fact, managed to see every one of the parks. Every one, that is, except the park outside of Washington DC. That would be where he was heading today. The difference this time was he was not going there with his family. He and some friends from school were making the trip.

Growing up in a family that moves a lot is not an easy thing. It can be very difficult on everyone, especially the children. Stephen found the best way to make new friends, as well as stay out of trouble, was to try out for sports when he got to a new school. "Try out for them all, you're bound to make at least one of them," was his motto. As it turns out he was pretty good at most of them, especially football. As he got older and stronger he started to attract attention of some college recruiters. He managed to spend his junior and senior years at Esperanza High School in Anaheim excelling at linebacker. Filling out a six foot two frame and weighing in at around two hundred thirty pounds, UCLA coach Tom Brennerman liked what he saw and offered him a scholarship to play there. Stephen accepted. Although things have not worked out as he would have liked on the playing field so far (he has been primarily a back-up and special teams player through his junior year), he made some great friends and received a free education. It was four of these friends that were going to accompany him on this trip to complete his quest of visiting every Six Flags in America.

"Honey, are you ready, I think Nick is here," his mother shouted from downstairs.

Denise Russo was an attractive woman in her mid-forties of solid mid-western stock. She met her husband at a Milwaukee Brewers game. She was there with a couple of girlfriends (one of them was dating the first baseman) and he was two rows in front of her sitting with his boss entertaining some business clients. A foul ball was hit in their direction and both went for it. They nearly collided with neither ending up with the ball. A conversation was struck and the rest, as they say, is history.

"Be down in a second," Stephen shouted back.

He grabbed his duffel bag and his Uni-phone. The Uni-phone was the latest and greatest in smart phone technology continuing man's never ending pursuit of the perfect handheld device. Heading downstairs Stephen threw his duffel in the foyer and went into the kitchen to grab a drink for the ride; the very long ride. They had all agreed to drive there; make it a real road trip. They planned on covering the 2,700 plus miles in three days. Each would take turns driving for the first 24 hours or so. That would put them somewhere near Memphis, Tennessee where they would spend the night. Then up early the next morning and on to Washington DC, arriving late where they would check into their hotel rooms and then hit the park first thing the next morning. No hotel reservations were made just in case the plans had to be altered. The return trip was more play it by ear as long as they are back by the 11th of June. Nick's summer job was set to begin on the 12th.

Stephen's mother was also in the kitchen taking some drinking glasses out of the dishwasher. "Have you got everything?" she asked.

"I think so."

"Did you grab your toothbrush out of the bathroom?"

"Yes," he said rolling his eyes. Mothers are all the same, always worried about things like packing underwear and bringing your toothbrush. They are never concerned about the important things; like having the right kind of music for the trip, or bringing enough snacks for everyone. He opened the refrigerator and grabbed a Vitamin Water, unscrewed the cap and took a big swig.

Stephen looked over at his mom where her attention was now fixed on the 36-inch TV recently installed into the kitchen wall just above the counter. She seemed very interested in whatever the woman on the TV was saying. Just then, the doorbell rang; his mother's gaze still on the TV.

"I'll get it," he said.

Stephen opened the door and standing there was Nicholas Van Arden. He was all of five-foot-seven and one hundred-sixty pounds. His skin was fair, especially for Southern California, and he had light brown hair that could be described as unkempt. A history major at UCLA, Nick was Stephen's best friend at school. They roomed together the first two years there. Nick was still living on campus while Stephen had moved in with a couple of other football players in some off campus housing.

Nick had required some serious convincing to go on this trip. He did not particularly like amusement parks as he has gotten sick on roller coasters and was not very fond of heights or traveling at high speeds. But, his father was the US Congressman representing the fine folks of the 40th congressional district so he did not get to see his dad that often. Nick thought he could swing by and say hi to the old man while he was in D.C. They were taking his car so they would have to go where he wanted anyway.

"You ready?" Nick blurted out as he walked past Stephen and into the foyer.

"Yeah, my bag's right there." Stephen said as he pointed to the duffel on the floor.

"I need to use the can before we go; the hatch on the car is open, you can throw your crap in the back." Nick, having been to the Russo residence a few times previously, headed straight for the bathroom.

Stephen returned to the kitchen to say goodbye to his mother and receive any last minute words of wisdom. As he entered he noticed she was still engrossed in what was on the TV. She was startled as he approached and turned to look at him. The look on her face was one of worry and confusion.

"Is everything alright Mom?"

"Have you heard about these strange reports of looting and vandalism in some cites back East?" his mother asked.

"No, not really, I had finals this week and have been getting ready for my trip. What's going on?" Stephen said.

"No one really knows. Reports are vague. There seems to be some looting and rioting going on in a lot of the cities back East. They think maybe something got into the water and people are acting weird … maybe you shouldn't go."

"It'll be fine, probably just some college kids blowing off some steam," Stephen tried to explain. His mother shot him a look; more precisely, the look.

"Not that we would ever engage in such behavior," Stephen answered trying to lighten the mood. He even added a wry smile. His mother was having none of it. She was clearly worried.

"I want you to call me every night so I know you're ok. Will you promise me that?" She said.

"Of course, no problem," he promised.

She hugged him tightly and kissed him on the cheek. He hugged her back.

"Tell Dad goodbye for me."

"I will. Behave yourself but more importantly, be careful."

"You got it Mom."

As Stephen turned around, Nick peered into the kitchen. "Hello Mrs. Russo," Nick said.

"Hello Nick. How are you?"

"Never better," Nick answered. Looking in Stephen's direction he said, "We ready?"

Denise Russo took a few steps toward them and said, "Have a good trip and take care of each other."

Stephen nodded, turned, and headed for the foyer. Nick followed and opened the front door. Stephen bent over, grabbed his duffel, and followed Nick out the door. His mother looked out the kitchen window and her gaze followed her son and his friend down the sidewalk toward Nick's car. Stephen turned around and glanced behind him. He caught his mother looking at them and offered a small wave. She gave a small wave in return. Turning back into the kitchen she grabbed the remote for the television to turn up the volume without possibly knowing that would be the last time she would ever see her son.

Once in the car, they headed toward the I-5 traveling south to Irvine to pick up the remainder of their group. They started off with the usual chit-chat and nervous excitement that begins any adventure but settled into listening to the hum of the tires on the highway pavement. Stephen began to drift off and could not help thinking about his mom and the worried look she had given him. She was genuinely frightened but did not want to come off as the over protective parent. He was sure she was overreacting. But still, he could not shake the feeling that she might be worried for good reason.

"Yo, dude, did you hear anything I just said," Nick blurted out jolting Stephen out of his trance.

"What?"

"I said do you have the address for the park so I can put it in the GPS?" Nick asked.

"Uh, yea … it's right here," said Stephen as he pulled a piece of paper out of his pants pocket. He read off the address to Nick.

The 2026 Hyundai Phoenix was all Nick's, passed down to him from his dad as he upgraded to a newer model. It was an early edition Sport Utility hybrid that had significantly improved ability to capture lost energy from braking and store that energy for later use, helping improve power and gas mileage. He loved this car.

"Where were you anyway, you totally zoned there for a minute," Nick asked.

"Nowhere, really, it was just my mom. She was telling me about this story she saw on the news, something about looting and other weird stuff happening back East. She seemed really freaked out. Have you heard anything?"

"No, nothing, I've been so busy the last few days preparing to cart your ass across this wonderful country of ours I haven't had time to catch up on recent events," Nick said.

"Did your mom say anything?" Stephen asked.

"My mom?!? For being married to a politician and raising a UCLA history major, she couldn't care less about current events," Nick said. He then added, "The one phrase I don't think I ever heard my mom say was 'do you know what I heard on the news today?'"

Stephen chuckled and felt a little more at ease. Maybe he was being a little over dramatic. He was on the verge of completing a great quest. What he needed to do was sit back, relax and enjoy the ride. At least until it was his turn to drive.

They arrived at the residence of Devendrakumar Patel a little after three in the afternoon. The pre-med major, who goes by "Dave," was waiting out front in the driveway along with his girlfriend, Emma Blackburn, and her friend Lucy Griffin and a fair amount of luggage. Stephen had phoned ahead to let them know they were on their way.

"How the heck am I going to fit all that in the back of the car," Nick shouted through the open car window, staring at the luggage.

"I guess you'll just have to manage because I'm not traveling across the country without the essentials," replied Emma.

Stephen and Nick got out of the car and headed toward the various bags strewn across the driveway. Stephen shook Dave's hand and gave him the universal "what's up" head nod. Dave was just shy of six feet tall and skinny as a rail. He had a dark complexion common for his race. His parents were from western India and had moved here before he was born making him a first generation American. Stephen and Dave met in an Intro to Biology class their freshman year. Stephen was required to take a science elective; all the cake courses were taken by the time he registered so he was forced to take Intro to Biology. His plan was to find someone who looked smart, sit next to them, and sponge as much information as possible; a standard jock trick.

He found Dave sitting by himself and saw an opportunity. As it turned out they had many things in common and became friends. Dave helped Stephen achieve a C+ in the class so he could continue playing football and their friendship was cemented.

Dave had met Emma later that freshman year as they kept bumping into each other in the science building. She was a nursing student and had to take some of the same introductory classes as the pre-med students. He was fond of her immediately. She had long dark hair and a medium build. But what really got him was her laugh. He loved to hear her laugh. She played a little hard to get at first, but he found out her favorite band was called "The Lowdown". When they came to Los Angeles, he snagged tickets before they sold out and invited her. She really wanted to go so she went and they have been together ever since. At first,

Dave's parents were not pleased with this arrangement. They were of a traditional Indian background and arranged marriages were the norm. However, it must be something about the relaxed nature of Southern California, as they finally relented.

The car was loaded and the travelers climbed into the car. Nick behind the wheel, Stephen riding shotgun. Dave sat in the back behind the passenger's seat with Emma in the center. Rounding out the group was Lucy sitting behind the driver's seat. The Phoenix actually had room for one more, at least that's what the owners' manual said, so the five of them fit comfortably.

Nick put the car in drive and headed toward I-15, the first leg of their trip; sort of the first step on the yellow brick road. The question was which one of them was the Tin Man or the Scarecrow, and how about the Cowardly Lion? And of course which of the girls was Dorothy? Perhaps time would tell. Would their adventure be fraught with the kind of peril those famous storybook characters had to endure? Of course not, what could possibly be worse than Flying Monkeys?

"I want to thank you for inviting me on this trip Stephen, I'm so excited," Lucy exclaimed.

Stephen was fiddling with Nick's Uni-phone as it was plugged into the car's stereo system. He was looking for a particular song to play, keeping in mind Nick's one standing rule: it was his car, so you listen to his music. That is not to say that he would not take requests for the sake of peace and harmony.

"Uh, you're welcome," Stephen replied.

Stephen had not actually invited her. When he was planning this trip his first invite was Nick, of course. He then mentioned it to Dave who jumped at the opportunity having never been to a Six Flags. Dave then asked if was ok to bring Emma; Stephen liked Emma and said sure. A few days before they left, Emma's best friend Lucy asked if she could go. So, Emma asked Dave to ask Stephen if it was all right.

Lucy and Emma have been friends since middle school. She came from a mixed household; her mother was Korean and her father Irish which explained her jet black hair and almond eyes and the last name Griffin. When they both decided to enroll at UCLA, Emma knew exactly what she wanted to study; Lucy on the other hand had no idea. She finally decided on a business major after hanging around all the students at UCLA whose families had money. She figured maybe a business degree would help get her get some of that money.

As they merged onto I-40 taking exit 184A heading toward Needles, Nick decided that it would be best if they limited the stops to make better time and that each of the guys would drive eight hour shifts. Not that he had anything against women drivers, it's just he didn't know them as well as he knew Stephen and Dave. As a matter of fact, if he could stay awake for the full 24 hours he would drive the whole way. This car was his baby after all.

Just before eleven PM they pulled into a rest stop just west of Holbrook, Arizona. It had a single building with rest rooms, a snack area and an information shack separate from the main building. A picnic area with tables and an area to walk dogs was situated off to the left. The highway sign said there was a gas station there but it was in fact about a mile and a half away. Nick decided to drop everyone off to use the facilities and he would go top off the gas tank and come back to pick them back up.

The place was deserted except for two tractor trailers at the far end of the parking lot. Both trucks had their engines running and were equipped with sleeper cabs. Everyone was out of the car and stretching as Nick drove off. The girls headed off for the restroom together. Stephen told Dave to go on ahead, he wanted to call his mom before she went off to bed, like he promised. He pushed the icon on his phone for his mom's phone and it started to ring and then abruptly stopped. Looking at his phone, it indicated a lost signal. Checking his reception it showed a weak signal but should have been strong enough to complete a call. He tried again with the same result. He decided to text her that he was fine and that he would call her tomorrow. That seemed to work. With his promise somewhat fulfilled, he headed off to the restroom.

After everyone had successfully relieved themselves, they met near the curb to await Nick. Emma reached into her purse and pulled out her phone and looked at it. She had a peculiar look on her face that no one except Stephen noticed.

"What's the matter?" Stephen asked glancing in Emma's direction.

"Not sure … I have part of a text from my dad."

"What's it say?" asked Dave.

"It says 'tried to call but kept getting disconnected … Just wanted …' then it ends," Emma answered.

"He probably just wanted to say goodnight," Dave reassured her.

"Yea, probably," Emma said.

Headlights from a car coming towards them diverted their attention from the cryptic text from Emma's dad. A few seconds later, Nick pulled up in front of them. He got out of the car and came around the front with the car still running.

"You're up," he said to Stephen. "Take good care of my baby."

Everyone piled into the car in the same seats as before with the exception of Stephen in the driver's seat and Nick in the unfamiliar role of riding shotgun in his own car.

"Anyone else hungry?" Nick asked as they got underway.

Neither Dave nor Emma was, but Lucy said she could go for a bite to eat. She reached behind the back seat and opened a small cooler that Nick had packed prior to picking Stephen up. She grabbed a small ham and cheese sandwich and handed Nick a tuna salad.

"Did you make these sandwiches Nick?" asked Lucy.

"No," he replied. "The guy at the deli did."

They all chuckled at that as Nick turned around to eat his tuna salad. Dave and Emma had begun to lean on each other and it was easy to see that sleep was not far off. Dave needed to rest anyway because he was driving next. As Stephen steered the car down I-40 passing through the town of Holbrook, he looked over at his friend in the passenger's seat and sensed something was wrong.

"You ok?" Stephen asked.

"I'm fine. Just a little tired I guess," Nick answered. "You need me to stay awake with you so we don't end up in a ditch somewhere?"

"Not necessary amigo … I got it all under control."

Lucy moved forward from the back seat and spoke softly so as not to disturb the sleeping lovebirds in the seats next to her.

"I'm wide awake, I'll make sure he stays on the road."

Nick looked at Stephen and then at Lucy and said with a knowing smile, "Sounds good to me," adding, "I'll be right over here if you need me."

Nick settled in and angled the seat back a little bit. He shifted slightly to get more comfortable. Surprisingly, sleep descended upon him quickly but before he nodded off he said quietly, "There was no one at the gas station."

"What?" Stephen said.

"There was no one at the gas station," he repeated. "There was no one working that I could see. There were no cars on the streets. I slid my debit card, pumped my gas, went to the restroom, and left and didn't see a sole. I know I was in a small town late at night but it was a little bit eerie."

"We are in the middle of the desert you know."

"I guess so," Nick replied as he drifted off to sleep.

Stephen drove on as the clock passed midnight and a new day was born. As he stared at the highway stretched out before him as far as the beams from the headlamps would allow, he realized that there were no headlights staring back at him from the other side of the road or any headlights in his rear view mirror. Come to think of it, he had not seen another car since he started driving.

There is only one rest area in the entire state of Texas on I-40 and it's just outside Amarillo. No gas, no food, no information

24

booth, just a bathroom and places to park. The sun had fully risen by the time Stephen had pulled the car into the parking lot and let his weary passengers out.

Despite her promise to stay awake with Stephen, Lucy had fallen asleep somewhere in New Mexico. Nick, however, had awakened at the Texas border and had helped him fight off sleep the last two hours. Everyone else started to stir when he put the car into park.

"Everyone out," Stephen announced.

"Smoke 'em if you got 'em," Nick added.

Actually, no one in their group smoked. This made for a smoother, cleaner ride. As a matter of fact, smoking among their peer group, had decreased dramatically over the last twenty years. This had, of course, been replaced with other addictions; namely, the Uni-phones. That is why they all agreed the shut them down for the trip. Forget about school, summer jobs, and other friends for the week and a half they would be together. Calls or texts to parents for any unforeseen emergencies would be allowed.

"Whose idea was it to drive all this way, anyway?" asked Emma.

"We all agreed," Stephen answered. "Your boyfriend is up next anyway, the faster he drives, the sooner we get to a hotel and a nice comfy bed."

Dave came up from behind her and picked her up at the waist and said, "Stop your whining."

She turned around and began playfully hitting him in the chest with her palms. "I'm not whining, I'm asking a question."

"We could strap you to the roof if you'd like more room," Nick offered.

"Have you really been to all the Six Flags parks except this one Stephen?" Lucy interrupted.

"Um, yea, the first was when I was six years old," He replied. "There are technically 17 parks but some are grouped together like the ones in New Jersey. I think there are about a dozen or so actual cities you'd have to visit."

"My goal is to one day visit all the rest areas on I-40," Nick chimed in. "So, let's get a move on."

The girls once again went to the rest room together and the guys went one at a time so that at least someone stayed with the car at all times. Stephen said he would go last. He stood in front of the car and looked out onto the highway he had come to know so well the last eight hours or so. Traffic had picked up a little bit, not much, but some. He glanced over to his right, across from where they were parked, at the only other people and car in the lot. They were too far away to hear exactly what they were saying but it sounded like they were having an argument. It appeared to be a family of four. The dad seemed to be hurrying everyone along to get back into the car. He was standing at the back of the car looking into what appeared to be a jam packed trunk. It did not appear to be luggage or duffel bags but blankets and maybe camping equipment. Stephen could not be sure. All he could be sure of was that after slamming the trunk as hard as he could, he heard the man shout, "We need to leave now, they say it's heading this way!"

Dave had assumed the driving chores even though Nick said he had rested plenty and could take over, but Dave convinced him he was perfectly capable. Another concession was allowing Emma to sit shotgun while her boyfriend drove. That now relegated Nick to the back seat of his own car.

He was not too sure how he felt about that, but thought to himself, *"Maybe I'll get to sit in every seat of my own car. How many people get to say that!"*

Stephen did not mention the conversation he overheard at the rest area. Mainly because he didn't really know what to make of what he heard. *"What's coming this way?"* he thought. Perhaps a storm, it was beginning to cloud up.

They got off the next exit to fill up on gas because the rest area did not have a gas station. Pulling into the station Stephen noticed a significant increase in activity than at any other time or place since leaving Los Angeles. As a matter of fact, they had to wait in a short line for gas. It was a full service station which might have been the reason for the line.

Upon reaching the pump, Nick handed Dave his debit card which he in turn handed it to the attendant and said, "Fill it up, regular please."

"Cash only," the attendant said.

Dave turned around and said to the rest of the car, "Cash only."

He gave Nick his debit card back and collected a total of fifty bucks from the car's occupants; turned to the attendant and said, " Fifty dollars regular please."

The attendant pumped the gas and when had he finished he came back to the car window to collect the money. Dave handed him five tens which the attendant counted and then said, "Good luck."

Dave considered a response to that odd statement but before he could come up with one the car behind him beeped its horn. Dave put the car in drive and pulled forward, and headed back to the highway.

"What did the guy who pumped the gas say to you Dave?" Stephen asked after they were back on the road.

"He said, 'good luck'."

"Good luck?"

"That's what the man said."

"Good luck with what?" Emma asked.

"Hell if I know," Dave said.

Just then the clouds opened up and it began to rain. Actually, it began to pour. The raindrops were hitting the roof of the car so loud one could barcly hear oneself think.

"Maybe he was wishing us luck making it through this storm, looks to be a doozy," Nick said.

The subject was dropped as the group's attention turned to the powerful rainstorm that was now enveloping them. Dave naturally slowed down as the driving became more and more treacherous. Most of the other drivers, however, did not. Cars passed them going in the opposite direction as if they were standing still. Stephen looked out the window and watched as the cars passed by. All of them were filled with people and belongings with little room for any more of either.

"Good luck," he thought to himself, *"it's coming this way?"*

The rainstorm lasted on and off for most of the day, it seemed to be following them. Each tried to call their parents but was unsuccessful, they blamed it on the rainstorm and that the part of the country they were traveling through was notorious for poor reception. After more than 24 hours in the car they were all exhausted. All any of them could think about was sleeping in a bed. It did not have to be a nice bed; any would do right about now.

Taking his cue from the group, Dave took the next exit and they found themselves in the small town of Wheatley, Arkansas; population 326. There was an Econo Lodge right off the exit which satisfied two requirements; they had beds and it would be cheap. Dave had done yeoman's work. The heavy rains had severely slowed them down. He had driven the better part of twelve hours. Perhaps preparation for those long shifts at the hospital when he became a doctor. It was now a little past eight in the evening and almost dark.

Dave parked the car and Stephen got out first. "I'll go see about rooms, one for the boys and one for the girls," he said.

There were two other cars in the lot. Stephen was not sure if they belonged to fellow travelers or employees.

After they were all out of the car, Nick yelled in Stephen's direction, "I thought I was rooming with the girls." Lucy and Emma both hit him with their handbags simultaneously.

"In your dreams," Emma said.

Dave tossed Nick his car keys and he opened the hatch and everyone searched for their luggage. As Stephen emerged from the office a short while later, he had a strange look on his face.

When he reached the car Nick asked, "Was the penthouse suite available?"

"I booked you in the broom closet," Stephen countered. "Actually, I was able to get two rooms but they're not next to each other," he continued. "The guy was a little strange; said he only had a few rooms currently available. He said he was the owner and has apparently had staffing problems the last few days and very few of the rooms have been cleaned recently. Just about his entire staff has been no call-no shows."

"Did he mention anything else?" Lucy asked.

"Yeah, that the TV's aren't working in the rooms but everything else works fine and, I quote, 'that doesn't bother me none because I don't watch TV anyhow 'cause there's nothing on there but bad news and worse shows'."

"Ohhh … Kaaay …" said Nick.

Stephen grabbed his duffel and the cooler, in case anyone wanted something to eat, and shut the hatch. Nick pressed the auto lock on the key chain which produced an electronic beep that echoed throughout the parking lot.

"The girls get room 206 the guys get 214; like I said, not next to each other but on the same floor," Stephen said and handed Emma the two keycards for the girls' room. He kept the guy's room keys. "What do you say we meet in the girls' room in 20 minutes and have a bite to eat?" Everyone agreed.

The rooms were neat, clean, and had beds. Stephen threw his duffel on one of the beds and went into the bathroom to splash some water on his face. As promised, the TV's weren't working. They turned on but all you got was snow. *"Probably didn't pay their cable bill,"* he thought.

The group met in room 206 as planned, had a bite to eat and engaged in some small talk but it was clear that they were all very tired and by ten it was time for bed. Stephen, Nick, and Dave went back to their room and left the girls in 206. Stephen got the one bed and Dave the other because they were both taller than Nick, who was able to fit on the couch. Nick did not mind at all because he was asleep before Stephen even turned the light off.

29

Stephen pulled his phone out of his bag before nodding off and tried his mom one more time and this time it rang and rang and rang and then the connection was lost. He was starting to think this trip may not have been the greatest idea he ever had.

Chapter 3
The Park

Stephen was awakened by a loud noise outside in the parking lot. It sounded like a garbage can falling over. He rolled over and looked at the turn of the century alarm clock on the nightstand; it read 9:42 am. *"Slept for almost eleven hours,"* he thought. He looked up and saw Dave still sleeping in his bed as Nick began to stir on the couch. Stephen got out of bed and went to the window. Looking out, he tried to discover the source of the noise that woke him up.

Located halfway across the parking lot, off to the left near a chain link fence separating the property from some dense woods, two large metal garbage cans were rolling back and forth after having obviously been just knocked over. The perpetrators, if any, were nowhere in sight.

"What time is it?" Nick asked groggily.

Stephen turned around and saw Nick sitting upright on the couch, "About a quarter to ten," Stephen replied. "How was the couch?"

"Lovely, like sleeping on a bed of fluffy white clouds."

"Wake sleeping beauty up," Stephen said nodding in Dave's direction, "and get in the shower, I'll go check on the girls."

"What? You want me to get in the shower with the girls?" Nick said with a grin.

"You heard me," Stephen said as he opened the door and headed down the hall towards the girls' room.

After everyone had showered and dressed they met downstairs in the lobby. Stephen settled up with the owner, whose name he found out was Jeremiah. Stephen also found out that he lived in one of the rooms in the motel and that he could cook a mean breakfast. Since they were the only guests at the hotel, he cooked all of them scrambled eggs, ham, and French toast. He offered to make grits but there were no takers.

Satisfied after the huge breakfast, they packed the car and headed back toward the highway. It was a little after noon and they were about sixteen hours from Six Flags. Nick was in his rightful place behind the wheel. Their first stop was a gas station on the other side of the highway overpass. Nick pulled in next to one of the two pumps. It was one of those old fashioned ones that operated automatically by lifting the handle and then pumping the gas. No need to pre-pay. When you were done you would lower the handle and replace the pump.

"I didn't think anyone had one of these anymore?" Nick said as he got out of the car.

He went into the small office located on the other side of the pumps.

"Anyone here?" Nick called.

There was no answer. He peered behind the counter; nothing was there except a couple of empty open boxes, their previous contents probably on the shelves.

Shouting a little louder this time he said, "Hello!"

Still there was no response. There was a small garage attached to the main office. He entered through a side door connecting the two buildings and saw a car up on the lift but no mechanic. Giving one last look around, he returned to the office and then exited heading back to the car.

"What's up?" Dave asked.

"Nobody home," Nick said.

Nick thought for a moment and then opened his gas tank and removed the gas cap. He reached for the pump and lifted the handle and started pumping gas.

"What are you doing?" Stephen asked.

"Fillin' her up. I'll leave enough money on the counter and we'll be on our way. If we play our cards right we should have enough to get there without having to stop for gas again."

Nick put the handle back in its holder after he finished and went back inside to leave money for the gas. He was about to turn around and leave when he thought about leaving a note to explain the money on the counter but unfortunately did not have a pen on him. He quickly looked and could not locate one but he did spot a Kit-Kat bar in a small candy holder next to the cash register. Reaching into his pocket, he pulled out a two dollar coin and threw it on top of the cash and grabbed the Kit-Kat. Opening it, he took a bite and then threw the wrapper into a small garbage can wedged between the wall and a Coke cooler, scoring two points. He turned to walk out of the door without noticing the blood-stained work boot sticking out from behind the cooler.

Nick drove them back onto I-40 east leaving Arkansas behind them and crossing into Tennessee by early afternoon. The storms from yesterday had yielded to sunny skies and temperatures in the mid-seventies. Stephen, back up front riding shotgun, took the opportunity to roll the window down and breathe in the fresh air. Looking back over to Nick who was driving, he noticed the heavy traffic over in the westbound lane. Significantly heavier than the eastbound lane they were traveling. As a matter of fact, the eastbound lane was nearly deserted.

"At least we'll make good time," Stephen thought.

The delicious breakfast prepared by Jeremiah had filled all their bellies and they decided on one last bathroom break before heading on to Six Flags. They had enough snacks and sandwiches to last the rest of the trip if anyone was hungry. By this point in the trip everyone was sick of driving and anxious to get to where they were going. At present course and speed, they would arrive very early in the morning, well before the park opened. Stephen figured they would find where it was, get the lay of the land, and then find a motel to crash in.

The last stop turned out to be a rest stop on I-81, just outside Wytheville, Virginia. This would leave them a little more than five hours away from the park. Nick steered the Hyundai into one of the parking spots and cut the engine.

"Last chance saloon," he called out.

Everyone got out and hung around the car for a minute looking around. Nobody wanted to say it but Emma finally did.

"There is no one here."

She was right. There were two cars other than theirs in the parking lot but no activity; nobody walking to or from their cars, no voices, no screaming kids. It was nearly ten at night on a Thursday but this was a major highway. It was unusually dark as only a couple of the street lamps were working to illuminate the rest stop. Most of the rest stop was cast in the deep shadows of a summer night.

Dave added, "Did anyone else find it weird that most of the traffic on 81 was headed in the other direction?"

"Yea, I did," Stephen agreed.

"Me too," said Lucy.

"And why haven't our phones worked the last two days?" Emma asked. They all looked at her. "I know we agreed to turn 'em off but you know, old habits die hard."

"I'm sure there is a reasonable explanation for everything," Nick said. "We're all a little road weary. Personally, I think it's great that we made it this far without killing each other."

There was some nervous laughter from the group but they were not totally convinced.

"The sooner we get back on our way, the sooner the real vacation begins," Stephen said.

With that, the girls headed off towards the rest rooms. Stephen and Nick followed behind them, with Dave remaining at the car.

Nick handed Stephen the keys as they entered the bathroom and said, "You've got the final leg."

The first thing they noticed when they entered the men's room was the smell. Rest area bathrooms are not known for their pleasant aroma, but this was awful. They looked at each other without saying a word; the scrunching of their noses was all that needed to be said. They made a beeline to the urinal to get their business over with as soon as possible and get back out to the fresh air. The bathroom was rectangular with six urinals on either side towards the front, and a long mirror along the left wall with six stalls lining the right side in the back. Beneath the mirror were a row of sinks.

They were heading to the sinks to wash their hands when they were stopped dead in their tracks by the oddest noise. The noise, a scraping sound like nails on a chalkboard but worse, seemed to be coming from the last stall. Stephen looked and noticed, for the first time, legs sticking out from beneath the stall door. He slapped Nick on the arm and pointed in that direction.

Nick looked at the stall and turned to Stephen, "What the f …" he whispered.

Stephen shrugged his shoulders. Both of them started moving in the direction of the occupied stall. The smell intensified. Stephen then realized that he was wrong, there were not a pair of legs sticking out from underneath the stall; there were two pairs. As they moved closer, Stephen decided that the noise was more of a sharp sucking sound … almost like someone … feeding.

Stephen did not notice the aluminum beer can on the floor and accidentally kicked it as they passed the second stall. The noise from the can vibrated loudly off the walls of the restroom. The odd sucking sound stopped. Silence gripped the restroom. Stephen and Nick froze where they were, about ten feet from the two pairs of legs sticking out from underneath the stall door.

Suddenly one of the pair began to move, slowly at first, then with more urgency. Whoever was moving in the stall was now standing. The stall door began to move as if it was going to open. Stephen grabbed Nick, who was rigid as a statue, and began leading him backwards toward the exit door. The stall door began to shake violently. Whoever was inside was desperately trying to get out but had locked themselves in and could not figure out that all you needed to do was slide the bolt to the right.

Snapping out of the state of fear that had gripped them, they turned and sprinted towards the exit. Escaping into the fresh air, they ran to the car as fast as they could. Emma and Lucy were just up ahead of them almost to the car.

They caught up with them and Stephen screamed, "Get in the car, NOW!"

Dave was waiting for them with a puzzled look, "What's going on?" he asked.

Stephen ignored him and ran around the front of the car while digging for the car keys in his pocket.

Nick came up behind Dave and said, "If you've got to take a piss, drop your pants and do it here … you don't want to go into that bathroom and you're not going in my car."

Dave was going to protest but he saw the look in Nick's eyes and he really had to go, so he did as instructed. The girls had already climbed in the car. Emma had left the door open for Dave to get in when he was finished. Stephen had finally fished the keys out of his pants and got the car started without ever taking his eyes off the men's room door. Dave finished his business and hopped in the back seat. Stephen had the car in reverse before Dave could close the door. Quickly turning around he put the car in drive and sped out of the parking lot back onto the highway with his eyes glued to the rear view mirror.

They rode in silence for nearly fifteen minutes until Dave finally spoke up. "What the hell happened in there?"

Stephen looked at Nick. It was Nick who finally said, "There was somebody in the last stall."

Dave countered with, "And that's unusual for a bathroom, how?"

"I'm not sure what was going on in that stall but there were two people in the one stall and I think only one of them was alive," added Stephen.

"Are you sure? Should we call the police?" asked Lucy.

The next several minutes were spent discussing whether or not they should contact the authorities. In the end they did not want to prolong their trip as they were so close to the park.

Stephen put an end to the matter saying, "To be honest, I'm not sure what we saw … or heard … or smelled for that matter."

"Smelled?" asked Emma

"Yea, it smelled like …" Stephen started to say.

"Death," Nick finished.

The next several hours were spent in relative silence as Dave, Emma, and Lucy drifted off to sleep in the backseat.

"It was easier for them", thought Stephen, *"they didn't see what I saw."*

He and Nick exchanged glances from time to time but no words were exchanged. It was hard to be sure what happened in the restroom but it seemed to Stephen that it was unlikely an innocent explanation. Neither of them was going to relax for a while.

They reached Interstate 66 around three in the morning and then the Beltway about an hour later. As they neared the exit for Andrews Air Force base, they slowed down as it appeared the road was closed. They came up to a sign that read "ROAD CLOSED> USE ALTERNATE ROUTE." As they slowly backed up, a pair of military helicopters flew overhead likely en route to the Air Force base. They turned off at Exit 7 and followed the signs for Six Flags.

The neighborhoods they were now driving through seemed eerily deserted, even for nearly four in the morning. No early risers, no garbage trucks, nobody making the doughnuts. They finally arrived outside the Six Flags America main entrance. A large parking lot lay out before them with the huge park rides, the

Skycoaster and the Batwing, off in the distance. They sat there for a few moments as the early sun began to creep over the horizon. It was almost five a.m.

Stephen sat behind the wheel of Nick's Hyundai Phoenix having completed a trip of nearly 2700 miles. Everything at first seemed normal. The park was closed as it should be. But as the sun came up and began to shed light on the property, Stephen noticed cars in the parking lot. The park did not officially open until 10:30 a.m. There was likely a night crew to clean up the park at night, as well as some security to ensure no one snuck in after-hours, but there were at least seventy-five cars in the lot; maybe even a hundred.

Most peculiar was the fact that they were fairly scattered within the lot; not like employees who would park in a designated area.

The passengers in the backseat began to stir. Stephen pulled forward and headed into the parking lot. Slowly making his way toward the park entrance, he began to notice that some of the cars had their doors open. In the distance, off to his left, he noticed some movement. It appeared to be a small group of people walking slowly toward one of the cars. They were moving awkwardly and with staggered steps. Stephen turned the car and headed toward the group.

They had nearly reached the car when Stephen thought he saw movement coming from within the Chevrolet they were targeting. All of a sudden, the back passenger's side door opened and a young woman burst out and began running toward their car. She was clearly panicked and was shouting something. Stephen swung the car around and rolled down the window so he could hear what she was saying.

"Help me!" She screamed.

Stephen was about to yell back and ask what the problem was, when someone emerged from behind one the other cars between Stephen and the young woman. The stranger startled her causing her to stop suddenly and lose her footing. Stephen made the decision to try to pull the car alongside and see if they could get her in. Unfortunately, he was not fast enough, the man who had been hiding behind the car was on her and the group that had surrounded her car was approaching fast.

She let out another cry for help but it would be to no avail. The group had descended on her and began to tear at her clothing. One of them got down low and appeared to bite her on the back of the neck while the rest held her down. Stephen, Dave, Nick, Lucy, and Emma stared in horror as the woman went limp. One of the attackers then seemed to realize that the Hyundai was there and turned to look at them. He began to rise, as the rest of the pack began to do the same. Stephen locked eyes with one of them as the group started to move toward their car. At that moment Stephen realized two things; first, these things that attacked that poor woman were not human, and second, he needed to get the hell out of there.

Chapter 4
Chester Boone

The sounds of the birds and the rustle of the leaves as a gentle breeze blew through the woods did little to improve Chester Boone's mood. He was already agitated that he had failed to bring down the doe with his bow earlier in the day. Now he was forced to track the blood trail through the woods for the last hour, instead of relaxing back at his campsite.

"*I can't believe I lost the trail again,*" he thought as he knelt looking for any sign of the wounded deer passing this way. His ability to track anyone or anything in these woods was stuff of local legend but that was not helping him now. He was about to stand when he noticed the glint of wet blood on a leaf to his right. Moving to the leaf, he could just make out the fresh blood trail continuing into the thick brush to the south, away from his campsite.

"Of course it can't be heading back towards camp," he muttered to himself.

With an annoyed sigh, he adjusted the pack on his back and slung his bow over his shoulder. As Chester eyed the brush he realized there would be no easy way to do this if he wanted to follow the trail directly. Wounded animals rarely made finding them easy. With a grunt, he pulled out his machete and began to hack a path through the thick foliage.

Chester Boone was a native North Carolinian, having been born and raised in a small town outside of Charlotte. Growing up, his family would visit the Great Smokey Mountains at least twice a year for camping, hiking, and hunting. To that end, Chester developed a fondness for all things outdoors. Even when he was attending college at the Virginia Military Institute he lived for the weekends when he could escape into the woods to camp and hunt. Upon graduation, he decided not to accept a commission into any of the branches of the US Military, but instead pursued a career as a Park Ranger.

Chester married a girl from his home town three years after graduating from VMI. Shortly after their fourth anniversary, however, his wife was tragically killed in a car accident. Since then, he has adopted an almost a hermit like lifestyle moving to a small house in the town of Waynesville, west of Asheville. He then obtained a job working for the United States Park Service in The Great Smokey Mountain National Park. Whether he was working or not, Chester spent most of his time alone in the woods.

At 47 years of age, he was of average build and height but had strength developed from years of hiking, hunting, and outdoor activity that belied his frame. Completing his stereotypical outdoor look was a head of curly dark brown hair and full beard that were just starting to show the signs of greying. His tanned leathery skin showed the results of years of outdoor living. When he actually had something to say, his gruff voice completed the image.

Movement in the brush ahead froze Chester in mid-swing. Peering through the dense vegetation he tried to see what had made the noise. The sound of breaking branches drew his attention to what appeared to a man slowly moving through the underbrush in roughly the same direction as the blood trail.

"Where did he come from?" thought Chester *"I haven't seen anyone in five days."*

Lowering his machete, Chester began picking his way through the undergrowth as quietly as possible. He did not know who this intruder was but Chester certainly did not like being surprised by other people, especially not in his woods. The man did not seem to notice that he was being followed even when Chester unintentionally stepped on and broke several twigs. The man continued to shamble forward following the trail of the deer.

"If that deer is still alive he is goin' to scare it off," thought Chester as the stranger continued to crash clumsily through the brush.

Suddenly, the mystery man stopped and began looking around as if he was lost. Chester could see him more clearly now. His hair was matted and his clothes were filthy and torn in some places. The man's arms hung limply at his sides and he stood awkwardly favoring his right leg. Just as suddenly the man began to move forward again. Chester moved a few feet forward and in the distance, slightly ahead of the stranger, he could make out the deer lying in a heap with the end of his arrow protruding from its neck. The man seemed to spot the deer as well, and moved slowly to it, sinking to his knees directly in front of the deer. Chester could make out the man reaching for the animal but could not tell what he was doing. It appeared as if the man had been tracking the deer all along.

"What is this fella doin'. That's my deer and if he even thinks he can take it for himself he's got another thing comin'," thought Chester angrily.

Not making an attempt to be quiet anymore, Chester moved through the brush and approached the man from behind.

"Hey, buddy. What do ya think you're doin'?"

With no response Chester tried again, "Hey, I'm talkin' to you! That's my deer. I don't know where you get off trackin' and stealin' other people's deer but that ain't happenin' today."

This time the man let out a grunt. As Chester drew close he could make out sounds as if the man was eating.

"Hey buddy, what's wrong with you? Can't you hear me?" asked Chester moving forward and poking the man in the back with his boot.

In an instant the man turned around still on his knees, his face and hands covered in blood from the deer. Chester could see the deer's belly had been torn open and the man had begun to tear out its entrails and devour them.

"Wha … what the heck are you doin'?" yelled Chester "Why are ya …"

Chester was cut short as the man moaned and lunged, hands outstretched towards him. He took two quick steps backward easily avoiding the man's grasp. The man fell face first onto the ground but pushed himself up slowly then stood and started moving again towards Chester. The man snarled at him as the blood and intestines of the deer dripped down his face and onto his tattered clothing.

"Don't come any closer buddy. I will hurt you." Chester warned raising his machete.

Paying no attention to his threat, the man continued moaning and moving forward grasping for Chester at every step. At last the man lunged, but before he could reach him, Chester's machete blade was flying through the air landing a blow on the man's right arm severing it above the elbow.

To Chester's shock the man staggered and then, seemingly unfazed by the loss of an appendage, leapt at Chester once again. Chester swung the machete with full force; it bit into the man's shoulder but failed to stop his aggressive advance. As the man clawed for Chester with his one good arm he gnashed his teeth and lurched forward again in an attempt to bite him.

Fueled by adrenaline, Chester now began to rain down blows on the man with his machete. To his horror the man kept attacking him and was only finally put down by a timely blow to the back of his head. The man fell to the ground unmoving and Chester, in a state of exhaustion, collapsed to the ground beside him. As he labored to catch his breath and calm himself Chester noted that the fatal strike had landed at the base of the man's head and cut almost entirely through the neck. He also noticed that his wounds were not bleeding profusely as should be the case but rather oozed a thick dark substance.

Chester shuddered at the grotesqueness of the entire scene and the realization that he had just killed a man. It was in self-defense he tried to tell himself. Unable to control his stomach any longer, Chester leaned over and lost his breakfast.

"*I don't know what was wrong with him but he did not seem human,*" Chester thought as he wiped his mouth on his sleeve.

Steeling himself against the sight and smell of the man, he searched his body to try and obtain some sort of identification with which he could report the incident to the authorities. Chester believed that this man needed to be examined as something was very wrong. The dead man had nothing in his pockets besides a key to one of the cabins that made up the "Blue Ridge Wilderness B&B"; located several miles away. Upon finishing the search, Chester wiped his machete blade with several leaves before sheathing it. Then making note of his currently location on his map, quickly made his way back to his campsite.

Chester's campsite consisted of a small tent assembled against the side of his pickup truck. A small fire pit ringed with tiny rocks filled with the ashen remains of last night's fire lay nearby. His bear bag moved slightly in the breeze as it hung suspended between two trees.

As he entered the clearing, a squirrel darted back into the underbrush unnoticed by Chester. He quickly reached his truck, opened the door, and pulled out his shortwave radio. Turning it on, he tuned it to the local emergency channel and tried to raise the nearest park ranger station. Unable to contact anyone he set the radio to scan and quickly went about breaking down his camp and loading his belongings into the truck.

Once all his camping and hunting gear was stowed in the bed of his truck Chester jumped in the cab with his radio. After one more futile attempt to raise anyone with the radio, he started the truck and headed down the access road. He planned to drive to the nearest ranger station to report what had happened and then onto the cabins to see if he could help the rangers identify the man from the woods. While he drove Chester set the radio to scan the airways until he could pick up a signal.

Thirty minutes later Chester arrived at the ranger station. It was a small log cabin with a watchtower around back which the rangers used to spot wildfires. When he was on the clock this was where he was assigned. The ranger's truck was gone and after a quick search he determined the building was empty. Curiously, all of the ranger's gear, including the radio, was gone as well.

The ranger on duty was not supposed to leave his post until he was relieved or in case of an emergency. As Chester climbed back into his truck he was just in time to hear the emergency broadcast tones coming across the radio. As he adjusted the volume the broadcast began.

"This is a reversal of our previous announcement. Charlotte and Raleigh are no longer safe zones. Repeat: Charlotte and Raleigh are no longer safe zones. All citizens are directed to stay indoors and wait until evacuation zones are established. This message will repeat until new information is available. Please stay tuned to this station, details to follow."

As promised, the radio broadcast began to repeat as Chester sat in his truck in a state of complete confusion.

"What in the world is happenin' out there?" he thought. *"I've been gone less than a week. There is no way all that riotin' and violence spread this far north. This is why I live alone in the woods, away from these idiots."*

Starting his truck and pulling away from the Ranger station Chester headed off to the "Blue Ridge Wilderness B&B" to get some answers about the man who had attacked him and what was going on in the world outside of his woods.

Pulling up to the large lodge house at the bed and breakfast, Chester could immediately tell something was very wrong. The door to the lodge was open and a body lay in the doorway. To the left of the lodge, smoldering logs was all that was left of one of the cabins. There were two cars in the gravel parking lot but Chester could see from the tire tracks that there had been one more that left in a hurry.

Leaving his truck running Chester got out and grabbed his hunting rifle off of the gun rack in the cab of his truck. As he carefully approached the body at the open lodge door, he noticed that it was mutilated and covered in blood. It looked as if something had ripped out the back of the man's neck. Wincing at the sight and smell of the man he poked his head in the open door.

"Hello, anyone here?" Chester called.

After receiving no answer, he moved slowly through the door with his rifle at the ready and began to search the lodge. It was a single floor building and consisting of a great room with dining tables and a buffet line behind which was a kitchen. In the back of the building was an office and bathroom, both of which were empty.

Finally moving around the buffet line and into the kitchen, Chester was surprised to see another man lying dead on the floor covered in bite marks and with the back of his neck ripped out as well. Covering his mouth and nose from the smell, Chester quickly backed out of the kitchen and ran out of the lodge and to his truck. Resting his hands on the hood of his truck while he regained his composure, Chester heard a sound behind him. Turning, he saw that he was not alone after all.

Chapter 5
The Walkers

Since purchasing the house nearly three and a half years ago, Marcus Walker has spent precious little time in the basement. He was planning to remodel it and use it as a second living space. Those plans were now on hold; indefinitely. After finding what he come down here for, two Coleman heavy duty flashlights with handles and extra D cell batteries, he headed back upstairs.

Closing the basement door and turning off the light, he headed into the den where his wife was finishing her packing. The power had actually gone out for good the night before but Marcus had purchased a generator a few years back for just such an emergency.

"Found 'em," he said proudly.

"Will wonders never cease?" she responded before considering the current implications of that statement.

Kimberly Walker and her husband were childhood sweethearts. Growing up in the same Richmond, Virginia neighborhood, they first met in middle school but did not date until junior year. After high school, he went on to J. Sargent Reynolds Community College and studied engineering with hopes of transferring to a four year college after graduation. Unfortunately, his mother got sick and he had to stay around the house to help his mom because his dad worked two jobs. His education on hold, he got a job at Berger's Department store as a cashier. After his mom passed, he decided that he liked retail and took a head cashier's job.

The Walkers were married twelve years ago almost to the day. She started working as a dental assistant and Marcus worked his way up the management ladder. Management opportunities without a degree can be hard to find, but four years ago the expanding Berger's opened a new location in Petersburg and asked Marcus to manage it for them. He saw this as an opportunity to get his family out of the city and to the suburbs so he happily took it. They purchased this house conveniently located near the store and have lived happily here ever since. That is until a few days ago.

"Are the kids ready?" Marcus asked.

"I'll go check on them," she answered.

As her husband headed outside to finish loading the car, she went upstairs to see about the kids. Heading up to the second floor bedrooms, she thought back to how this all started. Initial news reports started about a week ago. Unusual stories about large groups of people suddenly turning violent. There was destruction of property, looting, and people hurting others for no apparent reason. It originally started in the southern cities like Miami, Orlando, and Atlanta.

The government first said it was some sort of mass hysteria brought on by an unknown condition. Then they said it may have been a terrorist attack; a coordinated event where local water supplies were contaminated causing people to become delusional. It was recommended only drinking bottled water or boiling your tap water. They started referring to these unfortunate soles who had succumbed to this kind of madness as "infected". It was suggested that these people be avoided and not try to help them. Symptoms and characteristics of those infected were announced; a blank unresponsive stare and a staggered gait were two of the conditions to look for.

That all changed when the first city became overrun. People were then advised to stay in their homes until further instructions could be issued. Everyone was thirsting for information. Every television, computer, Uni-phone, and mobile device was tuned to the various news outlets. The last piece of information that was disseminated before the networks and servers began to crash was to pack only essential belongings and head north or west. Evacuation zones were being established near cities that were overrun; a list that was growing daily. Short wave radios were recommended as they were still a reliable source of information.

"So... here we are," thought Kimberly, *"packing to head north."*

She entered Jason's bedroom first. He was sitting cross legged in the middle of the room staring at a fish bowl. A small goldfish swam back and forth. Next to him was a gym bag filled with clothes.

"Why can't we take Oscar with us?" he asked.

"We don't have the room honey," she offered, "he'll be fine. We'll be back soon," she lied, "after we get back from Nanny and Grampa's house. Put a little extra food in his bowl, just in case."

Jason got up from his seated position and reached for the fish flakes adding a few pieces of food for Oscar. She hated lying to an eleven year old but, unfortunately, she felt she had no other choice.

"Grab your bag and bring it to your father downstairs," she instructed.

"Ok."

"I'm going to check on your sister," she said as he bent down to retrieve his bag. She saw the disappointed look on his face and grabbed his shoulder as he walked by.

"He's starting to get so tall," she thought.

"Hey," she said, "I love you."

"Yea, love you too," he said looking away and heading downstairs.

Moving down the hall she turned right into Danielle's bedroom. The precocious eight year old was standing in front of her bed with one doll in her left hand and another in her right and staring at the pink suitcase on the bed.

"Can't decide on Miss Molly or Sandra," Kim asked.

Danielle turned quickly around and said, "Mom, you scared me half to death."

"I'm sorry. Are you just about ready?"

"What do you think?" Danielle asked her mom showing her the two dolls, "Which one?"

"Personally, I think Miss Molly, but it's your decision."

"I think you're right," Danielle decided.

Kim grabbed her daughter's suitcase. Danielle, deciding not to pack Miss Molly but hold on to her, followed her mother out the bedroom door. They headed downstairs where Marcus was standing in the middle of the foyer with Jason by his side. He had finished packing their Honda Accord as full as it could get. The trunk was full of blankets, flashlights, camping gear, as well as a cooler filled with food. Also, in the back of the trunk, was something that Kim was unaware of. Marcus had purchased a hand gun before all this started. Now that they had belongings and a house to protect, he felt it was something they needed. Also, in the back seat, was a short wave radio he had purchased at Berger's. It was the last one they had. He also had an extra supply of batteries.

"Are we all set?" Marcus asked.

"I believe so," Kim replied as she looked down at her two children, waiting for any objections. None came.

Marcus grabbed the pink suitcase from Kim and said, "Let's go then."

They walked out the front door and down a sidewalk that curved to the right where it met the driveway about halfway down. Marcus opened the trunk and put Danielle's suitcase inside and slammed the door shut. They all turned around to look at the house they were leaving behind. The children were told they were going to visit Kim's parents in Burtonsville, Maryland and that they would be back in a few days. Kids being smarter than most parents give them credit for knew something was going on.

"Last chance," Marcus said, "anyone have to go to the bathroom before I lock up?"

"Not me," said Danielle.

Jason stood there looking like he might have something to say.

"Jason?"

"Maybe I should," he finally said.

Jason and Marcus started heading back into the house when Kim came up from behind and said, "I forgot my medication."

For about the last year, she has been taking Synthroid for a hypothyroid condition. She still forgot to take it from time to time and had forgotten to pack it.

She turned back around as she approached the front door and shouted to Danielle, "Stay right there, we'll be right back."

Marcus double checked the windows on the lower floor and that the generator was off while Jason went to the downstairs bathroom and Kim went to the upstairs bathroom where her medicine was. He was satisfied that the house was going to be as secure as possible while they were away and headed back to the foyer. He was fishing for the house keys in his pocket to lock the front door when he heard a loud scream coming from outside. It sounded like his daughter.

Marcus raced to the open front door and looked out. At the end of the driveway he spotted his daughter leaning against the passenger's side back door. She was clutching Miss Molly and screaming at the top of her lungs. She was frozen and looking away from the house toward a row of trees that separated their property from the Burton's next door.

Emerging from the trees were three … no four … four people heading in the direction of the Honda. Marcus immediately noticed a fifth coming up from the end of the driveway and finally a sixth person moving across the lawn and coming towards the house. The strangers exhibited all the characteristics the news reports said would help identify those who were infected.

There was no way Marcus could get to Danielle before at least one of the infected people reached her. He thought quickly, as he did, Kim and Jason came up from behind him and stood on either side of him in the doorway. The intruders had cleared the trees and were now in full view. Kim let out a scream of her own and Jason grabbed his father's left leg.

Marcus reached in his pocket and pulled out his keychain and yelled to Danielle.

"Danielle, sweetheart … open the car door and get inside."

Her father's voice snapped Danielle out of her stupor. She turned around and looked in the direction of her father. He repeated his request. She quickly turned back around and fumbled for the door handle. Finally getting it opened she dove inside and slammed the car door shut with all her might. Marcus used the auto lock on his keychain to lock the doors just ahead of the first infected. Safe for the moment, Marcus turned his attention to getting the rest of his family into the car.

He quickly stepped back into the house, opened the sliding door on the hallway closet where his new set of Taylor Made golf clubs sat. He reached in and pulled out two irons. He handed his son the three iron and kept the five for himself. The initial group of infected people had all reached the car and started banging on the windows. The last person, a female, was still heading up the lawn and had nearly reached the sidewalk.

Marcus turned to his son and said, "Listen to me Jason, I need you to go with your mother and head for the car. Take this club and swing it at anything that moves."

Jason, trying to be brave, shook his head up and down.

Marcus then looked at Kimberly and said, "I'll go ahead and distract them. Try to get them away from the car." He handed her the car keys. "When there is an opening, run for the car and get in."

"What about you?"

Marcus had already done the math. It was unlikely he would be able to fend them all off and get back to the car. He would, of course, try, but sometimes life is filled with sacrifices that you have to make as a man, as a father, and as a husband. Sometimes those sacrifices are bigger than others.

"Just get yourself and the kids to your mother's house. I'll find you there," he said.

Marcus realized he was running out of time and was about to run when he stopped, turned back around, kissed his wife and whispered, "I love you," and then said, "oh, it's 2-3-6-6," and then took off at a run.

He ran toward the closest ... person ... swinging the five iron. It was the woman coming up the sidewalk. His first two blows to the head seemed to have little effect. He backed up a step and regrouped. He then swung at the knee and was able to snap the woman's leg at the knee collapsing her to the ground. He turned around and waved for Kim and Jason to move up behind him. The woman was on the ground now only able to crawl and was not as much a threat as those surrounding the car with two good legs.

Marcus approached the Honda making wild gestures and waving his club in the air. The group surrounding the car took little notice. He moved closer and noticed his daughter looking out of the back window at him, scared but hopeful; her daddy was coming to save her. He was now close enough to bludgeon the nearest person. He tried the same trick as before, swinging the five iron into the back of the leg. The infected man started to go down but caught himself on the trunk of the car. It turned to face Marcus and for the first time he had a good look into the eyes of an infected person. They were empty and soulless.

He raised his weapon and swung the club backwards this time and connected with the man's chin. This knocked him back a step or two. More importantly, it seemed to get the attention of the others. Slowly, each turned away from the car and moved toward Marcus.

Marcus turned and sprinted a few steps away from the car hoping they would follow him. When he turned back around, he saw that his plan appeared to be working. The group of five had turned their full attention to Marcus. He looked over to his left to see his wife and son halfway between the house and the car. Jason was poised with the club ready to smash the infected woman on the ground if she got any closer.

When the car was clear of trouble, Marcus yelled over to his wife, "Go! Now!"

Kim ran as fast as she could, keeping Jason by her side. She got to the car and tried to open the driver's side door while Jason went for the passenger's door.

"*Oh no!*" she thought *"forgot to unlock the door."*

She fumbled with the keychain in her hand and pushed the unlock button. The click from inside the vehicle confirmed the doors were now open. She grabbed the handle and pulled the door open quickly getting inside. Once inside, she turned to the backseat to make sure Jason made it safely inside and to check on Danielle. Both were safe and sound for the moment. Kim then looked past the kids, out the back window to check on her husband. She did not like what she saw.

Marcus saw his wife and children make it safely to the Honda. A brief feeling of relief came over him. That feeling quickly vanished as he realized the predicament he now found himself in. The five of the infected verses the one of him. He had noticed a few things about them in the past several minutes. First, they were determined but slow. Second, they seemed impervious to pain. Third, they stunk to high heaven. That last observation would not help him much but the other two led him to a decision.

He would not be able to slug himself out of this but he may be able to outrun them. All he needed was a couple of swings to give him some space and then an end around towards the car. As he brought the club up behind his head to let loose with a couple of whacks, he froze. The last of the intruders, the one that had come up the driveway, was now directly in front of him. Looking at his face Marcus realized it was, or more accurately, used to be Benjamin King, his sporting goods department manager at Berger's.

As he was getting over the shock of seeing someone he knew, and liked very much in such a condition, he did not see or feel the two additional people come up from behind him. These new intruders had come from behind the house and grabbed Marcus' arms in mid swing. The surprise was too much for him and he lost his balance as the new people pulled him down from behind. The rest of the infected were quickly on top of him. He tried to fight them off but it was useless. As they tore at his clothing and the one who used to be Ben King knelt down to take a bite out of his arm, he could see the faces of his children looking out the rear window of the Honda.

Kim noticed the two people coming from the back of the house too late. Now that she was in the car, she thought about turning the car around and running these bastards over but there would be no way to make sure she did not hit Marcus in the process. She saw her husband go down and knew that there was nothing she or anyone else could do now.

"Get down and don't look!" Kim screamed at her children.

She reached behind and pushed her kids' heads down towards the backseat. She turned back around, turned the car on and put it in drive. Before stepping on the gas, she could not help but look in the rear view window. Her husband was nowhere in sight beneath the mass of bodies doing unspeakable things to him. She stared in horror but could not look away, holding onto the slimmest of hopes that Marcus could somehow fight his way out of it.

Those hopes were dashed when the tallest of the men stood back up and turned to face the car. His mouth covered in what could only have been Marcus' blood. She had her foot on the gas pedal before he could take even one step in her direction. The tires squealed as she and her two kids pulled out of the driveway and moved down the street.

As she headed toward I-95 and what she hoped would be the safety of her parent's house she thought of the last words Marcus said to her. "'*Get the kids to your mother's house*' and '*it's 2-3-6-6'. What in the world did 2-3-6-6 mean?*"

Chapter 6
Major Charles "Butch" Bradley

"Sir, the helos will be here in about ten minutes," said Captain Morris.

"Alright, make sure the civilians are ready near the tarmac," replied Major Bradley as he smoothed out the map lying before him on the table.

Major Charles "Butch" Bradley, an army lifer, made a name for himself during the North Korean War of 2017 leading his men in battle. Wounded twice and receiving the Silver Star for valor, Bradley quickly progressed through the post war ranks until he stalled out at Major due to his refusal to play army politics. Major Bradley was an imposing figure with stern features who demanded the best from the men he commanded while also inspiring their personal loyalty. His leadership and no nonsense style was one of the reasons he had been left to finish the evacuation of Washington D.C.

"*I don't know how it ever came to this,*" Major Bradley thought to himself as he looked at the operational map of the United States east of the Mississippi River.

No one had been prepared for this, whatever 'this' was. The people up the chain of command who were supposed to have the answers still had very little idea about what was happening. The government's response, and in turn the military's, to the crisis had been unsurprisingly slow. The higher Major Bradley had risen in the ranks, the more frustrated he had become with the inability to get anything done quickly. Everything required the meddling of government officials and approval by committee. It had not been any different with the current situation.

Because he refused to play politics and take sides, Major Bradley was assigned as the liaison between the Army and the Department of Homeland Security (DHS) when the first reports had surfaced out of Miami. At first, the Army and DHS did not give the events a second look. Local law enforcement and media outlets described it as a local gang war spilling into the streets of Miami.

However, this quickly proved not to be the case. By the end of the first day, the city of Miami was in chaos. Reports of roving bands of people attacking bystanders surfaced and the residents of Miami were warned to stay in their homes by local officials. Then the looting began, people taking advantage of the situation for their own personal gain. The following day the Mayor of Miami requested assistance from the National Guard. As usual, bureaucracy got in the way and the National Guard did not deploy until Miami was a complete loss.

At this point DHS was contacted. There were reports of, not only major rioting, but of a large number of people who reportedly had been attacked and bitten by others. DHS dragged its heels unwilling to get involved in another local problem; they did, however, decide not to disclose the latest developments to the public. They only acknowledged that some unknown condition was responsible for mass hysteria in the area. It was then that Major Bradley had been notified by his superiors of peculiar reports from the Florida National Guard. These reports corroborated the information from local law enforcement that the civilian population was turning on one another in an almost cannibalistic fashion.

After these reports the government, in conjunction with the military, issued a warning of possible terrorist attacks targeting the affected area's water supply. It was then that the term 'the infected' was first used to refer to those seen attacking and biting others. The Army, fearful of additional biological attacks, began to mobilize its bio-terrorism units. At the same time Major

Bradley was tasked with coordinating the Army's actions with those that DHS might be preparing to take.

By the time DHS had begun mobilizing, there was no communication from Miami and reports were flooding in that similar attacks were beginning to take place in Tampa and Orlando. The Army finally started to deploy small advance forces in Florida but these were soon overwhelmed with the fleeing civilians, rioters, and the infected.

As more reports flooded in, Major Bradley was stuck in Washington trying fruitlessly to coordinate a response between the Army and DHS. Completely unorganized and unprepared, the government continued to deny that the crisis was significant enough to warrant extensive federal intervention. Discussions on how to deal with the problem and limit collateral damage contributed greatly to the inaction.

On more than one occasion Major Bradley sat in on a meeting where one side wanted to go in with guns blazing while the other was very concerned about civilian casualties and infrastructure damage. By the time a compromised response was agreed upon and implemented, most of the major cities and towns in the southeast were over run. By then, reports were starting to filter in from Arkansas, Tennessee, the Carolinas, and Georgia of cases matching those first reported in Florida.

Then the biggest obstacle Major Bradley was dealing with, besides the unknown, was panic. Ever since the reports had first surfaced in Florida, despite the government's best efforts, rumors had started to fly about what was happening. These rumors, running unchecked, caused fear not only in the civilian population but also among the enlisted ranks of the military and police forces. Desertions had skyrocketed as soldiers left their posts, taking weapons and ammunition with them, to head home and protect their families. This severely hamstrung the military response as whole units were gutted including commanding officers. To make matters worse, the strain on the electrical and telecommunication infrastructure had caused major power failures and loss of communication. With so many people warned to stay home, as well as those directly affected by the outbreak, there were very few people left to maintain or repair these vital systems. The looting and rioting did nothing to improve the overall situation. The problem had become so wide spread that all military and emergency communication were being done via antiquated shortwave radios; and those were in short supply.

Two days ago when all communication ceased with forces deployed in Richmond, Virginia the decision was made to evacuate Washington D.C. and move the government to the secure base at NORAD. After the President, members of Congress and other high ranking government and military officials were clear of Washington, Major Bradley was ordered to stay behind and finish the evacuations of the civilian population. For the past two days the small force under his command was moving through the city clearing out the few civilians who had not already fled. Those who could not get out on their own were brought back to Andrews Air Force base where Major Bradley had his headquarters. From here they were picked up by transport helicopter and flown to newly constructed Red Cross camps out west.

Now, as Major Bradley reviewed his map he thought to himself. *"How could the world's most powerful military fail to contain this outbreak?"*

Shaking his head he turned from his map and surveyed his headquarters, if it could be called that. The small room just off the main hanger at Andrews had been hastily converted to Major Bradley's base of operations during the evacuation of D.C. After the government and military officials had gone, he could have had his pick of any of the offices but in typical fashion thought it a waste of time and resources to move his headquarters. Now, most of the equipment from the room had been packed into the Humvees waiting just inside the hanger. All that remained in the room was a small table covered in maps and a shortwave radio set up in the corner.

"As soon as the helos arrive I want that radio equipment in the Humvees," Major Bradley said to his radio operator.

"Yes sir," replied Specialist Simmons as he put the radio headset back on.

The door opened and Captain Morris rushed in. Struggling to catch his breath he said, "Sir ... sorry sir ... the civilians are ready."

"Very good Captain, you ok?" replied Major Bradley as Captain Morris doubled over gasping for air.

"Give me a minute sir," wheezed Captain Morris.

After he had caught his breath he continued. "Sir, the civilians are fine and the helos are inbound but the sentries at the north gate say those things are getting closer. I think they know we're here sir."

"It was only a matter of time Captain. Tell the guards not to fire unless absolutely necessary. We know noise attracts those things. Then make sure the convoy is ready to go the minute the civilians are off the ground. We'll pick the guards up on the way out," Major Bradley said.

"Yes sir," said Captain Morris giving a quick salute before heading back out, the door slamming behind him.

"Never mind what I said before Simmons, go ahead and pack the stuff up and get it to the convoy," said Major Bradley as he collected his maps from the table.

Looking over the small room one last time to make sure he did not need anything else, Major Bradley headed into the expansive hanger outside the office. It was a buzz of activity and noise as the soldiers were trying to prepare the civilians for departure. Everyone was talking, orders were being shouted, and children were crying. He barely concealed a look of frustration as he surveyed the scene before him. The far side of the hanger was a less chaotic scene as other soldiers under Major Bradley's command went about preparing the convoy.

At the last minute, Major Bradley had been informed that his command would not be flown out of Andrews but instead would leave on a convoy. The reason given was twofold. First, due to the amount of evacuations being performed along the East Coast, helicopter extractions were in high demand. Second, his commanders wanted him to look for any remaining civilians around D.C. which could be evacuated. Major Bradley was also told in no uncertain terms that his men should not have a problem fighting their way out if need be.

For the past two hours the members of Major Bradley's command had been scouring the base for vehicles, weapons, and fuel for the convoy. Besides the four Humvees that his men had arrived in four days earlier, they had found a couple of two and a half ton cargo trucks and a refueling truck. His men had surprised him by taking the initiative and filling the refueling truck by syphoning the diesel out of every available source on the base.

In terms of armament, his men had their standard issue weapons ranging from M4 rifles to larger S.A.W. machine guns. Several of the men also had their own personal side arms. Each of the four Humvees was equipped with a 50 caliber machine gun. A couple of his men had found the air base's armory and had taken extra rifles and what little ammunition was left. From a military stand point Major Bradley was appalled. He had an ill equipped and undersupplied patch work unit, with no intelligence of what to expect and only the vaguest of orders to go by.

Major Bradley's plan was to leave with the convoy the minute the helicopters left. They would then travel north on the D.C. Outer Loop from the airbase looking for any civilians who needed help evacuating the area. Once northwest of D.C., the convoy would head towards Fredrick, Maryland; their destination would be one of the few remaining evacuation zones in the region, Fredrick Municipal Airport. Military transports were scheduled to be making around the clock evacuation flights as long as it was safe to do so.

The sound of helicopters landing brought Major Bradley's attention back to the task at hand. Seeing Captain Morris approaching the hanger at a run, Major Bradley headed his way.

"Is everything alright Captain?" ask Major Bradley.

"No sir, those things definitely know where we are. They are starting to congregate outside the north gate. Enough of them will quickly push through the temporary barrier we erected. The guards have orders to hold until the last possible minute and then displace back here, taking out as many of those things as they can."

As if to emphasize Captain Morris' point the sound of gun fire erupted from the direction of the north gate.

"Sounds like they've breached the barrier, Captain get these civilians on the helicopters now! We'll cover you with the convoy. Once they are wheels up we'll bug out of here," Major Bradley ordered.

With a quick salute Captain Morris turned around and began herding the civilians towards the waiting helicopters. Major Bradley headed towards the convoy pulling his M9 from his hip holster.

"Mount up men," he shouted, "we need to buy these civies some time."

With a shout his men leapt into action. They ran to their assigned vehicles, drawing and checking their weapons in the process. The convoy's engines came to life almost drowning out the distinctive sound of the gunners cocking their 50 caliber machine guns. Jumping on the running board of the lead Humvee Major Bradley directed the convoy past the frightened civilians and into a blocking position between the helicopters and the north gate. As the gate's guards arrived at a full run behind them, Major Bradley could make out the distinctive movement of the infected that had crashed the gate.

"Alright men, we just need to hold them until the helos are off the ground. Make your shots count and remember aim for the head. That is the only thing that seems to bring these things down."

With that, Major Bradley jumped from the Humvee, gun still in his hand, and jogged to the nearest Chinook helicopter. As he reached one of the crew members, at the rear loading ramp helping people into the helicopter, the sounds of gun fire erupted behind him as his men began to engage the infected.

"You guys almost done here?" asked Major Bradley.

"Yes sir this is the last of them," replied the warrant officer.

"Good, get these birds in the air quick. Oh, and one more thing. The municipal airport in Frederick is still open for evacuations, correct?"

"The last I heard it still was sir. After we drop this load off, that is where we are headed next."

"Sounds good, my convoy will be headed there with any other civilians we find along the way. Just make sure you don't leave us," Major Bradley said with a small smile as he clapped the warrant officer on the shoulder.

"Yes sir. We'll see you there," was the reply as the warrant officer followed the last civilian up the ramp and into the helicopter.

With a salute he punched a button and the loading ramp began to close. As Major Bradley jogged back to the convoy, head ducked to avoid the prop wash, he heard the Chinooks engine's power up and felt the wind as they lifted off the ground.

Ahead of him his men looked like kids at a shooting gallery at the state fair. They stood next to, behind, and on top of the trucks shooting at the infected people who seemed to be coming from everywhere in front of them.

Reaching the lead Humvee Major Bradley yelled, "Cease fire, cease fire."

As the gun fire slowly stopped Major Bradley opened the passenger side door and stepped up on the running board. Seeing the rest of his men, including Captain Morris, mount up in their own vehicles he motioned with his hand and waved the convoy forward. He sunk in to the seat, slammed the door shut and rolled down the window.

Turning to his driver, Private Sinclair, he said, "Alright private, let's get out of here before we all get eaten."

"Yes sir!"

"Oh, and see how many of those thing you can run over on your way out," Major Bradley said with a hint of a smirk.

"It would be my pleasure sir."

The private gunned the Humvee's engine and with a lurch it sped forward turning towards the main gate. About 40 bodies littered the tarmac courtesy of his men but Major Bradley still saw another several hundred more infected people shambling their way.

With a sickening crunch the Humvee ran over its first victim as it picked up speed towards the gate.

The Humvee hit several more infected before they reached the gate and crashed through the fence next to what was left of the overrun barricade. Realizing he still had his gun out but had not fired a shot, Major Bradley stuck his head and arm out the window and drew a bead on the closest infected person. As they sped by, the bullet from the Major's gun entered the things head. It crumpled to the ground where it had stood and ceased to move.

"Nice shot sir," said Sinclair.

"That was for my mother, she never made it out of her retirement home in Florida," Major Bradley said solemnly.

As the convoy merged onto the capital beltway heading north, Major Bradley noticed the number of abandon vehicles. Presumably from people running out of gas and being forced to leave their cars. After the electrical grid had failed most gas stations could not pump gas leaving people with only the gas left in their cars. Thankfully his men had been able to fill their fuel tanker with the diesel required by the rest of the convoy. For now, he would not have to concern himself with that.

Turning in his seat Major Bradley said, "Simmons did you get all the radios working in the convoy vehicles?"

"Yes sir, they should all be on the same frequency as your comms system," replied Specialist Simmons.

"Good work Simmons."

Squeezing the button on his comm link Major Bradley spoke to his men.

"Alright men it looks like we made a clean exit from the airbase. Nice work. Now I want you all to keep an eye out for civilians. Try not to get trigger happy, sound seems to attract those things. If you see anything, report it, otherwise just follow the truck in front of you. Now I want everyone to sound off to make sure we can all communicate?"

A flurry of, "Yes sirs," came over the airwaves as one by one each of the men sounded off. For the next several miles, as the convoy sped along, Major Bradley studied the road maps of D.C. and the surrounding area. He made several notations along their path to Frederick, Maryland just in case they needed to find an alternative route.

Engrossed in his maps Major Bradley felt the Humvee begin to slow and looked up. He let out a groan as up ahead the road was blocked. It looked like there had been an accident. Unfortunately it was on an overpass so there was no way around. He could back up the convoy and take the previous exit and come back up the on ramp but that would take time and it looked like the cars could be moved easily. As the Humvee came to a full stop Major Bradley pressed the button on his comm link.

"Sanchez, Kowalski, and Stevens get out and see if you can move these cars out of our way. We'll use my Humvee to help push through. The rest of you stay on alert for any of those things."

"Private, once they make some progress see if you can use our bumper to push through. We don't want to be sitting still for too long. We need to make it to Fredrick as quickly as possible," Major Bradley said to his driver.

As the three soldiers passed the Humvee at a jog, Major Bradley stood up in the gunner's copula and survey the area around them. From his map he could tell that Route 214 ran under I-95 here with some residential and commercial areas around them. Taking out his binoculars he scanned the area for any signs of civilians. In the distance he could make out figures but from the way they were moving they were most certainly infected. As his soldiers finally moved the wreaked cars to the side his Humvee slowly rolled forward scraping the cars on either side as it push a path through them. After they were clear of the wreck Major Bradley turned to make sure the other vehicles in the convoy made it through. As the last Humvee cleared the cars the radio crackled to life.

"Major we've got a bunch of those things coming up the road behind us. Let's get out of here."

"Thanks for the heads up. Try to hold your fire unless absolutely necessary," Major Bradley replied.

Looking down into the Humvee Major Bradley said, "Alright private, let's get this convoy moving."

Private Sinclair accelerated towards the point where the on-ramp merged with I-95 but then began slowing down again.

"No need to be overly cautious son, just drive," Major Bradley yelled down into the Humvee.

"Um … sir, look over there," he said pointing toward the on ramp, "coming out of the woods."

Major Bradley looked towards the woods on the edge of the on-ramp just in time to see a group of people emerging from the trees at a full run. There appeared a man at the front of the group frantically waving his hands.

"Heads up men we have incoming. Not sure if they are friendly or not. Prepare to engage if necessary," Major Bradley said into his comm link.

As the Humvee closed in, and slowed to a stop, Major Bradley swung the 50 caliber machine gun around and leveled it at the people coming out of the woods.

Chapter 7
The Cowardly Lion

Stephen had his foot on the accelerator well before Dave and Emma screamed in unison, "Let's get out of here!" He turned the wheel hard to the right as the Hyundai's wheels screamed and smoke billowed behind them. With their focus on the group that attacked the young woman, they had not noticed the three other people coming up from behind. Stephen saw them as he straightened out the wheel and the car began to accelerate. Two were close, but off to his left, and were easily avoided. The third was directly in front of them.

Stephen expected her to move out of the way of the oncoming car, but she made no attempt to do so. This forced him to pull the wheel sharply to the right to avoid her. The car reacted quickly but she was knocked down by a glancing blow off the left front quarter panel. Stephen straightened the wheel again and hit the gas pedal while trying to avoid the disapproving look Nick was surely giving him.

There was now no one between the car and the exit. Stephen glanced in the rear view mirror in time to see the woman he knocked over getting back up as if nothing had happened. Trying to shake off the events of the last ten minutes, he focused his concentration on getting them safely away from whatever had just transpired.

They arrived at the end of the road that led out of the park and were faced with a decision; turn left or right on Central Avenue.

"Head toward I-95," Nick offered.

Stephen waited for an objection from anyone, none came.

"My dad may be able to fill us in with what the hell is going on," Nick added.

He pulled out his Uni-phone and attempted to call his old man but it was useless, still no reception.

"These things have turned into expensive paper weights," Nick said as he threw the phone into the center console.

As Stephen turned right heading towards I-95, the car was filled with a binging noise; the one all car owners hate. Stephen looked at the dashboard and saw the red gas pump illuminated.

"We need gas," Stephen said.

"She'll still go for a while," Nick said, "but we should probably find a gas station before we hit the highway."

In the back seat, Emma looked over at Lucy who had barely moved during the whole experience at the park.

"Are you ok," she asked. She got no response. She asked again. This time, Lucy slowly turned her head and looked at Emma. Her eyes were wet and her jaw slack.

After a few seconds she asked, "What were those things? They looked human but they couldn't have been. Could they?"

She was looking directly at Emma but then moved her head and looked at Dave, then Nick in the front seat, and finally Stephen through the rear view mirror. No one had an answer for her.

"This obviously has something to do with what your mother saw on the news before we left," Nick said looking in Stephen's direction.

"What did your mother see?" Lucy asked.

Stephen thought for a moment and then relayed to the rest of the group what he had told Nick in the car before they picked everyone else up.

"That's it?" Dave asked.

"Yea, that was it. Reports were vague and they didn't know very much at the time."

"Well, I'd say things have just gotten a whole lot less vague," Dave countered.

They all had to agree with that.

As they neared another intersection Nick pointed and said, "Over there."

On the corner Stephen saw a Hess station. He slowed down and hung a sharp left and pulled into the gas station. Stephen and Nick got out and looked around. Nick put his head back into the car and asked if anyone had any cash left in case they needed it. They were able to scrape up thirty-six dollars.

Stephen went to the pumps and tried his debit card. No luck. He tried lifting the pump and hitting start. No luck. He turned to Nick who had returned with the thirty-six dollars.

"You ever work at a gas station or convenience store before?" he asked Nick.

"No, but how hard could it be to start the pumps, have you seen some of the geniuses that work at convenience stores."

Nick headed off to the shop as Stephen stayed by the pump. He had a second to look around. The station was deserted. There was no traffic heading in either direction. There were what appeared to be several abandoned cars in the parking lot in a nearby shopping center. Looking further on up the road, it seemed like there was lots of shopping that could be done in the area.

The sun had fully risen by now and what would normally be a busy beginning to a Friday workday near the nation's capital, was nothing of the sort. For the first time Stephen began to worry about his parents.

The car doors opened and Dave, Emma, and Lucy got out. They began to stretch.

"There doesn't appear to be any of those things around here so I think we're safe for the moment," Stephen said.

As he was finishing that statement, Nick had emerged from the Hess store, but he was not alone. There were five men accompanying Nick out of the shop, followed shortly by a sixth man. They were young, probably about the same age as Stephen, maybe a little older. They were dressed in jeans and tee shirts. Two of them wore headbands, one a Washington Nationals baseball cap, two just had their greasy hair exposed and the last one wore a straw cowboy hat, the kind with the sides rolled up. It was the man in the cowboy hat who was immediately recognizable as the leader of the band of misfits.

Stephen looked at Nick who returned a look that was not easily interpreted; a combination of confusion, anger, and fear. The one in the red headband and one of the greasy haired guys each carried large canvas bags that were filled. Baseball Cap carried a lead pipe; the other two did not appear to have any weapons. Cowboy won the prize because he had a gun, and it was pointed in Stephen's general direction.

"What have we here?" Cowboy asked no one in particular.

Stephen moved from behind the pump to the other side so he was between the gang and the car as Nick joined him and turned to face his captors. Emma and Lucy were only a few steps from the car near of the rear passenger's door. Dave was directly in front of the open passenger's side door and he began to slowly move toward it.

"Hey! Where do you think you're goin' Habib?" Cowboy said waving his gun at Dave. "Everyone move over here … slowly." He motioned for the group to move to the right, away from the car.

After they had appropriately complied with Cowboy's request, Stephen asked, "What do you want?"

"What do I want?" Cowboy repeated turning to his posse and laughing as they dutifully followed in kind. "It's Christmas out here man, didn't anyone tell you? Everything is for the taking. We just loaded up at the plaza next door. Now we're heading to Target to finish our shopping."

"So," he continued, "to answer your question, what we want is something to put our loot in," gesturing to the two bags being carried by his associates. "And your car there will do just fine."

Nick was about to voice his displeasure with that arrangement when Cowboy asked, "Who gots the keys?"

Stephen reactively reached for his pocket and then stopped; but it was too late, Cowboy saw it. He motioned for the second greasy haired guy to get the keys. He moved toward Stephen but slowed as he got near, suddenly realizing how big Stephen really was.

He pulled out a knife from behind his back and shoved it in Stephen's face and said, "The keys." Stephen hesitated. Cowboy moved closer raising the gun to eye level.

"Is there a problem big boy?" he asked.

Stephen reached into his pocket and removed the keys to the Hyundai. "No, no problem."

Greasy Hair snatched the keys out of his hand and delivered them to Cowboy, who motioned for the rest of his posse to get into the car. As he moved toward the car he stopped and grabbed Baseball Cap and Blue Headband.

He looked in Emma's direction and said, "What our little shopping trip needs is a woman's touch."

Cowboy moved toward Emma and told his buddies to bring her with them. She screamed and struggled against their grip but could not break free. Dave made a move to help her but Baseball Cap used his lead pipe to keep him at bay hitting him in the shoulder and causing him to fall to one knee.

Stephen saw an opening to get the gun away from Cowboy. He stepped to the left behind Nick and moved toward him. He charged him like he was a quarterback. Cowboy, however, was ready for the move as he turned around and clipped Stephen in the side of the head with the butt of the gun. It was not enough to knock him down but it slowed him and knocked him to the side.

"You get that one for free," Cowboy said, "next time you get the bullet."

They hustled Emma into the car sitting between Greasy Hair One and Two. Cowboy got into the driver's seat. Baseball Cap opened the hatch and emptied all its contents onto the pavement and loaded their ill-gotten goods and himself into the back of the car. Red Headband got in the hatch with Baseball Cap and Blue Headband got in the backseat. Cowboy started the car, put it in drive and took off down the street.

Lucy ran over to Stephen to see if he was okay while Nick did the same with Dave. Stephen had a small gash above his right eye, it was bleeding but he would live. Dave had a welt already developing just below his shoulder. Nick helped him up off his knee.

"Did anyone pack Band-Aids?" Lucy asked looking at the luggage strewn about the pavement.

"No," Stephen said thinking that his mother would have wanted him to, just in case. Nick and Dave each shook their head no.

Lucy stood up, looked around, and headed into the Hess store. "I'll be right back," she said.

Stephen looked over at Nick and asked angrily, "Where did those assholes come from?"

"I was behind the counter attempting to figure how to get the pump started when I heard a noise coming from the back room. At first I thought it might actually be an employee, so I moved from behind the counter so I would not be caught trying to steal gas. Then I thought it might be one of those things from the park and thought about heading out the door when the idiot in the cowboy hat came from out of the back room. He looked out of the window and saw the car and asked if it was ours. I said it was and he sent me back out with his goons while he cracked open the register to grab some cash."

Lucy had emerged from the store carrying Band-Aids, disinfectant, and baby wipes. She approached Stephen and told him to bend over while she wiped the wound with the baby wipes, applied disinfectant, and put two Band-Aids above the eye.

"Thanks," he said. He was finally regaining his senses. He was still a little groggy but had begun to refocus.

"Are you ok?" he asked Dave.

"Yea, I'm all right," Dave replied.

Stephen spun around and looked down Campus Way heading south, the direction Cowboy took off with Emma.

"They aren't going to get too far, they're almost out of gas," Nick said reading Stephen's thoughts.

"Good thing for us we know where they're going," Stephen replied.

"Where's that?" Lucy asked.

"Target," Stephen answered.

"We don't even know where that is," Dave said.

"Yes we do," Stephen said pointing south. They all looked in the direction Stephen was pointing and could barely make out the forty foot beige pylon with the two red circles visible intermittently between the trees. It was probably half a mile away.

"We need weapons of some kind," Nick suggested.

They all turned and looked toward the Hess store. "There's nothing in there," Nick said; Lucy concurred.

There was a plaza behind the gas station. Stephen suggested that they could go there and maybe find something useful. They all agreed.

They were about to head out when Lucy said, "What about our stuff?"

Stephen looked around and asked, "Anybody really need anything out of their bags?"

No one did.

"Let's go get Emma," Stephen said.

"Yeah, and my car too," Nick added.

There was an Ace Hardware in the center of the Plaza. As they approached they discovered there was no need to try the door as the glass window was shattered. Perhaps compliments of their new friends.

"Grab the first thing that looks useful," Stephen instructed.

When they all met five minutes later back at the front of the store, Stephen had grabbed a chopping axe, Nick had a hatchet, Dave found a utility hook knife, and Lucy grabbed a locking knife. Having armed themselves the best they could, they headed back out.

"Be on the lookout for those things," Nick said.

They started heading in the direction of Target at a slow jog. Dave grunted with each step as pain shot down his arm forcing him to carry the hook knife with his good arm.

Ten minutes later they arrived at the edge of the expansive Target parking lot. To their immediate right there was a Giant supermarket which only served to remind them how hungry they were. As they stepped into the parking lot they had to carefully avoid several infected coming out of the supermarket as they made their way toward the Target located at the other end of the property.

Moving slowly across the lot, they hugged a tree line leading to the store. As they approached, they spotted Nick's Hyundai parked at an angle directly in front of the entrance doors. The driver's side door was open. The car appeared to be empty. No sign of Emma.

They crouched down and leaving the cover of the trees headed toward the car. When they reached it, they noticed the car was off. Nick went to the open driver's side door and looked inside; no keys. Cowboy must have them.

Trying to be quiet, they spoke barely above a whisper.

"What's the plan?" Nick asked.

"I got us this far," Stephen said attempting a smile. Looking at Dave he said, "You're the brains here mister pre-med."

Dave said nothing, having said very little since Emma had been kidnapped.

"Emma's in there," Stephen said. "She needs you."

Dave was about to say something when there was a gunshot from inside the store. They all instinctively ducked down behind the Hyundai and gripped their weapons a little tighter. As they slowly got back up to look over the car into the store, a second shot rang out followed by a woman's scream; Emma.

They split in two groups with Dave and Lucy heading around the car to the right, Nick and Stephen to the left. They entered the store and stopped immediately to look around. The shopping carts were off to the right, the registers straight ahead, and the bathrooms to the left. They listened and immediately heard the commotion coming from the back of the store.

The wide aisles made moving to the source of the noise quick and easy. With the domestics department on their left and woman's apparel on their right they came to the end of the aisle and turned left. At the far end, by the sporting goods department, the gang that had hijacked Nick's car found themselves surrounded by a dozen or more of those things. Cowboy's gun must have had only two bullets because he had it in his hand but was not using it.

The infected were closing in on them and it certainly was only a matter of moments before Cowboy and his band of misfits were finished. There was, however, no sign of Emma. Dave had moved off the main corridor down a side aisle, the others had done the same except one aisle up and on the other side.

Out of view of the carnage that was about to take place in sporting goods, Dave moved down the aisle he was in towards the back wall. When he reached the end of the aisle he peeked around the corner. Slouched down, hiding behind a row of bicycles, was Emma.

She did not see him at first. He grabbed a small rubber ball off the shelf and rolled it in her direction. It bounced off the rack that housed the bikes but it was enough to get her attention. She looked over and saw him. She started to get up but then ducked down again as one of the bikes fell of the rack. None of the infected seemed interested in the bike.

Dave waved at her to come toward him. She got up and, moving slowly, made her way toward him. He moved out into the back aisle and headed to meet her. As she passed the double doors that separated the back stock room from the sales floor, they suddenly burst open. Two infected leapt forward reaching for Emma. As she turned to run two more infected people appeared from the side aisle, pushing Emma back into the outstretched arms of the other infected. The momentum from the collision carried Emma and the four infected through the double doors and into the back room. As she was falling into the store room, she looked over at Dave locking eyes with him. She barely had time to scream as she disappeared from view.

Dave halted for a second and then moved forward toward the double doors. He stood there with his utility hook knife raised above his head with his good arm and put his other hand on the door. The sounds coming from behind that door were inhuman. He peered in but the lights were off. It was pitch black in there. Even if he went in he would not be able to see anything, to say nothing of finding Emma; his Emma. He wanted to go in. God knows he did. But he could not muster the will. He told himself there was nothing he could do. She was already gone. He would just be putting himself at risk. He slowly backed away from the door and started heading down the aisle across from the double doors.

It was then he noticed that the struggle down in sporting goods had come to an end. It had become very quiet. Dave, moving more quickly now, came to the end of the aisle and looked down to the right. The infected had finished their attack on Cowboy and his gang. Some were moving away, others were still hunched over their victims … feeding on them.

"Psst."

Dave turned to his left; Stephen was looking at him and mouthing the word 'Emma.'

Dave looked down and shook his head no. Stephen could tell by the look in his eyes that Emma was dead. Stephen motioned toward Dave to follow and he quickly crossed the main aisle to join Stephen, Nick, and Lucy. Without saying a word they made their way to the front of the store where there were three infected milling about at the front door.

Stephen figured they could outrun them and easily make the door before any of them knew they were there. He turned around and saw that some of the infected that were at the back of the store were making their way up front. It was now or never. The group burst out from behind a shelving unit up front and ran for the door. As expected, the infected people reacted slowly. Stephen leading the charge was out first with Lucy right behind him. Nick was next and Dave brought up the rear. Dave's shoulder was really bothering him and he was not able to move quite as quickly as the others.

One of the infected was able to reach out and get a hand on Dave just before he reached the exit. Dave reached for the knife to help extract himself from the thing's grip but no longer had it. He must have dropped it somewhere along the way. He started to panic as he used his one good arm to push the infected person off of him; it was not working. The creature moved closer and Dave could smell its breath. It was rotten. He thought of Emma and how this was the last thing she must have seen, and smelled, and felt. He was about to just give up, figuring he probably did not deserve much better anyway. Just as the thing was about to grab hold with a second hand, a utility hatchet came down with amazing speed in front of him severing the arm that had ahold of him. He stepped back and looked to his right and saw Nick.

Nick grabbed him and yelled, "Come on!"

The severed arm fell harmlessly to the floor as Nick pulled Dave through the door and into the sunlight.

"Where to?" Lucy screamed.

"Anywhere but here," Stephen answered.

Dave was standing next to Nick, still in a state of shock. Nick stood looking at his car.

"Forget it Nick," Stephen said. "No gas and no keys. Unless you want to go back in there and search Cowboy's pockets."

Through the front door four infected began to make their way into the parking lot. One of them was missing an arm. Stephen grabbed Lucy's hand and Nick grabbed Dave by the shirt collar and they began running. At first just to get away from Target and then with adrenalin kicking in, just to run. They ran across several more parking lots and through small clumps of trees. They ran past several roads avoiding numerous infected along the way. They eventually ended up back on Route 214 where they stopped for a second to catch their breath.

They decided to continue on as originally planned; head for I-95 and hope someone was passing by that they could flag a ride down from. They followed Route 214 for the next few hundred yards until they were forced to come to a stop. Up ahead several cars were pulled off to the side of the road. In one of the cars there appeared to be movement but it was difficult to see who or what was the source of the movement. They approached cautiously with Stephen in front, Lucy right behind him, then Dave with Nick bringing up the rear.

Slowly, they approached the right side of the car. Suddenly, the origin of the movement revealed itself. A man in a suit and tie turned to face them. He was, however, drooling uncontrollably and his white button down dress shirt was covered with blood. It did not appear to be his blood. He started to move in their direction when Stephen pointed to a wooded area off to the right.

They took off into the woods coming out into a hotel parking lot. Stephen looked around for a second and then froze. He heard something. The others did as well as everyone turned to the left and looked up towards the Beltway overpass. It sounded like trucks; a lot of trucks. Stephen also thought he heard voices.

They sprinted across the parking lot to the other side and entered a small patch of woods near the on ramp for I-95. As they emerged from the trees a convoy of trucks, military trucks, could be seen heading their way. Stephen ran onto the ramp and began waving his hands furiously attempting to get the attention of whoever was driving the lead vehicle. The convoy appeared to be slowing down. They must have seen him.

Chapter 8
Burtonsville

Kimberly Walker drove north on I-95 traveling at a safe 60 miles an hour. Traffic was very sparse heading north and nonexistent heading south. She would, from time to time, slow down to maneuver around an abandoned car in the road. Occasionally she would look in her rear view mirror to check on the children. Neither of them had said one word since they left their house. Kim had been quiet as well; she had no idea what to say to them.

Danielle sat holding Miss Molly tightly to her chest. She appeared to whisper something in the doll's ear but Kim could not make out what was said. Jason sat in the backseat leaning against the door looking out the window. The three iron that his father had given him he held firmly between his legs. Both of the kids' eyes were moist but neither had cried yet.

"They are probably in some kind of shock," thought Kim.

As they approached Richmond, I-95 was closed to traffic so she had to take Chippenham Parkway. This was a toll highway but there was no one around to take her money so she just drove on through. She was now alone on the road. Not just alone on the road but alone now that Marcus was gone. It was up to her to look out for their children. She needed to be there for them; needed to be strong for them.

The Parkway led to an ordeal of side routes which forced her to drive around the major cities, costing her time and gas. She was finally able to pick I-95 back up again north of Washington D.C. on which she stayed until she reached the Sandy Springs Road exit. Five minutes later she was pulling onto her parent's street.

She had attempted to talk to the kids on a couple of occasions by asking how they were or if they needed anything. Unfortunately, silence was the only reply she received. But now, as they pulled into her parent's driveway, Danielle and Jason began to stir. They sat up in their seats and looked anxious to get out of the car. It must have been the familiar surroundings or it could be simply that it was something not directly associated with the horror that occurred at their house.

Kim immediately noticed that the garage door was open but there was only one car, her mother's. Her dad's car was nowhere in sight. Otherwise, everything looked normal. Just as it had the dozens of other times she had been here with the kids. She parked the car as close to the front door as possible, just in case, and turned around to look into the back seat.

"We're here, everyone out," She said.

Jason and Danielle opened their doors and started to run to the front door.

"Hold up guys," Kim said. "Stick close to me at all times, ok." She turned and locked the car doors with the auto lock.

The kids stopped and turned around waiting for Kim to catch up. When she reached them, she stopped and put her arms around both of her children. She hugged them tight and said, "Let's go see Nanny and Grandpa."

Kim's parent's house was a two story blue and grey colonial built around the turn of the century. They moved here about eight years ago after Kim's father accepted a job offer with a local school to become its principal. It was in a quiet neighborhood which suited them just fine. The house had an attached two car garage off to the left with a small front yard and a fairly big backyard. The front door was large and painted white with a bronze knocker and matching door knob.

Using the knocker, Kim banged on the door twice, waited a second, and then tried the doorknob. It was locked. Luckily, she carried a spare key that her mom gave her several years ago, in case of emergencies. She opened her purse and fished around for it, eventually finding it. She unlocked the door and opened it slowly, peeking inside before letting herself or the kids in. After deciding it was safe to enter, she opened the door wide and the kids ran inside.

"Mom … Dad," Kim called out.

"Nana ... Grampa," Danielle yelled as she darted inside.

The door opened into a small foyer and then into the living room. Off to the right was the kitchen with a formal dining room behind it; to the left, a den and the downstairs bathroom. The upstairs contained three bedrooms and a second bathroom.

Jason walked in last looking around carefully, almost as if he had never been there before. As he moved into the living room, Kim noticed that he was still clutching the golf club and poised to use it if necessary.

Kim turned around to close the front door and paused for a moment as she considered whether or not to relock it. She turned back around and quickly surveyed the condition of the house. No windows were broken, the house was neat and orderly and the front door had been locked when they arrived. She concluded that it was unlikely that any of those … things … were in the house necessitating a quick getaway. She turned back around and locked the door.

Danielle had come back into the living room from the den.

"I don't think they're home Mommy," she said.

"I think you're right honey," Kim answered.

It had been five days since she last spoke to her parents. They had not mentioned anything about leaving but a lot has changed in the last five days. She walked into the den where there was a small closet. She opened it and looked up where there was shelving that would normally house a couple of blankets and their luggage set. Both were missing. She walked back into the living room where her children were now sitting on the sofa looking up at her.

"They must have gone on a little trip, like we're going on," Kim said.

She moved into the kitchen and motioned for Jason and Danielle to follow her. It was a good sized kitchen, square, with a small island in the middle. She went to the refrigerator and opened it to discover it was still working. They had arrived around noon so there was plenty of sunlight and there had been no need to turn on any lights.

"Is anyone hungry?" She asked.

No reply.

"Come on, I know you guys could use something to eat," she coaxed. "We got leftover spaghetti … or how about some chicken wings."

"Is there any mac and cheese?" Danielle asked.

"Let's look," Kim said opening the cabinet door to the right of the refrigerator. On the second shelf was a box of Kraft Mac and Cheese, a parent's best friend.

"We have mac and cheese."

"I'll have some too," Jason added.

Ten minutes later they were sitting around the island all eating mac and cheese. It was the first normal moment they had truly shared in the past few days and by the way they were devouring the contents of their bowls, it was clear that the kids were indeed hungry.

They ate in silence, their mouths full of cheesy goodness. Kim looked around the familiar setting. Her attention suddenly drawn to a piece of notebook paper attached to the refrigerator door by a magnet. She slowly got up from her stool and made her way to the piece of paper, surprised she had not noticed it the first time she opened the door. It was clearly in her father's handwriting.

It read: *Nearest evacuation center at the Frederick Municipal Airport. Departures will initiate at six am on Thursday May 29th. One bag per person allowed.*

"That must be where they went," thought Kim.

She turned around to see her children finishing up their lunch.

"Can I get anyone some more," Kim asked.

"No, I'm full," Danielle said.

Jason shook his head back and forth as he swallowed his last bite. She grabbed the bowls off the counter and went over to the sink to wash them. She turned on the water and the light above the kitchen sink, squirted some dishwashing liquid, and began scrubbing. Looking out onto the front lawn from the kitchen window, she noticed something moving across the street. At first she could not make out what is was then she realized it was someone emerging from behind the Bowman residence.

The light suddenly went dark and the house became eerily quiet as the power went off. She dropped the bowl she was cleaning and it shattered in sink below. A closer look across the street revealed two more people coming from behind the house. The slow methodical movement and the blank stare assured Kim that these were the same things that had attacked Marcus.

Jason and Danielle hurriedly got up from their stools and ran to their mother's side. They were not quite tall enough to see out the window.

"What is it Mom?" Danielle asked, panic creeping into her voice.

"Come with me," Kim said.

She grabbed both their hands and led them back into the living room. As she passed by she grabbed the note on the refrigerator, folded it, and put it in her pocket. She brought the kids to the couch and told them to sit down behind the sofa out of view of the windows looking out onto the front yard. She hunched down, moving quickly, went to the front windows and looked out. Their car was off to the right and seemed to be fine. Across the street the three infected people had become four. They were nearing the edge of the property and appeared to be crossing the street, heading towards Kim and the children.

She looked back at Danielle and Jason. Jason had gotten up and ran back into the kitchen to retrieve the golf club that he had left leaning against the island. He was just getting back now, plopping back down next to his sister. Kim, still hunched down, ran to the other side of the living room where a large picture window looked out on the backyard. Remembering the infected that had suddenly appeared from their backyard at home, she wanted to make sure it was clear before they headed for the car.

"*No more surprises,*" she told herself.

After ensuring it was all clear in the backyard, she went back to the children and put her fingers to her lips and shushed. Grabbing them both, they moved to the foyer where she grabbed her purse, reached in, and grabbed the car keys. Then she slowly unlocked the front door.

In a whisper she said, "I want both of you to run to the car as fast as you can. Get in on the side you were earlier, ok."

They both nodded their heads. Kim looked at Jason and the golf club. She thought briefly about asking for it so she could use it if necessary. The look in her son's eyes told her everything she needed to know. He was not giving up that club to anyone. Not even his mother. His father had given him that club to protect his mom and his sister and that is what he was going to do.

"Swing that thing at anything that moves," she whispered to him.

"Ready?" she asked them. There was more shaking of the heads.

Kim reached for the door handle, turned the knob and slowly opened the door far enough where she could see across the street. She had all four infected people in her sights. They were about halfway across the street. There was plenty of time for the kids and her to get to the car.

She opened the front door the rest of the way and in a loud whisper said, "Go!"

Danielle and Jason moved past her and headed straight for the car reaching it with no problems. Kim unlocked the car with the remote and quickly scanned the area for trouble; there were still only those four infected who were now at the near side of the road about to step on her parent's property.

With the kids safely in the car Kim ran around the front and quickly got in the driver's side door. Once inside, she locked the doors and told her children to keep their heads down, she was going to back out of the driveway. The car started right up and she threw it into reverse and stepped on the gas.

The infected had made it onto the property and taken a definite interest in what was in the car. They turned and headed for the driveway. The Honda lurched and headed straight back. It was almost a clean getaway except the first infected person to reach the driveway was clipped by the back end of the car and sent sprawling onto the front lawn. She told herself she had not purposely veered into the person.

"*But then again, payback is a bitch*," she thought to herself.

Kim drove for a couple of minutes before she realized that she had no idea where she was going. She drove past a grocery store parking lot, made a quick U-turn, and found a spot in the middle of the lot. Keeping the engine running, despite the fuel gauge reading less than a quarter tank, she scanned the area for any immediate danger. Finding none, she put the car in park and opened the glove compartment. She rummaged around looking for an area map but found none. To save a couple of bucks Marcus decided not to get the GPS option in the Honda. He said he always knew where he was going and did not need some machine to tell him when to take a left or right.

"*Marcus was also a practical man,*" thought Kim so there must be a map in here somewhere. Giving up on the glove compartment, she opened the center console, no luck there either.

"Why did we stop?" Jason asked.

"I'm looking for a street map so we can find the airport that Nanny and Grampa went to," she said.

Jason considered his mom's statement for a second then leaned forward; reaching into the pouch attached to the back of the driver's seat, and pulled out a folded street map.

"You mean like this one?" he said holding the map.

"Exactly like that one," she answered with a warm smile.

She took the map from him and unfolded it; all the while her eyes scanning the parking lot. One side was a map of the Virginias, Carolinas, and Tennessee. She flipped it over and there were maps of the Mid-Atlantic States. Looking over the map she decided on the best route to airport. She refolded it and handed it back to Jason.

"Keep an eye on this for me, make sure we're headed in the right direction," she said.

"You got it," Jason replied.

"Mom!" Danielle suddenly blurted out.

"What is it honey," Kim answered while jerking her head back up and looking out toward the parking lot.

"Over there," Danielle said pointing across the street.

Kim turned around and spotted what her daughter had seen. Two people walking toward them from the south. They did not seem to have any of the characteristics Kim observed from the infected individuals. They actually seemed to be weaving in and out of the tree line and using the buildings as cover as they traveled down the street.

Kim was not taking any chances. She had her children to consider. No hitchhikers. She was about to put the car in drive when she heard a muffled scream coming from one of the people walking down the street. She looked back to see them pass by a dry cleaners just as one of those things came out from behind the building. The people ran across the street trying to avoid the infected person, heading toward Kim's car.

Kim put the car in drive, pulled out of the parking lot, and headed north without looking back. *"I never would have done that two weeks ago, leaving someone who so obviously needed my help,"* she thought to herself as she shook her head. She felt like she was barely holding it together.

"How in the world are Jason and Danielle coping so well," Kim contemplated.

Unfortunately, she knew that was only temporary. Everything that happened today would hit them eventually; sooner more likely than later. She just hoped she would be strong enough for them when they really needed her. Right now, however, her job was to find this airport and get her kids and herself to safety. That was assuming that such a safe place existed.

"Take this exit Mom," Jason exclaimed.

Kim slowed the Honda down and turned off I-70 and headed down the off ramp. Jason had done an excellent job navigating and his mother let him know it. He beamed with pride. His father had taught him to read a map and since his dad was not here, the responsibility fell to him.

She followed the signs until she could see the airport in the distance. As she approached Aviation Way she noticed another sign, obviously hastily erected, that read: *Temporary Evacuation Site. Please Proceed with Caution to Gate for Processing.*

She took a left and headed to what must have been the processing gate. There was, however, no one there. She pulled the car up to the gate and put the car in park. Leaving the car running, she leaned in the back seat and told Jason and Danielle to stay put. She exited the car and walked up to the chain-link gate next to which was a guard shack about the size of an old telephone booth. There was a sign on the shack that read: *Please present Identification. Only one bag per person. All persons are subject to inspection.*

As she was reading the sign her attention was drawn to the noise coming from behind the airport tower. She observed three military helicopters slowly rising into the air. Quickly running to the gate she opened it and darted back into the car. She pulled forward, through the gate, and then put the car in park. Getting back out she swung the gate back closed all the while wondering why she was bothering.

"*Must be my OCD,*" she thought to herself.

Getting back in the car, she watched helplessly as the helicopters continued to elevate and head off to the west. She thought about getting out and jumping up and down or waving her hands but they would never see her.

"*Maybe they'll come back for another pick up,*" she thought; but deep inside she knew that probably was not going to happen. The guard shack was empty and there did not appear to be any ground personnel left. She pulled a little further down the road to the actual airport entrance just as the car began to sputter. She had not even noticed she was on fumes.

Reaching behind her into the back seat she grabbed the short wave radio that Marcus had packed. She turned it on and began scanning the stations for any information that might be useful.

"Are the helicopters coming back?" Danielle asked.

"I don't know sweetheart," Kim said. "I'm hoping the radio might tell us something."

As she finished that statement, the radio crackled to life. She moved the knob delicately to get the best reception possible. As she hit on the correct frequency, the speakers erupted with: "*... what the hell do you mean you're not coming back ...*" another voice answered "*... sorry Major, orders are we move to extraction point delta. This one is no longer active. Emergency broadcasts are being updated as we speak. Rescue Six, over ...*"

Chapter 9
Winchester

Three infected people covered in blood slowly ambled towards Chester as he stood frozen next to his truck. They were just like the one he had killed in the woods earlier that day. There was no doubt in his mind that these three were responsible for the death of the two people in the lodge.

As they drew closer, Chester could not tear his eyes away from them. He knew they had been people, but now they were something else. One of them looked like a worker from the bed and breakfast; the man's uniform shirt was covered with blood and other human remains. The second was most likely a tourist staying at the lodge. She wore casual clothes that were torn and bloody and walked with a limp caused by what looked like a large bite in her leg. However, it was the third person who disturbed Chester the most. It was a young girl, probably not yet a teenager. She wore a sun dress that, like the others, was covered in blood and dirt. She had bite marks on her arm and as she came closer Chester could only shudder at the vacant stare she gave him.

As a shiver ran up Chester's spine he finally snapped out of his trance. Running around the driver's door he jumped into the truck slamming the door behind him. Throwing it into reverse, he backed up into a parking spot and then jammed the truck's stick into first, spinning his tries on the loose gravel as he turned toward the road, away from the bed and breakfast.

By then, the three people had closed in on his truck and were almost in front of him. Chester swerved to miss the young girl and was rewarded with the heavy thud of the man hitting the corner of the truck's front bumper. As Chester maneuvered out of the parking lot and onto the access road, he looked into his review mirror to see the man slowly crawl to his feet, joining the other two people slowly following in the wake of his truck.

It had been almost an hour since leaving the grisly scene at the bed and breakfast but Chester could still not shake the image of the young girl. Despite his rough exterior, Chester had a small soft spot when it came to children. Finally shaking the image from his head, he began trying to puzzle out what was happening in the world around him. He had been in the woods for six days hunting, hiking, and camping.

Before he had started his trip, he remembered hearing reports about looting, rioting, and general unrest in Florida but could not imagine this was in some way related. The 'people' he had encountered were most definitely not looters or rioters; something more was going on. To take his mind off of what he had witnessed earlier, Chester turned on his shortwave to see if he could get any new information from the emergency broadcasts. As he continued to bump along down the mountain road he tuned his receiver until he found a broadcast.

"Attention all citizens, evacuation zones in North Carolina and Southern Virginia have been closed. Please proceed north or west to the next closest evacuation zone. Stay tuned for specific locations."

As the broadcast began listing various evacuation zones Chester had already made up his mind what to do. He would head to Winchester, Virginia to see if he could find the only friend from VMI that he still stayed in contact with, Douglas Stanton. Douglas had served in the military after graduating VMI and upon retirement went on to be a civilian analyst for the US Army Command. If anyone knew what was going on it, would be Douglas.

After consulting his maps as he drove, Chester planned to make his way over the Blue Ridge Mountains and into Tennessee where he could get onto I-81 and take it north through the Shenandoah Valley to Winchester. First he wanted to stop at the Park Ranger headquarters to see if anyone there could fill him in on what was happening.

Upon his arrival, Chester found the place abandoned. He was, however, able to restock some of his provisions and ammunition from the supplies there; as well as fill several jerry cans with extra fuel for the trip. Before he ran into any more of those things, Chester got back on the road and began heading north. To his surprise he encountered very little traffic on the road. He saw a few of the 'people' which he learned from subsequent radio broadcast were being called the infected. As he made his way across the state line into Virginia he saw fewer and fewer people traveling on the highway, until he was left alone driving with his thoughts and carefully avoiding the odd abandoned car.

Reaching Winchester just before dark, Chester was able to find his friend's home without mishap. He did not hold out much hope that Douglas would be there as most of the surrounding area seemed to be deserted. He had seen a number of the infected once he entered the suburban areas but had managed to avoid them. He also was certain he had seen a gang of looters inside a pharmacy he had driven by.

Not in the mood to deal with anyone, he had just kept on driving. Now, as dusk settled, he pulled up in front of Douglas' house and turned the truck off. It was a small split level with tan siding and over grown flower beds. It did not look like anyone was home. There was no car in the yard and none of the lights were on. Chester quickly realized there were no lights on in any of the others houses either, not even the street lights were lit. Grabbing his pack and heading to the front door, Chester knocked, but predictably no answer came. Looking around the front door he found the fake rock that Douglas had mentioned to him on a previous occasion he hid his key in. Retrieving the key he let himself into the house, closing and locking the door behind him.

"Douglas won't mind if I camp out here for the night," thought Chester.

Setting his pack down he quickly made his way through the rest of the house making sure Douglas was not home and that no one else had taken up residence. Now in the downstairs level, he found the closet were Douglas kept his camping gear and hunting equipment. Despite Chester's general dislike of people, Douglas and he had gone on a number of hunting and camping trips together. Both being men who only spoke when they had something useful to say made their friendship work. Chester opened the closet to find it mostly empty.

"He must have taken his gear and gone to his hunting cabin in Pennsylvania," Chester thought as he went through what little of the gear remained in the closet.

In the morning, Chester decided, he would head that way as well. If there was anyone he could stand being around in this situation it would be Douglas. He headed back up the stairs to the entrance landing and then out to his truck to retrieve his camp stove. Quietly making his way to the small shed around the back of the house, he looked around for extra propane tanks for the stove. Chester found three camping size propane tanks and two full size tanks. Knowing he could always use them later he put the full size and extra camping tanks in the back of his truck.

As he was about set up the small stove in the driveway he noticed movement down the road. There, slowly shuffling towards him, were two infected people. Quickly gathering the stove he silently made his way back inside. Peering out of the window he watched as the two infected gradually made their way by the house. Realizing he might not be as safe as he thought, Chester went around the house making sure all the doors and windows were secure before heading to the upstairs level with the camp stove. Making his way into a small office Chester set the stove on a small wooden desk under the window. He opened the window to vent the stove and turned it on. While he waited for the stove to heat up he went down stairs grabbed his pack and a couple bottles of water he found in the pantry.

As Chester settle down for a meal of rehydrated spaghetti he debated with himself whether or not to go back to his truck and retrieve his gun for the night. As he finished his meal he decided against it and instead went into the master bedroom. Getting down on his hands and knees he searched under the bed until he found what he was looking for. Taped to bottom of the box spring was a sawed off shotgun and a case of shells. Letting a rare smile creep across his face, Chester loaded the shotgun, shut the bedroom door, kicked off his boots and settled into the double bed for a good night's sleep; shotgun laying across his chest.

Chapter 10
Rescued?

Nick emerged from the woods in time to see Stephen waving his arms frantically in the direction of the convoy. As Nick came up beside him, Stephen said, "I think they saw us."

"I hope so," Nick said, and then added, "they better get here quick because I'm pretty sure I saw some of those things coming out of the hotel we just passed back there."

Lucy and Dave finally came out of the woods and walked to the edge of the on ramp. Dave's left shoulder was hanging low and he was obviously in a lot of pain. The run had taken quite a bit out of him.

Stephen's anticipation was quickly replaced with apprehension when he noticed the serious looking soldier in the first vehicle swing his large machine gun in his direction. He stopped waving his arms and held his arms straight up in a surrender position.

"Put your hands up in the air, like this," he said to the rest of the group. Everyone did as instructed except Dave who could not get both arms up in the air. Stephen heard the soldier behind the machine gun shout instructions to three other soldiers walking alongside the convoy.

The three soldiers began jogging toward Stephen with guns at the ready, prepared to use them if necessary. Two of the soldiers arrived a minute later while the third held back acting as a lookout, presumably to keep an eye out for any trouble.

The one whose name patch read 'Sanchez' looked Stephen's group over then spoke into his comm link saying, "We got four civilians Major." He listened for a second and then responded, "Copy that."

Turning his attention to the students he said, "Have any of you had contact with any infected persons?"

"You could say that!" Nick answered.

This caused Sanchez and the other soldier, whose name patch read 'Kowalski', to raise their weapons.

"Check them for bite marks 'Ski," Sanchez said to Kowalski.

Following orders, Kowalski inspected all of them for any evidence of contamination; bite marks, torn clothing, blood stains. Dave had some stains on his shirt from the arm that was severed back at Target, but they were black, not red. While Kowalski was examining the students, Sanchez took a small Maglite out of a pocket in his uniform and began scanning each of their eyes.

Kowalski glanced at the Band-Aids on Stephens head, to which Stephen said, "Don't worry, my head just ran into the butt of a pistol."

When he was done, Kowalski nodded at Sanchez who in turn spoke into his comm link, "They're clean Major."

Kowalski had taken the hatchet Nick had stuck in his waistband. Showing it to Sanchez, he addressed the other students, "Does anyone else have any weapons?"

Lucy reached into her front pocket and pulled out the knife she had concealed in her jeans and handed it over. Stephen reached down and retrieved the axe that he had placed on the ground next to him.

"We needed these to protect ourselves from those things," Stephen said as he offered the axe to Sanchez.

"You'll get them back," Sanchez answered. As he was about to take the axe from Stephen, shots rang out.

The serious looking soldier in the front Humvee of the convoy yelled down to Sanchez and Kowalski, "Sergeant, get those civilians into the second truck now!"

"*He must be the Major,*" thought Stephen.

Sanchez yelled at the students, "Follow me!"

He led them alongside the convoy, with Kowalski in the rear, passing several other Humvees. On the other side of the guardrail was the third soldier who had held back and Stephen saw that he was the one who opened fire. The infected Nick had seen earlier were now coming out of the same trees that the students had recently emerged from.

When they reached the second truck, Sanchez hopped in the back first to help the students into the truck. Lucy went first, grabbing hold of the soldier's hand, she was pulled in and told to sit on one of the bench seats on either side. Dave was next, offering his good arm to Sanchez he grunted as he fell into the truck. Stephen and Nick were nearly all the way in when Sanchez turned around to help them.

After everyone was seated, Sanchez pressed his comm link and said, "Civilians secure Major." He listened for a second and again said, "Copy that."

Moving to the end of the truck, Sanchez leaned out and said, "Ok Kowalski, time to …"

By the time Sanchez had seen the infected person it was too late. The thing had crawled up the hill and around the guardrail unseen. Everyone was looking up, not down. It had grabbed ahold of Kowalski's boots and pulled his feet out from under him. Caught by surprise and still holding the hatchet he had procured from Nick, he fumbled with his weapon and was unable to get off a shot before he hit the ground hard. The collision caused him to drop the hatchet. Before he knew it, the man was on him.

Sanchez, having placed his rifle down to help the students into the truck, reached for his sidearm. He took aim on the infected man and fired once, hitting it square in the head and removing most of its skull. The man went limp and Kowalski was able to push him off. Trying to get up, he rolled over and looked at

Sanchez. It was then he put his hand up to his neck and felt the deep gash left by the infected man. Looking at his hand he saw the blood dripping from his fingers.

Kowalski nodded in Sanchez' direction and said weakly, "Go ahead, you gotta do it man." Sanchez hesitated. His friend continued, "You can't leave me like this … please."

Looking down at his friend, Sanchez knew it was over for him. There was nothing anyone could do for him now. Well, almost nothing. Sanchez raised his sidearm one more time and did his buddy one final favor.

Sanchez moved back into the truck and sat on the bench across from Stephen. After holstering his weapon, he stared down at the ground for a second. Reaching for his comm button, he paused a moment as if to gather himself, then spoke in even tones, "Major, we lost Kowalski," then added with more urgency, "we need to move now sir, those things coming up from behind us will be here any minute."

This time he did not wait for a response, he took his hand off the button and leaned back against the side of the truck banging his head against the canvass lining. Turning his head to the left he looked out at the fuel truck behind them and then beyond it to the approaching horde of infected. A few seconds later, the truck lurched forward and they were once again moving.

Stephen looked at the soldier sitting directly across from him, the axe between his legs, and saw he was obviously distraught. He had lost one of his friends while saving Stephen and his friends. He did not know what to do or say. He felt like he should thank him but could not quite form the words. Would a thank you even be enough; it seemed to Stephen to be inadequate. Surely soldiers are trained, even prepared, for the loss of life. Be it the enemy, or a buddy, and even their own.

Finally, Stephen said, "Sorry about your friend."

Sanchez looked at Stephen with a hard stare but said nothing. He then looked at Nick sitting to Stephen's left and then to Lucy and Dave sitting to his right on the same side of the truck.

Gripping the butt of his rifle tighter he looked down and shook his head ever so slightly. He looked back up and locked eyes with Stephen. He was about to say something when his head jerked slightly and he put his hand up to his ear. Something was coming through his comm link.

Major Bradley was very upset. No, make that pissed off. He always loathed losing men under his command. He had lost quite a few during his time in Korea; but as an officer it was his job to make decisions and sometimes those decisions put people in harm's way. That, however, was not what had him really fuming; it was that this outcome, he felt, could have been avoided. Losing someone was one thing, losing someone unnecessarily, was another.

Major Bradley pressed the comm link button and then cleared his throat.

"Listen up," the Major began then paused, not for effect, but to make sure everyone was listening. "We lost a good man today. I want each of you, in your own way to pay your respects when you feel the time is right. But I also want this to serve as a lesson. We cannot afford to be lax in our diligence. We must remain steadfast in our attention to detail. We are in uncharted territory here men. We must be prepared for anything at any time." Pausing again; this time for effect, he concluded by saying, "We should be at the extraction point within the hour. That is all."

He hoped that his men would take his speech to heart. He could ill afford to lose another man. Not just from an emotional standpoint but from a cold hard analytical standpoint; he did not have that many men to begin with.

The convoy continued on the Beltway without incident, while the Major scanned the areas they passed with his binoculars for any sign of civilians. None were found. Although they had traveled this same route picking up civilians before, he was still a little surprised they had not encountered anyone else besides the four young people at the overpass.

He did, of course, spot plenty of infected people wandering around aimlessly. He instructed his men to leave them alone if they were not a direct threat to the convoy or any civilians. Thankfully, very few of the infected were on the highway and the convoy was able to maneuver around the abandoned cars with little trouble.

Exiting the Beltway the convoy headed west towards Frederick. As they neared the airport the Major trained his binoculars toward the tarmac. He spotted three Chinook helicopters preparing for takeoff behind the tower.

He turned in his seat and said, "Simmons, see if you can raise anyone on those helicopters."

"Yes sir," replied Simmons.

As the convoy turned right onto Monocacey Boulevard, Simmons said, "I have a Captain Jeter on the comm sir, pilot of Rescue Six."

The Major was about to speak when he saw the birds taking off. Speaking quickly he said, "Captain, this is Major Charles Bradley, I have four civilians en-route, ETA five minutes, I need you to remain grounded until I can deliver, over."

"Sorry sir, that's a negative, all three birds are full up, over," the Captain responded.

"When is your estimated return time, over?" Bradley asked.

"Sorry again sir, that's a negative on our return, this site has been shut down. It's been deemed too hot by Colonel Jepson. We are moving farther west, over."

Furious, Major Bradley yelled, "What the hell do you mean you're not coming back."

"Sorry, major our orders are to move to extraction point delta. This one is no longer active. Emergency broadcasts are being updated as we speak. Rescue six, over … and out."

Major Bradley was about to tell Simmons to try and reach Colonel Jepson when Sinclair said, "Sir, up ahead. What would you like me to do?"

The Major refocused his attention to what was in front of the convoy. It was the temporary processing gate. He surveyed the makeshift entry point and being in no mood to waste time, he leaned over and told his Sinclair, "Run it."

"Yes sir, no problem."

Private Sinclair hit the accelerator and crashed through the chain-link breaking the gate apart at the posts. The Major lifted his binoculars again and peered out toward the airport. Off to the left he noticed several rows of cars parked rather haphazardly; obviously left by those civilians who were fortunate enough to get on one of the helicopters. A group of what appeared to be three people, one adult and two children were making their way toward the parked cars. They were moving rather quickly so the Major assumed they were human but after what had happened to Kowalski, he was not taking any chances.

"Private, head to those parked cars over there," he said pointing to the left adding, "and be alert."

"Yes sir," Private Sinclair answered.

Kimberly Walker had decided to see if she could find her father's car among the several hundred that were parked in field of grass across from the airport. She figured if they made it here their car would be here. She really hoped the car was there. It would mean that her parents were probably safe. With Jason, still holding the golf club, and Danielle in tow, never more than a few feet away from her, they reached the rows of cars.

Kimberly was looking for a light blue 2028 Toyota Sequoia. The relatively short trip here from her parent's house hopefully meant there was still a fair amount of gas left in the Sequoia; which was good because the Honda was on empty.

For once luck was with her as she spotted the car almost immediately. It was in the last row, fifth from the end. Moving quickly, she ran to the car and read the license plate; indeed it was her dad's car. She motioned for the kids to get in. The doors were unlocked so she sat in the driver's seat while the kids jumped in the back. Now all she needed were the keys. She had a spare set in her pocketbook that her parents had given her. As she reached in her purse to look for the keys, she heard the undeniable rumbling of heavy vehicles coming her way.

She looked out the back window and saw a row of military vehicles pass by. It was hard to make out how many or exactly what kind because of the glare of the sun and dust the vehicles were kicking up.

What she did see was a number of men on foot starting to surround her car. She resisted the urge to open the car door and run out waving her hands in the air.

"Stay put," She told the kids.

Finally one of the soldiers surrounding the car yelled, "If you can hear me, exit the vehicle slowly with your hands in the air."

Kim nodded to Jason and Danielle that it was ok.

"Slowly," she said to them.

Kim cracked the driver's side door open slowly and put one foot on the ground, then the other. She gradually stood up, arms above her head, and turned to face the soldiers. For the first time she got a good look at the convoy. There were seven trucks and about a dozen men as far as she could tell.

"Now turn and face the vehicle, placing your hands on the car," came the next order.

She turned to comply, now looking at her kids on the other side. For some reason Jason got out on the same side as her sister. He was still, she noticed, holding the club.

After the woman and two kids had been checked for infection, the Major came down from his perch on top of the Humvee and introduced himself.

"Major Charles Bradley, ma'am," he said extending his hand.

"Kim Walker," she answered returning the gesture. Looking at her children she continued, "That one over there clutching Miss Molly is my daughter Danielle and the one holding the golf club is my son, Jason." The kids nodded but said nothing.

The Major took a step toward Jason and hunched down to get nearly eye level with him.

"What's the golf club for?" he asked.

"For protection," Jason answered. "I have to make sure my mom and sister are safe because my dad isn't around now to do it."

"Oh," Bradley said looking at Kim. She didn't need to say anything; he read the whole story in her expression. Returning his attention to Jason he added, "Well Jason, looks like you've done a great job so far." The Major stood back up but never took his eyes off Jason. "Do you think it would be ok if I helped you look out for your mom and Danielle?"

Jason looked at his mom and then the Major and then his mom again. Thinking for a second he finally said, "I guess that would be ok."

The Major clapped Jason on his shoulder and said, "Sounds like a plan, son."

Moving closer to Kim and turning his back slightly so the children would not easily overhear him he said, "Ms. Walker, I don't believe those helicopters that you must have seen leaving are going to be coming back. I don't know what plans, if any, you may have but I'm going to have my communications specialist try to contact a Colonial Jepson and see if we can't get one more chopper here to pick you up. But, to be honest, I think that it's a long shot. We're going to camp here for the night and if no helicopters arrive by first light, we're going to move out. You and your children are welcome to travel under our protection."

"Thank you Major, that's very kind of you," Kim said. "But is it safe to stay here?"

"The buildings behind you should afford us a certain degree of safety and we are in an open field, we should be able to spot any trouble easily enough," Major Bradley said.

"Then I accept your offer," she said.

"Then I suggest you grab any personal belongings that you think you'll need out of the car and hop in that second cargo truck."

"Where?" she asked.

He smiled and said, "The one in front of the fuel truck."

"Oh, ok," she replied and grabbed her kids by the hand and started off toward the Honda.

The Major noticed this and said, "Aren't you going to grab anything out of your car?"

She stopped, hesitated for a second, and then let out an actual giggle. "This," pointing to the Toyota, "is actually my dad's car. I was thinking of taking it because my car," she said pointing to the Honda about one hundred yard away, "is out of gas."

"I see. Hold on one minute for me will you?" said the Major.

"Stevens!" the Major shouted.

Jogging over was Private Stevens, "Sir?"

"Please escort Ms. Walker and her children to their car and help them retrieve their belongings."

"Yes sir," Stevens replied, turning his attention to Kim he said, "after you, ma'am."

As they walked over to the Honda Kim was doing a mental inventory of what they had packed.

Noticing that, Stevens offered, "I would suggest bringing only what is necessary. We may have to move quickly."

She nodded as they got to the car. She opened the back door and grabbed the radio. Nothing else in the car seemed important enough. She moved around to the trunk and opened it up. Staring inside she saw the cooler, two blankets, three suitcases and some camping equipment including the Coleman flashlights.

Stevens could not help himself and peered inside. "We definitely could use those flashlights if you'd consider donating them to the cause."

"Of course," she said and pulled them out of the trunk handing them to the private.

She decided to take all of the kids' and her luggage and go through it later, deciding then what to keep and what to leave behind. She would bring the blankets to have something to sleep on but leave the camping equipment behind. After removing the kids' bags, she reached in to grab her luggage but hesitated. She noticed a small black hard plastic case behind where Jason's bag was. She lifted her luggage and dropped it on the ground then reached deep into the trunk and removed the case.

Placing it on the edge of the cars bumper she stared at it.

"What's that Mommy?" Danielle asked.

"I don't know," was Kim's only response.

Private Stevens looked at the black case and said, "Looks like a gun case ma'am."

"A gun case?" she repeated, "but we don't own a gun."

"Looks like you do now," Stevens replied.

"How do you open it?" she asked Private Stevens.

"Usually with a key or a combo lock," he answered. Studying the case he said, "Look, right there," pointing to a four digit dial combination lock on the case's handle. "You just need to move the numbers on the dial to whatever the four digit code is and it should open."

"I don't have any idea what the com ..." she stopped in mid-sentence and lifted the case upright to better view the combo lock. Slowly moving her fingers over the numbers she turned the first digit to a '2'; then, a little more quickly, finished the code with a '3' and a'6' and finally another '6'. Leveling the case she began lifting the top half. It easily separated from the bottom half revealing a shiny black handgun.

She was about to start cursing Marcus under her breath; buying a gun without consulting her, he knew how she felt about guns. She hated them, especially if the kids got ahold of it and it went off by accident. She shuddered just thinking about it. The question now, however, was what the hell she was going to do with it.

"What am I going to do with it?" she mumbled to herself letting her internal thoughts come out.

It was loud enough, however, for Private Stevens to hear.

"If you don't mind me sayin' ma'am, given our current situation, it's probably the only thing in that car I would consider a necessity."

Chapter 11
All Flights Cancelled

As the convoy rumbled onto the tarmac Major Bradley was pleased to see there were no signs of any infected. He shook his head as this confirmed his suspicions that Colonel Jepson had been wrong about this extraction zone being unsafe. Not that the surrounding area was devoid of infected, but at least the airport did not look overrun. Surveying the airport's buildings he knew exactly where they would be spending the night. The airfield's control tower rose above the other buildings giving a commanding view of the surrounding area.

Major Bradley activated his comm link and said, "Alright gentlemen we'll be lodging in the control tower tonight. Get the deuce and a halves and fuel truck right up next to the front door. The Humvees will form a half circle security ring in front of them. Then we'll clear the building. Make sure you stay alert."

As the convoy positioned itself in front of the control tower, Major Bradley got out of his Humvee and walked towards the back of the second deuce and a half. As the civilians hopped out of the truck he waved over his soldiers as well.

"I am going to give it to you all straight. It looks like the helos might not be coming back for us. We'll spend the night in the tower and I'll see if I can get ahold of someone to send something back to pick us up. If not, we'll head out bright and early tomorrow morning."

Turning to his soldiers Major Bradley continued, "Captain Morris take some men and clear this tower, I don't want any nasty surprises during the night. Simmons, once the tower is clear you get up to the control room and set up your radio, see if you can contact anyone. The rest of you keep watch until the tower is clear."

Looking back at the group of civilians he said, "You folks just hang tight here, I don't want you wondering off. Once the tower is safe and we get inside, you can do as you like as long as you stay in the tower."

As soon as Captain Morris and his men had cleared the tower Major Bradley ushered the civilians inside and placed a guard at the door to make sure nothing got in and no one snuck out. Heading back to his Humvee he found Specialist Simmons gathering up his radio gear.

"Simmons, I want you to get up to the top of the tower. See if you can plug into their communications equipment and contact someone at NORAD," Major Bradley said.

"Yes sir!"

Simmons headed into the building lugging his radio equipment with him. As he disappeared Captain Morris came out and headed for Major Bradley.

"Sir, there's no way anything is getting in that tower without going through us first."

"Very good Captain we should be safe here tonight then. Is there anything else?"

"Yes sir, we don't have much in the way of food for the civilians. Our men have their MREs and the lady with the kids had some food in a cooler but that's it."

"I figured we would eventually have to address the food supply, especially with civilians involved now." Gesturing down the road Major Bradley continued, "We passed some warehouse buildings on the way in and I saw a number of semis parked outside of them. Top off all our vehicles with diesel and then take some of the men along with the fuel truck and refill it. While you are there, see if the men can find a break room and vending machines that might have some food and drinks. Then check over at the offices buildings across the street for the same. I know they'll have coffee and I'll need that in the morning."

"Sounds good sir we'll get right on it."

"You and your men keep a low profile Captain, and get back here before dark. We can't afford to lose any more men."

As Captain Morris gathered his men and headed to the fuel truck Major Bradley turned to the group of civilians huddled next to the truck.

"Ok folks it's safe to go inside. Make yourselves comfortable but do not try and leave the building. We will stay here for of the night."

Speaking up from the back of the group Dave asked, "Did I hear you say something about food?"

"Don't worry about that, I have men out gathering some," replied Major Bradley.

"We could always help look for supplies," said Stephen.

"I don't think that's a good idea son. My men are trained and armed. I don't want to have to worry about a bunch of civilians running around. You folks just make yourselves at home in the tower."

Major Bradley turned and motioned for one of his soldiers to herd the civilians inside. Once they were in the tower, Major Bradley grabbed his map case and headed up the stairs to find Specialist Simmons.

Stephen held the door as the others made their way into the control tower. With an annoyed look back at Major Bradley he followed the others inside. The tower was a small building to begin with but Stephen was surprised to see that the ground floor contained only an office and a stairwell leading up to the observation deck. The others shuffled into the office in front of him. The room had a window with a shade half way drawn allowing enough of the early evening light in to see a small desk with a computer, a conference table, and four chairs around it. In the corner was a file cabinet and the walls were decorated with memo papers and maps. Out of instinct Stephen closed the door behind him and sunk to the floor next to Nick. Lucy and Dave took a seat at the conference table while the lady and the two kids huddled together on the floor on the opposite side of the room.

Clearing his throat Stephen said, "I guess we should all introduce ourselves."

"I'm Stephen, this is Nick, that's Dave and Lucy," he continued gesturing around the room.

"Nice to meet ya'll, I'm Kim and these are my kids Jason and Danielle."

"Hi," said the two kids in unison.

"That's a nice doll you have there Danielle," said Lucy, "what's her name?"

"Miss Molly," Danielle replied sheepishly, hugging the doll closer to her chest.

"So what's with the golf club Jason," asked Stephen.

"My, my … dad … um gave it to me … for um … protection," stammered Jason. "Why do you, you know, have an axe?"

"Same reason as you, for protection," answered Stephen with a slight smile. "Well it's nice to meet you guys considering the circumstances. Where are ya from?"

"We're from Petersburg, Virginia; what about you guys," replied Kim.

"Believe it or not we are from Anaheim, California."

"California? What in the world are you doing out here?

"Kind of a funny story, but this ugly lug over here has visited almost every Six-Flags except for the one outside of D.C. so he dragged us all out here," chimed in Nick dryly.

"And you wanted to visit your dad," Stephen said giving Nick a look.

Stephen continued, "It's been an interesting trip to say the least. We had no idea what we were driving into. When we left we heard of possible riots in Florida and then drove straight through and didn't hear anything else. Things just kept getting stranger and stranger the farther east we went."

"Yeah, things got out of control faster than anyone realized, including the military," Kim replied nodding to the door. "I heard you guys talking about food outside, we've got a little in this cooler we can share until those army guys find more."

"That would be great," said Dave speaking up for the first time.

"Ok I'll divide it up; I think we should save some for later too."

Opening the cooler Kim took out some peanut butter and jelly sandwiches and began splitting them in half and handing them around the room. Dave grimaced as he reached for the sandwich but soon had the whole thing stuffed in his mouth.

"Are you ok?" Kim asked Dave noticing the dark stains covering his shirt. "You didn't get bit by one of those things did you?"

"No, no bite. It's just my shoulder. We had a run in with some looters," Dave replied.

"Sounds like we've all had a rough couple of days," said Kim looking down at her two kids.

"This is the first chance we have to process it," said Stephen. "It all happened so fast once we got to D.C."

In the silence that followed it finally began to sink in for Stephen, Nick, Lucy and Dave. So much had happened in the past few days, all with no time to really understand what was happening.

Finally Nick broke the silence, "So what is going on Kim. Like Stephen said, we've been traveling the past couple of days and once we realized something was going on none of our Uni-phones worked. All we know is we saw a lot of people heading west, people biting and eating other people, and looters. Those …

those cannibal people or infected people or whatever the army guys call them even got Emma."

With that Dave let out a sob and buried his head in his hands.

"Real nice Nick see what you did," said Lucy has she put a comforting hand on Dave's shoulder.

"Who's Emma?" asked Kim.

"She is er ... was Dave's girlfriend. Some looters kidnapped her and stole my car. That's when Dave hurt his shoulder," answered Nick. "We tracked them down but we all got attacked by those things and then Emma ..."

"Shut up Nick, you're not helping," growled Lucy.

"Sorry," mumbled Nick looking down at the ground.

As Dave continued to sob Kim got up and went over to him. Kneeling down in front of him she grabbed his hands and looked him in his eyes.

"I know what you are going through," she said comfortingly. "I watched my husband get taken by those things. He saved our lives. I am sure you did everything you could to save her. There's just no stopping those things."

Dave sputtered out thanks and went back to sobbing as Kim went back to her kids and pulled them both in close as they began to quietly cry.

"I am sorry to hear about your husband," Stephen said quietly. "It sounds like he was a brave man."

"He was, thank you," replied Kim as a tear rolled down her cheek.

"It seems like you've got a little better handle on this then we do but could you tell us what the heck is going on?" asked Stephen.

Wiping her eyes Kim responded, "It started in Florida, around Miami. At first there were just reports of rioting and random violence. But that grew out of control and then the government thought that maybe there was something causing mass hysteria. Soon they blamed it on terrorism and thought something was contaminating the water supply. Then it started to spread, quickly. Lots of cities were being overrun with the violence. Rumors were coming in that people were eating each other. They referred to them as 'the infected.' Before the news stations starting going dark and the power went out we heard there were evacuations zones being set up. We decided to head north to find one and well, here we are."

"Wow, no wonder we couldn't get anything on our Uni-phones," said Nick.

"That would explain a lot of what we saw driving out here," said Stephen.

"Yeah but why couldn't the government or army stop this?" asked Nick.

"I don't know, but I think those would be questions for Major Bradley," answered Kim.

For the next hour the small group of civilians talked sporadically with each other, sharing their stories and their grief. They were only interrupted when Major Bradley and Captain Morris knocked on the door and entered the room each carrying a box.

"Here are some blankets and a couple couch cushions my men were able to round up for you," Major Bradley said setting his box on the table.

This is Captain Morris he's my XO," he said eliciting quizzical looks from the civilians. "Kind of like my right hand man. So if any of you need anything or have a problem he'll have the solution. His men were able to round up some food from a couple break rooms and vending machines."

"I'll leave you to it Captain," Major Bradley said with a nod and then exited the office.

Captain Morris set his box on the table began to hand out a small assortment of candy bars along with a bottle of soda for everyone.

"You don't have a diet one in there do you?" asked Lucy absent mindedly.

"Miss, I think that's probably the least of your worries," replied Captain Morris.

"We'll have to ration out the food and drinks as we don't know when we'll find more of it," Captain Morris continued. "I am leaving a guard right outside this door tonight so you all can sleep easy; you look like you need it."

As he finished passing out the food, Captain Morris noticed the black gun case nestled in the few belongings that Kim had brought into the office.

"Is that your gun ma'am."

"Um, well it was my …. my … husbands … but I guess it's mine now," Kim replied looking at the floor.

"Do you know how to use it," asked Captain Morris.

"Not really," replied Kim.

"It would probably be a good thing to know. Anyone here know how to use a gun?" asked Captain Morris as he looked around the room.

Everyone shook their head except Nick who spoke up, "Yeah I do. I used to go shooting with my dad."

"Ok then. Let me give the rest of you a quick crash course. You know, just in case," Captain Morris said uncertainly.

The nods around the room reassured him and he reached for the case.

"First things first, what's the combo in case someone needs to get in," he asked.

"Umm, 2, 3, 6, 6," said Kim.

Captain Morris applied the combination and then opened a case to reveal a brand new Glock semi-automatic pistol. Holding it up for all the civilians to see he showed them how to hold and aim the gun. He then proceeded to show them how to turn the gun safety on and off and how to make sure there was no bullet chambered in the gun. Passing the gun around so everyone could get a feel for it, Captain Morris talked about when and how to use it safely. Finally when it came back to him, he showed how to insert and eject the ammunition clip of which there were three in the gun case. After everyone had a chance to practice loading and unloading the gun and asking any questions they had Captain Morris returned the gun to the case, locked it and handed it back to Kim.

"I hope you all can remember most of what I said. It could save your life or the lives of those around you one day," said Captain Morris.

"Anything else before we turn in," he asked surveying the room.

"Will we be leaving in the morning?" asked Kim.

"If we can't get into contact with anyone we'll leave early tomorrow."

"Anything we can do to help?" asked Stephen.

"Tonight, no," replied Captain Morris. "For now try to get some sleep and we'll see you all in the morning."

Turning on his heel Captain Morris left the room, closing the door tight behind him. The group ate their meager rations in silence and then each grabbed a blanket. Finding as comfortable of a position as they could, they settled in for a fitful, albeit much needed night's sleep.

Chapter 12
The Benefactor

"It really is a spectacular view," thought Dr. Sanderson. He was standing, arms folded, in front of a large row of picture windows looking out onto the beautiful snowcapped Rocky Mountains. He had been admiring this view for over a week now but was beginning to run out of patience.

The nebbish Doctor stood at five foot nine with dark brown hair that was speckled with white. In his early fifties he had, up until now, been able to maintain his slim build. He wore glasses that were usually found atop his head.

He turned around and headed back into the large den where he had spent most of his time during the past week. It was a large office space with a set of two steps leading back down from the picture windows. To the Doctor's right was a large mahogany desk and leather chair, with rows of books lining the shelves behind it. Straight ahead of him was an oval conference table with six chairs on either side and one at each end. Notepads, folders, and various documents littered the table along with the Doctor's personal computer. To his left, a couch was flanked by two living room chairs and a small coffee table in front of the sofa. The furniture faced a roaring fireplace with a large screen television above it. At the far end of the room were the office door and a small bar stocked with the finest spirits.

"The rest of the house is just as impressive as the view," the Doctor mused.

After he had discovered what had happened in the Florida lab, he contacted the man who, for the last several years, had been funding the project. His generous gifts to the sciences had been well documented and he had taken Dr. Sanderson's project to heart, claiming he thought it to be the single most important work presently being done. No one else shared his view.

After the fateful incident in Florida the Doctor had been unable to reach the benefactor directly, but through his people arranged for a meeting. The Doctor had grabbed all the mini data discs and personal notes from the lab and was picked up by helicopter and flown to Tampa International Airport where he was then flown, by private jet, to this mountain lodge located near Silverton, Colorado.

He had spent the last week going over his notes and reviewing the data discs trying to figure out what had happened. All he was able to discern was that all ten test subjects expired at about the same time. Data recordings showed no pulse, respiratory function, or brain activity for any of the test subjects for the better part of an hour. Shortly after he had received Keith's frantic call, the subjects began to move. Unfortunately, that was impossible; or as impossible as modern medical science would allow. The raw medical data was at odds with what the data recordings were displaying.

By the time he reached the lab, all ten subjects had escaped and there was nothing but the nearly devoured body of his former assistant. A quick search of the premises yielded nothing; and a more thorough search of the surrounding area had been unsuccessful. He spent the next two days cleaning up the mess left behind by the test subjects before being picked up by the helicopter. His notes, thus far, had yet to shed any light on how or why this happened. He did, however, have an idea of how to proceed.

Moving into the living area, Dr. Sanderson sat on the couch and opened the drawer in the coffee table where a data disc player was housed. He put in the disc he had watched earlier and pressed play on the touch screen remote. Although it was difficult to watch, he wanted to reassure himself of his idea. It was the recording of the brutal attack on his lab assistant. He watched as Keith entered the lab for the first time to check the equipment, and then as he pressed the reset button, the lights flickering on and off. When the lights came on for good, the subjects began rising to their feet.

Dr. Sanderson sat up and leaned forward as he stared intently at the television screen. He wanted to make sure he got a good look at what happened next. As the test subjects cornered poor Keith, he began to scream for help. Test subject Number Five approached and placed a hand over the mouth of the doctor's assistant. The others then attacked and began to tear at his clothing. Using the remote, Dr. Sanderson hit the rewind button and watched again as Number Five deliberately muffled the scream of Keith McFadden. He was sure of it.

The door to the den suddenly opened, diverting Dr. Sanderson's attention from the TV. Entering the room was Benton Worthington III. He was in his late forties and just a tad over six foot, with a full head of dark brown hair, wearing khaki pants and a thin dark blue cable knit sweater over a stripped blue pinpoint oxford shirt. After closing the door behind him, he strode purposefully toward the Doctor who rose from the couch to meet him halfway.

"Sorry to have kept you waiting, Doctor," Benton said while offering his hand.

"With all due respect, Mr. Worthington," Dr. Sanderson said as he extended his hand, "that's something you say to someone whose been waiting an hour for you, not almost a week."

Unfazed, the billionaire replied, "Again, allow me to apologize, but unfortunately my delay was unavoidable. I had important business to tend to overseas and every time I thought I was going to be able to leave, I was forced to stay. I kept my staff informed and instructed them to relay the message."

"Yes," said the Doctor, "your staff was very diligent in informing me every day that you would be here soon."

"I hope you were treated well, and your stay a comfortable one," Benton said.

"Very comfortable, and I don't wish to seem ungrateful, but I was hoping that I had impressed upon your staff the urgency for us to meet."

Benton began to make his way over to the semi-circular bar in the corner of the room. He slid behind the counter, reached down, and retrieved a bottle of very expensive cognac. He slid a glass off the rack behind him and turned back around.

"Would that urgency have anything to do with the events unfolding back East?" Benton asked.

"Yes," the Doctor responded. "I'm afraid it does."

Benton lifted the soon to be filled cognac glass in the air and motioned in the Doctor's direction.

"No thanks," the Doctor replied thinking it was too early for a drink.

"Suit yourself," Benton said.

He poured the amber colored liquid into the glass and replaced the cap. Leaving the bottle on top of the bar in the event the snifter needed refilling, he came around the bar and joined Dr. Sanderson by the couch. Putting the glass to his nose he took a deep breath. He raised the glass to his lips, swallowed hard, and let out a small sigh. Satisfied, he turned his attention back to Dr. Sanderson.

"I left Paris, as a matter of fact, just in time," Benton said. "My understanding is that most European airports have discontinued any and all outbound flights to the United States. They are also turning away any inbound flights as well. Unfortunately, it might be too late. Reports similar to those coming out of the Eastern United States had begun in a few European cities as I was leaving. Having your own jet does have its advantages."

Benton motioned to the couch and they both sat down.

"Why don't you fill me in Doctor as to how your research in Florida is connected to the terrible state of affairs that is undoubtedly heading this way."

Dr. Sanderson filled Benton in on the events at the lab and the escape of the test subjects; then the escalation of the infected and how cities began to be overrun. Those that were infected seemed to be passing the virus to the people they attack. The descriptions of those people wreaking havoc in the cities matched that of the test subjects the Doctor had observed on the data disks; the blank stare, the unsteady gait, the unprovoked attacks. Finally, he mentioned that systems outages across the country have made it very difficult to get any reliable information.

"So," Benton said, "you're saying that the test subjects from your lab escaped, after apparently dying, and have been the cause of this epidemic."

Dr. Sanderson said nothing. He was not sure if Benton believed him or not. Was he was being made fun of or if Benton was just summarizing the facts as he understood them?

Benton leaned back on the couch and took the last swig of cognac. His mind was racing, that much was obvious. But what was going through his mind, Dr. Sanderson could only guess at.

After nearly a minute of silence, Benton leaned forward and said, "What is it that you need from me to help resolve this crisis that you have created?"

"That we've created," Dr. Sanderson countered.

Benton said nothing and turned his attention to the television for the first time. He finally noticed the images from the med lab on the screen.

"What have we on the TV?"

"This is where I believe we need to begin," the Doctor replied.

He picked up the remote and played the attack scene in the lab. Benton watched, his face revealing nothing. After the scene finished, the Doctor turned to Benton.

"I believe that the key to solving this problem and perhaps reversing the condition or providing an antidote lies within the body of test subject Number 5."

"If you say so Doctor, I of course yield to your expertise, but finding one infected person in a sea of infected people will prove daunting at best," Benton concluded. "And fatal at worst," he added.

"You would, of course, be right except for one thing."

"What would that be?" asked Benton.

"All the test subjects had small transponder microchips embedded in them when they first arrived."

Before he was test subject Number 5, his name was Richard Kimbro; a twenty-nine year old with a wife and young son from Lynnwood, Washington. He was an account executive for an advertising company in Seattle. Being very good at his job, even at his fairly young age, he was allowed to make presentations to prospective clients. It was after one of these presentations that his life changed forever.

The clients he had just presented to loved his ideas and were all but ready to sign on the dotted line. It was going to be the most lucrative contract of his short career. He was naturally very excited. After leaving the meeting, he got into his Ford Fusion and headed back to the office to report the great news. Unfortunately, he could not wait and started messaging his boss. Being in such an excited state, he neglected to fasten his seatbelt.

Richard did not notice the traffic light had turned red and flew into the intersection at around forty-five miles an hour. Sideswiped and thrown from the car, he was thought to be dead. The paramedics, however, were able to revive him but his normal brain functions had ceased. His family was, of course, devastated. There did not seem to be any hope and they were considering pulling the plug. Then the Brain Research Centre of nearby Vancouver contacted them about an experimental procedure in need of test subjects in Florida. With nothing to lose, the family signed the waiver form and he was transported to Florida and put under Dr. Sanderson's care.

The treatment started and at first nothing happened. Then everything happened. He awoke, regained full brain function, and seemed to be on his way to a full recovery. Even then, Richard felt as though this was happening to someone else. He could not quite explain it but it was as if someone, or something, was inside his body with him. It sounded crazy he knew, but the Doctor told him it was natural and not to worry. He became more withdrawn and was soon barely talking. That, however, was the outward appearance; inside he was screaming for help.

Whatever was inside with him was taking over and there was nothing he could do about it. Then suddenly, while lying on a hospital bed attached to monitoring devices, he ceased to be Richard Kimbro. He awoke and was filled with an unusual need; the need to feed on flesh; specifically, human flesh.

He could not deny the need, but he also seemed to be able to control it somewhat. More accurately, whatever was inside with him controlled it. He did not need to feed all the time. When he did not, he simply bit his victims and added to the army he was creating. This same temperament seemed to be passed onto those he infected. They would feed when needed and infect when the hunger was satisfied. The others that became infected and those they infected, however, lacked Number Five's basic ability to reason. They acted on pure primal desires; feed or infect and move on. Test subject Number 5 seemed more cognitive. He also seemed to be able to manipulate, in some small way, others that were infected. There was, of course, no verbal communication above the occasional grunt, but somehow he was connected with them.

As he moved on, feeding and infecting, he survived on what could be best described as instinct. Driven by that force that had taken up residence inside him; its purpose unknown. All Number 5 knew was that he could hear your heart beat and if he found you, he would have no choice; he could not be bargained with, reasoned with, or stopped. He was a Zombie.

Chapter 13
The Search

Benton Worthington III got up from the couch and slowly walked around behind it. Using his free hand he ran his fingers through his thick brown hair. Looking at the other hand, he considered the empty brandy snifter and began walking toward the bar. When he arrived he grabbed the bottle of Cognac, unscrewed the cap, and poured himself another glass. Turning back around, he looked in the direction of Dr. Sanderson.

"If the test subjects have transponders implanted in them, why was this technology not employed to locate them when they went missing?" Benton finally asked.

"Well," Dr. Sanderson began looking a little embarrassed, "we were unable to locate the receiver."

"I see," said Benton.

"The microchips we imbedded were made up of three components," the Doctor continued. "There was a microprocessor that relayed valuable medical data to the computers. Second was a GPS transponder. We placed these inside the patients because several of them suffered from Alzheimer's and dementia. They would be prone to wonder off. In the unlikely event that we actually misplaced one, we would be able to quickly find them. And lastly, the chips are powered by a small lithium battery which will likely run out of juice in about," the Doctor thought for a moment and concluded, "a little over a month."

Benton had made his way back over to the couch, still standing; he took a sip of his drink.

"So, if I follow Doctor, what you require of me would be a new receiver and a method of transportation so that you may go and find your missing test subject?" Benton asked.

"For starters, yes," Dr. Sanderson replied. "Assuming I am able to locate Number 5 and somehow capture him, I will also need a laboratory to work in."

"Of course, Doctor," Benton said. "My facilities are at your disposal."

"Thank you Mr. Worthington."

"I assume we are talking the sooner the better," Benton said. Dr. Sanderson nodded. "Might I also suggest some company on your trip?"

"Company?"

"It would not be very wise heading back East, traipsing about with scores of infected looking to take a bite out of you," Benton suggested.

"I suppose not, I hadn't considered that," Dr. Sanderson admitted.

"I can provide you with a private plane complete with pilot," Benton said with a wry smile, "a new receiver and a security detail to keep you safe. We can't have anything happening to you Doctor, you may be mankind's only hope."

Dr. Sanderson nodded. He was trying to get a read on Benton Worthington III. He had been ever since he had first met him. He's never done anything to overtly arouse suspicions but the Doctor could not help feeling that the billionaire's motives are not always one hundred percent altruistic. Then again, it just may have been his overactive imagination.

"It's settled then," Benton said. "All I need is the GPS transponder code for the test subject you are looking for so that I can program it into the receiver."

The Doctor remained quiet.

Benton, finishing his drink, turned to the Doctor and said, "You do have the code?"

"Yes, I have the code. It's on my computer," Dr. Sanderson replied. "But, unfortunately, the codes for all ten test subjects are the same.

"Why would that be Doctor?"

"The GPS was designed just to be a beacon of sorts. The microchip that relayed the medical data was encoded to identify which patient it came from. Since the test subjects are no longer exhibiting any brain activity, the microchip has no need to send any information. The receiver will be able to acquire the GPS signal from each subject; we just won't know which one until we make visual contact."

"It will make your job all that much harder," Benton said.

"Yes, I'm afraid it will."

"Well then," Benton said putting the glass down on the bar and springing into action, "there truly is no time to waste. Collect anything you may need to assist you on your quest Doctor and wait here for me while I assemble everything we discussed. Oh, and please find that code for me."

With that, Benton Worthington III exited the room.

About an hour later the door to the den opened and Benton returned as promised. He was, however, not alone. He entered the room with a mountain of a man. He may have been the largest human being Dr. Sanderson had ever seen. Six and a half feet tall and most likely made of granite, the stranger wore black trousers with casual dress shoes. A navy blue sport coat covered a snug fitting microfiber tee shirt. Underneath the jacket was a conspicuous bulge that was likely a not so concealed hand gun. He had a chiseled face topped with a head of cropped blond hair. The only thing the Doctor could not see was the throwing knife hidden under his right trouser pant leg.

The Doctor was standing at the far end of the conference table after having just finished organizing his notes and retrieving the GPS codes from his computer. Benton moved toward the conference table to meet Dr. Sanderson with the massive stranger in tow.

"Doctor," Benton said, "I'd like you to meet my chief of security, Gunner Johansson."

The Doctor extended his hand to meet Gunner's and it was swallowed up whole. Even though he had a feeling that Gunner was easy on him, it took a lot of self-control not to rub his hand and cry out in pain after the handshake.

"Doctor," Gunner said in a thick Swedish accent.

"Nice to meet you, Mr. Johansson," Dr. Sanderson said.

"Please call him Gunner. He will be accompanying you on your journey," Benton informed him, "as well as his team."

Dr. Sanderson seriously wondered if this man would be able to fit on a plane. He did not know if he felt safer with Gunner around or terrified. Either way, it was not like he had much of a choice.

"Hopefully we will find Number 5 quickly and return as soon as possible," the Doctor said.

"Speaking of Number 5 Doctor, have you the code?" Benton asked.

Dr. Sanderson handed a piece of paper where he scribbled the GPS transponder code to Benton. He took it, turned and handed the paper to Gunner and said something to him in a language the Doctor did not understand. Gunner nodded and headed towards the door.

"Gunner will meet us at the plane," Benton said as he escorted Dr. Sanderson out of the den.

"Do you have everything you need?" Benton asked.

"Most of my notes will only be useful if and when we have Number 5 back here in the lab. The most important things right now are the GPS receiver and making sure we have a way to transport Number 5."

"All of that is being taken care of Doctor," Benton replied. "If you need to get in touch with me for any reason, Gunner will assist you. He has my express orders to aid you in any way you need. You will be in charge Doctor, but I would suggest you let Gunner take the lead when it comes to matters of safety."

"Of course," replied Dr. Sanderson adding, "could I ask a favor?"

"What can I do for you?" Benton replied.

"I was hoping you might be able to locate my wife and daughter. I have been unable to reach them and am quite concerned. My son lives overseas and I haven't been able to get in touch with him either. I have their address in Vancouver …"

"That won't be necessary Doctor," Benton interrupted, "I have that information already. I will do what I can to locate them."

"I would appreciate it very much Mr. Worthington."

"Consider it done."

They left the den and headed down a long hallway then went down a flight of stairs. Turning left, they headed out a side door into an expansive garden accessed by a maze of cement walkways. They walked along these paths passing some of the most ornate shrubbery the Doctor had ever seen. Suddenly, they turned sharply to the right and went through some sort of tunnel and emerged on the other side where the garage was. Benton motioned Dr. Sanderson to get into the passenger's side of a Bentley Mulsanne. He did as instructed as Benton got in on the driver's side. Benton pulled a set of keys from his pocket and started the car. He pulled out of the driveway and headed down a steep hill that connected to a mountain highway.

Benton noticed the Doctor admiring the automobile. "Goes from zero to sixty in 5.1 seconds," he said.

"Impressive," the Doctor said.

They drove in silence for a few minutes as the Bentley moved effortlessly through the mountainous terrain. If the thing had wings, thought the Doctor, the car would fly.

Breaking the silence, Benton asked, "How many infected soles do you think are out there?"

"Well," replied the Doctor, "that's really hard to say. If you look at it from a strictly mathematical standpoint by taking the original ten test subjects and assume they could infect one person every three hours, you would have twenty infected people after three hours, forty after six hours and so on. After only seventy-two hours the infected total would be," the Doctor thought for a moment and turned to face Benton.

"What is it Doctor?"

"The infected total would be over 160 million people."

For the first time since coming to know Benton, the Doctor was able to discern an actual human emotional response from the man. Quickly recovering, Benton said, "We'd better get you to that plane then," and punched down hard on the accelerator.

Shortly thereafter they arrived at a small airstrip cut out of a valley between two sizable mountain ranges. On the tarmac was a Gulfstream G 670; the latest in corporate jet technology. On the fuselage, starting at the wing and moving to the cockpit, in big block letters and at a slight upward angle was the letters W-O-R-T-H. It was Benton's corporate insignia.

Benton pulled alongside the plane and cut the engine. Dr. Sanderson reached in the back seat and grabbed his computer and backpack filled with his lab notes and data discs. After he closed the door and turned to face the plane, he saw that Benton was already walking up the stairs heading into the plane.

Dr. Sanderson reached the top of the stairs and entered the plane. It was just as impressive on the inside as it was on the outside. Looking down the aisle to his right he saw two ultra large seats on the left side and two more on the right. There were four men he had yet to meet already sitting in the seats; undoubtedly members of Gunner's crew. There was one more seat on the right side facing inward and behind that a medium sized couch also facing inward. Beyond that there appeared to be a small conference table with seating.

As he looked to his left, he saw Benton coming out of the cockpit with a man dressed in a pilot's uniform. The pilot was right out of central casting, about five foot eleven with jet black hair, solid build, and a confidence that all air jockeys have.

"I'd like you to meet your pilot, Captain John Bannon," Benton said.

"Nice to meet ya," the Captain said.

"Likewise Mr. Bannon, I just wish it was under different circumstances."

"Please," Captain Bannon said, "call me John."

Before the Doctor could reply, Gunner emerged from the back of the plane and informed Benton that they were ready to go. He turned toward Captain Bannon.

"Have you completed your pre-flight checklist Captain?"

Not waiting for a reply, Gunner followed Benton to the edge of the stairs and had a few last words with his boss before raising the stairs and locking the door.

Captain Bannon turned to the Doctor, putting his hand on his back while leaning in and whispered in his ear, "Watch out for that one," nodding in Gunner's direction.

"Where to first, Doctor?" Gunner asked after he had finished sealing the cabin door.

"Do we have any signals to follow yet on the receiver?"

"Not as of yet, but we should have something soon, after we are airborne," Gunner said.

"Without any other information to go on I would suggest heading to where they were last seen, Florida."

"You heard him Captain," Gunner said, "set a course for Florida."

"Off to Disney World," Captain Bannon responded.

Dr. Sanderson turned and headed toward the back of the plane. As he walked past the members of Gunner's crew, he said hello but received no response. He was about to try again when Gunner came up from behind him.

"My associates do not speak English, Doctor," he said.

"Oh, I wasn't aware."

"If you need anything from them, please ask me," Gunner said. He motioned to the couch and said, "Sit here Doctor and buckle up; we'll be airborne in a few minutes."

"Förbereda för avresa," Gunner said to his crew.

They checked their belt buckles and sat straight up. Gunner sat next to the Doctor on the couch.

Now in the rear of the plane for the first time, Dr. Sanderson noticed a small galley behind a partition separating it from the main cabin. On the other side of the galley was the lavatory.

The intercom came alive as Captain Bannon announced they were ready for takeoff and to remind them to buckle up. As the Gulfstream taxied to the end of the runway, the Doctor, for the first time, pondered the probability of their mission succeeding. After considering all the variables, he decided it would be best not think about it.

The airplane picked up speed as it hurled itself down the runway attempting to achieve takeoff velocity. A few seconds later they were in the air, traveling to where this whole nightmare began; into the lion's den as it were.

Chapter 14
Up in Smoke

Early the next morning, after a peaceful night's sleep, Chester made a modest meal of eggs and bacon that he had found unspoiled in the now room temperature refrigerator downstairs. As the morning mist was just lifting, Chester packed up his gear and grabbing the sawed off shotgun quietly making his way out of the house and to his pickup truck.

Throwing the gear in the back of the truck, he grabbed one of the jerry cans and topped off his tank of gas. Putting the can back in the bed of the truck he grabbed the shotgun and made his way to the other side. As he was reaching for the door handle a sound behind him made him stop mid-motion and turn.

There, coming around the corner of the house, was an infected person. Without thinking, Chester raised the shotgun and fired hitting the man square in the chest. The man staggered and then continued coming towards him, as a second blast from the shotgun to the man's head finally put him down.

Chester climbed into the cab of the truck and started it up. As he slowly backed down the driveway he realized the noise from the shotgun blasts had attracted several other infected people. Anther came from behind Douglas' house as three more came from across the street. Not waiting to find out if there were any more Chester spun his tires on the pavement as he pulled away from the house.

As he drove through the neighborhood he noticed that the infected were coming from everywhere. It was like he had kicked an ant pile. Speeding up, he managed to navigate his way out of the suburban maze while bouncing a couple of the infected off of his front bumper.

As he drew closer to I-81 he took a wrong turn and ended up in the middle of Old Town Winchester. Out of nowhere a rock suddenly flew by the windshield and bounce off the hood of his truck. Slamming on the brakes and whipping his head around Chester saw a group of people coming out of a side street. They were armed with an assortment of bats, sticks, and rocks. It looked like the looters from the night before.

Not wanting to stick around Chester slowly began to steer around some debris in the road. He noticed in the review mirror that the thieves had begun to run after him. As a shower of rocks rained down on his truck, Chester floored the gas pedal and sped off. He navigated several more side roads before finally coming upon an onramp for I-81. Merging onto the highway, Chester noticed the road was only occupied by several abandoned cars and several infected people. As he headed north, he turned the shortwave radio on to see if there was any new announcements. However, the message was the same as before and he quickly turned it off.

As the sun slowly rose in the east, Chester passed by Martinsburg and from the highway could not help noticing a number of smoke columns rising from the small town. Curbing his instinct to explore Chester continued north. In the distance Hagerstown came into view as he crossed the Potomac River. More cars began to litter the road forcing him to slow down.

Again, the area surrounding the highway was littered with burning fires. Here and there Chester could make out infected people moving without purpose through the deserted streets. As he passed under the I-70 interchange he saw another person coming down the road. However, this person was moving at full speed unlike the infected he had previously seen.

As he drove closer Chester slowed and was able to make out a woman waving her arms at him. She was young with light brown hair and wearing black Capri pants and a soiled blue tee shirt. Still wary of strangers Chester readied his shotgun in his lap and rolled down his window as the woman reached the truck. Instead the woman ran to the passenger's side, opened the door, and jumped in the truck.

"Hold it right there lady, what do ya think you're doing?" asked Chester gesturing with the shotgun.

"Chill out mister, we got to get out of here, there are a bunch of those zombie things after me."

"Zombie things? Oh, you mean the infected people?"

"Yea, those people who died and come back from the dead all cannibal like. Seriously, we got to go."

"Who the heck are you?"

"My name is Donna, now let's go."

"Well Donna, I never said you could get in my truck so what makes you think I am gonna to give you a ride?"

"'Cause I'm not getting out until we are clear of these zombies," Donna said as she pointed to the group of them coming down the highway.

"This is why I don't get involved," Chester muttered angrily.

Looking around Chester saw roughly 30 zombies about 400 yards away shuffling towards them from all directions around the highway. As they converged on the highway they began to form a small group. Directly in front of his truck were several empty cars in the middle of the road leaving only a small path for the truck to fit through.

"Alright, Miss, I'll get us out of this mess but then you get out of my truck."

"Sure, whatever you say mister. What are you gonna do?"

"I've had about enough of runnin' from these things; I think it's about time I went huntin'. I'm going to rig a trap for them in that group of abandoned cars up yonder. We'll draw them through that pathway and set it off. Then you leave."

"Ok, but how are you going to take them all on by yourself?"

"Just wait and see. Help me grab these propane tanks."

Getting out of the truck with the shotgun in his hand Chester met Donna at the rear of the truck. Grabbing one of the large propane tanks he motioned for Donna to grab the other. Moving to the abandon cars in front of the truck Chester set down the tank and moved to each car, crawling underneath and knocking on the gas tank trying to figure out which contained more gasoline.

A silver Dodge was the lucky winner and Chester placed one of the propane tanks underneath the car's gas tank. Moving to the car across from the Dodge he took the second propane tank from Donna and placed it under that car's gas tank. By now the zombies were about 150 yards away but had not seemed to notice Chester and Donna moving around the cars. After he had finished he ran back to his truck.

"Get in; I'm gonna to go draw those zombies into the trap."

"Ok but I still don't understand what you are doing with those propane tanks," Donna replied.

"Just wait and see."

Chester moved off through the gap in the cars. Leveling his shot gun at the nearest zombie he fired hitting it in the chest. The zombie stumbled but got up again and began moving straight for Chester. The other zombies in the area, having heard the noise, all began to converge on his position. After getting off two more shots just to be sure, he turned and ran back to the truck.

"Here goes nothing," Chester said jumping into the driver's side of his truck.

He slowly turned the truck around and began repeatedly beeping the horn. The zombies seemed to pick up on the new target and began to move between the abandoned cars as they drove off down the highway.

As he drove, Chester kept an eye on the review mirror watching as the zombies made their way to the cars. When the majority of them were in and around the cars he had booby trapped, he slammed on the brakes and jumped out. Retrieving his rifle from the bed he braced himself on the side of the truck, held his breath, and squeezed the trigger.

In an instance the propane tank under the Dodge exploded triggering subsequent explosions from the now exposed gas from the car's tank, the second propane tank, and the other cars. Car and body parts rained down around the area as a huge fire raged in the pile of destroyed cars. A large dark plume of smoke rose slowly and drifted skyward. Chester's ears were ringing and he was rubbing his eyes as some of the debris fell around him. It looked like most of the zombies had been destroyed by the explosion. Scanning the area he noticed movement as several zombies which had been thrown by the explosion got up and began to move towards them down the highway again.

Moving back to the cab Chester said, "Hang tight, I am going to deal with these stragglers."

Slinging the rifle onto his shoulder Chester picked up his shotgun out of the front seat and then retrieved his pack from the bed of the truck. The pack contained his extra shotgun shells, just in case. Moving towards the raging fire he quickly dispatched three zombies that had survived the blast with shotgun rounds to the head. He shuddered as he dealt with a fourth that was still moving along the ground but was missing most of the left side of its body.

Chester let out a gruff cough from the smoke in the air around him and then stepped back from the heat of the fire. Standing there he admired the effectiveness of his plan and allowed himself another of his rare smiles. This was quickly replaced with a scowl as he turned back around in time to see Donna landing in the driver's seat of his truck and speeding off down the highway with his truck and all of his camping supplies.

Chapter 15
All Together Now

It was well before the first rays of light painted the Maryland sky that Major Bradley awoke. Specialist Simmons was snoring, face mashed into the desk in front of him, having unsuccessfully tried all night to raise someone via the radio. Looking down from the observation deck he could make out a few of his soldiers on guard at the entrance below. The others would hopefully be fast asleep inside their vehicles. There was a light knocking on the observation room door and Major Bradley smiled as he knew who it would be.

"Enter."

"Morning sir," said Captain Morris as he shut the door behind him.

Coming up the two steps from the door to the observation deck he continued, "An uneventful night sir. A couple of the infected came within 20 yards of the perimeter but the men stayed calm as none of them posed a threat. Any luck with the radio?"

Gesturing to Specialist Simmons Major Bradley said, "That poor boy was up most of the night with no luck. It looks like we are going to have to do this the hard way."

Shaking his head Captain Morris asked, "How did you sleep sir?"

"As good as can be expected considering the circumstances. I woke up to the sound of gun fire in the distance a couple of times; probably just some locals taking pot shots at the infected. At around two this morning I got up to stretch my legs. Looking out towards the town, I am pretty sure I saw car lights heading south on I-70. Not sure where they are going but that might not end well for them."

"Yeah we heard the gunfire to, spooked the men a little, but hopefully that means fewer of those things."

Handing Major Bradley a canteen Captain Morris continued, "Here's your coffee sir, it's not warm but it's better than nothing. So what's the plan?"

Taking the canteen from the Captain, Major Bradley took a swallow and then gestured to the maps laid out on a table in the middle of the room. "Logic would dictate that since Command abandoned this evacuation zone they probably have done the same with anything nearby. Our best bet is to head west."

"What about some of the other regional airports, would they be used as evacuations zones?" asked Captain Morris.

"Most likely, but they will also be the first to be abandoned when the shit hits the fan. I think our best bet would be one of our army bases or an air base. They should be better protected and could hold out longer then a civilian airport."

"We could head to Fort Campbell; I did some training there and they should be well protected."

"We could, but I was thinking something closer. I really want to get these civilians off our hands if possible and I am not sure we want to drive all the way there with them."

Pointing to the map Major Bradley said, "I was thinking of Wright-Pat Air Force Base in Dayton, Ohio. They've got a pretty secure base up there and we can just take I-70 straight to it. If we leave in the next couple of hours we could even make it before nightfall."

"You want me to load 'em up?" asked Captain Morris.

"No, give them another hour of sleep" Major Bradley replied looking over at Specialist Simmons. "But I want to leave no later than 0800; dismissed Captain."

The sudden banging made everyone bolt wide awake as Captain Morris opened the door and stepped into the office.

"Rise and shine folks we've got to be on the road in about half an hour."

Tossing some more candy bars and bottles of soda on the table he said, "We've also got some room temperature coffee out here if anyone is interested." He then turned on his heel and left the room.

Stretching and letting out a big yawn Nick said, "Well at least we've got room service."

As the others slowly woke up it appeared that Nick was the only one to have gotten anything resembling a good night's rest. They all felt a little rested but none of them had truly gotten a full night's sleep. Between the gunshots heard outside and the thoughts running through each of their minds, it had been a long listless night.

"Mmmm, a breakfast of champions," Nick said as he finished his candy bar and downing the last of his soda.

"Easy there Nick. Save some for the rest of us," said Stephen.

They all rolled up their blankets and grabbed the few things they brought in with them and headed out into the already muggy Maryland morning. Outside the soldiers were milling around the convoy vehicles packing up their gear. Up on top of the Humvees several of the soldiers manned the machine guns keeping an eye on the surrounding area. As they stood awkwardly awaiting instructions on what to do, Major Bradley, with Specialist Simmons in tow, came out of the tower.

"Morning folks," Major Bradley said greeting them. "Hope you got some sleep."

"It was better than nothing," said Kim to the nods of the others.

"So I am assuming no one is coming to pick us up?" asked Stephen.

"That's right son, it looks like we are going to be on our own 'till we find another evacuation zone," replied Major Bradley.

"And where might that be?" asked Stephen.

"We'll be taking I-70 straight through to an Air Force base in Dayton, Ohio. We should be there sometime early this evening if everything goes smoothly."

"Does that mean showers and some real food," asked Lucy.

"I hope so," replied Major Bradley. "If any of your need to use the facilities now is the time to do it as we won't be making very many stops. When you are ready, I want you to load up into the same truck you were in yesterday; any questions?"

When no questions came he turned to his soldiers and continued, "Load up and be ready to move out."

The convoy was loaded and ready to move about twenty minutes later. Stephen, Nick, Lucy, and Kim all chatted casually with each other in the back of the truck while Dave sat sullenly looking at the floor. Jason and Danielle were drawing with some pens and paper that Kim had found in the office. As the convoy left they watch the control tower recede into the distance as they made their way onto I-70. Here and there they could see an infected person stumbling around through the town. As the drove out of Frederick and into the countryside the talking stopped. It was still early but the temperature was already starting to rise. They settled in for what was sure to be a long hot ride in the back of the truck.

The convoy was making good time despite the number of abandoned cars that littered I-70. Every now and then Major Bradley would climb in the gunner's cupola and survey the surrounding area. The farther away from populated areas they were the less infected he saw. Although every once in a while he would see one staggering out of the tree line or through a field. They were passing through the outskirts of Hagerstown when in the distance the Major heard an explosion followed by a large plume of black smoke rising skyward.

"Slow down Sinclair," said Major Bradley to his driver. Again climbing into the gunner's copula he examined the smoke column through his binoculars.

The smoke seemed to be rising about two miles away. The origin at this point was unknown. Looking at his map Major Bradley assumed it was most likely coming from the interchange of 1-70 and I-81.

Leaning down again in his turret he said, "Private, stop up here on this small over pass."

As the convoy slowed to a stop Major Bradley got on the radio, "Captain, do you see that smoke plume up ahead?"

"Yes sir. What do you think it is?

"I'm not sure but you are going to go find out for me. It looks like it will be in our line of travel. Take your Humvee, your driver, and gunner and go recon it."

"On it sir."

Soon thereafter, Captain Morris' Humvee drove past the head of the convoy and minutes later disappear around a bend in the highway.

On the radio once more Major Bradley said, "We are somewhat protected up here on the over pass but stay alert as we're still in the open."

Twenty minutes later Captain Morris' Humvee appeared in the distance speeding towards them. Major Bradley dismounted his Humvee as the Captain's slowed to a stop.

"What did you find Captain?" he asked looking up at the Captain who was in the gunner's turret.

"A couple of blown up cars and the guy who blew them up," he replied with a nod of his head down towards the inside of his Humvee.

As Major Bradley looked he saw a man climbing out of the passenger's side of the Humvee. His hair was a mess and through the dirt and soot that covered him, the Major could make out a beard and an unhappy expression. He wore a pack on his back and slung over his left shoulder was a rifle. In his hands he gripped a sawed off shotgun.

"He hasn't been bitten as far as we can tell. Not that he would let us search him," Captain Morris called down. "And don't even ask about him giving up his weapons."

As Major Bradley surveyed the man trying to decide what to do, the man spoke up.

"With all due respect Major, you need to teach your Captain over there some manners," Chester said tightly. "Ya'll won't be taking these weapons unless it's off my cold dead body. Unless of course I come back to life and start gnawing on ya first."

"Fair enough," replied Major Bradley extending his hand. "I'm Major Bradley and I see you've already met Captain Morris."

"The name's Chester Boone," replied Chester shaking the Major's hand.

"You a military man Mr. Boone?" asked Major Bradley.

"Not so much sir, but I graduated with a degree from VMI so I know my way around."

"If you don't mind me asking what are you doing out here by yourself blowing stuff up?"

"It's a long story."

"Give me the short version Mr. Boone."

Begrudgingly Chester filled him on the events of the morning culminating with Captain Morris arriving and picking him up as he was trying to get away from a horde of zombies.

"Well you are welcome to travel with us Mr. Boone," offered Major Bradley. "We are trying to get to another extraction point."

"Seein' as I ain't got my truck any more it don't look like I got another choice."

"Captain, show Mr. Boone back to the truck and then we'll be on our way. And let the man keep his weapons."

Chester began walking back along the convoy as Captain Morris' Humvee followed. Reaching the truck Chester threw his backpack in and pulled himself up into the truck's bed. He let out a bothered sigh as he looked around and saw eight faces looking back. Settling in on the end of the bench nearest the tail gate he signaled to the soldier across from him that he was ready to go. The soldier spoke into his radio and a minute later the convoy was on the move again. Chester stared out the back of the truck as it rumbled down the road intent on avoiding any unnecessary conversation with the others unfortunate enough to be stuck with him in the back of the truck.

Chapter 16
Ground Zero

They had reached their cruising altitude shortly after takeoff and Captain Bannon announced over the intercom that is was safe to move about the cabin. The Doctor had unbuckled his safety belt and taken a seat at one end of the small conference table across from the couch. He had his notes spread out before him and was feverishly pecking away on his computer.

Gunner was speaking with his men in the front of the cabin. The Doctor could not hear what they were saying and even if he could he would not be able to understand them. He was too busy anyway, trying to figure out what vital piece of data he was overlooking. He was sure that Number 5 held the key to figuring this whole thing out but he had been unable to work out exactly how. One of the items he had brought back with him from the lab in Florida were samples from the last dose given to each of the ten subjects. Dr. Sanderson was confident that if he could compare the original sample against its current state deep within Number 5, he could determine what happened; and then subsequently try to reverse it.

The Swede, as Dr. Sanderson had begun referring to him in his own mind, joined the Doctor at the conference table bringing with him his PDA. He was staring intently at it but said nothing. The Doctor was about to ask if he had received any hits yet from the tracking signal when the door to the cockpit opened and Captain John Bannon emerged.

He walked past Gunner's men without acknowledging them. As he approached the conference table he announced with a smile, "Gotta go see a man about a horse."

Dr. Sanderson, looking genuinely concerned, asked "Who's flying the plane then?"

"Not to worry Doctor, these planes practically fly themselves," he replied, patted Dr. Sanderson on the shoulder, and continued on to the lavatory.

The Doctor looked at Gunner who revealed nothing. He looked back at the cockpit and then at the lavatory still awaiting an answer to his question. Realizing he was not going to get one, he turned his attention back to the paperwork in front of him.

When the Captain had returned from the bathroom Dr. Sanderson asked, "Where are we at the moment Captain?"

"Right smack dab in the middle of the good ole US of A," Bannon replied. Clarifying for the Doctor, he added, "Just south of Wichita, Kansas."

"Thanks."

The Captain nodded and headed back to the cockpit.

"Right smack dab in the middle of the ...," Dr. Sanderson cut his thought off in mid- sentence. He began to quickly shuffle through the papers in front of him looking for a particular report. Finding it, he brought up a file that he had stored on his computer's hard drive. Alternately looking at the piece of paper and the computer screen he started jotting down some notes.

His concentration was broken when Gunner asked, "Found something of interest Doctor?"

Dr. Sanderson lifted his left hand and raised his index finger indicating he needed a minute. Gunner obliged by remaining quiet. A few minutes later the Doctor looked up to see Gunner staring at him with genuine interest. He made one last check of the information he had written down.

"The bacterium," Dr. Sanderson began, "was discovered in an underground cavern. Samples were collected from different areas of the cave and catalogued. We administered the Principle by alternating samples and dosages until we achieved a favorable result. I just cross referenced the samples given to the test subjects with their location in the cave." He looked at Gunner to make sure he was following along.

"Continue Doctor," Gunner said.

"The collection pattern looked something like a starburst. When the samples are plotted against the pattern, we can see where exactly in the cave and simultaneously where in the collection area the samples were located. It appears that test subject Number 5's sample was smack dab in the middle of the collection area. The pattern would seem to indicate that the bacterium spread in a circular design. That would make the middle of the starburst the likely origin of the bacterium."

Dr. Sanderson stopped to catch his breath. He was talking fast as he often did when a significant discovery was made. He looked again at Gunner who was now very quiet and just staring at him.

"It's sort of like the ground zero of the bacterium," the Doctor continued. "It could easily explain why Number 5 reacted differently than the others. When bacteria cells replicate through binary fission, mutations sometimes occur. I would have to reexamine the sample but I would guess that its cell structure would be slightly different than those on the outer edge of the pattern."

It looked like Gunner was about to ask a question when his PDA began to make noises. Looking down at it, he pressed the touch screen a couple of times.

"Looks like we have a signal Doctor," he said.

The Gulfstream had a mobile transceiver and digital signal processor not unlike the common Uni-phone tower. It was able to send and receive signals and then transmit them to the portable GPS receiver that Gunner had brought on board. An alert was set up on his PDA to notify him when a signal was discovered.

Gunner got up from his seat at the table and walked to the rear of the plane where the GPS receiver was and checked the coordinates of the signal's origin. Jotting them down on a slip of paper, he moved through the cabin to the front of the plane where he knocked on the cockpit door. A second later he opened it and went inside.

A few minutes later the cockpit door opened and Gunner made his way back to Dr. Sanderson at the conference table. He sat back down and said, "It looks like we have a signal originating just outside Rogers, Arkansas. We are going to land at the Northwest Arkansas Regional Airport."

"Captain Bannon will begin the descent in about ten minutes so I suggest you gather up your materials Doctor and then buckle up on the couch for the landing," Gunner said.

They landed about fifteen minutes later without incident. Captain Bannon taxied the Gulfstream to the terminal right next to Airport Service Road. He would stay with the airplane while Gunner and his team, along with Dr. Sanderson, followed the signal on foot. They would get a more accurate reading on the test subject's position once they disembarked but at the moment it appeared that the signal was about one mile away.

Gunner opened the hatch and performed a quick scan of the immediate area, finding no trouble. The airport was truly in the middle of nowhere; the infected would be easy to spot. Gunner motioned to the Doctor that it was safe to exit.

Dr. Sanderson walked down the steps into a beautiful, sunny, Midwestern sky. He brought with him folders of each of the ten subjects containing their name, a photograph, and the serial number of the microchips implanted. He had these in a small backpack that was slung over his right shoulder.

Gunner was at the top of the stairs issuing instructions to his team. When he was finished, they came down the stairs and headed to the underside of the plane. One of the men (Dr. Sanderson had yet to be introduced to any of them) reached under the fuselage and turned a latch that revealed a small cargo hold.

They immediately began removing items from the cargo hold. Smoothly and efficiently they started covering themselves with body armor. They had forearm guards, chest plates, and shin protectors. A long thin pole with a loop or lasso at the end was removed along with a canvass bag. The bag contained other restraining devices such as hand cuffs and leg irons. Finally, the men pulled out weapons; lots of weapons. Each was carrying a handgun with holster and a semi- automatic rifle.

"Armalite AR-10 A2's," Gunner said coming up from behind Dr. Sanderson and scaring him half to death. "Accurate, fast, well-balanced, and easy to carry," he added.

The Doctor turned around facing the hulking Swede and replied, "Good to know, thanks."

"Redo?" Gunner said to his men who all nodded in unison as one of them closed the cargo hatch.

Gunner grabbed a small walkie-talkie from his hip and pressed a button and spoke clearly into it, "Comm check, comm check ... do you copy Captain?"

"Loud and clear, good hunting," was the response.

Gunner replaced the walkie and motioned to one of his men to take point with another on each side and the fourth bringing up the rear. Gunner and the Doctor were in the middle as they moved out heading northwest.

The Doctor could not help notice that Gunner had none of the armor that his men did. He was not even sure if they made any that would even fit him. All he had was his sidearm, his walkie, and the portable GPS receiver at which he was now staring at.

"This way Doctor," he said as they continued to move.

They crossed the road and then a small field to find themselves on, according to the street sign, Phillips Cemetery Road.

"How appropriate," thought the Doctor.

It was rural country with no one in sight. They moved swiftly as Gunner monitored the tracking device.

"Vara uppmärksam," Gunner said to his men. Again, they nodded.

"What does this Number 5 look like Doctor?" Gunner asked.

"Um, he is … er was ... 30 years old, five foot ten, white male, probably wearing the hospital scrubs top and matching sweats he had on at the lab."

"The signal does not seem to be moving," Gunner said.

"As far as I know they don't require sleep, or rest. Given the rate at which the infection spread, they must just keep going," the Doctor answered. "If he's not moving it could be he's currently feeding or he's … dead … or whatever you would call it."

They crossed a small creek and passed a collection of buildings that looked like an abandoned mill works. Off to the right, in a large open field about 200 yards away, someone was walking across the field. The Doctor observed the slow pace and unsteady nature of the individual and immediately concluded it was an infected person. He was about to turn and tell Gunner who had apparently already seen the man.

Using hand signals, he directed one of his men to the edge of the field. Taking a knee he raised his weapon, adjusted the scope, and fired. It was easy to see, even from this distance; the zombie's head explode as he fell harmlessly to the ground. Gunner's man rose to his feet and returned back to formation without saying a word.

With the zombie dispatched, they continued walking for another 100 feet or so until they had come to a fork in the road. Straight ahead of them was a white, rectangular one story house with a grey roof. To the left was a ramshackle detached garage that probably had not housed a car in twenty years. Behind that was a moderately sized shed.

"The signal appears to be coming from inside the house," Gunner said.

Again using hand signals Gunner directed his men in a two by two formation to the front of the house, using the trees in the front yard as cover. The Doctor stayed back, constantly looking over his shoulder. For the first time he almost wished he had a weapon.

Gunner and his men had reached the front porch, two of them taking flanking positions on either side of the door, which the Doctor noticed was slightly ajar. The third man ducked under a large window that looked onto the front lawn. He rose slowly and peered inside. His view was obscured by grey curtains and a fine coat of grime on the window. Shaking his head, he quietly leapt off the porch and took a kneeling position in front of the door. The fourth man stood directly in front of the door. Gunner stood off to the right side. Each man had his weapon trained on the door, including Gunner who had removed his sidearm for the first time. After a moment's pause, Gunner gave the signal and the man standing in front of the door raised his right boot and kicked it in.

The two men flanking the doors spun around quickly and were the first in the house with the man who kicked the door in third. The last of Gunner's men stayed back ensuring no trouble appeared from either side of the house. Gunner moved to the front door and looked inside.

"Alla Avmarkera," said one of Gunner's men from inside the house.

Gunner turned around and waved for Dr. Sanderson to enter the house. The Doctor moved across the lawn and walked up two steps and onto the porch. He looked both ways and then cautiously entered the structure.

The door gave way to a small living room. A tattered couch was to the left against the wall with the window above it. Against the far wall was a cheap entertainment center with a television on top of it. To the left was a narrow hallway that probably led to a bedroom. An archway to the right of the entertainment center opened into a dated kitchen with a linoleum floor. A partially open closet was to the right. Looking in, the Doctor noticed a few lightweight jackets and a pair of work boots on the floor. A well-worn rug covered the entire living room. Standing near the hallway was one of Gunner's men; another was in front of the archway.

Gunner and the third man were standing next to the most striking feature of the room; the corpse lying face down in the middle of it with a large kitchen knife protruding out from the back of its skull. There was a fair amount of dried blood on the rug as well as the small coffee table next to it. The thing that Dr. Sanderson found most interesting was the color of the blood. It was a mixture of black and deep red.

"Don't be alarmed Doctor, it's dead," Gunner said. "Is this one of your test subjects?"

The Doctor looked more closely at the figure in the middle of the room. It was wearing hospital scrubs similar to those issued by the Doctor and his staff in Florida. He could not be sure though until it was turned face up. He slid the back pack off of his shoulder and unzipped it. He removed the folders containing all the pertinent data on each test subject.

"Could he … be turned over?" asked the Doctor.

"Tur den personen over," Gunner instructed his men.

They moved quickly to the corpse and removed the large knife from the back of its head. As one grabbed its legs and the other its shoulders, they flipped it on its back. The face was distorted with decay and filth. Much of the lower jaw was missing and the eye sockets had receded into the bone. Identification would be difficult. The Doctor was confident it was not Number 5 but he wanted to make certain it was one of his test subjects so he could eliminate it from his list. The photographs were little help but based on probable age and gender, he narrowed it down to three possible candidates.

"I don't believe it is Number 5," he admitted to the group, "but we should be sure."

"How do we do that?" asked Gunner.

"We could remove the microchip from the back of its neck," the Doctor answered pointing to a spot behind the right ear at the base of the skull. "I have all the serial numbers on file and could positively identify it that way."

Gunner instructed the third man in the room to do just that. The man bent down and opened the bag containing the restraining equipment, pulling out a knife with a six inch blade and a pair of latex gloves. Leaning over the corpse, he put the gloves on and inserted the knife where the Doctor had indicated and began to root around. He removed bits of flesh and rubbed it between his fingers looking for the small plastic microchip. After the third try he held a small piece of plastic between his thumb and forefinger. Cleaning it off with a rag he pulled out of the bag, he deposited the chip in a small candy dish that was conveniently left on the coffee table and handed it to Dr. Sanderson.

The Doctor used a pair of tweezers he had brought with him to bring the chip closer and squinted at it. He could not read the numbers on it, they were too small. Absentmindedly, he moved past Gunner's man and into the kitchen. He began opening cabinet drawers. He finally found the drawer he was looking for; the junk drawer that every house has. Rummaging through, he removed the item he was searching for; a fold out magnifying glass. He opened it up and trained the glass on the chip. Looking through the lens, the numbers were now easy to read. The Doctor memorized the number sequence and then turned to his sheet containing all the numbers corresponding to the test subjects. There it was, test subject number seven, Michael Lembeck. As he suspected, not Number 5. The Doctor turned to see Gunner, taking up most of the available space in the archway, looking at him.

"Is this our subject?" he asked.

"No, I'm afraid not. He's one of mine, but not Number 5."

The Doctor turned to put the magnifying glass back in the drawer but decided he should keep it in case he needed it again. It was at that moment that he noticed two things. First, there was a wooden butcher's block on the kitchen counter with an empty slot where the largest knife would be. This discovery simply answered the question of where the knife sticking out of the zombie's skull had come from. Second, and much more alarming, was the strange noise coming from behind the door at the far end of the kitchen.

Gunner had heard it also and moved into the kitchen along with his three men. The door, Dr. Sanderson surmised, could open into a moderately sized pantry or it could lead into a basement. It had two sliding bolt locks on the kitchen side of the door; one near the handle and one up top. The noise was a scraping sound that quickly escalated into a banging. Gunner had one of his men squat down and peek under the door. He was able to see movement but it was impossible to make out whom or what was making the noise.

"If you can hear me, please answer me," the Doctor said.

He waited a second for a response. He then repeated his request; still no answer. The banging began to intensify. It now sounded like there could be several things trying to get out. The problem was they simply could not tell. If they opened the door and a bunch of infected poured out, it may be difficult to fight them off given the tight quarters. And since they were not answering, one had to assume the worst.

The Doctor looked at Gunner and it was clear he had reached the same conclusion. The risk of opening that door outweighed the reward.

Gunner instructed his men to exit the building. They all filed out the front door and out into the front yard. The fourth man who had remained outside was right where they left him.

"Alla tecken av problem," Gunner asked his man outside.

"Nej," he answered.

"Back to the plane," Gunner ordered. That was just fine with the Doctor.

They headed back the way they came and in the same formation. As they passed the old mill a second time, they noticed several zombies on the grounds that were not there before. Gunner ordered his men to eliminate them, which they did in usual efficient fashion.

Moving now with more urgency, they retraced their steps along Phillips Cemetery Road. As they neared the airport, Gunner removed the walkie from his belt and pressed the button. Speaking into it he said, "Captain, come in Captain."

"This is Bannon, go ahead."

"Captain, we are about five minutes out, no additional passengers, are we clear to come aboard, over."

"All clear, I am right where you left me. Will be ready when you arrive, over."

"Copy that, over and out," Gunner finished and put the walkie back on his belt.

Five minutes later they were on the edge of the tarmac. Gunner did a quick visual sweep of the area and confirmed the Captain's assessment; no zombies in sight.

As they approached the plane, Captain Bannon lowered the stairs. Gunner's men removed their body armor and replaced everything they had taken from the cargo hold.

Once everyone was back on board, the Captain closed the hatch and sealed the door.

He looked at the Doctor and said, "Where to now?"

"Um, I guess we continue on to Florida … unless we get another hit," the Doctor answered.

"You got it," Captain Bannon said as he spun around and headed toward the cockpit. "Buckle up; we'll be airborne in five."

Dr. Sanderson put his knapsack down on the couch next to him and strapped himself in. As the Gulfstream began making its way to the runway, the Doctor suddenly realized how truly exhausted he was. The little adventure they just had was draining; both physically and mentally. He was not sure he was up to having to repeat it perhaps nine more times. The only problem was he did not have a choice.

Chapter 17
Hit and Run

Dr. Sanderson was attempting to eavesdrop on the conversation Gunner was having with Benton. He had resumed his position at the conference table once Captain Bannon had the Gulfstream in the air. Gunner was standing in the galley speaking quietly into a satellite phone. As he strained his neck to get a better angle, Dr. Sanderson finally was able to make out a few words. Unfortunately, those words were spoken in the language the Doctor now recognized as Swedish. Realizing he was not going to understand anything that was said, he turned his attention back to the folders containing information on the nine remaining test subjects.

He decided that reacquainting himself with the pertinent details of his former patients would be useful. In the future, they may not have as much time as they had in the house to determine the infected person's identity. Quick and decisive action may be necessary.

Gunner returned to the main cabin after finishing his conversation with Benton. Along with the satellite phone, Gunner had a tuna sandwich and a bottle of water with him. He put the food on the table across from Dr. Sanderson and then headed toward his men. After saying something in Swedish, he returned to the table.

"Hungry Doctor?" he said.

"Yea, I could eat I guess," replied the Doctor.

"Help yourself, the galley is well stocked."

Dr. Sanderson was about to get up when he was nearly knocked over by Gunner's men as they passed by him heading to the back of the plane.

"On second thought, I'll grab something in a minute," the Doctor said.

After dining on a grilled chicken breast sandwich and a Sprite, Dr. Sanderson looked out of the window and noticed it was getting to be late afternoon. They had left mid-morning from Colorado but after their stop in Arkansas, and the fact they were heading east, daylight was slowly slipping away. There was, however, several hours of sunshine left as they were nearing Florida's western coastline. They still had some time left in the day.

The Doctor had become acutely aware of how the definition of time had been altered. There were no schedules to keep, no clocks to punch, no soccer matches to bring the kids to. In his mind, the only thing that really mattered about time was that it was running out.

Gunner had returned to the couch and sat there with his head leaning back and his eyes closed. His PDA was on his lap and Dr. Sanderson had a feeling that even in this relaxed state, Gunner missed nothing. He put the folders back in his knapsack and zipped it back up. Maybe he would try to follow Gunner's lead and grab a few minutes of shut eye. They would likely be receiving another signal soon.

Just as the Doctor had drifted off he was awakened by Gunner standing over him holding his PDA. "We have two separate signals very near each other Doctor."

This time the Doctor accompanied Gunner up front and stood in the doorway of the cockpit. Captain Bannon entered the coordinates provided by Gunner into the Gulfstream's computer.

"Miami," the Captain said, "roughly three miles southeast of Miami International. We can land there. Mr. Worthington has a private hanger complete with a fuel truck and ground transportation. That is, of course, if it hasn't been compromised."

"ETA Captain?" Gunner asked.

"On the ground in twenty," was the response.

Gunner waited for the Doctor to step aside before heading back in the cabin to relay the information to his men. The Doctor turned back into the doorway and was about to close the cabin door when Bannon turned around slightly to add, "Better strap in tight Doc, wind is picking up, we could be in for a rough landing."

"Thanks," the Doctor said and closed the cabin door. He was going to mention the weather update to Gunner but decided not to. He thought it might be interesting to watch the usually unflappable Swede handle a bumpy landing.

The landing was, as promised, a rough one but Captain Bannon deftly guided the Gulfstream to a successful touchdown. To the Doctor's disappointment, Gunner remained calm through the entire process.

Captain Bannon, having been here many times with Mr. Worthington, knew exactly where to taxi the airplane. After about ten minutes, they were in front of a small hanger on the north side of the airport. The doors slid open with a touch of a button from inside the cockpit. When the entrance was fully open, Captain Bannon slowly moved the plane into the hanger.

Gunner and the Doctor were out of their seatbelts looking out the port windows for any signs of possible trouble. The hanger appeared to be clear. It would have been difficult for any infected to get in. The hanger was always kept locked and was accessible only through the large sliding doors or a side door that had a keypad lock.

The plane came to a stop near a large fuel truck. Gunner immediately went to the hatch and opened it up. As before, he looked out and deemed it safe. The Doctor grabbed his knapsack and a bottle of water from the pantry and headed down the steps and into the hanger. It was a large open room with a fuel truck to the left of the plane. At the far end of the hanger, in the left hand corner, there appeared to be a small office. Off to the right, parked near the entrance, were two metallic black Range Rover Land Rovers; complete with alloy wheels, luggage rack, and front grill rack with fog lamps.

Gunner came over to where the Doctor was standing as his men began the process of arming themselves again.

"We'll be taking the Range Rovers into the city," he said, "the Captain said there is an entrance to 36th street behind the hanger.

The Doctor was about to ask about the seating arrangements when Gunner continued, "You will sit with me and Olaf in the first vehicle, the others will ride behind us in the second."

Gunner removed the walkie from his belt and performed a comm check again with Captain Bannon adding, "Please be prepared to open those sliding doors at a moment's notice Captain. We may be coming in hot."

"Copy that."

Dr. Sanderson started making his way to the Range Rovers. As he approached the cars, the headlights flashed and the doors unlocked. He opened the door and got in the passenger's seat of the first car. Gunner soon followed along with Olaf. The Doctor was pleased to finally learn the name of one of Gunner's men. He could see the others get in the second car through the side mirror. Once everyone was in and the cars loaded up, Gunner started up the car and put it in drive.

Captain Bannon had opened the sliding doors enough so the vehicles could get out and quickly closed them. They made a U-turn and headed onto 36th street. To their left, a heavy residential area was teeming with infected. They were moving into and out of houses obviously looking for potential victims; but it appeared there were none to be had. Looking out over what had been, until recently, an affluent neighborhood complete with local country club and specialty food stores, the Doctor was beginning to fully understand the magnitude of the situation they were in.

They turned onto the on ramp to Route 953 heading south. The infected were mostly clear of the roads but the abandoned cars were a real problem. They could average only twenty-five to thirty miles an hour.

Gunner had his GPS, hooked onto the dashboard, leading them to the source of the signals.

"What do you make of the signals Doctor," Gunner suddenly asked, "that they are moving but seem to be confined to a small area."

The Doctor considered the question and answered, "It would appear that this area is significantly contaminated and there are probably very few, if any, survivors. The test subjects could be looking for humans but are unable to find any and have become … confused?"

Gunner turned the Land Rover onto the Dolphin Expressway as the Doctor continued, "Or it could be they are trapped somewhere and can't get out. The reports I have read and what little I have actually witnessed would indicate they don't have a real ability to reason."

"With perhaps one exception," the Doctor thought.

Gunner nodded and continued to drive, weaving in and out of what could be best described as traffic that was standing still. He reached down and removed the walkie from his belt. He turned the knob to change the channel from the one he used to communicate with Captain Bannon.

He pushed the button in and said, "Få klart vi är nära."

Gunner put the walkie back and began to slow down. The Doctor tensed up as he thought Gunner had seen some infected that he did not. But it was because the GPS unit indicated that they were close. Scanning the immediate area and looking at the GPS unit, the Doctor figured that the signal was just off to the southeast.

Arriving at the same conclusion, Gunner took the next exit and headed down 17th Street. They were now in a heavy residential area. Given the architecture and the businesses they were passing, the Doctor assumed they were in what was referred to as 'Little Havana'. As they neared their destination, rising up before them, was a huge stadium complex. Gunner took a left onto 5th Street and came to a complete stop.

In front of them was Marlins Stadium, former site of the famous Orange Bowl and current home of Miami's baseball team. More importantly, a combination of police SWAT trucks and abandoned cruisers choked off their path to the stadium to a narrow gap barely wide enough to get the Land Rovers through.

The greatest concern, however, was the dozen or so infected moving through the restricted space heading in their direction. Gunner briefly considered backing up and returning to 17th Street but a glance in the rear view mirror dissuaded him as more infected were closing in on their position from behind.

"Our test subjects are inside that stadium," Gunner said.

He grabbed the walkie again and began speaking in rapid fire Swedish to the men in the car directly behind them. As he finished barking orders he put the walkie back in his belt and turned to the Doctor and said, "The windows are bullet proof but you should probably keep your head down anyway."

Before the Doctor could respond, Gunner floored the Land Rover and sped forward toward the opening. The car reached about 45 miles an hour before smashing into the first zombie. Despite the tight space, Gunner was able to maneuver the car slightly to the left or the right so as not to collide with any of the zombies head on. They were flying off the Rover's front grill and landing on the hoods of the cruisers. After about 50 feet or so the street widened. It would have been easier to simply avoid most of them now but Gunner continued to use the car as a battering ram, crushing as many as he could. As they approached Marlins Way, Gunner took a sharp right and ended up in front of the main entrance. Much to the Doctor's surprise, Gunner's men were still right behind them.

The first thing the Doctor noticed was that the main gate was barricaded. Jersey Barriers were piled high across the entire entrance. He thought it might be possible to climb them and pull oneself over to the other side. There were two problems with that; first, would one be able to get over before any of those things grabbed ahold of their feet or legs and pulled them back down and second, it was impossible to know what was waiting on the other side. To their left were the ticket booths but there was no door for them to access from the outside. The only way in was through the windows and that was implausible. Next to the booths was the door to the administrative offices. It did not appear to be blocked from the outside but it was difficult to tell from their current view. There was sign, knocked over on its side, that read *Emergency Evacuation Site* with an arrow underneath it that would have been pointing to the main entrance had it been right side up.

The most immediate concern, however, was what to do about the zombie that was crawling up from the front grill and was making its way onto the Land Rover's hood. Gunner must have plowed it over but it had somehow hung on and now that the vehicle was stopped it was attempting to reach its prey. As it arrived at the top of the hood the Doctor noticed it was missing its lower extremities. He did his best not to vomit at the sight.

Meanwhile, Gunner had been assessing the situation and decided their best chance was to head for the administrative offices. The door had a window so he could see what was on the other side and even if it was locked, one well-placed gunshot would remedy that problem. They should be able to reach it safely. He again used the walkie to communicate his plans to his associates. When finished, he turned to Olaf in the back seat and said something to him. Olaf then reached into the back hatch and removed the bag containing the restraining devices.

Gunner then turned to the Doctor and said, "We're heading for the door to the offices; I'm getting out first and will take care of our friend on my hood. Then you get out and follow right behind me."

The Doctor nodded.

Wasting no more time Gunner grabbed the GPS tracker and removed his weapon. Opening the car door, he stepped out and using the crevice between the door and the windshield as protection, he quickly dispatched the zombie climbing on the hood. The Doctor swung the passenger's side door open and stepped out into the hot Florida sun. The shock initially slowed him down. He had been in the plane, then the hanger, and then the car. He was not ready for the blast of heat he received upon stepping out of the Land Rover.

"Please hurry Doctor," Gunner prodded.

Snapping out of it, the Doctor ran around the front of the car avoiding the slumped half body of the zombie Gunner just shot. Moving in behind Gunner, the Doctor saw Olaf fall in behind him with Gunner's other men sliding in on either side. They reached the door to the offices with little difficulty but realized they were drawing a great deal of attention. Gunner peeked in the window and did not see any trouble. He tried the door. It was locked. Taking one step back he leveled the handgun at the door handle and fired once. The door shuttered and Gunner pushed it open. They all followed in behind him.

The door led into a hallway with corridors heading down either side, office doors; some open, some closed, lined the hallway. The end of the hallway on the left side opened into a work area housing several cubicles. Gunner ran across the hall into the first office and emerged a second later dragging a moderately sized office desk. One of his men ran to his aid and helped him place it in front of the door they just entered. He and the same man went into the next office and repeated the act.

The Doctor noticed the offices seemed to be clear of any infected. As Gunner and his associate heaved the second desk on top of the first, the Doctor also noticed the gathering of infected outside peering in the window. It was probably only a matter of time before they tried to get in.

Gunner pointed to an open space at the end of the hallway to the left, in front of the cubicles. They made their way there and gathered in a small alcove next to a water cooler. Gunner looked down at his GPS tracker.

"One signal is about 200 yards from here in that direction," Gunner said pointing east. "The other … appears to be right on top of us."

That declaration caused the Doctor to tense up and look frantically around. He quickly realized that the GPS signal did not account for altitude. Any signal on the first floor would look the same if it was coming from the second floor and so on. It most likely meant that the test subject was directly above them.

Moving toward a door at the other end of the alcove, Gunner had one of his men open it and then step back. Nothing happened. Olaf and another man stepped through the door and spun to face opposite directions in the hallway. Olaf nodded and the rest of them entered the corridor. There was a sign that read *Ticket Office* with an arrow pointing right and another sign that read *Stadium Field* with an arrow pointing left.

A loud noise coming from the administrative offices indicated that the infected were indeed trying to get in. Gunner shut the door behind them and they followed the sign for the stadium. After a few turns, they found themselves in an open area with a set of wide stairs leading up to the field level seats. A stream of bright sunshine shone through the opening.

Looking again at the GPS receiver, Gunner said, "We head up those stairs, then double back heading that way," pointing in the direction from which they had just come. Turning to his men he relayed the same information.

Two of Gunner's men went ahead first hugging the wall on each side as they went up the stairs. Gunner followed with the Doctor right behind him. The other two followed from behind. The first two men reached the top of the stairs and the spun around and out of the Doctor's view. Before reaching the top step, he flinched from the unmistakable sound of gunfire.

Gunner leapt up covering the last three steps in one hop. He moved forward and opened fire. The others followed and moved between Gunner and the first two men forming a semi-circle around the top of the stairs. The Doctor moved slowly up the final two steps looking once behind him, just in case.

The steps opened up into a large concourse. Straight ahead were the field level seats. To the left and right were all manner of food vendors and merchandise displays. Also littering the concourse were several dozen infected. Gunner and his men had already dropped five or six but they seemed to be coming out of every corner of the concourse, drawn by the noise of the gunfire.

Gunner motioned for his men to tighten up their formation and once they had cleared some space, head to the right in the direction of the signal. The Doctor was in the middle as the group moved as one down the concourse. It narrowed somewhat as they moved away from the steps and headed toward the seating behind home plate. Infected were now appearing from behind the food stands, coming out of the gift shops and restaurants that filled this part of the stadium. Fortunately for the group, the zombies were slow and unsteady and Gunner and his men were managing at the moment.

The Doctor began to feel secure enough to begin looking at individual zombies to try and spot one of his test subjects. At first nothing looked familiar. Then, meandering near one of the circular tables that fans use to lean on while eating their hotdogs, the Doctor spotted the familiar hospital scrubs used by his patients.

Tapping Gunner's shoulder and pointing in that direction he shouted, "There!"

Gunner slowed his pace and began moving his men into position. Olaf unzipped the bag containing the restraints and the collapsed lasso harness in preparation for the possible capture and transportation of the … prisoner. As they approached the test subject, the group began to fan out in an attempt to surround and isolate it. Unfortunately, the Doctor soon realized that it was definitely not Number 5. This subject was one of the two females. His best guess was test subject number two, Evelyn Phelps.

"Not who we're looking for," he finally said.

Without missing a beat, Gunner retightened the formation and with one pull of the trigger, ended the unfortunate existence of test subject number two.

Immediately back to business, Gunner checked the GPS unit. The second signal was definitely coming from the playing field. They turned and headed toward a sets of stairs leading down to the field. The Doctor finally had an opportunity to look at the field for the first time. It was a beautiful diamond filled with brown dirt and Bermuda grass. The white bases were still anchored in their respective locations. Behind second base was the most interesting feature, one not usually seen at a ballpark; a National Guard UH-72a Lakota Utility Helicopter.

The field had thirty to forty infected wandering around. The signal seemed to be sending them in the direction of first base. When they had reached the short wall separating the playing field from the stands, they stopped to regroup.

"Doctor, I will need you up front this time," Gunner said, "we need to identify the test subject as soon as possible. If this is our subject, we will need to move quickly."

The Doctor agreed, but was silently wondering how the hell they were going to get themselves out of this mess to say nothing of bringing an infected person with them. Gunner hopped over the fence and onto the field with his men in tow. Dr. Sanderson moved out in front as they followed the dirt warning track behind home plate and past the home team's dugout. Up ahead five zombies took notice of their arrival and started closing in on them.

Gunner did not want to prematurely fire upon a zombie without first making sure it was not who they were looking for. Not to mention they needed to conserve ammunition. They were coming to realize that the noise from the gun blasts attracted the zombies.

Number 5 was not amongst the first group they encountered and Gunner and his men took care of them. As they neared first base, the Doctor once again spotted a zombie wearing the familiar hospital scrubs. He moved closer and could tell it was a male. Thinking back to the images and features of the test subjects he had spent an hour on the plane memorizing, he attempted to determine if this was Number 5. There was no time to consult his folders or try to pin it down and remove its microprocessor. He processed all the information as quickly as he could; height, weight, hair color, as it was now no more than five feet from him. He could smell the blood and bile covering the scrubs. The face was in no better shape than the one inside the small house in Arkansas. He had to be right. He made mistakes all the time as a research scientist. Trial and error were the name of the game; but the stakes were higher now.

The zombie was three feet from the Doctor and had its arms outstretched. He had been concentrating so hard on positively identifying this test subject; he had hardly noticed the increase in gunshots surrounding him.

Finally he blurted out, "Not him, it's number six."

Before he could finish his statement a gun shot rang out next to his left ear and test subject number six fell in front of him, his skull now in pieces. The sound snapped Dr. Sanderson out of his intense concentration. He now looked around to see that their situation had become significantly more precarious.

Dozens more infected had suddenly appeared from out of the home team's dugout and were closing in on their position. They had little chance of returning the way they had come and were being forced out into the playing field by the sheer number of zombies. They would have to find another way off the field and then find a different stadium exit and work their way around to where they left the Range Rovers.

Gunner moved them further into the field toward second base. Suddenly he shouted instructions to his team and for the first time they looked at him like he was crazy. He did not, however, have to repeat himself.

"Follow me," he said to the Doctor.

His men were up ahead clearing a path to the helicopter. As they reached it, his men surrounded the Lakota. The pilot's door was already open and Gunner wedged his sizable frame into the pilot's seat.

"Get in!" he shouted to Dr. Sanderson. He did as he was told lifting himself into the back seat. It was spacious enough to fit at least six people in the back and two in the front. The Doctor remembered the sign he had seen out front about this being an evacuation site. The authorities must have shut it down when it became too dangerous and then barricaded the infected in so they could not get out. At that moment he wondered what happened to the pilot. Instinctively, he started looking around to make sure it was just he and Gunner in the helicopter. They were, for the time being, alone.

Gunner's men were holding the infected at bay as Gunner worked the controls of the chopper trying to get it started. They would not, however, be able to hold out much longer. Dr. Sanderson was going to ask Gunner if he knew how to fly a helicopter but just then the rotors started to slowly move as the engine roared to life. The Doctor assumed that since the helicopter was evacuating civilians out of here that it would probably be ready to go. All it needed was a pilot.

Gunner yelled at his men, this time using their names, as one of them, Mikael, got in the copilot's seat and closed the door. Two others, Stefan and Ludvig, got in on either side of Dr. Sanderson. Olaf was last as he continued to fire away at the approaching zombies. Gunner was waiting until the blades reached takeoff velocity before calling his last man to board the aircraft.

A few seconds later, Gunner turned to Olaf about to instruct him to climb aboard. He was surprised, however, to see the number of infected between Olaf and the helicopter had doubled. They must have come from the rear of the aircraft. It was now impossible for Olaf to get to the rest of the group. He could not fire in the direction of the helicopter without endangering the others or the aircraft.

Gunner looked beyond Olaf toward the right field corner and saw that it was currently clear of infected. Gunner shouted at him to make his way to the outfield and he would land there to pick him up. Olaf turned and opened fire clearing a path for himself.

The Doctor became alarmed as dozens of infected converged on the helicopter. He hoped that Gunner could get the helicopter in the air soon or they would have some unwanted passengers. Just then the aircraft began to rock slightly and separated itself from the stadium grass. Several infected reached the helicopter and began fumbling for the landing gear. Gunner was able to lift the aircraft high enough to avoid the infected on the ground; turning around, he focused his attention on Olaf.

Olaf had managed to extract himself from the congregation of infected surrounding the helicopter and now stood in the right field corner on the edge of a dirt warning track. His movements, however, had been followed by a few infected occupying the centerfield warning track and the first base line. They were headed his way.

Gunner was having some trouble steadying the Lakota but had it at a safe altitude. He slowly piloted the aircraft toward the right field corner and attempted to land but each time he descended a group of infected moved into the area. Olaf was running out of time as the infected moving around the track would soon be on him. The noise of the helicopter was also attracting the attention of those zombies in the promenade as they began stumbling down the stairs toward the playing field.

Olaf decided his best move was to climb the wall separating the playing field and the stands and see if he could leap into the helicopter so that Gunner would not have to land. He turned and started to climb the wall.

It was much higher here than near home plate where they had entered the field. He reached for the top and pulled himself up. The weight of his rifle and the black bag slowed him down not to mention the overall physical exertion expended during the day had begun to take its toll.

He had pulled himself about halfway up as he took a second to rest his forearms on the top of the wall. He made a final push to get his lower half up and over. Suddenly he felt something pull on his left leg, then his right. He took a second to look down to see two infected had ahold of both legs and were trying to pull him down; or maybe they were trying to climb up. Either way, Olaf had to shake them off fast. He began to violently kick his legs using the wall for traction. He then peddled his legs as fast as he could, propelling himself upward and over the wall falling onto the hard concrete.

He stood back up and looked down onto the field and saw several more infected had joined the other two and were trying to get up the wall. They were neither strong enough nor coordinated enough to make any progress. He determined they were no longer a threat. Looking out toward the helicopter he saw Gunner had positioned himself so that Olaf could jump out toward the aircraft and grab the landing gear. The only problem was he could not get the Lakota low enough or close enough to make such a jump feasible. Olaf had to get higher up.

He briefly considered his options. He could try getting to the upper deck giving Gunner more room to get closer. If he should misjudge his jump, however, he would fall over one hundred feet to his likely death. He could make his way to the outfield stands. He would not be much higher but at least the foul pole would not be in Gunner's way.

"The foul pole!" thought Olaf.

The foul pole had three feet of netting extending upward to the top. He could climb up about half way and use the net as a springboard and grab the landing gear. It was dangerous but probably his best option as the nearest infected stumbling down the stairs were nearly upon him.

Olaf grabbed the netting and began pulling himself up. It was sturdy nylon rope and easily held his weight. He wedged the tip of his boots into the holes in the netting and climbed higher. The infected had reached the bottom of the pole and started to climb up after him. They lacked the strength to pull their undead selves up but seemed to be climbing on top of one another and slowly began closing the gap. Some fell off landing hard on the concrete or playing field below. It would be some time before they would be able to reach him, if at all. One thing was certain however; he could not climb back down.

Olaf had reached a good point on the pole and, using hand signals, imparted his intentions to Gunner. He slowly moved to the other side of the pole and began to rock back and forth attempting to create a sling shot action that would help propel him toward the chopper. Gunner moved into position and tilted the landing gear slightly so that it was as close as possible to Olaf.

Gunner had actually considered leaving Olaf behind as he felt attempting to rescue him was putting the rest of the group at risk. But, Olaf had the restraining devices and most of their ammunition in the black bag. Luckily for Olaf that made him a very valuable commodity.

Olaf was slightly above Gunner. In theory he figured he would fall down and outward and be able to grab ahold of the landing gear. He was about to count to three and leap when he noticed his left ankle had begun to throb with pain. He hoped it would not affect his ability to push off the netting. As Gunner steadied the Lakota, Olaf counted down from three and tried to time his jump so it coincided with the proximity of the landing gear.

He leapt forward, arms outstretched as far as he could. Gunner's men were leaning out of the helicopter waiting to grab Olaf as quickly as possible. Olaf soared toward the chopper for a second or two before the weight of his weapon, the bag, and his protective gear, succumbed to gravity and he began to rapidly free-fall. But he had propelled himself enough and one last maneuver by Gunner allowed Olaf to reach the chopper and grab hold of the landing gear.

His feet swayed in the open air as his weight caused the helicopter to pitch and roll slightly. Gunner was, however, equal to the task and quickly regained control of the aircraft. Olaf desperately tried to maintain his grip on the gear as his associates reached down to assist him. Gunner's men were finally able to grab Olaf's left hand as he pulled himself up into the back of the chopper. Olaf was clearly shaken. Stefan relieved him of the black bag and sat him down near the edge of the helicopter.

Gunner moved the helicopter high enough to clear the stadium and started heading northwest. With the immediate danger of the infected behind them, he turned his attention to Olaf.

"Har du blivit biten?" he asked.

Receiving no answer he asked again more urgently.

"Kontrollera honom," he said to the other two. They looked at Gunner, then at Olaf who appeared terrified. The other two men grabbed Olaf and pinned him to the floor of the helicopter and began poking and prodding him. They checked him all over as he squirmed. Gunner removed his hand gun and leveled it at Olaf's head. Olaf stopped moving.

Lifting Olaf's left pant leg revealed blood stains. Further examination exposed the source of the stains; a sizeable bite mark just above the ankle. Olaf looked at Gunner. The sheer terror in Olaf's eyes was obvious and his face was ashen.

Gunner looked down and then back up. "Kasta honom överbord," he said to the two men holding Olaf down.

They did not move. Gunner raised his weapon again; this time at one of the two other men. Unblinking, Gunner stared at his associate. Everyone in the helicopter new what had to be done except no one wanted to do it. A second passed, then another. When they were finally clear of the stadium, Gunner reached back and with a swift stroke, grabbed ahold of Olaf and pushed him out of the aircraft. Turning back around he continued to fly the helicopter.

"I'm sorry Doctor, it had to be done," he said.

Dr. Sanderson had spent most of his adult life trying to find ways to improve the quality of life for all mankind. He had trained himself to believe that there was always hope; always a chance. It was this belief that was partly responsible for this adventure they were currently undertaking. But as the sun began to set over the western horizon, Dr. Sanderson agreed; it had to be done.

Chapter 18
Captured

Test subject Number 5, the former Richard Kimbro, had just finished infecting an unsuspecting pizza delivery boy. He was traveling north and had almost reached the Florida-Alabama border. His need to feed, however, was growing again. His next victim was likely going to be devoured and not added to the zombie army he had been accumulating for the last 72 hours.

His thirst for flesh was primarily confined to humans whereas those he infected and those even further down the line seemed content with either human or animal flesh such as deer or boar.

The need for rest eluded him. He had been moving nonstop for the better part of three days traveling with a small group of zombies since leaving the Orlando area. They seemed to respond to him in a way that was hard to describe. He was using them as … protection. They surrounded him as the group moved wherever fresh prey was in great supply.

They were currently ambling near I-10 just outside Tallahassee Florida. Up ahead, they were drawn to the smell of human flesh and the sound of beating hearts. A group of humans were standing off to the side of the road. Number 5 followed their scent and moved in closer. He was in reach of his next victim when suddenly it was gone and a steel door slammed in front of him. Unable to move forward, Number 5 turned around only to bump into one of his own.

Moving in circles and unable to escape, Number 5 could still smell the humans nearby. Determined and persistent, he continued to head toward the sound of beating hearts but was stymied at every turn.

Shortly after Miami fell the President of the United States ordered the military to find and capture several infected persons so that they could be studied at length and perhaps a cause could be determined and then a proper course of action could be undertaken. Since the National Guard was already in position in Florida, it fell to them to round up potential guinea pigs for the experiments. A small unit of Guardsmen had positioned themselves outside of Tallahassee after they received word that several groups of infected were heading that way.

They had set a trap for them that included a portable iron cage large enough to easily hold 8 to 10 infected; basically a portable jail cell. It was driven down in the back of a climate controlled 18 wheeler that the Guard used from time to time to haul emergency supplies to affected areas after natural disasters.

They drew in the first group of infected they saw by placing two Guardsmen inside the cage as bait (unsurprisingly no one actually volunteered). There were two doors on the cage, each on opposite ends. The plan was to lure them inside the one door and then have the Guardsmen slip out the other door locking them in while another soldier would nudge the stragglers into the cage using a large pole.

Once the first infected entered the cage the guardsman exited using the back door closing it tightly behind him. He barely escaped the reach of the prisoner as it extended its arms through the narrow space between the bars. The next three followed right behind the first. The last two hesitated before moving forward into the trap. They began to take an interest in the other Guardsmen occupying the area to the cage's left. Two other soldiers came around from the back side of the pen holding six foot poles that looked like small battering rams. They shoved the last two infected into the cage with the end of the poles. A third soldier ran to the door and slammed it closed.

Overall, it went as well as could be expected with no casualties and six infected locked in the pen. The cage was then lifted into the back of the truck using a forklift and then pushed back toward the middle of the truck bed. The lights inside the truck were turned on so that the infected could be observed during transport.

A closed circuit camera had been set up inside to monitor the infected and record on their activity. As it turned out, they mostly charted their inactivity. The scientists felt that the captured infected people's behavior might shed some light on how best to reverse whatever it was that was happening to them. All that the Guardsmen witnessed was a lot of standing and pacing. The infected seemed to barely acknowledge the existence of one another; while at the same time, constantly bumping into each other or the iron walls of the cage.

The soldiers, however, made two noteworthy observations. First, at no time during the trip did any of the infected sit down or lean against the walls of the cage. It was a ten hour trip to Fort Campbell, Kentucky and they showed no sign of fatigue. The second observation was a little more subtle. None of the infected made any real attempt to escape. They all aimlessly moved about inside the cage. None of them attempted to open one of the locked doors or tried to climb upwards to see if the top of the cage could be lifted up.

That is except for one. An adult male of indeterminate age wearing what appeared to be hospital scrubs tried opening both doors. It was almost imperceptible. He moved to one of the doors and instead of just running into the bars as the others did; he reached for where the lock was and pulled. It might have been an accident or pure chance if not for the fact that when he was unable to open the first door, he tried the same thing with the second door.

Fort Campbell was the home of the 101st Airborne and had the distinction of being the most deployed unit in the armed forces. This basically meant that when there was trouble out there, they were the first to go. It also meant that the base was often sparsely populated with army personnel.

Upon arriving in Fort Campbell, Number 5 was unloaded with the rest of the test subjects into a holding pen. Soldiers in full armor entered the pen a short time later to subdue and strap each of the six subjects onto a hospital gurney. Number 5 could smell the soldiers through their armor but could do nothing about it. His attempts at feeding were in vain. He could not penetrate their protective gear. He was very hungry now.

Number 5 was moved into a medical lab along with the others. Each were placed in a small cubical separated by a sliding glass window. Blood (if you could call it that) was drawn, x-rays were taken, spinal fluid tapped, and hair samples were examined.

Over the next 24 hours the test subjects had transformed from a maniacal bloodthirsty group into a docile like condition. It was as if they were sleeping or in a coma. It was impossible for the researchers to tell. All the data from the tests were inconclusive. They were no closer to figuring out what had caused their illness then when they were brought in. It frustrated and agitated the medical personnel.

Number 5 was perfectly aware of his surroundings and the movements of the staff. He could still hear their heartbeats and smell their flesh but had outwardly shut down. The virus that had invaded his body and controlled his actions had induced a trance like state; perhaps simply waiting for an opportunity to feed.

The researchers were working long hours and most had not rested since the subjects arrived. They understood the urgency to produce results and had failed to do so thus far. They began to rush and they began to get sloppy.

If the test subjects needed to be moved in order to retrieve samples from particular parts of the body they would be unstrapped and held in place, the samples taken, and then re-strapped. The subjects' current condition had lulled the staff into a false sense of security. The need for answers combined with the perceived safety was a dangerous combination.

32 hours after arriving, the test subject that had been given the code name Bravo was unstrapped and skin tissue was removed from several areas of the body. The researchers were in such a

hurry to properly store the sample for testing, they forgot to re-strap the subject's restraints. After repeating the procedure on the other test subjects, one of the researchers left the lab to bring the samples to the testing facility. The second researcher, returning to the test subject's cubicles, noticed the loose straps on test subject Bravo. Moving over to the hospital gurney he reached for the left arm strap. As he was about to grab it, Bravo's hand came up and closed tightly around the researcher's neck. The test subject's head came up as he pulled the researcher's neck down at the same time.

Number 5 was finally feeding again. He took a bite out of the researcher's neck and let him fall to the ground. He started to rise up only to be stopped by the strap on his right wrist. Rotating his wrist back and forth he was able to slowly remove his arm from the leather strap. He was soon sitting upright. His leg straps had not been refastened. A few moments later he was standing next to his gurney.

He bent down next to the research assistant and hovered over him for a moment. Number 5 paused for a second and then gradually rose to his feet. He stepped out of his cubicle and looked out into the lab. He could not smell any humans nearby. He turned to the right and staggered to the only exit in the lab. He pushed on the door and it did not move. He reached for the door handle and pulled and that did not work. Moving back a few steps and to the left he stood silently waiting for the door to open.

Fifteen minutes later a former research assistant with a large gash in his neck and blood splatter on his lab coat moved next to Number 5 and stood there staring blankly at the door.

Chapter 19
Reservations

The convoy had been rumbling along for over an hour before anyone said anything in the back of the truck. Kim was whispering to her kids as the students tried in vain to get a few more minutes of sleep. The soldier kept inspecting his gun over and over again while Chester stared out of the back of the truck. With sleep impossible to obtain the students resigned themselves to being awake and started making small talk with Kim and Sgt. Sanchez. As the drive wore on, the civilians tried to relax as much as they could on the hard wooden troop seats. Passing the time in idle conversation nobody noticed Danielle shuffle over to Chester and tug on his pant leg.

"Hey mister, what's your name?" she asked.

Hearing her daughter's voice Kim's looked up, "Leave him alone Danielle. Come back over here." Looking in Chester's direction she added, "Sorry about that sir."

Chester looked down at the girl and let out a grunt as he turned back to stare out of the truck.

"She asks a good question, sir," said Stephen. "It looks like we might be together for a while so you might as well let us know what to call you."

"My name's Chester."

"We'll it's nice to meet you, Chester," said Kim trying to be polite. "I'm Kim; these are my kids Danielle and Jason."

"And I'm Stephen and these are my friends Dave, Lucy and Nick," Stephen said motioning to the others.

Without saying a word Chester turned to survey the others in the truck, gave them a nod, and then turned back to staring out of the back of the truck.

"A real conversationalist that guy," said Nick with a chuckle.

"How come he won't talk Mommy?" asked Danielle.

"I think he just wants to be left alone honey," replied Kim.

"Hey Danielle, you want to come over here and I'll braid your hair?" asked Lucy.

Looking to her mom and receiving a nod of approval Danielle went over and sat down in front of Lucy who began to comb her fingers through the young girl's hair. The others went back to quiet conversation while Sgt. Sanchez continued inspecting his weapon. Chester stared into the distance beyond the convoy wondering where the hell his truck was.

Around noon, Sgt. Sanchez suddenly put his weapon across his lap and put his hand to his ear as he listened to his comm. When the message was over, Sanchez turned his attention to everyone in the truck.

"Alright listen up everyone. The Major said we will be stopping in the next half hour. He's looking for a place that has a restroom and that might also have food. When we arrive he wants us to move as quickly as possible so we can get on the road again. I'll let you know when we are about to stop."

The conversations ceased as everyone contemplated having to leave the safety of the truck. Even though most of them were hungry and could use a bathroom break they did not relish having to face whatever was out there. Sgt. Sanchez went back to looking his weapon over while Stephen picked up his axe from the floor and gripped it tight in his hands. Kim glanced at the pistol case next to her but decided against opening it up here in front of her kids.

A short while later Sgt. Sanchez spoke up again.

"It looks like there might be a small convenience store and gas station down the road at the next exit. I'll get out first and once we know it's all clear, the rest of you can get out."

Everyone, except Chester, gave Sanchez a nod. The truck bumped along for a couple more miles before it slowed. As the convoy pulled into a small parking lot Sanchez raised his weapon to the ready position. Before the truck had even come to a stop Chester had hopped out, shotgun in hand, and disappeared around the corner.

"Hey buddy ... oh never mind," said Sgt. Sanchez as he jumped out of the truck.

Looking around he put his hand to his ear again as he received a message. Coming back to the truck's tail gate he motioned for the civilians to get out.

"It looks all clear but make sure you are paying attention. The building is being cleared. Make it fast; when you are not using the restroom look for food in the store. Let's go."

Major Bradley slowly got out of his Humvee and stretched his legs as he barked orders at the soldiers around him. He had picked a small isolated gas station convenience store to stop at. The Major was counting on few zombies being in the area. He was also hoping that this would not only offer a restroom for the convoy but also a possible source of food and supplies. Two of his soldiers caught his attention as they emerged from the store and gave him the all clear signal.

"Alright, get the civilians into the building and keep a sharp eye out," he said into his comm. "The rest of you can relieve yourselves around the convoy."

He watched as his soldiers escorted the civilians into the store and set a guard at the door. It was a typical backwoods gas station; a rundown building with two pumps and a small garage to the side. Through the dirty glass windows in the front of the store he could see shelves that seemed to still hold most of their goods.

The civilians milled around in the back of the store waiting on the restrooms.

"Major, the perimeter is secure and the men are checking to see if they can get any diesel out of the pumps. We haven't encountered any infected yet," Captain Morris said as he appeared around the side of the convoy.

"Very good Captain, the sooner we get out of here the less of a chance we have of running into them."

"I want you to get in the store and see about getting some supplies," Major Bradley continued. "Put the civilians to work gathering them; food and drink should be a priority but take any medicine, clothing, or other items that might be of value. I hope we won't need them but who knows what awaits us in Dayton."

"Yes sir," replied Captain Morris with a salute. "We'll load it into the second truck."

Captain Morris headed off into the store and Major Bradley pulled out his map and laid it out on the hot hood of the Humvee. One more time he went over their route to Dayton as well as his secondary routes should their primary route be inaccessible.

Inside the store the civilians had already begun shopping for supplies as Captain Morris entered. A bell jingled as the door shut behind him.

"Alright ladies and gentlemen listen up," said Captain Morris. "We need to be loaded up and ready to move in ten."

Looking around and finally finding Sgt. Sanchez, Captain Morris continued, "When we are ready to move, I want a head count from you before we roll."

"Yes sir, but umm … sir … uh I don't know where that Chester fellow went, he jumped out as soon as we stopped and he didn't come in here with us."

"I knew that guy was gonna be trouble. Don't worry about him; he's a problem for the Major and I."

"When the civilians are finished with the bathroom, I want you to gather up any supplies you might need or want," continued the Captain. "Food and drink is the most important but don't neglect medicine, toiletries, clothing etc. I'll be back in five to help load it all up."

Not waiting for a reply, Captain Morris turned and headed out of the store towards Major Bradley.

"Major, we've got a problem. That guy Chester we picked up, he jumped out of the truck before we stopped and we aren't sure where he went."

"That's alright Captain, if he wants a ride he'll be back," replied the Major. "He's one of those loner types so don't expect him to want to hang around with the others."

"You gentlemen looking for me?" Chester said as he materialized from around the corner of the store giving the Major and Captain a scare.

"Yes, in fact we were," answered Major Bradley. "You can't be going off on your own like that if you want our protection and you definitely can't be sneaking up on us like that unless you want to get shot."

"I don't think I'll need much of that protection Major, I got past your perimeter guard goin' out and comin' in."

"Yes, you proved your point," said Captain Morris, "but we would appreciate it if you let us know where you are going so we don't shoot you by mistake."

"I can tell you can take care of yourself Mr. Boone," added Major Bradley, "so I won't subject you to the same rules as the rest of the civilians but work with us here. You can come and go as you like but inform me first and make sure you are back when we are ready to leave as we won't think twice about leaving you behind."

"Fair enough Major," replied Chester.

"So where did you go Mr. Boone?" asked Major Bradley.

"I went lookin' for some supplies. There is a house through the woods aways," he said pointing in the direction of a small clump of trees off to the side of the convenience store.

"It had a deer skinnin' rack in the back so I figured it might have some useful things."

"And did you find anything?"

"Yes sir, I got a mess of shot gun rounds and a couple boxes of rifle ammo," Chester said patting his pack as he slung it around front and put it on the ground.

Opening the pack he pulled out several large bags. "I also found six sealed bags of fresh deer jerky. It should be good for a couple of weeks. Its good eatin' when there isn't much else to be had."

"Thanks Mr. Boone, I think your skills will come in handy …"

"Don't mean to be rude Major but I thought you should probably know there are about fifteen of those infected things comin' down the road towards us. They'll be here in a few minutes."

"You should have said that first Mr. Boone. Captain, get those civilians and supplies back in the truck immediately; we roll out in two minutes. Mr. Boone if you wouldn't mind getting back to your truck as well."

The Major spoke into his comm and the convoy came to life with activity. Captain Morris quickly shepherded the civilians, and what few supplies they had obtained, back to their truck. Within minutes the convoy was loaded up and rolling out of the parking lot towards the highway. As the last truck drove out of the lot, zombies began to appear in and around the gas station.

It was getting to be late afternoon as the convoy neared Columbus Ohio. Major Bradley had stopped gazing out his window to study his map again. They were several miles from I-270, the route they would be using to skirt around Columbus. With the speed in which cities had become infected Major Bradley did not want to find out how many of those things were in Columbus. He was just about to inform Private Sinclair about the upcoming exit when his comm came to life.

"Um, Major we have a problem with the fuel truck."

"What's wrong McCutchen?"

"I am pretty sure we have a bad axle here."

"Alright hold on, we'll stop and come have a look."

"Stop the convoy son," said Major Bradley to Sinclair.

The convoy came to a stop as Major Bradley jumped out and walked back to the fuel truck. As he did his soldiers began setting up their security perimeter. As he passed the truck holding the civilians, Chester jumped down and gave him a nod.

"I'm gonna go have a look around Major."

"If you insist Mr. Boone but I don't need to remind you to be back when we are ready to go."

As Chester jumped the guard rail and disappeared into the woods near the highway, Major Bradley reached the fuel truck and found Captain Morris watching two of his men working under the front axle of the truck.

"What's going on Captain?" asked Major Bradley.

"Looks like the front axle is broken sir."

"Can they fix it?"

"No sir, there is no fix for it. They are telling me they would need a replacement axle rod."

"I am going to go out on a limb and say we didn't bring one of those along?"

"No sir."

"That was rhetorical Captain. Well, I'd rather not leave the fuel truck. I hate to say it but if there is nothing in Dayton then we will need all the fuel we can get our hands on." Looking at the Captain he added, "So what are our options?"

"Well, we can leave it but like you said that's not viable. We could continue to drive it but very slowly and it will eventually completely fail. The final option is letting the boys here swap the front axle out with the second deuce and a half but then we have to leave that behind."

"You can just switch out the axles like that?" asked the Major.

"That's what the boys tell me. The fuel truck and deuce and a half are the same truck body with a different bed mounted on them."

"That makes sense. I guess we don't need the second truck if it's just holding supplies and sucking down diesel. We'll make it all fit in the other vehicles. So how long will this take Captain?"

"The boys say a couple hours minimum, sir, and it will take at least three of them."

"Well, it will start getting dark by then. I don't think we'll make it to Dayton tonight."

Looking around the Major continued, "We're too exposed to change it out here. I think I saw some signs for hotels at the next exit. Do you think we can make it there on the axle?"

"We'll give it a shot sir."

"Alright Captain load 'em up. It looks like we'll be spending the night in comfort. What do you think; Holiday Inn or Best Western?"

"I've always been partial to Best Western sir. I believe one more night's stay and I get one night free," Captain Morris said with a smile.

"Best Western it is then. Let's move."

Major Bradley made his way back to the lead Humvee as Captain Morris got the convoy ready to move. All Major Bradley could do was shake his head as he saw Chester appear out of the woods and jump into the back of the truck right before the convoy drove off.

The convoy moved slowly but eventually made it to the parking lot of the Best Western. By the time it came to a stop Chester was already out of the back of the truck but did not wander far. Having been given very little information about what was going on; the civilians were relieved when Captain Morris and Major Bradley showed up at the back of their truck.

"Alright folks here's the plan," said Major Bradley. "We broke an axle on the fuel truck so we are stuck here for the night while my men switch it out with one from the second truck back there. We'll get to spend the night in actual beds tonight and hopefully by morning we'll be good to go. If you have any questions speak with Captain Morris."

Finishing what he had to say Major Bradley motioned to Captain Morris and then headed back to his Humvee.

"Once my men finish clearing the first floor and blocking off the stair well and entrances we'll move into the first couple of rooms for the night. You all can split them up however you see fit. We don't want you moving around so once you are set we'll bring food and water to you. Then it's up early before we head out. Any questions?" asked Captain Morris.

"Yeah I've got one," answered Nick. "It's not like we've got a reservation; how are we gonna get in the rooms?"

"Trust me, it won't take much to knock down one of the doors, but that shouldn't be necessary. There should be a master key card behind the reception desk," answered the Captain.

It doesn't look like there is any electricity," said Stephen, "do you think we can get some of those flash lights we found at the gas station?"

"Sure, I'll have them brought to your rooms. Now figure out who's sleeping where and how many rooms you'll need and I'll be back in a minute."

As the Captain walked off Chester stopped him and said, "I'll just take a couch in the lobby. But right now I am going to go scout around, I'll be back before nightfall."

Before the Captain could respond, Chester had turned around and was walking away. Shrugging his shoulders he continued on to find the Major and assist in securing the perimeter so the axle could be changed as soon as possible.

"Well, I think the kids and I will take one room," said Kim. "Lucy you are more than welcome to join us, I think Danielle is kind of fond of you."

"I would like that, thanks Kim," responded Lucy.

"We'll get a room across the hall so we aren't too far. What do you guys think," Stephen asked looking at Dave and Nick.

Dave shrugged his shoulders and continued to look sullen as he sat at the far end of the truck.

"Doesn't matter to me as long as I get one of those nice soft hotel beds and some of the complimentary shampoo," Nick said.

"You gonna be alright Dave?" asked Stephen.

Dave nodded but did not say a word.

"Just give him some space Stephen, he'll be alright," said Lucy.

Just then, Captain Morris came around the corner and interrupted their conversation.

"The hotel is ready for you guys; we've got rooms 101 and 102 open for you just past the check-in desk. We need to get inside quickly, we've seen some infected in the area; although our new friend Chester seems to be dispatching a few of them with his machete."

"Does he need some help," asked Jason picking up his golf club.

"No son, you stay with your mom, she might need you and your club. And Stephen you've still got your axe, right?" asked Captain Morris.

"Yeah, I do," replied Stephen.

"Alright that's good, let's go get settled for the night."

Major Bradley and Captain Morris stood shoulder to shoulder outside in front of the lobby door. They were supervising the soldiers replacing the fuel truck axel and things seemed to be progressing well but it was an involved process and was taking time. They were using the Coleman flashlights donated by Kim to provide much needed light under the truck beds.

Captain Morris looked over at the Major who appeared to be deep in thought. Turning his attention back to the busy soldiers he asked the Major, "If you don't mind me askin' Major … how did you get the nickname 'Butch'?"

"What?" the Major asked having his concentration broken by the question.

"I've heard people call you Butch, just wondering where the name came from," the Captain responded.

"Well, if you must know Captain," the Major said with a smile. "When I was a kid, even into my teenage years, I loved to blow stuff up. Give me a firecracker or some incendiary device and I would find something to blow up. One of my favorite things to do was to try to lift things off the ground, like a rocket using the firecracker as fuel."

"And you still have all your fingers?" Captain Morris interjected.

"And all my toes," the Major continued. "One day my best friend, kid by the name of Donald Grimaldi, got his hands on some M-80's. He brought them over and I thought it would be a great idea to lift something heavy off the ground so I grabbed one of our old wooden chairs from the basement."

"I think I see where this is going …" Captain Morris said.

"The day before, it was a rainy day so Donald and I were stuck inside my house and watched that old Paul Newman western *Butch Cassidy and the Sundance Kid.*"

"Yea, I've seen it."

"Remember the scene where Newman blows up the train to steal the money but he uses too much dynamite and blows up the money as well. They have to run for cover as all the burned up cash is raining down on them."

"That was the best scene in the movie."

"Well, I placed the M-80's under the legs of the chair and lit them in hopes of lifting that chair as high off the ground as possible. We ran for cover behind a nearby tree and waited. When the M-80's exploded, the chair simply fell over and the bottom of the legs were a slivered mess as small shards of wood came raining down on Donald and me," the Major said chuckling at the memory.

"He turned to me with a huge smile on his face and quoted that famous line from the movie, '*Think you used enough dynamite there Butch*'. We both fell over laughing so hard it hurt. From then on he started calling me 'Butch' and I guess it kinda stuck," the Major concluded.

The Captain laughed then added, "I have a feeling we're going to have to blow some stuff up before this whole mess is over."

Major Bradley just nodded and looked straight ahead at his soldiers working diligently on the fuel truck.

After getting situated in their rooms, everyone met in the lobby for a dinner that consisted of more vending machine snacks, some stale pastries, and overly ripened fruit meant for the hotel's breakfast buffet. They ate in silence and watched out the window as some of the soldiers worked feverishly switching out the two axles under the watchful eyes of Major Bradley and Captain Morris. Using the other vehicles, the remaining soldiers had formed a semi-circle around the men working in front of the lobby doors. There they stood guard keeping a close eye out for zombies.

Chester was nowhere to be seen for the rest of the evening until, just as the last rays of light slipped below the horizon, he showed up at the lobby doors. Covered in dirt and what everyone assumed was zombie parts, he had a brief conversation with the Major before coming inside and finding a couch to bed down in for the night. He slipped out of the soiled clothing and put on some clean clothes he found during one of his excursions. The others, with no daylight left to see in, retired to their rooms for what they hoped would be a comfortable night's sleep.

Chapter 20
Heading North

"Come in Captain," Gunner repeated into the walkie. He was nearly screaming in order to be heard above the noise of the helicopter's rotors.

"Bannon here, over," finally came the response.

"Captain, we are three minutes out. We will be arriving via helicopter. Please be prepared to open hanger doors, over," Gunner replied.

"Did you say helicopter?" Captain Bannon asked.

"That's affirmative."

"Copy that; be advised there has been some activity around the hanger. When you exit the chopper, use the side door to enter, over."

"Copy; over and out."

Gunner returned the walkie to his belt and turned around to talk to Dr. Sanderson. He was shouting now.

"We will be entering using the side door. Captain Bannon said there has been some activity in the area. When we land, Mikael and Stefan will exit first and clear the area if needed. You, Doctor, will follow behind Ludvig and I will bring up the rear," Gunner said. He repeated his orders to his remaining men in Swedish.

The Doctor could see the airport in the distance. Gunner would have to land off to the side of the hanger, in between Mr. Worthington's and a much larger hanger next to it. It would leave them about a fifty foot dash to reach the side door. He took notice of some movement below and as they started to descend further; he saw exactly what Captain Bannon was talking about. It appeared their arrival had attracted some attention.

Their probable landing spot was clear but a dozen or so infected had congregated in front of the hanger doors. Gunner slowly piloted the Lakota down to the asphalt exactly where the Doctor assumed they would land. They would have a clear path to the side door unless there were any infected hiding around the corner.

The helicopter touched down and bobbed up and down for a brief second before settling onto the tarmac. Gunner killed the engine and waited a few seconds for the blades to come to a stop. He motioned for Mikael and Stefan to get out of the helicopter. Mikael, who was in the front with Gunner, opened his door and took a position facing away from their hanger; looking toward the larger hanger next door. Stefan jumped out of the other side and faced their hanger and the increasing zombie presence in front of it.

Gunner motioned for Ludvig to grab the Doctor and get him inside the hanger which he literally did by grabbing his shirt collar and removing him from the helicopter. Stefan was holding his fire as long as he could as some of the infected became aware of their position and began moving toward the helicopter. Mikael noticed movement from within the larger hanger next door; about 75 yards away. Gunner reached into the backseat and retrieved the black bag that Stefan had relieved poor Olaf of. He opened the door and ran around the front of the helicopter and tapped Mikael on the shoulder and pointed to the side door.

As Ludvig and the Doctor reached the hanger entrance they heard shots ring out. Resisting the urge to turn around and look, they headed into the hanger through the side door being held open by Captain Bannon. Mikael followed a few seconds later.

Gunner moved in next to Stefan and helped slay a couple zombies wearing olive green flight suits. Between them they had killed the majority of infected in front of the hanger. They started to move backwards together away from the front and toward the side door. After a few more steps they turned around and bolted for the door, reaching it with no problem. Captain Bannon closed the door tightly behind them and started to turn away when he paused for a second. He quickly turned back to the door and peered out, scanning the immediate area. Then turning back, he stared at the group before him.

The Doctor could tell he was doing a head count.

"We lost Olaf," Gunner said matter of factly while exchanging a few words with Mikael.

Captain Bannon turned to the Doctor with a quizzical look.

"He was unfortunately bitten," Dr. Sanderson replied.

"Oh."

"Are we ready to depart Captian?" Gunner asked as his team was already heading toward the plane to once again remove their armor and stow the weapons in the cargo hold.

"All gassed up and ready to go," he answered.

"Mikael said there were a large number of infected pouring out of the larger hanger next door and they seemed to be heading this way," Gunner added.

"Then we should be going," the Captain replied.

They all moved quickly to the Gulfstream. Gunner's men had finished and were already moving up the steps into the plane. The rest boarded with the Captain heading to the cockpit and the Doctor strapping himself into the couch and placing his knapsack beside him. Gunner sealed the hatch and joined Dr. Sanderson on the couch.

They felt, and then heard, the Gulfstream's engines roar to life. It was much louder in the enclosed hanger than it was out in the open air. The Captain had already turned the plane around so that it was facing the sliding doors. It moved slightly forward as he opened the hanger bay doors.

Suddenly, the plane came to a stop and jerked its passengers in their seats. A second later, *"Gunner to the cockpit, Gunner to the cockpit,"* came blaring over the intercom.

Gunner swiftly removed his seatbelt and ran to the cockpit. When he arrived, he noticed the alarmed look on the Captain's face. Without saying a word, Bannon simply pointed out the cockpit's windows toward the sliding bay doors that had by now opened all the way revealing a mass of zombies piling into the hanger.

The infected Mikael had seen indeed had made their way over to Benton's hanger and were now pouring into the opening. There was no way, given the size of the plane; they would be able to get through the opening without striking quite a few zombies.

"Could we plow through them?" asked Gunner.

"We could," answered Captain Bannon, "but we would likely damage the plane's landing gear or the flaps. Maybe even the fuselage or the slats."

Gunner peered through the cockpit window for a second then turned to Captain Bannon and said, "Can you back her up?"

He thought for a second and said, "I could use the reverse thrusters but that would be dangerous, especially indoors. It would also be difficult to control the speed; I might end up inadvertently creating a back door to the hanger."

"I just need you to create a little bit of space between the plane and those things out there," Gunner said.

"Yea," the Captain said, "why not, and I might even knock a few of them on their asses in the process."

Gunner turned around and quickly moved into the cabin shouting instructions to his crew in Swedish. As he reached the back of the plane he grabbed the black bag that held the restraints. He did not have the time earlier to store it in the cargo hold and was forced to bring it on board.

"Please remain seated, we have encountered some trouble," he said to Dr, Sanderson.

Captain Bannon had backed the plane up as best he could, buying time for Gunner and his crew to disembark. Gunner instructed the Captain to pull forward as space was created and exit the hanger at the first available opportunity; then wait for them out on the tarmac.

Gunner opened the hatch and he and his crew headed out of the plane. When they reached the bottom of the stairs, Captain Bannon lifted the hatch and closed the door. Gunner got down on one knee and unzipped the black bag. He pulled out extra clips for each of his men for their handguns and tossed them each two and kept two for himself. He reached deeper into the bag and pulled out a canvass strap that housed six M67 fragmentation grenades. He closed the bag and slung it around his shoulder.

Getting to his feet he quickly surveyed the situation. The zombies were too many to count and had not fanned out as they entered the hanger but had remained fairly close together. Gunner instructed Mikael to move to the left of the plane and to eliminate the zombies in the front of the pack. Gunner, Ludvig, and Stefan moved to the other side of the plane and attempted to act as bait to draw them off to the side of the hanger.

Mikael began plugging the zombies up front attempting to clear space for the Captain to move the plane forward. He was having some success but he had emptied his original clip and was now working on the first of the spares.

Gunner, meanwhile, had managed to draw several zombies away from the front of the plane without wasting any ammunition. He and his men were standing in front of the office acting as bait and waiting until the last possible minute to move. As they began to draw more and more attention away from the plane and onto themselves, Captain Bannon started to move the plane slowly forward.

Mikael had managed to drop over two dozen zombies but was now on his last clip. He moved under the plane's left wing and continued to fire upon any zombies that were in the way of the wing. He had his nine inch combat knife sheathed on his belt if needed when he ran out of ammo. Although he was not wearing his armor, and hand to hand combat would be dangerous, he would have little choice but to use the knife if necessary.

The plane had managed to push forward about halfway to the bay doors without any contact. It was the last several feet that would be the trickiest. Especially since bullet riddled zombies littered the hanger floor.

Gunner ordered his men to walk under the other wing, using it as a shield, and eliminate any zombies in the way of the right wing. They had yet to open fire and had the full complement of bullets at their disposal. Gunner would follow from behind.

Mikael had done such a remarkable job clearing the left side of the hanger, Captain Bannon was able to move the plane slightly to the left and then move forward as the bulk of the zombie horde had taken the bait set by Gunner and his group. Mikael had fired his last round just as the Gulfstream's nose was exiting the hanger.

The setting sun would make it difficult to spot any additional zombies that were still outside in front of the hanger. Ludvig and Stefan were rapidly depleting their cartridges as well but had managed to clear a modest path for Captain Bannon to guide the plane out of the hanger and onto the tarmac.

Gunner was following the plane out with his head ducked under the tail fighting the heat and noise generated by the aircraft's engines. The zombies were having trouble maneuvering around the wing and rear landing gear so Gunner was currently well protected. Any that managed to get close were quickly dispatched.

Once clear of the hanger, the Captain accelerated and directed the plane past the helicopter Gunner and the Doctor arrived in and headed toward the nearest runway. Bannon grabbed the walkie and tried to hail Gunner. He was not answering.

As the plane moved out of harm's way, Gunner instructed his men to follow it and wait for the Captain to stop the plane and get back on board. Not having to be told again, they ran after the plane. They encountered little resistance as most of the remaining zombies had made their way into the hanger.

Gunner turned to face the open hanger doors and grabbed the walkie off his belt. He had heard Captain Bannon calling him but was unable to respond until now.

"Captain, come in."

"There you are, I have been ..." the Captain responded but was immediately cut off.

"Close the hanger doors now Captain," Gunner said with what he hoped was sufficient urgency.

"Uh, copy that, over," replied Bannon as he reached for the remote that controlled the hanger doors.

The zombies that remained in the hanger were wondering what had happened to their prey. Some started to figure it out and headed for the bay doors as they began to slowly close. Gunner removed two of the grenades from the canvass belt, pulled the pins and threw them inside; one to the left side and the other to the center of the hanger.

He turned and ran heading for the plane as the last shreds of daylight faded from the sky. Eight seconds later the darkness was briefly again filled with light as the grenades exploded inside the hanger. The explosion was significantly greater than Gunner had anticipated as the ground shook and nearly caused him to lose his footing. He stopped briefly and turned back around to admire his handiwork. The damage caused and the ensuing fireball was impressive but it took Gunner a second to figure out what really happened. His first grenade must have traveled a little farther than he intended and landed under the fuel truck parked inside. Nothing could have ... survived that explosion.

Satisfied, he turned back around and continued on to the plane all the while contemplating how he was going to explain the destruction of his hanger to Mr. Worthington.

When he reached the plane, the hatch was open and the stairs were down. Captain Bannon was out on the tarmac inspecting the plane for structural damage. The rest of his crew was already on board.

"What the hell was that?" Bannon asked Gunner.

Ignoring the question Gunner asked, "Did the plane suffer any damage Captain?"

"None that I can see … nice work."

The Captain made one more pass around the plane as Gunner went up the stairs.

Dr. Sanderson was waiting for him at the top of the stairs.

"I can't believe we made it out of there," he exclaimed. "Are you hurt?" He wanted to ask if he had been bitten but did not dare.

"No," was all Gunner said as he walked past the Doctor heading to the lavatory. His men were already in their seats strapped in ready for takeoff.

Captain Bannon had climbed back aboard and was closing up the hatch. He turned to the Doctor and said, "That was a close one, wouldn't you say Doctor?"

The Doctor, not sure how much more of this he could take, said nothing.

"Anyway, where to next?"

"Head north," was the Doctor's reply.

He turned around and headed back to his familiar seat on the couch. As he was fastening his seatbelt Gunner came out of the lavatory. He had obviously cleaned himself up and looked more like his old self then when he entered the plane.

He stopped for a second to consult his PDA which he had left on the plane during his encounter with the zombies in the hanger.

"No additional contacts Doctor," he said.

"I told John to head north," replied the Doctor.

Gunner just nodded and settled back into his seat on the couch as the Gulfstream started to move again.

For the first time Dr. Sanderson sensed something wrong with the usually stoic Swede. It could be the loss of Olaf. Or it could be that this mission was turning out to be more difficult than he planned on; or perhaps something deeper. The Doctor had enough trouble getting a read on Benton Worthington III. Trying to penetrate the mind of this man would likely prove impossible.

Chapter 21
Getting Closer

The sun had fully retreated behind the western horizon as the plane reached its cruising altitude. Gunner remained seated on the couch while Dr. Sanderson returned to his position at the conference table bringing with him his knapsack. He pulled out the folders containing the information on his ten test subjects.

He spread the files out in front of him and pulled out the ones they had already eliminated; test subjects number two, number six, and number nine. That left seven more. Seven more chances to reverse the wrong that had been done.

He admitted to himself that doubt had begun to creep into his mind. Even if they located Number 5, would they be able to get him on the plane and would he be able to learn enough to figure out a cure. Was Number 5's GPS still generating a signal? Was this nothing but a wild goose chase?

He was lifted out of his doldrums by Gunner as he passed by and took a seat across from him.

"We're going to have to put down soon," he said. "Captain Bannon will need to get some sleep and we can't go hunting those things at night without night vision equipment."

"I suppose that's true," the Doctor answered.

"I'll go talk to Bannon and see about finding us an out of the way airstrip somewhere."

Gunner moved forward through the cabin and entered the cockpit. Dr. Sanderson was considering the probability of getting any sleep while on the ground knowing those things were out there. He was, however, very tired. It had been a long day and the Doctor had seen things today that two weeks ago he could not have imagined.

The sound of the cockpit door closing drew the Doctor's attention to the front of the plane where Gunner was moving toward his men. He stopped briefly and spoke to them. They nodded. As Gunner continued down the cabin toward the Doctor, Stefan and Ludvig got up from their chairs and followed behind him.

Gunner sat down across from the Doctor again as Stefan made his way to the lavatory and Ludvig headed into the galley.

"We're heading to Middleton Field. It's a small municipal airport just outside Evergreen, Alabama. It only has two runways and is fairly isolated. It should be reasonably safe. Captain Bannon said it's used primarily by the navy for flight training."

"Sounds reasonable," the Doctor answered.

"My men will take turns keeping an eye out for any trouble during the night. We'll get started again at first light," Gunner said adding, "you can have the couch."

"How long before we are on the ground?" asked Dr. Sanderson.

"Captain says about twenty minutes."

The Doctor nodded as Stefan and Ludvig emerged from the galley carrying a couple of sandwiches and two Cokes. He thought briefly about eating and decided he simply did not have much of an appetite at the moment. He started gathering his folders from the table and putting them back in his knapsack.

He figured it was probably around 9:00 pm local time. That would mean that it had been over ten hours since they left Colorado and the comfort of Benton Worthington III's mountain resort. For the Doctor, it seemed more like ten years ago.

He had already strapped himself in for the landing when Gunner sat next to him and did the same. The touchdown was rougher than usual as Captain Bannon was a little long on his approach and had to use full reverse thrusters and slam on the brakes in order to stop before overshooting the runway. Landing in the dark with no running lights and only the luminosity of the moon and GPS calculations is challenging at best.

Once down, the Captain turned the plane around and assumed takeoff position so that he could depart at a moment's notice if necessary. Gunner and his men quickly unstrapped themselves and went to the windows to survey the surrounding area. It was too dark even with the full moon to accurately assess their situation.

Captain Bannon opened the cockpit door and said to everyone, "Sorry about that landing gentleman, I overshot it by a hair."

No one responded so the Doctor felt it necessary to reply, "No problem Captain, I have heard it mentioned by some of your brethren that any landing you can walk away from is a good one."

"How right you are Doctor."

Gunner spoke up, "My men and I are going outside to secure the perimeter."

He opened the hatch and headed down the stairs with his men following close behind. Gunner had the black duffel bag and his sidearm at the ready as he disappeared from sight.

The Captain moved toward the Doctor in the rear of the plane surveying the condition of the cabin like a flight attendant moving down the aisle prior to takeoff. Dr. Sanderson had unfastened his belt and was standing a few feet from the couch. Bannon sat down at the conference table and motioned for the Doctor to join him.

"Hell of a day wouldn't you say?" he asked as Dr. Sanderson sat down across from him.

The Doctor nodded in agreement and after a moment of silence asked, "How did you come to work for Benton?"

"Well," he began, "I spent eight years flying fighter jets for the navy; F-18 Super Hornets and then at the end, the new F-20's." He leaned back in his chair and continued, "I had enough of navy life so I left and took a job flying commercial jets for American. I don't know if you remember that accident five years ago just outside Oklahoma City. The airplane stalled at 24,000 feet and the pilot couldn't restart the engines. Complete mechanical failure. So he had to treat the plane as a glider and try to land with no engines. He managed to land in a large grassy field with no one getting hurt and minimal damage to the plane; a real miracle actually."

"I do remember that," Dr. Sanderson replied looking at Bannon with interest.

"I was that pilot," Bannon said. "It made the news and got the attention of one Benton Worthington III. He offered me a job at three times the salary I was making for the airline; so I accepted and here I am."

"Are you glad you took the job?" the Doctor asked.

"As with any job there are good days and bad days. There aren't the regulations and restrictions or bureaucratic bullshit you deal with as a commercial or navy pilot. I am, however, at the beck and call of an eccentric billionaire. I see myself as a well-paid indentured servant," Bannon said with a chuckle.

"What's Benton like?"

Captain Bannon leaned in closer to the Doctor and spoke softly, "He is a man who gets what he wants Doctor. I have flown him around the world a dozen times and have overheard conversations that would make your hair stand on end. Be very careful in you dealings with him. He will tell you what he wants you to know and no more." He leaned back and added, "And anything you say around him," nodding out the window toward Gunner, "you might as well be saying to Mr. Worthington himself."

"I appreciate the advice John," Dr. Sanderson said.

They both sat back in their chairs and looked out the Gulfstream's windows.

It was Captain Bannon who broke the silence this time, "So why are you here? As I said, Mr. Worthington tells you only what he wants you to know."

The Doctor thought for a moment and then said, "I'm the one who inadvertently started this nightmare."

Gunner and his men reported no infected activity in the area and deemed it safe to stay for the night. Captain Bannon returned to the cockpit where he would be able to get some sleep. The Doctor had grabbed a blanket out of the storage compartment and moved to the couch. Stefan and Ludvig leaned their chairs back while Mikael stood to take first watch. Gunner took the large chair that faced inward and reclined back.

Dr. Sanderson moved back and forth adjusting the blanket and the pillow in a vain attempt to get comfortable. His mind was racing with the events of the day; starting with Benton's arrival through the narrow escape out of the hanger in Miami. As sleep finally overtook him, the last image he had was the look on Captain Bannon's face when he told him that he was responsible for the current situation they found themselves in.

The Doctor awoke to the sound of shuffling feet in the cabin. He slowly opened his eyes and noticed the cabin was still dark. He sat up and started rubbing the sleep out of his eyes. The shuffling had stopped and he sensed someone standing over him. Actually, more like hovering. As his eyes adjusted to the darkness he also noticed an unpleasant smell; one not unlike the odor in the house in Arkansas. He looked up and saw an imposing figure moving toward him. It bent down revealing the face of Gunner Johansson. Except it was not the same face he had remembered. The eyes were sunken in, the face thinner, and the teeth discolored. The Doctor suddenly realized why as Gunner lunged at him. He was able to move just enough so that Gunner was unable to hit him head on. He rolled off the couch and onto the floor of the cabin. Gunner was quickly on top of him and had the Doctor pinned to the ground. His teeth exposed as his hot breath washed over the Doctor.

Tilting his head back and looking upside down at the rest of the plane he saw Gunner's men strewn about the cabin. They were hanging off of chairs and lying upside down on the floor. There was no sign of Captain Bannon. He turned his attention back to Gunner who was now leaning in ready to take a bite out of the Doctor's neck. Unable to hold him off any longer he let out a scream for help …

Bolting upright from his prone position on the couch the Doctor instinctively started moving backward pushing himself against the cabin wall. He was in a cold sweat, his clothes were soaked. It took a few seconds to realize that he had just awoken from a terrible nightmare. The cabin was bathed in early morning light. Standing in front of him was the hulking presence of Gunner Johansson looking nothing like the he had in his dream.

"You were having a bad dream Doctor," Gunner said.

"This whole endeavor is one bad dream," thought the Doctor as he just simply shook his head up and down.

"The lavatory is open, go ahead and wash up," Gunner said adding, "and by the way, we received another signal during the night."

Chapter 22
Dorothy and the Tin Man

The morning's first light was just peeking through the room's window as Lucy awoke, confused at first as to where she was. Having finally enjoyed a sound night sleep, it took her a minute to come to grips with where she was and why she was there. As she slowly woke up, she stretched and let out a yawn.

"Sleep well Lucy?" asked Kim from across the room.

Suddenly remembering she was not alone in the room, she replied, "Better than I have in a week, how about you and the kids?"

"I got a couple hours of sleep, but my kids slept like rocks," Kim said motioning to the still sleeping children.

"I guess we should start getting ready before Captain Morris shows up," said Lucy.

"Yeah, I think we should pack up some of these blankets and toiletries for the road; oh, and the water seems to be working even with the power off but you can only get the cold to work."

Looking around the room for the first time in full light Lucy located the bathroom just inside the door. There were two double beds, a small desk and dresser with a TV. Next to the dresser was a locked door that connected their room to an adjoining room.

"If you and the kids want to use this bathroom I'll see if I can go through the door to the adjoining room and use that bathroom," said Lucy.

"Sounds good, I'll get the kids up. I have a funny feeling we'll have to go wake the boys up," Kim said with a smile.

As Kim began to wake her kids up, Lucy moved to the door between the two rooms and unlocked it. Opening their door she found the door to the adjoining room half open. She cautiously looked around the door and into the next room. No one was immediately visible but it looked like someone had been staying there when this all started. The place was a mess and it smelled of spoiled food.

Holding her breath Lucy quickly walked to the window and opened the shades letting enough light into the room to see what she was doing. Then, walking to the bathroom, she opened the door and let out a blood curdling scream. There, on the floor of the bathroom, were two zombies staring back at her. The female zombie had several bite marks on her legs and arms and the male zombie had a large bite taken out of his shoulder. The floor around them was strewn with empty medicine bottles. Each of them let out a chocked moan as they slowly got to their feet. Lucy turned and went running from the room as fast as she could. Tripping over an open suitcase, she caught herself on the bed and launched herself at the door to the next room. She considered turning around and closing the door behind her but was gripped by fear and thought only of the safety of her room.

"Kim, help, there are infected here!" she screamed as she burst through the door into their room.

Lucy paused in bewilderment as she looked around and found it empty. Just then, Kim stuck her head out of the bathroom.

"Quick, get in here!" she yelled.

Lucy ran to the bathroom and dove inside as the two zombies stumbled through the adjacent room's door after her. As Lucy hit the floor hard Kim slammed the door shut and leaned against it. Danielle and Jason had both crawled under the sink; Jason still gripping his golf club. In unison both girls started pounding on the bathroom walls and screaming for help.

Stephen had been up for a couple hours unable to sleep any longer. All he could think about was his family and if they were safe or not. He had no way of contacting them, no way of knowing, and it was eating him up inside. As the sun was just coming through the window, Stephen got up and shook Dave and Nick awake. Dave turned out to already be awake, curled up in the fetal position just staring at the wall. Nick pulled the covers over his head and tried his best to ignore Stephen.

"Come on man, just five more minutes. You're as bad as the military guys," said Nick from under the covers.

"I want to be ready when they come for us."

"Yeah, yeah, yeah, I'll be up in a bit just give me a minute," groaned Nick.

Stephen busied himself gathering up some of the spare blankets and towels and making an improvised sack wrapping up the room's coffee and toiletries inside. As he was setting the sack by the door he thought he could hear banging coming from somewhere outside his door. Unlocking the door he opened it a crack and peered into the darkened hall. It came again from across the hall, this time accompanied by muffled screams. Realizing in horror it was coming from the girls' room Stephen turned back into his room and grabbed his axe.

"Dave, Nick, something's wrong in the girls room, go see if you can find the Major!" Stephen yelled.

As Stephen dashed out of the room and across the hall, Nick threw the covers off. Jumping out of bed he hurriedly put his pants on as he hopped towards the door.

"Come on Dave get up," he said to Dave who was still lying curled up on the bed.

Without waiting for him, Nick finally got his pants pulled all the way on and sprinted out of the door down the hall to the lobby. Stephen had reached the door to the girls' room and had his ear pinned against it listening. He could hear the girls pounding on the walls and screaming from where the bathroom should be. He could also make out sounds just on the other side of the door.

Fearing the worst, Stephen glanced at the door and then began to hack at it with his axe.

As he swung the axe he yelled, "Hold on girls, I'm coming!"

"Hurry," screamed Lucy, "there are infected in here trying to get through the bathroom door!"

As the door to Room 102 began to splinter Stephen could make out two zombies trying to claw their way through the bathroom door. Finally, when enough of the door had been hacked away, he gave it three swift kicks and knocked what was left of it off its frame and into the two zombies. The zombies, now covered in splinters of wood from the door, turned their attention to Stephen. Both began squeezing through the broken doorway towards him. Letting out a yell, he swung his axe connecting with the female zombie on the right, cutting deep into its shoulder. It staggered but kept coming at him as he pulled his axe free and began backpedaling away from the doorway. The second swing from his axe landed square at the base of the zombie's neck severing its head from its shoulders. The momentum of the swing knocked Stephen off balance and he crashed forward into the decapitated zombie.

Falling to the floor, with the now headless mass of undead flesh landing on top of him, Stephen had the wind knocked out of him. Looking up in horror he saw the male zombie reaching down for him. Kicking desperately with his legs, Stephen was unable to stay the murderous advance of the second zombie. Struggling with all his might there was nothing Stephen could do to protect himself. Then suddenly two deafening shots rang out in rapid succession in the hallway. The male zombie was flung back against the wall and slumped to the floor motionless, a dark substance from inside its skull splattered all over the hallway.

Looking up Stephen saw Chester standing calmly with a smoking shotgun as Nick ran to take the dead body off of him. As he got to his feet he suddenly remembered the girls.

"Quick, the girls and the kids," he said as he ran to their room.

Stepping through the broken down door he saw the bathroom door covered in claw marks from the zombies who had tried to gain entry.

"Open up, it's okay, it's me Stephen, they're gone now," he yelled as he pounded on the door.

Stephen took a step back as the door unlocked and slowly opened. There, behind the golf club wielding Jason, stood Lucy and Kim who was holding Danielle. Seeing it was Stephen, Jason lowered his golf club and Kim sank to the floor with Danielle. Lucy ran out of the bathroom, arms outstretched, and straight into the still stunned Stephen. It took him a minute but he finally hugged her back.

"Everyone alright?" asked Nick.

"Yeah we're fine," replied Kim, "just really freaked out is all."

"I hate to break this party up kids but we need to get out of here, those things are attracted to sound. Who knows how many are locked behind these doors, the soldiers only cleared the common areas and the rooms you were staying in," said Chester as he reloaded his shotgun.

"Yeah where did those things come from anyways Lucy," asked Nick.

"I … I … went through the adjoining door to the next room and they were … in the … bathroom," Lucy replied as she finally released Stephen.

Just then the Major and two soldiers arrived.

"What's going on here, is everyone alright," Major Bradley demanded.

His question still hung in the air when he noticed the headless zombies in the hallway and the black splatter on the wall. He was able to quickly piece together what happened.

"Everyone's ok, they just found a couple of those things in the room next door," said Nick.

"Good, now get to lobby … we move out shortly," ordered Major Bradley.

He directed the two soldiers to stand guard and then turned and headed back down the hall. Everyone quickly grabbed the few items they wanted to bring with them, while Nick finally got Dave out of bed. They all gathered in the lobby a few minutes later. Looking outside, they saw the soldiers transferring the supplies from the second truck to the Humvees and the truck they had been riding in.

"The truck is fixed folks and we are ready to go. Outside is crawling with infected but we don't think they've noticed us yet. We'll have to skip breakfast here and eat it on the road," said Captain Morris to the group.

"Now let's load up and get out of here before we have any other problems," he added.

The trucks all started up in unison as the civilians climbed into the back of the deuce and a half that now had decidedly less space than before due to the supplies it was carrying. Stephen helped Lucy aboard and was jumping in behind the others when shots rang out. Sgt. Sanchez jumped aboard and readied his weapon as the convoy began to pull away from the hotel. More shots were ringing out now and as everyone looked out of the back of the truck they saw zombies converging on the hotel parking lot as well the abandoned truck.

"Where is Chester?" asked Stephen looking around. "I need to thank him for saving my life. We didn't leave him did we?"

"No, I think he is riding in one of the Humvees," answered Sanchez, "there isn't much room left in here."

The convoy, now down to four Humvees, a fuel truck and the cargo truck quickly drove onto the highway as the soldiers took shots at the zombies who got too close. Once on the highway Major Bradley radioed a cease fire order and settled in for what he hoped would be a short and uneventful trip to Dayton.

"You saved a lot of lives back there Mr. Boone," Major Bradley said to Chester who now rode in the back seat alongside of Specialist Simmons.

"I hope you seriously consider sticking with us when we get to Dayton, but if not, then I am sure we can find a vehicle for you to use if you so wish," he continued.

"Mighty appreciated Major," replied Chester. "I'll let you know when I've made up my mind."

Almost two hours later the convoy approached Wright-Patterson Air Force Base in Dayton, Ohio. Major Bradley's heart sunk as they neared the main gate and he saw that this place would offer no signs of hope or life, but only the undead who now roamed the base.

Chapter 23
Practice Run

Dr. Sanderson's appetite had returned after he splashed some water on his face and changed his shirt. He made his way to the galley and microwaved a Jimmy Dean breakfast sandwich and poured himself a cup of orange juice. The cup, of course, had the WORTH insignia prominently displayed on the front. Feeling much better, he returned to the main cabin where Gunner was talking to his men.

Gunner noticed him entering the cabin and cut his conversation short; turning to the approaching doctor he said, "Feeling better?"

"Yes," he replied, "thank you."

"As I mentioned before, we received a signal during the night," Gunner said. "It passed fairly close to here but has moved north. It would be too dangerous to try to pursue on foot so we need to get closer. I was just heading to the cockpit to see the Captain."

"Mind if I tag along?" replied the Doctor.

Gunner said nothing and nodded his head in the direction of the cockpit. Assuming that meant to come along, the Doctor followed behind Gunner as they moved past his men and into the cockpit where Captain Bannon was checking his instruments in preparation for takeoff.

"I understand we have a new signal," Bannon said as they entered the cockpit.

"Yes," Gunner said handing Bannon a slip of paper, "here are the current coordinates."

Captain Bannon entered the information into the computer and studied the information displayed before him. Checking his map, he turned to the other two men in the cockpit.

"The signal looks to be about seven miles northeast from here right alongside I-65," he said pointing to the map in his hand. "Unfortunately, this is the closest airstrip to the signal."

"It would be difficult, not to mention very dangerous, to try on foot. Is there any way to get us closer Captain?" Gunner asked.

"If the signal keeps moving in its current direction it will end up near Montgomery. We could land there and you would be closer."

"I'm not sure about you guys but after what I saw in Miami, I think avoiding the major cities if at all possible would be preferable," the Doctor added.

Captain Bannon remained seated and was clearly in deep thought. Suddenly, he got up and moved to the other side of the cockpit where various flight manuals and plane schematics were housed. After a few seconds he found what he was looking for and sat back down.

He turned back toward the Doctor and Gunner and said, "Back in 1919 a young Army Captain was part of a military vehicles convoy that traveled from the White House to San Francisco. I believe they referred to it as the 'Transcontinental Motor Convoy'. It took them over two months to complete their journey. The young officer was so frustrated by the lack of a proper road system that he vowed someday to do something about it."

Gunner looked dubiously at the Captain and said, "Your point being, Captain?"

"Thirty some years later, as President of the United States, he championed the Federal Aid Highway Act of 1950 something that led to the interstate system that we all now enjoy. It even bears his name 'The Eisenhower Interstate System'."

"I've seen those signs before," the Doctor said.

"Of course Doctor," the Captain continued. "It's said that if you add up the entire cost of the endeavor since the beginning it would be the most expensive public works project since the Pyramids. But my point is that, although the project had many standards to make the roads easy to use such as using odd numbers for interstates traveling north and south and even numbers for roads traveling east and west, the one that we're interested in is that the system was designed so that planes could land on them during times of war or emergencies."

"Really?" said the Doctor.

"Actually, not really Doctor," the Captain responded.

Gunner and Dr. Sanderson exchanged confused looks.

"It's an old urban legend that the highways were designed so that at least one mile in every five were flat and straight so that a plane could land on it. Although Eisenhower, as a military man, saw the benefit of such a plan there was no practical way of accomplishing it. But that didn't stop some bored pilot with way too much time on his hands to research the entire interstate system and list any area in the country where you might actually be able to land a plane. He measured road width, looked for level ground, a straight road, and most importantly, no over passes. He then organized it into this book I now hold in my hand."

"So you are suggesting that we land on the highway?" Gunner asked.

Captain Bannon was busy flipping through the small paperback and either didn't hear or ignored the question. He was staring intently at the page he had stopped on, comparing what was on the paper to the map he had on his lap. After a minute or so he looked up and pointed to a spot on the map.

"Just above County Route 36, on I-65, there is a stretch of highway that would be adequate for us to land on. It's not wide enough for a commercial jet but should be fine for our purposes. That would put you less than a mile from your signal."

"Let's do it," Gunner said.

"Only one thing that could hold us up," Captain Bannon said.

"What's that?"

"The highways have been littered with abandoned cars everywhere we've gone. I'm going to need enough space to land and then take off again. As long as the road is clear, I should be able to get her down."

"We'll cross that bridge when we come to it," Gunner said, "prepare for takeoff Captain."

As they closed the cockpit door and headed back into the cabin, Dr. Sanderson was not sure but he thought that they just decided to land somewhere on I-65.

The Gulfstream was airborne fifteen minutes later. The trip was going to be a short one so the plane climbed to only 3500 feet before starting its descent as Captain Bannon approached I-65 from the southwest. His plan was to pass overhead first and ensure the road met the criteria for a successful landing and, just as importantly, survey the interstate for abandoned cars. If everything checked out, he would then circle back around and attempt his landing.

I-65 was a four lane north south highway separated by a grass median. As Bannon lowered the Gulfstream to about 1000 feet he saw a straight, flat road open up before him. *"Perfect,"* he thought. As he descended a little further he noticed the cars on the highway. There were not a lot of them but enough that would make landing impossible. Leveling off at 500 feet he observed that the cars were primarily on the northbound side of the highway; the southbound side was clear. Passing over the proposed landing site, he calculated the distance he would need to land and then takeoff. It appeared there would be just enough room.

Captain Bannon banked the plane and began to circle around for the landing. His first priority was to line up with the "runway". The two lanes plus the shoulder would provide just enough room to land but there would be little room for error. The

Gulfstream descended to 300 feet as the Captain used the slats to slow the plane down. He then used fully extended flaps to slow the plane down further in order to help land using the least amount of road possible. With fixed landing gear, all that was left was to raise the nose of the aircraft roughly five degrees and find the middle of the road.

Captain Bannon had landed many planes under many circumstances but had never landed on an interstate highway before. The rear wheels touched down first and skipped along for a few feet before grabbing hold of the road. Bannon lowered the nose quickly so that he could use the reverse thrusters and apply the brakes as soon as possible. The plane began to slow down as it traveled down I-65 coming to a stop about 2500 feet later.

"All things considered, not a bad effort," Bannon thought as he finished his landing procedures. He looked out through the cockpit windows at the road before him. He would need a minimum of 5000 feet to takeoff; 6000 feet was recommended. He grabbed a pair of binoculars from the storage bin in the cockpit and trained them on the interstate up ahead. There were two cars in the distance just as the road began to slope slightly downhill. Years of takeoffs and landings told Captain Bannon that it would be close. Very close.

Dr. Sanderson looked out one of the oval windows on the plane and half expected to see a car pass by. John had done it by God; landed on the interstate without killing them all. He started gathering his belongings when Gunner approached him.

"Captain Bannon has put us very close to our signal, no more than a half a mile," Gunner said.

As if on cue, Bannon emerged from the cockpit all smiles. "Not a bad bit of flyin' if I do say so myself, I'll have to check that one off my bucket list."

Gunner almost managed a smile before turning his attention to his men. They were preparing to open the hatch and head down the steps.

"Well done Captain," Dr. Sanderson said.

Gunner and his crew had already descended the stairs as the Doctor waited at the top anticipating the all clear signal. Bannon came up from behind him and firmly grabbed his arm and spun him around so that they were face to face. The Captain's demeanor had changed. He was suddenly very serious and staring directly at the Doctor.

"You can fix this can't you Doctor?" he said.

Dr. Sanderson looked into the man's eyes and saw fear in them for the first time. He desperately wanted to tell him yes ... absolutely ... no problem ... but he could not lie.

"I will do my very best John," was the only thing he could muster. He knew it did not sound reassuring but it was all he had.

Bannon nodded, slowly at first, then quicker as he reached out and slapped the Doctor on the shoulder and turned back around and headed into the cabin.

"Doctor!" Gunner yelled from below.

Dr. Sanderson whipped his head around to see Gunner at the base of the stairs with the black bag slung around his shoulder and replacing the clip in his sidearm.

"Time to go," he said.

The Doctor, moving swiftly down the stairs, joined Gunner, Mikael, Stefan, and Ludvig in the passing lane on the southbound side of I-65. He instinctively looked around scanning the area for infected.

Gunner took notice and said, "We're clear for the moment Doctor."

Dr. Sanderson shifted the knapsack on his shoulder and looked at Gunner and his men. They had already gathered their weapons and covered themselves in protective gear. A group of mercenaries following orders on a mission they did not fully comprehend; accompanied by a middle aged research scientist trying desperately to save the world from a plague he created.

"*Quite a group,*" thought the Doctor.

He motioned to Gunner and said, "Lead the way."

They moved across the grass median as Gunner used the portable GPS tracker to get a fix on their target. The Doctor occupied his usual position in the middle with Gunner out front, Stefan to his left, Mikael to his right, and Ludvig bringing up the rear.

Crossing the northbound lane they entered a dense but narrow group of trees. The ground was uneven and difficult to traverse. Sudden darkness enveloped them as if an eclipse had occurred. Twenty yards later they emerged from the trees into a vast field of tall grass and with a clear view. It was at least a quarter mile across and a half a mile in length. A dirt road from the north cut the field in half.

Gunner checked his tracker and said, "The signal is straight ahead, about a quarter mile."

Dr. Sanderson looked in the direction Gunner indicated, but saw nothing unusual. At the far end was another row of trees similar to the ones they had just come out of. The Doctor stared at the tree line for several seconds before noticing movement in the underbrush. Someone was materializing out of the woods. Upon closer inspection it was definitely a man. By the way he was moving Dr. Sanderson immediately assumed it was an infected person. He appeared to be alone and was too far away to notice the Doctor and his group yet.

As they crossed the dirt road closing the distance between them and the infected, Gunner instructed his men to fan out and attempt to surround the creature. Meanwhile, the Doctor was struggling to identify him. He was still too far away.

Gunner carefully opened the black bag and removed the collapsible pole with the loop on the end. His men had closed within 500 feet and had formed a semi-circle and stopped. They were waiting for the infected to come to them.

Dr. Sanderson, walking alongside Gunner now, was still too far away from the test subject to positively identify him. There were three males in the group that were approximately the same age. They had encountered one at the stadium. The other two remained at large. He did appear to be wearing the appropriate hospital scrubs and was definitely the source of the signal.

The Doctor looked around and saw they were alone in this field. His mind raced as an idea had begun hatching in his head.

"Gunner," he said in a hushed voice.

Gunner turned and replied, "Yes, Doctor."

"Have you tried your restraining devices yet?"

"What do you mean?" Gunner answered along with a 'now is not the time for this conversation' glare.

"What I mean is there's no one else around, infected or otherwise. It might be a good time to use the restraints on this test subject. If it's Number 5, we're done. If not, we can ... put it out of its misery and move on but at least we might be better prepared the next time."

The Doctor waited patiently for a response; like a child waiting to get the okay to stay up a half an hour past their bedtime.

The test subject was now less than a football field away.

"We have the advantage. It shouldn't be difficult," Gunner finally responded.

Gunner moved toward his men, called them over, and explained the plan. Dr. Sanderson noticed this was the second time they looked at him like he was crazy but the Doctor had no doubt they would follow orders. Gunner removed the hand cuff like arm restraints and gave them to Stefan. He gave the leg irons to Ludvig and finally the muzzle to Mikael. Gunner kept the pole.

They fanned out as before but this time with Gunner in the center position. The Doctor remained a few yards back continually on the lookout for any trouble. He did not need to identify the subject until it had been subdued.

Gunner had dropped the black bag as the test subject was less than 100 feet away. Jerking its head in their direction, it had begun to take an interest in Gunner and his crew.

The test subject's arms rose up and extended toward Gunner. He had allowed himself to act as bait in order to apply the noose first before the rest of the restraints were used. It was moving closer now as its prey was within reach. Gunner had extended the pole to its full length, approximately six feet.

Gunner raised the pole up as the test subject came within range. He brought it down hard on top of the subject's head but the rope had bent slightly and slid off the side and onto its shoulders. Gunner gave the loop more slack as he backed away from the approaching zombie. Stefan, Ludvig, and Mikael had closed in from behind and waited for Gunner to apply the lasso.

His second attempt was successful as he pulled the rope down around the creature's head and pulled tightly around its neck. The pressure Gunner applied would have choked an ordinary man to death but since this thing before him was already dead, it tried to continue forward.

Gunner had plenty of strength to keep the test subject at bay as Stefan came up from behind and with the all the swiftness of a seasoned police officer grabbed both arms and pulled them behind the subject. He quickly applied the hand cuffs and pulled them tight. The zombie thrashed back and forth as Stefan began pulling it down from behind. Gunner pushed the pole forward at the same time. The combination was too much as the test subject, uncoordinated to begin with, lost its footing and was soon on its back.

Ludvig came in and grabbed the legs to steady them. He kneeled down on the creature's shins as he opened the circular clamps of the leg irons. He attached the left leg, then the right and quickly stood back up. As he backed away, Mikael come from behind and lifted the test subject's head. The zombie suddenly snapped its head around and tried to take a bite out of Mikael's hand. He moved his hand away just in time. He pushed its head forward and tried again. This time he was able to carefully affix the Hannibal Lecter like muzzle.

Dr. Sanderson approached the captive test subject who was lying in a beautiful wide open field of grass. He bent over slightly to get a good look. Even with the muzzle covering part of its face it only took a few seconds to determine that this was not Number 5 but test subject number eight, Jacob Hester.

He allowed himself a moment to think about how he once had tried to help this man, maybe even save him; and how this whole thing went so terribly wrong. It was at that instant that he vowed to finish the job. In order to find an antidote, he had to stop thinking of these … things as once being human. All that mattered was finding Number 5 and finding a cure.

He turned to Gunner and said, "Not him I'm afraid."

Dr. Sanderson turned around before the bullet from Gunner's pistol exploded in his former patient's skull. They waited a minute to make sure the thing had stopped moving for good before they removed the manacles.

As Gunner's men were collecting the restraints, his walkie went off. It was Captain Bannon's voice, "Gunner, come in Gunner."

He grabbed the walkie, pressed the button, and said, "Gunner here, over."

"I recommend you get back here as soon as possible, we got infected coming up I-65 from the south; lots of them, over."

Gunner turned to his men who had just finished collecting their restraints and were heading to the black bag to put everything back.

"Skynda dig, tillbaka till flygplanet nu!" he shouted.

They threw the stuff in the bag and grabbed it without zipping it up. Gunner and the Doctor had already started for the trees at a full run. As they approached the tree line they slowed down. No telling what was in the woods. They moved slowly through the trees in a tight formation looking in all directions.

A minute later they were safely out of the woods and found themselves about 50 feet north of where they originally entered. Looking left they saw the Gulfstream. It was blocking the southern view of I-65 so they could not see what was behind it. They turned and ran toward the plane.

It was not but a few seconds later when the horde of zombies coming up the road came into view. There were probably a couple hundred of them and they were headed toward the plane. Luckily, they were still several thousand feet away.

Gunner reached for his walkie and pushed the button and said, "Captain, please open the hatch."

"Copy."

A few seconds later the hatch was opening as they came around the front of the plane. There was no time to stash the equipment or firearms in the cargo hold so everyone ran for the stairs. Once aboard Gunner closed the hatch as Captain Bannon hurried into the cockpit and closed the door behind him.

Gunner's men had to remove and stow their armor so they would be able to fit in their seats. Everyone knew the drill by now and had begun buckling their seatbelts.

Captain Bannon had secretly wished that they had time to back the plane up so he had more room for takeoff. But, with the approaching army of infected coming from behind, that was now impossible.

The plane was already set for takeoff. He strapped himself in and began to accelerate forward. He would have to increase speed above the normal 85 knots in order to shorten the distance needed to achieve takeoff.

If he knew the exact distance he had to work with he could accurately determine how much flap to use. Unfortunately, increased flaps increases drag; he would have to make his best guess.

The plane moved past fifty knots as the cars Bannon spotted earlier were quickly approaching and were now visible with the naked eye. He was perfectly centered on the highway and was hoping for a big gust of wind to pick the plane up.

Unfortunately the opposite happened. Calm overtook the area and the added lift Bannon needed was not going to be there. As the Gulfstream passed eighty knots he was able to raise the nose about five or six degrees. The cars were less than 1000 feet away.

He decided to increase the flaps another four percent as the plane accelerated past ninety knots. He felt the plane jerk itself up as the rear wheels scraped along the ground trying to release themselves from the pavement. The cars were 300 feet away. He was not sure if they were going to make it.

Then, out of nowhere, the wind that Captain Bannon desperately needed arrived. The plane left the ground and was now airborne. The last hurdle was to clear those cars.

As the G670 passed over the abandoned cars the right rear wheel rolled on top of the roof of a Subaru Outback. The plane briefly shuttered as the wheel moved along the top of the car and made terrible screeching noises as the weight of the plane caused metal to bend and twist and glass to shatter. The contact, however, acted almost like a springboard as the Gulfstream continued to climb higher and higher.

Once the Captain had cleared the cars he banked to the left to survey the situation on the ground. He passed back over I-65 and was able to get a bird's eye view of the zombies they had left behind. Looking down he could not believe what he was seeing. It was truly disturbing. What he originally thought was a group of several hundred or so infected had increased to over a thousand lost soles on some unholy pilgrimage.

Chapter 24
Last Hope

The once fortified gate house at Wright-Patterson Air Force Base was now little more than a choke point. The cars lined up leading to the gate told the tale of the many panicked civilians seeking the safety of the base. The number of zombies seen through the gate lumbering around spoke to the numerous civilians and soldiers that never stood a chance. It was a disheartening scene as Major Bradley surveyed it from the gunner's cupola. As the convoy came to a halt he climbed down and jumped out.

"Keep the engine running," he yelled back into the Humvee.

As he jogged towards the rear of the convoy he noticed that Chester had also exited the vehicle. Thinking about turning and saying something Major Bradley decided against it and continued on. Spotting the Major coming, Captain Morris dismounted from his Humvee and came to meet him.

"Let me guess," said Captain Morris, "the base is deserted."

"Worse," replied Major Bradley, "it looks like it's overrun with infected. It appears things did not go well during the evacuations here."

"So what do we do now?" asked Captain Morris.

"Well, we can't stay here. I don't think any of those things have noticed us yet but we need to decide quickly," said Major Bradley as he pulled his map from his jacket.

He continued, "I think it's safe to assume we should continue heading in a westerly direction."

"What about Fort Campbell, Major?"

"What about it Captain?"

"If I remember correctly when this all started in Florida the boys in the 101st captured a number of the infected and shipped them to Fort Campbell where some scientists where supposed to study them and figure out how to stop this."

"Yeah, I remember hearing about that, I think they got four or five of them. The last thing I heard they were performing tests and then all hell broke loose in D.C and we lost contact with the colonel so who knows what's happened since then."

"It's worth a shot sir, if they found a way to cure these people then that's where we need to go. Plus, there is no way the 101st would let their base get overrun. They've got to still be evacuating civilians from there."

"I would normally agree Captain but with a third of the 101st's strength deployed overseas and a majority of what was left spread out across the country to deal with the outbreak; who knows how strong their garrison is there."

Glancing at his map again Major Bradley continued, "But it does make sense to check it out, especially if they've found a cure, but I won't hold out much hope."

"Major, you might want to get this convoy movin' again," said Chester as appeared around the corner of the Humvee.

The Major and Captain jumped at the unexpected arrival but quickly collected themselves and looked where Chester was pointing. In the distance, at the gate of the air force base, a large group of zombies were clumsily making their way through the abandoned cars and heading towards the convoy.

"Good call Mr. Boone but you need to stop sneaking up on us like that," said Major Bradley.

"Not my fault none of ya'll can keep a good watch 'round here," replied Chester as he walked away and jumped up in the back of the truck carrying the other civilians.

"Alright, mount up Captain and we'll get moving."

"Yes sir," said Captain Morris as he saluted the Major.

Major Bradley quickly made his way back to his Humvee and directed Private Sinclair to get the convoy moving away from the growing horde of zombies that were heading their way.

Chester climbed into the cargo truck to the surprised looks of everyone inside, including Sgt. Sanchez. For a minute no one said anything until the truck started to rumble forward with the rest of the convoy.

Finally breaking the silence Stephen said, "I thought you got left back at the hotel Chester. We never got a chance to thank you for saving our lives."

Turning his attention from looking out of the back, Chester surveyed the people in the back of the truck, his eyes catching those of little Danielle staring back at him.

Shaking his head he turned back to look out of the truck and said, "No thanks required, I was just doin' what needed doin'. But ya'll should try and be more careful."

"Well, we all really do appreciate it and I think I can speak for everyone when I say we are glad you are still with us," said Kim.

"Not to switch the subject but why are we driving away from the air base," asked Stephen.

"Probably has something to do with the welcoming committee," replied Nick as he pointed to the large group of zombies stumbling around the entrance to the base.

"The base is overrun, we won't find help there," said Chester, all the while staring out of the back of the truck.

"So where are we going then?" asked Lucy.

"Don't know. We'll find out when we get there," replied Chester.

Obviously not wanting to talk anymore, Chester concentrated on some point in the distance while the others sank into an uneasy silence as the convoy continued down the road.

The convoy quickly left the airfield, skirted Dayton and began to head southwest with Fort Campbell as their destination. Major Bradley had learned in the early days of the outbreak how fast the infected multiplied inside cities with their dense populations. With this knowledge he planned to travel around the cities as much as possible in order to keep the convoy away from what he considered high risk areas.

However, he also worried that the suburbs surrounding the cities would not be any better. He hoped as long as he stayed on the highways they would be relatively clear of zombies. He also knew they would need to find some food supplies as his men's MREs were running low and the civilians had been consisting on vending machine and gas station food. Major Bradley was not holding out much hope of finding help in Fort Campbell and was already planning for the likelihood of a trip further west.

It was slow going, but the convoy passed through Cincinnati without incident. However, they did see plenty of infected people off the highway as well as a number of them roaming aimlessly among the many abandoned cars. The signs of rioting and looting were evident in the pillars of dark smoke that rose above the city, which was deserted by all but the undead and those opportunistic fools who dared to enter. They observed no survivors although the Major was prepared to pick any up they encountered.

As they left Cincinnati behind, the scenery was replaced by the bluegrass of Kentucky. The serene nature of the countryside was almost surreal to the members of the convoy compared to the horrors they had witness during the previous few days. Lulled by the peacefulness around them they were all jarred back to reality as the convoy come to an abrupt halt about twenty miles outside of Louisville. In front of them both sides of the I-71 bridges which cross the Kentucky River had been, for all intents and purposes, destroyed.

Major Bradley stepped out of the Humvee and walked as far out on the bridge as he could to survey the damage. Looking over the bridges he knew that there was no way either of them could support the convoy. It looked to the Major as if someone had tried to blow them up. It was obvious that it had been done by amateurs as the explosion had failed to completely destroy the bridge. However, it had done enough damage to render them impassable.

As he stared at the world around him, with the sound of the river running below, he was overcome with a sense of hopelessness. It seemed to him that no matter which way they went they were met with disappointment and less of a reason to hope for safety and answers. The bridge was a minor impediment as the Major was sure they could circumvent it. However, it was just another item to add to the growing list of frustrations. Here alone, out on the bridge, he could let his guard down and feel these emotions. Something he would dare not do in front of his men and especially not the civilians. Gathering himself, Major Bradley turned and headed back to the convoy.

After consulting his map Major Bradley found that the quickest route to crossing the river would take them northwest through the town of Carrollton, Kentucky, a small town located at the joining of the Kentucky and mighty Ohio Rivers. They would be able to cross a small bridge just outside of town and then follow several country roads back to I-71. The convoy was quickly turned around and five minutes later found themselves entering the outskirts of Carrollton. Besides appearing deserted, it was a town seemingly untouched by the unfolding horrors around it.

As the convoy rolled through the surprisingly empty streets of Carrollton, Major Bradley began to get an uneasy feeling. The main street was completely empty, no cars, no sign of the living or the undead. However, a number of the side streets were clogged with parked cars looking as if they have been driven in haphazardly and then abandoned.

Getting on the radio Major Bradley said, "Keep your eyes open boys something is not right in this town."

Then turning to his driver he said, "Keep the convoy moving and let's get out of here as soon as possible."

"Yes sir," replied Private Sinclair.

The radio crackled to life with Captain Morris in the rear of the convoy exclaiming, "Major looks like we've got company. Two pickups with several armed civilians aboard."

As the Major was listening to Captain Morris he looked up and saw in the distance, at that the base of the ramp leading up to the bridge, two more pickup trucks roared in from the side streets and blocked their way. Several men jumped from the back of the trucks and began to brandish weapons.

Picking the radio up again Major Bradley said, "Men, looks like we have some armed civilians and I've got a bad feeling. Keep your weapons ready but do not fire unless I give the order. And Sanchez, get those civilians down in the bed of the truck."

The convoy slowed as they neared the two pickup trucks. Major Bradley climbed up in the gunner's cupola behind the 50 caliber machine gun. To the rear of the convoy he saw the two trucks Captain Morris had reported cutting off the road behind them. Looking around he saw the side streets were still clogged with abandoned cars. There was nowhere to turn. Finally, the Humvee rolled to a stop and a man in worn ball cap stepped forward.

"Afternoon gentlemen, welcome to Carrollton. The name's Jeb Stalworth and I am the, how would ya say, newly elected Mayor of this here town," he said to the snickers of the men behind him.

"Afternoon. My name is Major Charles Bradley of the United States Army."

"Where are ya'll headed," asked Jeb.

"We are heading to an evacuation zone. The highway bridge is out so we had to detour through your town," Major Bradley said with conviction, hiding the uneasiness he felt.

"Ain't that a shame," replied Jeb smugly.

"You gentlemen are welcome to join the convoy if you are looking to head to safety."

"Look 'round you, this is as safe as it gets. Not a 'biter' in sight. I think we'll be just fine here."

"Well, if you don't want to join us that's your decision."

"Oh, I think we can manage," Jeb said with another smile creeping onto his face. "I think we'll manage just fine."

"Have if your way Mr. Stalworth. Now if you would kindly move your trucks, we'll be on our way."

"Well, ya see it's not quite that simple, Major. If you want to come through this here town and use our bridge over yonder then you'll have to pay the toll," Jeb said motioning over his shoulder to the bridge behind him.

"You're kidding me right," asked an incredulous Major Bradley.

"Afraid not, them is the new rules here in Carrollton."

"With all due respect, Mr. Stalworth, given the recent events and the fact that martial law has been declared, you have no right to be charging a convoy of the United States Army a toll," Major Bradley replied coolly.

"As I am sure you're aware Major, there ain't no functionin' government no more; at least not 'round here. So we do as we see fit to protect our own."

"We aren't looking for any trouble, we are just trying to get somewhere safe," said the Major.

"We wouldn't want to stand in the way of that now would we," responded Jeb, "but you've got to pay the toll to use our bridge, simple as that."

"Exactly what kind of toll are we talking about here?"

"Now we're getting somewhere. It looks like you got a fuel truck back there which I am guessin' is full," said Jeb as he looked over the convoy. "And some of them there weapons you got would be nice too."

"And what happens if we don't pay the toll?"

"I don't think none of us wants to find that out now do we?"

"I think we both know that's not going to happen. If you need some medical supplies or perhaps some food, I might be able to help you there but I'm afraid we cannot part with any of our weapons or our fuel truck. It does, however, appear that you have managed quite well on your own."

"I guess it's one of the perks of being Mayor," Jeb said with a laugh.

"It appears then, we are at an impasse," responded Major Bradley sternly.

"It appears so. I'd rather not have to take them there supplies the hard way. So if you could be as kind as to hand them over and the truck as well, we'll let you be on your way nice and peaceful like."

"You are trying my patience Mr. Stalworth. Please do not force me to do anything we will both regret."

"Whoa, easy there Major. There won't be anythin' to regret if you just step down from that vehicle," Jeb said lowering his rifle at the Major.

Behind Jeb the other armed men around the trucks shifted nervously readying their weapons. Major Bradley turned to look behind the convoy and the armed men blocking their escape were doing the same. In the rear Humvee he could see Captain Morris manning the machine gun anxiously awaiting his orders. Just as Major Bradley was about to respond to Jeb the radio in his ear came to life with the voice of Sergeant Sanchez.

"Um, Major, sir. That Chester guy, well he … uhh … he just jumped out of the back of our truck without saying a word. I think he's going to do something stupid."

"Understood Sergeant; Captain Morris prepare to follow my lead," Major Bradley responded back into the open channel.

By now Major Bradley knew enough about Chester to know he was not one for sitting on his hands. He also knew that Chester was up to something and that he should be prepared for anything. Major Bradley did not like it but realized it was probably his best chance out of this mess.

"Who are you talkin' to up there," yelled Jeb.

"Take it easy, I am just telling my men to hold their fire. I wouldn't want any of you civilians to get hurt." This time it was the Major's turn to smile.

"I've had about enough of this now," said Jeb taking a step forward with his gun aimed at the Major.

"Take one more step forward and I'll be forced to shoot you sir," said Major Bradley as he tighten his grip on the handles of the machine gun.

"I seriously doubt you woul …"

A gun shot rang out as Jeb stepped forward, his right leg shattering just below the knee. Jeb crumpled to the ground with a shriek and reached for what was left of his bloodied leg. A stunned silence followed as no one on either side knew where the shot came from. Then, just as quickly as the first a second shot rang out, unmistakably from under Major Bradley's Humvee, and found its target in the chest of one of the men by the pickup trucks.

Chester had quietly crawled unnoticed under the trucks and taken up position right below Major Bradley's Humvee. The civilians at the trucks finally began to react and lift their guns to return fire. However, it was too late as Major Bradley opened fire with his fifty caliber machine gun. Following his lead at the rear of the convoy, Captain Morris unloaded on the men and trucks boxing the convoy in. As Captain Morris and Major Bradley rained deadly fire on the men and their trucks, the other soldiers dismounted from the convoy and added their fire power. Bullets ripped through flesh and metal as Jeb's men went diving for cover, many of them taking their last breath. The gas tank of one of the trucks exploded engulfing the others in front of the convoy in flames and smoke. Jeb's men, who were not killed by the explosion or gunfire, cowered behind the cover of the trucks. As Major Bradley let off the trigger Chester rolled out from under his Humvee and jumped up on the running board.

"I think we better move before more of 'em show up Major," Chester yelled over the roar of gunfire still going on around them.

"My thoughts exactly," replied Major Bradley.

Speaking into his comm link Major Bradley ordered the soldiers to mount up and make ready to move. Once the men were back in their vehicles Major Bradley leaned down into the Humvee and ordered Private Sinclair to get the convoy moving.

The few remaining men scattered from the demolished trucks as Private Sinclair slowly maneuvered the Humvee through the narrow gap created by the explosion. Moving between two of the trucks, he pushed them apart with his front bumper to make room for the rest of the convoy. As the sound of metal on metal scrapping filled the air, Major Bradley swiveled in the gunner's cupola and watched what was left of Jeb's men running away. He held his fire thinking to himself that the lesson had been learned and too much blood had already been spilled.

Major Bradley looked down at Chester, standing on the running board, and gave him a knowing nod which Chester returned before turning his gaze to the Ohio River to their right. Doing a quick check over the radio Major Bradley conducted a head count and was relieved to hear that there were no injuries just some frightened civilians.

As the convoy eased over the bridge, Major Bradley shook his head as he watched the burning trucks in Carrolton disappear from view as only the columns of black smoke remained visible. He knew he should not be surprised that the baser instincts of human kind came to the surface in a crisis. It saddened him to think that there were people out there that were taking advantage of this mess for their own personal gain.

Chapter 25
They're Everywhere

Dr. Sanderson had seen the collection of infected moving north on I-65 through the window as the Gulfstream dipped its wing, banking slightly, and headed north. It was, by far, the largest gathering of undead he had seen in any one place at one time. He leaned against the back of the couch, as Captain Bannon piloted the plane upward, trying to get the image out of his head. Regrettably, it was there to stay.

Captain Bannon continued on the same course they were on prior to receiving the latest signal. He briefly thought about turning the plane around and flying south, maybe to the Caribbean. The islands were isolated from the rest of humanity and probably still uninfected. He could fly in, lie on the beach drinking a pina colada and let someone else deal with this problem. Unfortunately, the sense of duty that was drilled into him during his time in the navy was preventing him from doing so.

When they had reached cruising altitude Captain Bannon engaged the auto pilot and headed out into the cabin. The sight of the pilot coming out of the cockpit surprised the Doctor.

"*Must be okay to get up,*" he thought.

Bannon moved past Gunner's men and walked up to the Doctor and said, "Did we find what we're looking for?"

"We located the source of the signal," answered the Doctor as he unbuckled his seatbelt, "but, unfortunately, it wasn't who we were looking for."

"What, or should I say who, is it exactly that we are looking for Doctor?"

"One of my former patients," he said, now standing.

"He's one of those things now?"

"Yes he is," the Doctor answered. "As a matter of fact, he was the first one of these things."

Captain Bannon said nothing and just stared into space. He seemed to be looking past the Doctor instead of at him.

Gunner broke the awkward silence by announcing he was going to update Mr. Worthington on their progress.

"Could you ask him if he has located my wife and daughter yet?" requested the Doctor.

Gunner nodded as he went into the galley where the satellite phone was kept. Dr. Sanderson was going to attempt to eavesdrop, hoping he would not converse in Swedish again. Unfortunately, the Captain was still standing in front of him and looked like he might have more to say.

When it became apparent he did not, the Doctor asked if he was alright.

"Yea, I'm okay," he answered. "I continued on our northern heading, I assume that is acceptable?"

"Yes, that would be fine," the Doctor said adding, "we are just waiting for another signal."

Bannon nodded and began to turn around and head back into the cockpit when he abruptly stopped and asked, "How many more signals are out there?"

"Um … Six more," the Doctor answered.

Nodding again, this time he did turn and head back toward the cockpit as Gunner returned from the galley. He did not look particularly happy.

"Has he located my family?" asked the Doctor expectantly.

Gunner ignored him and headed toward his men who were still sitting in their seats. After a brief conversation, he returned to where the Doctor was standing.

With the Doctor's question still hanging in the air, Gunner walked past him and said, "Not yet."

About forty-five minutes later Dr. Sanderson was jolted out of a daydream about a beautiful summer's day twelve years ago with his wife and two children vacationing in Napa Valley, California, by the alarm from Gunner's PDA. Another signal had been discovered.

Gunner was sitting at the conference table sharpening the throwing knife he had stashed in his trouser leg. The PDA was on the table and began to wobble slightly as the message arrived from the GPS receiver. He returned the knife to its sheath and picking up the PDA, headed into the galley to consult the receiver. After returning, he placed the receiver on the conference table and made his way to the cockpit.

He returned a few minutes later and sat next to the Doctor.

"We have another signal," he said, "it is a few miles south of Knoxville. We're heading to the McGhee Tyson Airport. It will keep us further south of the city than the downtown airport. We should be able to stay clear of trouble that way."

As the Doctor was about to respond he heard the familiar sound of Gunner's PDA going off again. It was still in his hand as he glanced down at it.

"A second signal," Gunner said.

Turning around he picked up the GPS tracker from the table and jotted down the coordinates.

"I don't think it's near the other one," Gunner said.

He returned to the cockpit to determine the location of the new signal. A few minutes later Captain Bannon's voice came over the intercom asking for the Doctor to come to the cockpit.

When he arrived, Gunner spoke first.

"The second signal is coming from the Tennessee-Kentucky border" he said. "It's about the same distance away as the other signal from our present position."

"Is there any way to determine which signal is the one we're looking for?" Captain Bannon interrupted.

"I'm afraid not," the Doctor answered. "All the codes are the same."

"Do you have a suggestion as to which signal to follow first?" Gunner asked.

The Doctor thought for a minute and decided he had absolutely no reason to follow one signal over the other. He also had detected an edge to both Gunner and Captain Bannon as of late. They were likely discouraged at the lack of progress and in some way blamed him for it. The several close brushes with death probably had not helped their mood any either. He needed to answer with authority. Get everyone back on the same page. With his best doctor's voice he responded.

"Follow the first signal, head toward Knoxville," he stated without waiting for a response and turned around heading back into the cabin.

Captain Bannon completed a slight adjustment to their heading and made the notation in the log. He was not even sure why he was even keeping a flight log. There probably was not a functioning FAA anymore. Mr. Worthington could care less and would never ask to see one. It was, he figured, simply out of habit.

As he started his descent, the contact alarm from his onboard radar went off. He looked down at the circular screen to ensure the system was not malfunctioning; it was not. At first he felt a combination of surprise and excitement. They had not come into contact with any other aircraft since leaving Colorado (if they did not include Gunner's borrowed Army National Guard helicopter). Another airplane meant a sign of normalcy to Captain Bannon. Perhaps there are people out there, living somewhat regular lives.

The plane's computer identified the aircraft as US Airways Flight 1665. It was an Airbus 319 at 18,000 feet heading toward Knoxville from the opposite direction as the Gulfstream. The Captain did not have a visual confirmation yet but would have it soon.

As he descended past 20,000 feet, Captain Bannon grabbed the binoculars and looked out the cockpit windows scanning the sky for the mysterious airplane. After a few minutes he spotted it just off the starboard side of the aircraft. It was now at 15,000 feet and dropping rapidly. It appeared to be in duress.

Captain Bannon decided he was going to attempt to hail the troubled aircraft. He worked the communication controls and began to speak clearly.

"US Airways Flight 1665, come in," he said.

He waited a few seconds and tried again. A third and fourth try ended with silence. He tried once more this time adding, "Please respond," at the end.

Captain Bannon was about to try again when his headset crackled with static and garbled sound that could have been voices. He waited a second but nothing else came through.

"US Airways Flight 1665, please repeat."

This time a blast of sound came through the headset that nearly caused Captain Bannon to jump out of his seat. The voice was clear and sharp this time.

"Please help us … they're everywhere!" came the chilling cry for assistance.

Captain Bannon was about to respond but the mic on their end was still on. As the plane came into view with the naked eye he could see the aircraft was now in a complete nosedive. He focused his attention back on to the headset just in time to hear what was most assuredly a gunshot and then the line go dead.

The doomed US Airways flight continued its spiral downward as the Gulfstream dipped below 12,000 feet. Captain Bannon made one last attempt to contact the aircraft but to no avail. He briefly hoped that somehow the pilot could pull the aircraft out of its nosedive. Unfortunately, it appeared to be hopeless; not like he would have been able to do anything anyway. The G670 emerged from some clouds to a clear view of the surrounding area. The excellent visibility allowed the Captain to follow Flight 1665 all the way down to its inevitable demise.

The plane struck the ground and erupted into a giant fireball. The Captain could almost feel the explosion at 10,000 feet. He, of course, felt a kinship with the pilot and crew. There is a tight bond among those who make their living flying the friendly skies.

To make matters worse, it looked as though the Airbus landed in a small residential neighborhood. Anyone who had managed to stay alive in that area was probably no longer so lucky.

He did not have time to lament over the poor folks in that plane and on the ground; he had his own plane to land. Turning his attention to his instruments he saw that he was still on course to land at McGhee Tyson Airport. As he started his landing checklist there was a knock on the cockpit door. He did not like being disturbed during takeoffs and landings. He had half a mind not to open the door but decided it would be easier just to see what whoever it was wanted.

He got up and opened the door to a slightly annoyed looking Gunner. He had the portable GPS receiver in his hand.

"What can I do for you Gunner, I'm getting ready to land," the Captain said.

"I'm afraid that won't be necessary," Gunner countered.

"What?"

"We lost the signal. Most likely due to that explosion on the ground," Gunner explained.

"Do we know if it was the one we're looking for?" Bannon asked.

Dr. Sanderson stuck his head in the doorway and said, "Did you see that explosion?"

Gunner and the Captain exchanged glances but said nothing.

Gunner finally said, "The Captain wants to know if the signal we lost was the one we're looking for?"

"Like I said before, they all have the same signal, we'll only know for sure with visual confirmation," the Doctor replied.

"Mark the last known location of that signal and if we exhaust all other possibilities, we'll come back and sift through the wreckage," suggested Captain Bannon.

Gunner nodded. Dr. Sanderson looked uneasy about the prospect of pouring through crash site debris looking for all or part of his test subject.

"I suppose we should set a course to the second signal. I'll need those coordinates again Gunner," the Captain said.

Gunner nodded again and left the cockpit with the Doctor right behind him closing the cockpit door as he left.

Captain Bannon leveled the Gulfstream at 7,000 feet and started to turn the plane around and head west. As the plane finished banking and straightened itself out, the Captain could see tendrils of smoke from the crash site rising past his cockpit windows.

Chapter 26
The Calm

The back of the truck was silent save for the gentle sobbing of Danielle and the clicking of Sgt. Sanchez nervously turning his gun's safety on and off. Kim was comforting Danielle on the floor of the truck while Jason sat on the bench seat above them tightly squeezing his gulf club. Dave sat hunched over, sulking on the bench in the front corner of the truck bed. Lucy had her face buried in the side of Stephen's shoulder trying to hold back the tears. She had not released her grip on his arm since the shooting had started. Stephen exchanged a 'what do I do now' look with Nick, to which Nick shrugged.

After escaping Carrollton the convoy found its way back onto the main highway before Major Bradley halted the trucks and came back to check on the civilians. No one was hurt but everyone was a little rattled especially after lying on the floor of the truck during the exchange of gun fire. Several bullet holes could be seen in the canvas that covered the truck bed. After ensuring everyone was okay, Major Bradley informed them they would not be stopping again until they reached Fort Campbell; about four hours away. The Major put on a brave face telling them that they should be safe there. However, they could all see that even the Major had doubts about that. The convoy started on its way again as the truck holding the civilians bumped along in silence, each person lost in their own thoughts.

"Is Danielle going to be alright Kim," asked Stephen, finally breaking the silence.

"Yeah, she'll … be fine, just a bit shaken," said Kim looking up from her daughter.

"You gonna be okay Lucy," Stephen asked finally looking down at the girl clinging to his arm.

"Uhh, yeah I'll be alright, umm … sorry," responded Lucy quickly releasing her grip on Stephen.

"We can get you two a room when we get there," Nick said.

Lucy growled through gritted teeth at Nick.

"You okay back there Dave," Stephen said quickly changing the subject.

Dave mumbled something back in reply and then went back to examining his shoes.

Leaning in and lowering his voice Stephen said, "We really need to keep an eye on him, he is not taking this well."

"You wouldn't either if you just lost your girlfriend," said Lucy.

"I know but there is just something else," replied Stephen.

"Yeah, I know what you mean," said Nick.

Sitting back up Stephen turned to Jason, "How you holding up there Jason?"

"I'm okay as long as Mom and Danielle are safe."

"That's very sweet of you Jason," said Kim reaching up to give her son a hug.

"Hey Sergeant do you have any food or water, I'm starving," asked Nick.

"Really Nick, after that you're hungry?" asked Stephen.

"Hey what can I say, a man gots to eat," Nick said with a shrug.

"There is some snack food in that box at the end of the truck," said Sergeant Sanchez pointing to a cardboard box with a

Little Debbies logo on it. "You'll have to split it up amongst yourselves."

"Well, I guess we had better eat when we can," Stephen said heading to the rear of the truck.

As they passed the foodstuffs around, Danielle stopped crying and wiped her eyes dry.

"Umm, Mommy how much longer till we get there," she asked.

"I don't know honey. Why?" asked Kim.

"Umm … I might need to go to the bathroom soon," replied Danielle sheepishly.

"Oh, I'm sorry honey but we can't stop. Can you hold it?"

"I think so Mommy."

"I'm going to have to use the restroom soon to," Lucy said chiming in.

"Well how about we stop talking about it before all of us have to go," said Nick.

"Good idea," chimed in Sergeant Sanchez. "We've got just over an hour before we'll be there."

"Then what?" asked Stephen.

"Then hopefully there will be someone there to evac you civilians and tell us what to do next. If we are really lucky we will all just wake up and realize this is a nightmare. But I'm not holding out much hope of either," replied Sanchez.

"I guess all we can do now is prepare for the worst and hope for the best," said Kim.

"I never thought I would say this but I hope they have something more than vending machine food when we get there," Nick said.

"And maybe a soft bed," said Stephen stretching his back.

"Mmm … and a warm shower. None of us have bathed in a while and you boys are starting to stink," said Lucy giving Danielle a wink.

Danielle giggled and then nestled up against her mom who looked down at her and smiled.

"I haven't heard that giggle since … well since before we left home," said Kim longingly.

"It's interesting to notice the things we took for granted before all this happened and now we miss them," said Stephen with a sigh.

"Way to bring the mood down dude," said Nick.

With that, everyone in the back of the truck returned to their own thoughts. As the truck bumped along, silence engulfed them once again.

Captain Bannon was still a little shaken as he tried to look over his maps. Looking up, he stared at the flight controls. This was more than he had signed up for. He just wanted to fly his plane. Even with everything going on down on the ground he knew that up in his plane he was away from of the horror of it all. Unfortunately, that comforting thought had now been cruelly taken from him as well. Looking back down at his guidance computer he discovered the coordinates that Gunner had given him were right in the middle of Fort Campbell, home of the famous 101st Airborne. He had flown into the base a couple times before so he was somewhat familiar with the army airfield there. They would be there shortly and the Captain knew he had to prepare himself.

He had decided to attempt a silent landing. He had seen how the noise of his plane's engines had attracted the infected before and that was not a mistake he wanted to make again. Once he had lined up his approach he would cut the engines and glide in for a landing. He had done it before but not by choice. However, this time there would be no ground crew if something went wrong. Clearing his mind of the recent events in the air, the Captain adjusted his heading and buckled into his seat.

Back in the cabin, Gunner and his men talked quietly in the rear of the plane. Dr. Sanderson buckled his belt and stared out of the window.

"According to the GPS our next signal is coming from Fort Campbell," Gunner said, startling the Doctor.

"I do not expect this to be easy, but we will find what we need," he continued as he took his seat near the Doctor.

"I hope this is Number 5," said Dr. Sanderson. "I really don't know how many more times I can do this. This … this whole thing has gotten out of hand."

Gunner sat expressionless, as if he was not even listening.

"I should really thank you for your help and protection Gunner," said Dr. Sanderson after a minute of silence.

"Just doing my job Doctor," replied Gunner.

"Of course you are Gunner."

Giving up on trying to converse with him, Dr. Sanderson resumed staring out of the window to the miniature world moving past below them. From the air everything looked so normal. No one from this vantage point could imagine the hell that was unfolding below them. The plane began to descend and as it circled the area Dr. Sanderson could make out the army base along with the small airfield just north of it. As the plane banked, to line up its final approach, he sat up right in his seat as he stared out of the window. There, below them, he thought he could make out a small convoy of what appeared to be military vehicles.

As the plane leveled, Dr. Sanderson was about to say something to Gunner when suddenly the noise from the engines stopped. With a shudder the plane began to glide and all the Doctor could hear was the sound of the wind keeping the plane aloft.

"What … what just happened?" Dr. Sanderson asked in a state of near panic.

"Relax Doctor. I believe the good Captain is attempting a silent landing," replied Gunner calmly.

"A silent landing? Like gliding?"

"Exactly. This should make things considerably easier for us once we are on the ground."

"I hope so," said Dr. Sanderson as he tightly gripped his seat.

As the convoy reached the northern outskirts of Fort Campbell Major Bradley called for a halt. Climbing up into the gunner's cupola he surveyed the area. The base, at least from this vantage point, appeared to be deserted. As he was about to order Private Sinclair to start the convoy up again, Major Bradley paused; in the distance he thought he could hear the sound of an engine. Scanning the horizon he could not see any vehicles. As he looked around a glint of something in the late afternoon sky caught his attention. Looking again he realized it was a plane making the noise he heard.

The plane slowly grew larger as it began to descend and circle the base. It looked to be some type of corporate jet. Through his binoculars Major Bradley could see an emblem on the side of the plane but could not quite make out what it said.

As the plane pulled out of its bank and straightened, it suddenly went quiet. It seemed as if the plane's engines had stopped working. Incredulously Major Bradley watched as the plane silently descended and then disappeared out of view towards what he could only assume was the base's airfield. With a renewed sense of hope that they may not be alone after all Major Bradley clamored back down inside the Humvee.

"Was that a plane sir?" asked Private Sinclair.

"Yes, yes it was," replied Major Bradley. "Now let's get this convoy moving. Let's hope whoever is in the plane is here for the same reason we are."

"What's that sir?" asked Private Sinclair quizzically.

"Maybe they've found a cure."

Chapter 27
Blanchfield

Fort Campbell is a sprawling army base covering over 100,000 acres. It has been in operation since the end of World War II and the home of the 101st Airborne Division since 1956. It has the capacity to house and train nearly 50,000 soldiers and their families. Complete with lodging, a dog park, tennis courts, movie theater, elementary school, sportsman lodge, restaurants, and a full service hospital. In other words, it is its own city; completely self-sufficient. It is also, typically, one of the most secure locations in the country.

Captain Bannon applied the brakes as the Gulfstream came to a stop. While the others were gone he would have to find a tug to get the plane across the tarmac and onto the other runway and into a takeoff position. If there was one thing he has learned over the last two days it was that he needed be prepared for takeoff at a moment's notice. There was no telling who or what Gunner was likely to come back with.

Gunner and his men were already out of their seats scanning the windows for trouble as the Doctor unbuckled his seatbelt. He grabbed his backpack and slung it over his shoulder. He did not need to be told to wait in the plane until Gunner and his men had cleared the immediate area. Unfortunately, he had been through this drill before.

While he waited, the Doctor looked out the windows and saw no activity. It appeared to be clear. Gunner and his men had opened the hatch and lowered the stairs and were now on the tarmac surveying the area. He slowly made his way to the front of the plane anticipating the signal from Gunner.

"All clear Doctor!" Gunner's voice shouted from below.

As the Doctor made his way down the stairs he thought it odd that Captain Bannon was still in the cockpit and had not come out to see them off as he had every other time. Perhaps he was trying something different this time. Change things up and maybe get a different result. The Doctor sure as hell hoped so.

Gunner was replacing his walkie onto his belt when the Doctor reached the bottom of the stairs.

"I was just talking to the Captain and he informed me he observed a convoy of, what appeared to be, military vehicles on the other side of the base," Gunner said.

"I thought I had seen them too. Maybe the base hasn't been overrun yet," Dr. Sanderson offered.

"Maybe not, Doctor," Gunner conceded, "but my instructions are clear. We are to find and return with your patient. Nothing else matters."

Dr. Sanderson did not exactly know how to take that but it was certainly said with a definite … tone. Unsure how to respond, he just nodded.

Gunner's men had finished their ritual of applying armor and arming themselves. It seemed to the Doctor they had a more determined look on their faces. It may have had something to do with Gunner's conversation with Mr. Worthington.

"We don't have a lot of light left and the signal is about two and a half miles southeast of here, so we should get moving," Gunner said.

Major Bradley halted the convoy in front of Gate Four. He had been here a few times previous and had a vague recollection of Fort Campbell's layout. Entering here would serve a couple of purposes. First, once inside, it had a wide dual lane with room to turn the convoy around and prepare for a quick retreat if necessary. Second, it is the closest entrance to the army hospital inside the base. At least as far as the Major remembered.

It made sense that if the National Guard or 101st brought infected here; they would have ended up at the medical center. Blanchfield Army Hospital was a large facility with modern equipment capable of handling nearly any situation.

His first concern, as he pulled up in front of the entrance, was the fact that no one was manning the toll booth style checkpoint just inside the base. He scanned the area with his binoculars and saw no movement; infected or otherwise. He was not sure if that was good news or not. It was possible that the remaining personnel would have moved inside the base to shrink the perimeter they had to defend.

"Captain Morris, we will be entering at Gate Four," the Major said into his comm.

"Yes sir," Captain Morris replied.

His second concern was the plane he saw landing. It was not military, he was sure of that. It looked to be a private jet such as a Dassault or a Gulfstream. He was not sure why a plane like that would be landing at a military base. It was possible whoever they were, they might be helping with the evacuations or helping transport a vaccine to various safe zones. Either way he would investigate that after he checked out the hospital.

Private Sinclair led the convoy down Screaming Eagle Boulevard driving in the exit lane as the large vehicles in the convoy would have had trouble getting through the checkpoint. The exit lane had no such impediment.

After they had passed the gate, the convoy moved into the proper lane and continued down the boulevard for about a hundred yards coming to the first intersection. The Major had the convoy turn around and move back into the exit lane. Once they were all in line he opened his comm link.

"Captain Morris and Sergeant Sanchez report to the lead Humvee," Major Bradley said.

A moment later he was standing under a large oak tree just off to the side of the convoy with Captain Morris and Sgt. Sanchez. The late afternoon sun was setting behind him as an eerie calm had taken over the base.

"What's the plan Major?" Captain Morris asked.

"Have either of you seen any infected on the base?" the Major asked.

"I haven't seen anyone, Major," Sanchez replied.

"Nothing except for that plane," Captain Morris added.

The Major thought for a second and then said, "There is no way we would be able to maneuver the convoy effectively inside the base. We need to leave the vehicles here, prepared to evacuate quickly. I will take a few men and scout out the hospital. Captain Morris, you stay here and guard the civilians and secure the convoy. We'll keep comm lines open and update each other as needed. Captain you remain on channel two, me and my group will be on four."

"What is your ETA to the hospital?" Captain Morris asked.

"It's probably about half a mile, maybe a little more," the Major replied. "I would say ten minutes."

"Any questions?" he added.

"Why don't you take my Humvee Major?" Captain Morris asked. "You can get there faster plus you'll have the 50."

"We may need to move in and out of buildings or around obstacles. If the place is filled with infected, there may be abandoned cars or telephone lines down. Plus, from what I've seen, they move pretty slowly. We should be able to avoid them if necessary," Major Bradley said.

"Anything else?"

Neither Sgt. Sanchez nor Captain Morris had anything else to add. The Major had made his decision and that was usually that.

"Okay, Sergeant I need you to grab McCutchen, Stevens, Sinclair, and Diaz. Meet me back here in five. Make sure you pack extra ammo, we may need it."

"Yes sir," Sanchez replied and headed back to the convoy.

"Captain, I need you to have Simmons try contacting anyone inside the base. Maybe we can get a fix on their location and perhaps a status on the base itself. Let them know we're here and inquire about any progress on a cure," the Major said.

"Yes sir," Captain Morris said as he turned to find Simmons and relay the Major's orders.

Major Bradley took a minute to look around. It was quiet; too quiet. If this was Korea, he would think they were being set up for an ambush. Across the street, back from where they came, was the visitor's center. At the intersection just ahead was the Turner Building; essentially lodging for anyone visiting the base. On the other side of the street was an army training center. Each building appeared to be empty. It was unnerving.

He reached for his sidearm and checked his clip. He did an inventory and found he had two spares as well.

Sanchez returned with Privates Sinclair, McCutchen, Stevens, and Diaz.

"All set Major," Sanchez announced.

"Very well Sergeant," the Major answered. "We'll be heading in that direction," he said pointing southwest. "I'll take point, Sinclair and Stevens fan out to the left; McCutchen and Diaz to the right. Sanchez, take up position to the rear."

"Be alert. We're heading to the base hospital. If we engage any infected, make your shots count. We have limited ammo; understood?"

No one said a word. He could sense their apprehension.

"Move out," the Major ordered. As they started to move the Major turned to Sergeant Sanchez and asked, "Can I get another clip Sergeant?"

The Doctor and crew moved along a service road from the airstrip that had several maintenance buildings to the left and a dense group of woods to the right. He had seen some strange things come out of the woods in the last couple of days and eyed them with suspicion as they passed.

Gunner halted the group at the first intersection. He preferred to stay on the main roads if possible. Although they would be more in the open it would be easier to spot any infected. The seemingly peaceful surroundings were not lost on him as the hairs on his neck began to stand up. Gunner had been in enough tight situations before that he always trusted the hairs on his neck.

Up ahead was a moderately sized residential area; presumably to house the soldiers and their families. Gunner consulted the GPS tracker and decided the quickest way to the signal was through the development. Locating the source of the signal quickly outweighed the risk of traveling around blind corners and small backyards. The sun was setting and it would be dark soon.

Staying in formation, Gunner led the group in between the first two houses, stopping at the end of each corner. Mikael and Stefan took turns darting into the open spaces between the houses making sure the coast was clear. They crossed Bell Road onto the other side of the development. As they moved through the backyards of two houses, the Doctor noticed movement in the narrow alley between them. He slowed and turned his head to get a better look.

Kneeling down and hunched over were three adults, their backs towards the Doctor. Their attention was fixed on something directly in front of them. Dr. Sanderson's line of site was obscured and he was unable to see what it was. They had not, however, noticed him yet. Ludvig came up from behind the Doctor and ushered him forward, out of view of the crouching adults. As he turned his attention forward he caught a glimpse of what had kept them occupied. The legs of a fourth person of indeterminable age and gender had been separated from its abdomen. The group appeared to be feeding on the rest of the corpse. It was an image the Doctor would soon not forget.

They reached the other side of the development and it looked as if following Indiana Avenue, which was directly in front of them, would get them to the signal the fastest. The Doctor was relieved to be out in the open. He would prefer to see trouble coming rather than to have it sneak up on him.

They passed a recreation center and an indoor sports complex. Both seemed to be empty. A few minutes later they passed another housing complex that looked more like apartments that were in a V-shaped formation with the point of the V facing the road. Filling the space between the two spurs of apartments was an open courtyard that could easily be seen through a break in the buildings.

Meandering down the stone pathways and grass fields of the courtyard were at least a hundred infected. Dr. Sanderson looked at Gunner and saw that he had seen them as well. Gunner moved the group to the other side of the street and tightened up the formation. There was apparently significantly more infected here than they originally thought.

Gunner stopped and turned to talk to the Doctor, "We need to pick up the pace, Doctor. The GPS has us about a mile and a half from the signal. We haven't attracted any attention yet but I feel it's only a matter of time. Are you up to it?"

Looking back at the infected milling about the courtyard and thinking back to the horrific scene in the alley he looked Gunner square in the eye and said, "Let's move."

Captain Morris checked in with Specialist Simmons to see if he had made contact with anyone on the base.

"Not yet Captain, but I've only been at it for a few minutes. I'll let you know as soon as I do," Simmons replied.

"Carry on," Captain Morris said as he left the Humvee.

Simmons was right; it had only been a few minutes. Time seemed to be dragging since the Major left for the hospital. It had only taken a couple of minutes to secure the area. There did not seem to be any infected on this side of the base. Maybe there was a group of soldiers holed up somewhere inside the base with a cure and a plan to distribute it. It could be what that plane they saw was doing. He was hoping anyway. It would explain why he was pestering poor Simmons.

With the area secured it was time to go get the civilians. Let them stretch their legs and hit the restrooms.

Stephen looked over at young Jason who was standing with his legs crossed and hopping up and down; the classic signal of a distressed bladder.

"But I gotta go …" Jason pleaded with his mom.

"I know honey … it'll be just a minute," Kim said trying to calm her son down.

The convoy had stopped nearly fifteen minutes ago and they had been sitting there by themselves for the better part of it. Chester was nowhere to be seen and the soldier that was in the cargo truck with them had jumped out as soon as they had arrived.

Captain Morris suddenly appeared out of nowhere at the back of the truck. Alongside him was another soldier Stephen had yet to meet. He peered in and looked around.

"Anyone seen Mr. Boone?" asked Captain Morris.

"Not since he jumped out of the truck and started shooting at some rednecks a couple of hours ago," Nick answered.

"My kids really need to go to the bathroom Captain," Kim said.

"That's actually why I've come. The immediate area has been secured. Corporal Levine will escort you to the lodge across the street so that you can take care of any business. So, anyone who needs to go or just wants to stretch their legs, please follow the corporal."

Stephen and Nick jumped quickly out of the truck, happy to escape the suffocating confines. Stephen helped Lucy down as Nick grabbed ahold of Danielle and gently lifted her up and put her on the ground. Jason did not need any help as he jumped out of the truck and landed hard on the ground nearly finishing with a somersault. After getting back up he returned to the truck and retrieved his golf club. Kim was helped down by both Nick and Stephen.

"Thank you gentlemen," Kim said with a smile.

Stephen looked back inside and saw Dave still sitting on the bench. He was staring straight ahead; face pale, wringing his hands.

"Let's go Dave, come and get some fresh air," Stephen said.

Dave turned his head and looked at him with his sunken eyes and said nothing for minute.

"Naw, go ahead I'm fine. I'll stay here … it's safer," Dave finally said.

Stephen was going to say something when Lucy grabbed hold of his arm and shook her head.

"Okay … see you in a few," Stephen said.

Danielle pulled on Kim's shirtsleeve and said. "Mom … let's go."

Corporal Levine motioned for everyone to move and said, "Follow me folks."

Stephen and Nick followed from behind and exchanged glances. They were both worried about Dave. He has steadily gotten worse since they lost Emma at the Target outside D.C.

Major Bradley had led his men down Screaming Eagle Boulevard until they came to the proverbial fork in the road. Straight ahead was an old Apache attack helicopter poised majestically on a platform with a sign welcoming them to Fort Campbell, home of the 101st Airborne Division; the Screaming Eagles.

Moving his left hand back and forth he signaled his men to take the left fork and continue moving. He was sure they were near the hospital. They had yet to run into any infected. That was the good news. The bad news was they had yet to run into anyone from the base. His uneasiness was growing.

As they moved down the boulevard another few hundred yards passing by the RF Sink Library, the Major stopped in his tracks. The hospital was on the other side of the library, he definitely remembered that. The last time he was here he visited an old buddy of his that had been wounded in Korea. His friend had asked him to get a particular book from the library for him while he was stuck in the hospital.

The Major repositioned his men in a single file as they crossed the sidewalk and took up position on the left side of the library. He could now see the hospital across Joel Drive. He moved slowly past the large windows of the library. The first two had their blinds drawn tight and he could not see inside. The third window, however, had its blinds raised revealing the library's interior.

The Major crouched down and instructed his men to do the same. As he passed underneath the third window he straightened up just enough to peer inside. What he saw froze him in his tracks. He was unable to move. The only thing more disturbing than what he was looking at was what was looking at him.

Dr. Sanderson's group had continued following Indiana Avenue, traveling southeast. They passed by a couple of more housing developments with more infected wandering around the grounds. They passed a large athletic field that had infected roving the outfield. It looked to the Doctor like a bizarre intramural softball game.

They hugged the east side of the road and had, to this point, managed to avoid any direct contact with infected. Gunner was instructing his men with hand signals as he did not want to bring any undue attention to the group. It seemed to him that noise was more likely to attract them than motion.

Twenty minutes later they had arrived at the intersection of Screaming Eagle Boulevard and Indiana Avenue. Gunner held up the group as he consulted the GPS tracker. They were close; a couple hundred yards away. The signal had moved only slightly since it had been acquired but was now still.

On the corner directly in front of them was a moderately sized one story building. A sign on the front window indicated it was the Baldanado Indoor Pool. Gunner figured it would provide adequate cover as they cut across heading south. He anticipated that their prize awaited them on the other side of the pool building's parking lot.

They moved alongside the building in a tight formation with Gunner in front; Mikael, the Doctor, and Stefan in the center and Ludvig bringing up the rear. As they reached the end of the pool building, Gunner looked past the parking lot to a large three story building. It had a smaller building in front of it and a small parking lot could be seen off to the side. It was readily apparent that this must be a hospital or medical center of some kind.

The other thing of note was that the hospital, if that's what it was, was surrounded by an army of infected. The parking lot, the small building in front, as well as the main entrance had infected everywhere. It was the most disturbing sight Gunner had ever seen. He was about to move away from the building to get a better look and take shelter behind some trees off to the right when movement from an adjacent building caught his attention.

Looking to his left he saw several men dressed in army fatigues and brandishing weapons, move quickly from behind a brick building fifty yards to their left. They appeared to be moving around to the other side of the hospital. Gunner immediately assumed these were the men that Captain Bannon alerted him to shortly after they landed.

Gunner turned to his men and was about to issue instructions when he noticed the Doctor looking upward toward the hospital. He started absentmindedly walking forward out into the open, never taking his eyes off the roof of the hospital. Gunner followed the Doctor's gaze and saw he was staring at several zombies standing on the roof. With all the infected surrounding the building on the ground, Gunner had never looked up at the roof.

He let the Doctor take a few more steps forward before reaching out and grabbing him firmly by the arm.

"Doctor?" Gunner said. There was no reply. He said it again.

Dr. Sanderson turned his head slightly and looked at Gunner. His mouth opened and he said, "Number 5," as gunshots rang out on the far side of the hospital.

Major Bradley was looking in on the reading area of the library. Long wooden tables with small reading lamps and wooden chairs covered grey carpeting. The problem was no one was reading. The wooden table closest to the window had the sprawled body of a woman. She was partially devoured and two infected were standing over her feeding.

Even more disturbing, if possible, was the infected male standing in front of the window staring directly at the Major. It leapt forward and lunged at him. The only thing keeping the creature off the Major was the glass window separating the two. It was only a matter of time, however, before it smashed through the window. Its aggressive actions also seemed to be drawing the attention of several other infected in the library.

Not wanting to open fire unless necessary, the Major led his troops out into the open, through the library parking lot and across Joel Drive. They crossed the street and ended up at the entrance to the small staff parking lot of the hospital.

The Major had wanted to move away from the immediate threat of the library so quickly that he had not noticed the hundreds, maybe several hundreds, of infected in front of the hospital. When he finally came to a stop at the edge of the parking lot, he had a moment to evaluate their situation. It was bleak. They were seriously outnumbered and their arrival had attracted attention.

He quickly decided they would move left, around the building and see if the backside was as infested. If they could not get into the hospital, they would head back to the convoy.

Moving swiftly, the Major led his soldiers over a grass median and past an outdoor generator. They turned the corner and saw a small clump of trees just ahead. Moving out from behind the trees were more infected. There was no way they were going to make it around them and trying to go through them would be difficult at best. He decided retreat was their best move.

They turned around heading back from where they came only to find that a few infected had followed them. They were trapped. They had no alternative. The Major gave the order to open fire; and open fire they did.

Corporal Levine led the civilians into the reception lobby of a two story lodge. It was actually a separate building from the where the rooms were located. In order to access the rooms, you would have to leave this building and drive, or walk, to your room.

The lobby was appropriately decorated. There was a sitting area with comfortable looking chairs and a couple of wooden coffee tables. The walls were decorated with framed pictures of helicopters and old soldiers. The reception area was a simple desk with a computer and a large aerial photograph of the base behind it.

The restroom was located off to the left of the reception desk and down a short hallway. It was a universal restroom. After the corporal cleared the restroom it was decided the girls could go first. Jason decided to stay with the boys.

"What grade are you in Jason?" Nick asked a minute later trying to keep things as normal as possible.

"I'm in fifth grade," Jason answered. "I'm going into the junior high next year … or at least I was," he added.

Stephen was going to add something when the bathroom door opened and Kim, Lucy, and Danielle came out.

"All yours boys," Kim said.

"Try not to make a mess," Danielle added looking at Jason.

Stephen let loose with the first smile in a long time. Jason and Nick followed him into the bathroom as Jason said, "Girls, huh."

They finished quickly and exited the restroom to find Corporal Levine waiting for them. The girls had apparently left the lobby and were already outside. The corporal instructed them to exit the building.

They emerged into a fading sky as the last rays of sunlight covered the large open field in front of them. Stephen stopped for a second as everyone went ahead of him. His large frame had cramped up pretty good while sitting in the truck. He began to stretch and bend, using the axe as a counter weight, trying to work out the kinks. He stood back up and looked around.

He noticed some people coming out of the visitor's center at the far end of the grassy field. Looking closely, he saw they were not wearing the army fatigues of the soldiers. Closer inspection revealed that they had the familiar awkward gait of the infected. Looking over at the rest of his group it appeared no one else had seen them. He started to get a very bad feeling when he felt a cold hand on his right shoulder.

Chapter 28
The Storm

The Major, along with McCutchen and Diaz, opened fire as they returned from where they had come. Sanchez, Sinclair, and Stevens covered their retreat as they mowed down the infected coming out from the trees. Stray bullets and those that passed through the skulls of their intended targets ploughed into tree bark causing wood chips to rain down on the zombies.

As they turned the corner of the building and faced the entrance to the hospital, undead that had been attracted by the noise of gunfire started making their way toward the Major. Looking back, he saw that Sanchez and company had bought them some time by eliminating most of the zombies approaching from the rear.

He decided that there was no possible way that there was anyone alive in the hospital much less a group of dedicated research scientists working overtime to produce a cure. They needed to head back to the convoy. He pressed his comm link and was about to inform Captain Morris of his intentions when he looked across the parking lot, past the administration building, and spotted a group of people huddled between a row of trees and the pool building. He guessed these might be the people from the plane he had seen land.

Letting up on the comm link he changed out the magazine in his handgun and pulled back on the chamber. He turned to his men and pointed in the direction of the strangers.

"Over there," the Major said.

His men saw the group across the street and nodded.

"We need to find out what they are doing here and what, if anything, they know. We'll cut across the parking lot and move to the other side of the street."

Sergeant Sanchez led the way blasting through the oncoming zombies with his M16A2. He was doing his best to comply with the Major's order of ammunition conservation but it was difficult given the growing number of infected in the area. He had brought the extra ammo the Major had asked for but he was not sure if they had enough to deal with the problem at hand.

The others followed Sanchez's lead in a tight formation and fired only when necessary. They had to watch were they stepped as they were forced to maneuver over decapitated zombies and avoid slipping on puddles of the blackened fluid that oozed from them.

As they reached the end of the parking lot and were about to cross the street, Private Stevens felt something grab his left leg. As he spun around and looked down he lost his balance and fell backwards and landed hard on the ground. Quickly lifting his head up and sitting, he saw an infected woman with most of her lower jaw and the left side of her face missing. Somehow she was still crawling forward and was about to place her other hand on his leg.

Regaining his composure he leveled his sidearm at what remained of the zombie's head and fired. The advancing zombie crumbled to the ground releasing its grip on Stevens' leg. Before he could steady himself to try and get up, he felt two strong hands reaching under each arm and lift him up.

After Major Bradley and Private Sinclair had gotten Stevens to his feet, they continued on across the street ending up in the library parking lot. As they regrouped, checked their ammo replenishing as necessary, the Major attempted to visually reacquire the strangers he had seen a moment ago.

They were still in the same place as before. The Major had to decide the best way to play this. He could approach them with guns drawn and demand they drop their weapons and insist they tell him who they are and why they are here. But given the current state of affairs he doubted they would comply; he sure as hell would not. He decided a more tactful approach would be best.

Moving along Joel Avenue they closed the gap between the two groups. The Major now had a better look at the strangers. There were five of them. One of them was the size of a tank and armed. Three others were also armed and covered in body armor, staring at the Major and his group as they approached.

The Major immediately recognized them as guns for hire or mercenaries of some kind. All except the final member of the group. He was a middle aged man with glasses and physically much smaller than the others. He also appeared to be unarmed which made the Major think he may be crazy.

As The Major and his men were about ten yards from the large man in the slacks and short cropped blonde hair, he instructed them to stop. Major Bradley lowered his weapon slightly and visibly released his finger from the trigger. Taking one additional step forward, he stared at the man he assumed was in charge.

"My name is Major Charles Bradley, United States Army, and with whom am I speaking?"

The enormous man with the blonde hair and the stone face stared at the Major but said nothing. His associates tightened the grips on their assault rifles and pointed them in the Major's direction. He took one additional step forward and lowered his weapon even further. He knew his men behind him had their weapons trained on the strangers and would not hesitate to unload on them if necessary.

A prolonged standoff would do no one any good. If the Major was correct and they were guns for hire, it could be a good thing. They typically were focused on their present assignment. The one that would get them paid. Anything else was irrelevant and right now the Major and his group were irrelevant.

The infected across the street would soon be making their way over and then all bets were off. He was about to repeat his request when the older man with the glasses stepped between the blonde giant, whose gaze was still locked on the Major, and another of the mercenaries.

"Perhaps I can help clear things up Major. My name is Dr. Lemuel Sanderson and these are my associates," he said motioning to the men behind him.

"We have been searching for one of my patients for the last several days. One that I believe holds the key to solving this whole mess."

"I'm sorry to be the bearer of bad news Doctor," the Major interrupted, "but if your patient is in that hospital, they're dead … or worse."

"Actually, he's not in the hospital … he's on top of it," the Doctor said pointing to the roof of the hospital.

Major Bradley looked up to where the Doctor was pointing. On the roof stood the silhouette of a man against the backdrop of the setting sun. At first the Major thought his original analysis of the Doctor was correct; he *was* crazy. But as he continued to stare, something struck him as unusual. The man on the roof was obviously infected, he could see that from here, but he was not roaming the roof aimlessly like the other infected in the area. As a matter of fact it almost looked as if he was staring back at him.

"We could use your help Major," Dr. Sanderson added. "I don't mean to be abrupt, but we don't have much time."

Major Bradley looked at the Doctor and saw that he was serious. The Major was not convinced that he was completely sane, but he was right about one thing; they did not have much time. And there was something … different about that infected man on the roof.

The other thing that concerned him was the humongous mercenary still watching his every move. But if capturing this … patient was his job; then helping him accomplish his mission would allow the Major and his men to remain irrelevant and maybe just put an end to this madness.

His thoughts were suddenly interrupted by the sound of breaking glass originating from the library. The Major turned around, as did his men, and saw infected pouring out of the building's windows.

With his easterly escape route now compromised and an increasing zombie presence moving across Joel Avenue, the Major looked at his men. Without a word each man nodded slightly. He turned his attention back to the Doctor.

"What's your plan?" he asked.

Number 5 had eventually made his way to the roof of the Blanchfield Army Hospital. After the door to the research lab had opened and the unsuspecting research assistant entered, it was only a matter of time before the entire base was infected. It was populated predominantly with families and support staff. Most of the soldiers were currently stationed elsewhere. The end for the majority of the inhabitants came swiftly.

He was now standing on the edge of the hospital rooftop looking down at the throng of undead in front of the main entrance. On the rooftop with him were a dozen other zombies. Although they could not comprehend why they were there, they had no ability to think or reason, they were there because Number 5 wanted them there. A number of hospital staff had fled to what they hoped would be the safety of the rooftop. Number 5 had followed them and quickly infected those who did not jump.

The "survivors," without knowing it, were acting as bodyguards; protecting the bacterium that had taken control of Number 5. The same bacterium that to this point had directed his actions and, for reasons yet to be understood by Number 5, created this army of the undead.

His attention, if you could call it that, was now drawn to a group of humans that had arrived a few moments ago. They had emerged from behind a building across the street and were now standing next to a small row of trees at the edge of the street. One of the humans had separated from the others and moved slowly out into the open; staring directly up at Number 5.

He looked down and their eyes met. There was seventy-five yards or so between them; but that would not have mattered.

If Number 5 had the ability to remember, he would have known his old doctor; even from this distance.

They say, however, that the eyes are the window to the soul. Number 5's soul had been taken over, hijacked if you will, by an unknown force bent on some evil intention. It was through these eyes that the entity inside him was able to see the outside world. And if the Doctor was close enough to see the expression on his face he would have able to discern it immediately. It was the unmistakable look of recognition.

A few minutes later a second group of humans arrived. They also seemed to take an interest in Number 5 who turned his head and looked in the direction of three other zombies near him. They stopped, turned, and began heading toward the edge of the roof.

Without stopping they continued forward even when they ran out of roof. Each fell and landed hard on the ground in a way that would have killed someone who was not already dead. All three zombies struggled to get up but each managed to do so. One had broken a leg and dragged the wounded appendage behind him as he moved forward. Another snapped its spine and walked in one direction while facing a slightly different direction. The third zombie had broken its left arm and after a few steps the arm fell to the ground.

The one thing all three zombies had in common was they were headed in the direction of the humans who had recently arrived.

Chapter 29
Alone

Stephen instinctively pulled away from the hand that gripped his shoulder and once free, turned quickly to see what had snuck up behind him. He found himself face to face with an infected man wearing overalls and a solid blue shirt. His dark hair was matted down and the left side of his face was sliced open with pieces of dried skin flopping up and down as he moved, his arms were outstretched and he was stumbling forward toward Stephen.

He raised the axe, gripping it at the bottom of the handle, and swung upward targeting the zombie's head. He did not have enough time to take proper aim, or to ensure the sharp end of the axe was facing the correct way, resulting in the blunt end of the axe glancing off the zombie's shoulder and redirecting upward hitting it square in the temple.

It collapsed immediately to the ground but continued to move. It started to roll around and attempt to right itself. Stephen never gave it an opportunity as he flipped the axe in his hand, sharp end now pointing down, and came down hard just above the shoulder blades separating the zombie's head from the rest of its body.

When it stopped moving he looked back up only to see several more infected coming into view. They were approaching from the building that housed the lodge's guests. There was now over a dozen infected heading his way.

He turned around and screamed at the top of his lungs.

"Corporal!"

Corporal Levine had been walking back toward the convoy with the rest of the civilians. They were about twenty yards ahead when Stephen let out his cry for help.

Turning quickly he saw Stephen, axe in hand, standing over the decapitated zombie. He then noticed the other infected emerging from both sides of the complex. His wider view allowed him a more comprehensive picture of what was unfolding. There were now over two dozen zombies heading toward the front of the registration building. Stephen was going to be in real trouble soon.

"Get back to the convoy now!" Corporal Levine shouted to the rest of the group. "Find Captain Morris, I'll radio you're on the way."

Kim and the children, Lucy, and Nick turned and began running as fast as they could. Kim picked Danielle up and Jason ran ahead holding his golf club up and in front of him.

Corporal Levine darted toward Stephen, gun raised. He pressed his comm link and said, "Captain Morris, come in."

"Morris," came the response.

"I've got the civilians headed your way Captain and we've got infected spotted coming out of the lodge, engaging now."

"Copy," replied Captain Morris.

Corporal Levine arrived just as Stephen had taken a few steps back and had the axe cocked behind his head ready to take aim at another zombie. This time it was a man in army fatigues. The single bar on his shoulders indicated that he was a lieutenant; emphasis on was.

Stephen had long ago decided that these things were no longer human and that their fate, cruel as it was, had been decided for them and was irreversible. He took no pleasure in killing these things, but he did not hesitate either. The former lieutenant suffered the same fate as the man in the overalls when Stephen swung his axe and connected with the zombie's neck.

Corporal Levine began targeting the nearest zombies hoping to buy a few minutes so that they could fall back and regroup.   He could have opened fire and sprayed bullets everywhere but was aware of the ammo shortage and decided to be more judicious with his targets.

Stephen raised the axe a third time and was prepared to fend off a woman who was stumbling in his direction.   Her summer dress, plastered with purple and pink lilies, was torn at the bottom and covered with blood.   He was about to bring the axe down when her skull exploded as a result of a round from Corporal Levine's semi-automatic.

It was then that Stephen finally noticed the infected emerging from the other side of the lodge. He quickly realized that staying here was not an option.   They had to get back to the convoy and get as far away from the base as possible.

He looked over at Corporal Levine and nodded his head backwards. The Corporal was thinking the same thing and nodded in agreement.   They turned sideways and had taken a few steps backwards when Stephen was sure he heard gunfire coming from the other side of the convoy.

Nick stopped dead in his tracks halfway between the lodge and the convoy when he heard gunfire coming from the other side of the line of trucks. Everyone else did as well except Jason who continued to run.

"Jason!" Kim screamed at him.

Moving again, Nick had taken a few long strides forward as he reached out and grabbed Jason by the shoulder.   The combination of his Mother's voice and the firm hand on his shoulder broke his concentration.   He stopped suddenly and whirled around, golf club raised, and took a whack at Nick.

Luckily for Nick, he had seen it coming and easily blocked it with his hand. It stung a little but did no damage. Jason was struggling to pull the club from Nick's grip and began to scream out.

"I'm going to get you for what you did to my dad!" he yelled as he continued to pull at the club. Nick was afraid to let it go. He did not feel like getting hit again.

Kim came up from behind them, putting Danielle down, she bent down slightly and looked into her son's eyes. They were filled with hate and fear and rage. Mostly, however, they were filled with sadness.

"Jason baby," Kim said. "It's Mommy. I'm right here."

She slowly put her arms around her son and squeezed tight. He finally stopped fighting Nick for the club and then just let it go; both physically, by releasing the grip on the golf club, and emotionally, by letting all the pent up emotion spill out in one long outburst.

Lucy came up from behind and put her hand gently on Danielle, who turned and looked up at her, her eyes were moist and her body trembling.

Nick kept hold of the club as he turned to see Stephen and Corporal Levine running full sprint in their direction. The gunfire from the other side of the convoy had intensified. He looked at Lucy, and then back down at Kim holding her son as tightly as she could. He suddenly felt as helpless as he ever had.

Dave sat, alone, in the middle of the cargo truck looking down at his shoes. He had been trying his best to get the image of Emma disappearing into Target's stock room out of his head. He was failing miserably.

He was almost thankful for the sound of gunfire that snapped him out of his painful thoughts. The first couple of rounds seemed to be far off. He was not even sure if it was anyone from the convoy. Maybe there were some others nearby.

That line of thinking was soon dispelled when the next round sounded as if was coming from right outside the cargo truck. He finally looked up and peered out the back. He only saw the front of the fuel truck. No sign of the Captain though.

He could hear men shouting over the sound of gunfire and the crunch of dirt under the boots of the soldiers running outside. He briefly thought of getting up and going to the end of the truck and seeing what was happening outside. Obviously the soldiers had encountered some infected. Maybe he could help. *"Like I helped Emma,"* he thought.

He did not even have a weapon. He had dropped it somewhere in that Target store. If he had a gun, maybe he could ... a gun! Kim had a gun in the truck somewhere, the one Captain Morris showed them how to use.

He got up and moved to the other side of the truck and unzipped the luggage Kim had brought. He felt kind of weird going through someone else's belongings. Lucky for him the black case was right on top. He was reaching for it when he heard a noise coming from the open end of the truck. Looking, he saw nothing. It sounded like someone moving along the canvass outside.

He turned back to the luggage, grabbed the gun case and closed the luggage flap. Sitting back down, he held the case in his lap. He looked at it and tried to remember the numbered code needed to unlock it. Kim said she would not leave it open because of her kids.

His fingers fumbled over the digits as he continued to search his memory for the numbers. His concentration was interrupted by the same sound he heard a few seconds ago, only this time much louder. He looked again out into the dusk and this time thought he noticed movement.

He was shocked to see a pair of hands reaching into the back of the truck. Even more so when he realized those hands were attached to an infected person. It was a man in a dark blue jogging suit. He was trying to pull himself up into the truck bed.

Dave frantically turned his attention back to the black box on his lap. He started moving numbers into combinations he thought it might be; 3-2-6-3, 6-2-6-6, 2-3-9-6. None of them were able to reveal the prize inside the box. He looked back toward the end of the truck. The man in the jogging suit was now almost all the way inside. Unfortunately, he had now been joined by two others. One was a woman wearing jeans and a soiled grey T-Shirt and another man; this one in a hunter green flight suit.

Now in a full panic, Dave realized that if he did not get the gun case open in the next five seconds he was going to be in serious trouble. The strange thing was he had spent the last two days thinking that he did not really want to live. That he did not deserve to live. But now, all he could think about was staying alive. He tried 2-2-6-6 and then 3-3-6-6; nothing happened.

He had two choices. Stay in the truck and try to fight them off or attempt to somehow get past them and run and find help. He decided the latter was his best option. Using the still unopened gun case as a weapon he got up and stood on the wooden seats and ran along the boards. His head down and the case in his right hand he swung it at the nearest zombie.

He connected solidly with the jaw of the one in the jogging suit, knocking it off balance just enough for him to get past the outstretched arms of the zombie. He made it safely to the end of the truck as the other two zombies had managed to climb about halfway into the truck bed. They were, however, blocking the exit. He would have to propel himself off the wooden bench and out into the approaching night.

He leapt off the end of the bench but his left foot slipped and his body twisted in midair. He fell out of the truck more so than launching himself out. The loss of speed and control caused him to fall short of his intended goal. His feet hit the back of the cargo truck as he fell backward. It caused him to land on his head instead of his back or his side. He landed hard but not hard enough to knock himself out.

The gun case flew out of his hand and landed on the ground several feet away. He lay motionless on the pavement for several seconds before he realized what had happened. If he had not slipped, he would have landed on his side and rolled to safety.

He tried to get up but his head was pounding. He was dizzy and disoriented but was conscience. As he struggled to get up he was pulled back down by a fourth zombie that he had not seen. He struggled to free himself as his head pounded worse than any migraine and his shoulder still ached with pain.

It was only a few seconds later when the two zombies at the end of the truck had turned around and pounced on top of him. He did what he could but it was hopeless. As the first zombie leaned in and sank its teeth into his flesh and the others tore at his clothing, he thought of Emma and wondered when she was lying on her back on the cold cement floor of the stock room, did she think of him.

Chapter 30
Friendly Fire

Captain Morris was about to walk over to the northern side of the convoy and await the civilians and also check how many infected Corporal Levine had spotted when he heard the gunfire erupt behind him. He turned around quickly and saw two of his men opening fire on a large group of infected that had suddenly appeared. They had apparently come from inside and around back of the army training center.

The large two story building had provided perfect cover for the massing zombies. They now were spread out evenly over a fifty or sixty yard span and roughly seventy-five yards from the convoy. He immediately assessed the situation and realized they were being attacked on two fronts. Corporal Levine was going to have to handle the infected near the lodge. Captain Morris decided he was going to need everyone else to manage the infected coming from the training center. Their numbers had quickly swelled to well over a hundred.

He saw Privates Rivers and Loomis were already engaging the infected. Private Benson and Corporal Ripley had immediately joined the fray without having to be ordered to do so. That left Privates Adams, Romaliga, O'Connell, and Specialist Simmons.

He opened his comm link and spoke with urgency.

"I need all personnel with the exception of Levine to the south side of the convoy on the double. Prepare to engage infected." Before releasing the comm link he added, "This includes you Simmons."

He had no sooner finished when Specialist Simmons ran by him, weapon raised and ready to engage. Captain Morris sprinted to the second Humvee and opened the cargo door. He removed what was left of the ammunition. Looking at what he had in front of him and then looking back at the growing number of infected heading their way, he was not sure they had enough.

Stephen and Corporal Levine reached Nick and the rest of the group as Jason had finally begun regaining his composure. He was still obviously upset but had stopped sobbing. Nick was still holding the golf club. Stephen looked at him and then the club. Nick responded with a shrug.

Corporal Levine reached for his comm link and listened for a second.

"Looks like they got infected on the other side of the convoy," he said having to raise his voice in order to be heard above the gunfire. "Captain has left me alone on this side to take care of these infected."

"Us," Stephen said.

"What?" Corporal Levine said.

"We can handle them," Stephen said.

A minute ago he felt their only hope was to get as far away from them as possible. With infected on the other side of the convoy, it appeared at least for the moment, leaving was out of the question.

"Nick, get back to the truck and get Kim's gun. Lock the kids and the girls in one of the Humvees. They should be safe there until we can leave."

"I'm afraid I can't let ..." Levine started to say but was interrupted by Stephen.

"There's no time to argue ... Nick, go and take the girls with you. Oh, and see if you can find Dave."

Nick grabbed Danielle and scooped her up and started running. The rest followed as they headed to the cargo truck in search of Kim's gun.

Captain Morris met his soldiers in the open field about twenty yards south of the convoy. They had set up a perimeter stretching from one end of the trucks to the other. The infected were now less than fifty yards away and closing. He dropped extra magazines on the ground at each man's feet, keeping a few for himself.

They had room to retreat if necessary but he was hoping it would not come to that. The men were making their shots count as per the Major's standing order. If they did run out of ammunition, each man was equipped with a standard issue combat knife.

As the infected approached, the Captain moved back and made his way to his Humvee and climbed up into the gunner's cupola to man the fifty caliber machine gun. He was not sure how much ammo the big gun had left but no matter what was left, he had a feeling it would all be used before this was over.

Nick was the first to reach Screaming Eagle Boulevard. He started crossing the entrance lane when he noticed a small black object in the white median separating the entrance lane and the exit lane. When he came upon it he immediately recognized it as a gun case; more specifically, Kim's gun case. Before he had time to consider how it ended up here, he detected movement coming from behind their cargo truck.

Nick bent over and placed Danielle on the ground. She turned ran toward her mom. Nick picked up the gun case and slowly made his way across the median. Dropping Jason's club, he raised his hand and turned around to alert the rest of the group to his discovery. He motioned them to stay back as he approached the truck.

Moving slightly to the left so he could come up from behind, he was startled to see a group of three … no four infected hunched down over something between the cargo truck and the fuel truck. The full horror of what was unfolding became apparent when one of the infected, a man in a jogging suit, turned around to face Nick and began to slowly stand up.

It revealed the familiar white polo shirt and faded blue jeans of one Dave Patel; the shirt now torn and covered in blood. Nick froze for a second. The sight of his friend lying on his back, covered in blood, made him want to vomit. Somehow he managed to keep all the junk food he had eaten over the last few days in his stomach. The zombie in the jogging suit now started moving in Nick's direction. The other infected took no apparent interest in him at the moment.

He looked down at the gun case in his hand. He could not remember the combination. Turning around he screamed in Kim's direction.

"Kim! The code."

Kim, still unable to see the other zombies huddled over Dave but could see the one heading directly at Nick, had to think for a second.

"2-3-6-6," she yelled. It was Marcus' father's birthday; February 3rd, 1966.

Nick turned the case so the lock was facing up. He quickly moved his thumbs over the tumblers so that it read 2-3-6-6. The lock clicked and he opened the case revealing the Glock. Grabbing it, he checked to make sure there was a clip in the handle; there was. He grabbed the other two spares and shoved them in his jeans' pockets.

The zombie was no more than five feet from Nick now as it approached the far side of the exit lane. He dropped the case, pulled back on the chamber loading a round, and leveled the weapon at the zombie's head. He pulled the trigger but nothing happened.

"Damn it, the safety," he thought.

He clicked the safety off and took aim again. He stared at the zombie in front of him; arms outstretched and blood dripping from his lips; Dave's blood. He pulled the trigger again, this time the Glock discharged ripping through the zombie's nose and out the back of its skull. It fell with a thud at Nick's feet.

He stepped over the fallen zombie and took aim at the other three hovering over Dave's body. They were now aware of Nick's presence. Each started to get up one by one and turn towards him. He never let any of them get to their feet as he blasted holes in each of their skulls: the last one falling back on top of Dave.

Nick waited a second to make sure they were not getting back up before approaching the back of the truck. He carefully kicked the zombie in the dark green flight suit off of Dave's corpse. He was obviously bitten but was otherwise intact. It must have just happened.

He started to turn away and rejoin Lucy, Kim, and the kids to make sure they were alright when a chilling thought occurred to him. Would Dave turn into one of them? Was he dead? Should Nick make sure he did not … wake up?

He looked down at the Glock in his hand. The butt of the gun was wet with sweat. It felt like it could easily just slip out of his hand. He looked back down at Dave who was just lying there. The sound of gunfire from the other side of the convoy rattled in Nick's brain.

He turned around and pointed to the Humvee at the front of the convoy.

"Lucy, you guys head to the first Humvee and climb inside. Lock the doors and keep your heads down."

Lucy nodded and ushered Kim and the kids toward the Major's Humvee. Jason picked up his father's club. Lucy looked back and met Nick's gaze. He did not have to say anything. She knew Dave was dead; first Emma, now Dave. She was not sure how much more of this she could take.

Nick turned his attention back to his friend lying on the pavement in front of him. His hands began to tremble as it became clear to him what he needed to do. He wiped the sweat from his upper lip with his sleeve as he lowered the gun and pointed it at Dave's head. He double checked to make sure the safety was off.

His concentration was broken by the sound of coughing. He looked around and saw no one. The zombies he had shot earlier were still lying on the ground, as dead as before. When he heard it a second time he stared down at Dave. His body began to twitch and his mouth had moved slightly.

Nick suddenly felt a great sense of relief. His friend was okay. He took a step forward but something told him to be careful. It was the culmination of everything that had happened the last week. Nothing these days was as it seemed. The world he grew up in did not exist anymore.

His suspicions were confirmed when Dave's eyes opened and he turned and looked at Nick. Those were not the eyes of his friend. They were the eyes of the undead. Dave started to rise and was now sitting on the pavement. He started to drool and utter growling sounds.

Nick had seen enough infected that he recognized the symptoms immediately. He again lowered his weapon and aimed it at his friend. He knew the only thing left to do was pull the trigger, but he could not do it.

The thing that used to be Dave stared at Nick as he pointed the gun at it. They both remained motionless for a few seconds. Dave suddenly rose up and lunged as Nick finally pulled the trigger hitting his friend in the side of the head just above the ear. It convulsed once and then was still.

Nick fell to a knee and put his free hand in his face. It was by far the most difficult thing he had ever had to do. It *was* something he had to do he told himself. He was certain, however, that he had never felt worse in his life. His brief moment to mourn his friend was interrupted by Lucy's voice.

"The door won't open!" she yelled from the front of the convoy.

Nick stood up, flipped the safety back on the gun, and jammed it in his waistband.

"*Just as well,*" he thought. He suddenly did not feel safe around the convoy.

Stephen and Corporal Levine headed back toward the lodge, stopping after running about twenty-five yards. They now had a full view of the infected in front of them. There was still almost two dozen left but it appeared no more were coming from the buildings.

Corporal Levine began targeting the nearest zombies as soon as they arrived. Stephen used his axe to take care of any that the Corporal missed. They had a pretty good system working. He found that coming down hard on top of the cranium worked better and more efficiently than attempting to decapitate them.

One zombie had taken a wide route around them and had actually snuck up on them from behind. Corporal Levine had lost sight of him but Stephen caught his arrival out of the corner of his eye. He pivoted quickly and chopped down at an angle catching the zombie just above the left ear. It was enough to knock it down but it still moved. Stephen finished him off with a final blow to the head.

He was about to turn around and continue helping Corporal Levine when he took notice of the arm band the zombie was wearing. It was black with white letters: MP. He was a member of the base's military police. Stephen kicked him over so he was lying on his back. Looking down at his waist he saw what he was looking for, a holster with a sidearm attached.

He bent down quickly and unbuttoned the holster and removed the gun. It was similar to the one Captain Morris showed them how to use at the airfield. He checked for a clip, there was one already loaded. He pulled back on the chamber and heard it click. Finding the safety he flipped it to the off position and took aim at the closest zombie. He pulled the trigger. The gun fired. He was a little surprised by the recoil but it did not affect the accuracy of the shot much because he was at such close range.

Corporal Levine was startled at the sound of gunfire originating so close to him that did not come from his gun. He looked over at Stephen who had a look on his face resembling that of a teenager who just asked the prettiest girl in class out and she actually said yes. Levine just shook his head and went back to removing the skulls of the approaching zombies.

Captain Morris watched from the gunner's cupola as the zombies closed the gap between themselves and the soldiers. The field was littered with fallen bodies but there was still a large group of infected moving toward the convoy.

He was waiting a few more seconds before opening fire with the fifty caliber machine gun. When fired on fully automatic, what the weapon lacked in accuracy it made up for in ferocity. As he gripped the machine gun's handles preparing to fire he thought about Major Bradley. The infected had appeared so suddenly that he never had time to inform the Major.

He switched his comm link to channel four and pushed the button.

"Major Bradley, come in."

He waited for a second but got no response.

"Major Bradley, Come in. Please acknowledge."

There was nothing but silence. Dead silence.

Chapter 31
The Plan

Gunner explained his idea to the Doctor as they crossed Indiana Avenue and traveled along the western side of the road heading south making their way to the back side of the hospital. He said it loud enough for the Major to hear but never spoke directly to him. Dr. Sanderson cleared up any details that the Major missed. The plan, as conceived by Gunner, was fairly straight forward.

Gunner and his team, minus the Doctor, would enter the hospital through the emergency doors which Gunner assumed were around back. This was confirmed when they crossed back over to the eastern side of Indiana Avenue and saw the signs for the emergency entrance. They would make their way up to the third floor and look for a maintenance room or supply closet that likely had an access hatch to the roof. They would find and capture Number 5 and return with him out the same door they entered.

The Major and his men would take up positions behind a small group of trees in a median southwest of the emergency entrance that separated two different parking lots. Their job was to keep the exit clear of infected. The trees were about sixty yards away from the entrance. Close enough for the Major and his group to hit their intended targets but far enough away to not draw a crowd in front of the emergency entrance. It was also the Major's responsibility to ensure Dr. Sanderson's safety. That part of the plan was the only piece communicated directly to him by Gunner.

"I need him alive when I return," Gunner said in no uncertain terms.

The back of the hospital was mostly devoid of infected. The approach to the emergency room door would be easy. The biggest question would be what awaited Gunner and his men once inside the hospital. If the interior of the hospital was as infected as the front, they would have a very difficult time getting in and out alive.

Gunner and his men left the Doctor with the Major and his soldiers at the median and headed for the emergency entrance. They followed the access road in a tight formation; Gunner up front, Mikael and Stefan in the middle, with Ludvig bringing up the rear.

They arrived at the entrance a minute later. There was a circular patch of grass in the middle of a paved area in front which helped create a sort of cul-de-sac. Arriving ambulances could pull up, drop off their patients, and then pull ahead and exit all without turning around. Of which, there was an ambulance parked haphazardly to the far left of the cul-de-sac.

The entrance had a wide berth with an overhead cover that narrowed quickly at the doors. There were large automatic sliding glass doors used to wheel patents on gurneys in and out of the ward. To the left, was a standard door with a lever style handle.

Looking through the glass sliding doors, Gunner could see that the reception area of the ward was free of infected. To the right was a long counter that stretched out of Gunner's sight. To the left was a waiting area with chairs and a water cooler. A few magazines were scattered on a coffee table in the middle of the room and on the floor as well. A wide corridor headed straight back to a set of large white double doors.

Gunner thought of entering through the sliding doors but decided if he opened the doors and could not get them shut it might be too inviting for the locals to come wandering in. He decided on the single door.

Pulling on the handle he was surprised to find it open. As he and his men moved inside he was hoping that was the only surprise awaiting him.

The Major, along with Sergeant Sanchez and Privates Sinclair, Stevens, and Diaz, huddled between a small cluster of trees in the middle of a grass median. It provided a good vantage point to keep an eye on the emergency entrance. To their right was a wide open field that would make it easy to spot any infected coming their way. Behind them was a parking lot that led into Indiana Avenue.

Sanchez was keeping an eye on their six while the Major and Private Stevens had their weapons trained on the emergency doors. Diaz kept watch over the large field and Sinclair's job was to keep the Doctor in his sights at all times.

The Major watched as Gunner and his team entered the hospital. By his calculations it should take them no more than ten minutes to get to the third floor and locate the access hatch. Capturing and returning with an infected person was a little bit more of an unknown. He figured they had about fifteen to twenty minutes of usable daylight left. After that it would be very difficult to see who or what was in front of that entrance.

There were only a few infected on this side of the hospital and they were currently no threat to either the Major or Gunner. He could easily have dispatched them but the sound of the gunfire would most likely attract more infected.

"That Gunner is quite a guy," the Major said to Dr. Sanderson.

"That he is," the Doctor responded. "He is what you might call a necessary evil. I must admit though, he has saved my skin a number of times so far and I never would have made it this far without him."

"He works for you I take it?"

"Actually, he works for Benton Worthington III," replied the Doctor.

"Worthington?! What's *HE* got to do with this?"

"He had been funding my most recent work. I needed him to help me find my missing patient. So he offered his help, his plane, and his muscle."

The Major did a quick scan of the area; there was still no infected to be concerned with. From where they were positioned, it would be unlikely they would be able to see the far side of the roof. Therefore, there was almost no way to track Gunner's progress. One thing was for sure, if Gunner did not come back out, he was not going in after him.

"I've had the pleasure of meeting Worthington on a couple of occasions," the Major said sarcastically. "He's made several trips to D.C. over the last few years lobbying for one thing or another. The kind of money he has can buy a lot of influence."

"I know, I've been to his mountain retreat in Colorado. His money has money," the Doctor responded.

"I wouldn't trust him if I we're you Doctor," the Major warned.

Dr. Sanderson has been worried about that for some time now. After the warning from Captain Bannon and now the Major, it seemed that Benton Worthington III had not earned a great deal of trust from those he has come in contact with. The Doctor's own dealings with him have produced mixed feelings.

If he was able to find a cure or some kind of antidote, he would need help distributing it. He figured Benton with all his connections would be the perfect person. He was now thinking he may need a plan B.

"If by some miracle I am able to develop a cure, I will need some help getting it out to the masses … whatever masses are left," the Doctor said. "Do you think the military would be able to do that?"

"To be honest, I have had little contact with any other military personnel recently. I'm not sure how much of an organized military is left," Major Bradley answered.

"Well, if you think you may be able to help, once we have my patient in custody we'll be heading back to the lab at Mr.

Worthington's estate in Colorado." The Doctor unzipped his knapsack and reached into his bag pulling out a piece of paper.

"Here is the address of his house there; if you can organize someway to deliver whatever I come up with, please help," the Doctor added.

The Major took the piece of paper and looked at it briefly before putting it in his jacket pocket. He was not sure what, if anything, he could do to help. But he felt that the doctor in front of him was confident of his ability to produce some kind of vaccine. Maybe standing in front of him was mankind's only hope.

"I'll see what I can do Doctor," the Major said.

"Major," Sanchez said suddenly, "we've got infected coming in from across the street."

After Gunner and his team had made it all the way inside, he went back and made sure the door did not automatically lock on him. He wanted to be able to open it quickly if needed when they returned. It had not.

Performing a quick scan of the area it appeared to be clean; no one in the reception area, waiting area, or in the hallway. Gunner motioned for his men to head to the large double doors. They stopped just in front of them.

Gunner moved over to the wall and placed his hand over the push button that would normally open the doors automatically. With Ludvig in front and Stefan and Mikael on either side; Gunner pressed the button. Nothing happened.

He did not expect it to work but thought he would give it a shot. It was safer than having to manually open it given they had no idea what was on the other side. They were, however, about to find out.

The doors would likely swing both ways to open. Doctors and nurses pushing patients on gurneys would need to get through those doors quickly. Gunner moved to the center and leaned against the doors and listened. He heard nothing.

He told Stefan to push on the left door, Mikael on the right, as he pushed in the middle. Ludvig stood behind, his automatic rifle ready to take out anything that came through the door.

With the black bag slung around his shoulder, Gunner gave a nod to his associates and they pushed on the doors. They gave way slowly at first. The creaking of the hinges combined with the swoosh of the rubber bottoms echoed in the hallway.

After a few seconds the doors parted revealing the hallway on the other side. Ludvig stood ready to fire upon any infected. As the opening widened, Gunner looked up and saw an empty hallway. He let go of the doors and allowed Stefan and Mikael finish the job. Grabbing his sidearm he raised it to eye level prepared to use it if necessary.

Stefan and Mikael joined Gunner after the doors were completely open; weapons drawn and focused. They moved into the hallway. A triage station was set up to their left. Three separate stations separated by plastic curtains contained hospital beds, medical equipment, and surgical supplies. To the right were doors leading into operating rooms. All areas seemed to be empty. On the far end of the room was another, smaller, set of double doors.

Gunner moved his group slowly down the hallway. They were heading toward the doors at the far end checking each room as they passed. Arriving at the last operating room they were startled as a man in hospital scrubs fell out of the doorway in front of them and landed face first on the tiled hallway floor.

He did not move or attempt to get up. As they all were looking down at the man in scrubs lying on the ground, they did not notice the infected woman standing in the doorway. She stepped over her victim and launched herself at Gunner. He caught the movement out of the corner of his eye and deftly moved out of her way at the last second.

As she passed by him, he shoved her down to the ground with his left hand and took aim at her head with the gun in his right. Before he could get off a round, however, Ludvig lowered his weapon and fired directly into the back of the zombie's skull.

Convinced it was dead, Gunner moved into the operating room to ensure it was empty. He found a collapsible ambulance gurney off to the side as well as the usual items one would expect to find in an operating room. No other infected were visible.

Gunner backed up into the hallway, stepping over the man on the ground, and turned his attention to the smaller double doors in front of him. The emergency room was connected to the main hospital through the doors in front of them. It was on the main roof that their target was last seen. Once through this door, they would have to locate the first set of stairs and get to the third floor as quickly as possible.

Chapter 32
Up On the Roof

Gunner noticed that one of the double doors was slightly ajar. He moved closer to it putting his ear near the gap and listening, he again heard nothing. Weapon drawn, he pushed the door open and stepped through into a small corridor that connected the emergency ward with the main building of the hospital.

The hallway was empty. Gunner instructed his men to move swiftly as they left the hallway and entered an area of the hospital that housed the laboratories. They moved down the narrow hallway looking in each lab window checking for infected. So far, none had been seen.

Gunner was surprised that the interior of the hospital had been, to this point, reasonably empty. He was hoping it would stay that way. After passing the labs, they came to a small nurse's station on their left and a door on their right labeled *STAIRS.*

It was what Gunner was looking for. He assumed that all the stairwells went up to the third floor so this one was as good as any other. He moved to the door and peeked through the rectangular window in the middle; it looked clear. Not taking any chances, Gunner had his men take flanking positions on both sides of the door. Ludvig stayed behind Gunner.

On the count of three he opened the door and went straight to the ground. Stefan charged in and turned facing the stairs heading up. Mikael turned completely around to check their blind spot behind the door. Ludvig positioned himself in the doorway checking straight ahead.

After Gunner gave the all clear signal they quickly climbed the first set of stairs. Using a two by two formation, they cleared the first landing and headed up to the second floor. The door to the second floor was closed. With nothing that would be of interest on that floor, they continued to the landing between the second and third floors.

Looking up, Gunner noticed the third floor door was propped open by a hospital gurney. Moving slower now, they climbed the last set of stairs finally reaching the third floor. At first he did not notice the blood soaked sheet draped across what appeared to be a body. The sun was setting and light inside the building was becoming scarce.

Upon noticing the blood, he trained his handgun on the end of the gurney that was exposed through the door. Gunner instructed Stefan to pull the gurney out of the doorway and onto the third floor landing. After it was completely on the landing Mikael grabbed hold of the bloody sheet and pulled back in one quick motion revealing a mangled body of what appeared to be a middle aged male.

He was best described as partially devoured. Most of his torso and lower left leg were missing. His face was the only feature still somewhat intact. Gunner, holding the open door with his left hand, reactively pulled the trigger of the gun in his right hand and shot the man between the eyes.

The gunshot startled his crew as they did not expect it. Gunner immediately regretted doing it. Regret was an emotion completely unfamiliar to him. He was not even sure why he did it. Noise attracts those things and this poor fellow was half eaten and likely no threat. It must have been that this whole business was finally getting to him. Pushing the gurney to the side he bulled his way through the door and found himself on the third floor of Blanchfield Army Hospital.

Major Bradley turned to see what Sergeant Sanchez was talking about. Two distinct groups of infected were crossing

Indiana Avenue and moving in their direction. Each group had about twenty infected and were separated by thirty yards.

The Major put his index finger to his lips ordering his men to remain silent. There was no indication that either group had seen them yet or was targeting them specifically. He hoped they would just pass on by. He did not want to open fire on infected that were not threatening them or the emergency entrance.

Both groups entered the hospital property at the same time. If they kept moving in the same direction they were currently heading, one would pass on their left side, the other to their right. The Major and his men had moved slightly so they were behind the trees, attempting to use them as camouflage.

The group closest to the hospital started to peel off and head in that direction. The Major briefly considered that good news until he saw why. Coming from around the front of the hospital was another, even larger collection of infected. This new group was, it appeared, led by a zombie with a broken leg and another who was missing his left arm. It looked to the Major as if the smaller group was planning on joining up with the larger group.

This is something that Major Bradley had never noticed before. The infected seemed to be moving in a herd mentality. He considered this for a moment as he thought of how he might use that to his advantage. Nothing immediately came to him so he turned his attention to the other smaller group to his left.

They did not seem, at first, to be interested in joining the party near the hospital. Then all of a sudden the group stopped. The infected in the front of the pack turned and faced the Major. They seemed to look past him as they began moving toward their position.

The Major raised his weapon as his men did the same. The infected were now moving just a few yards ahead of the trees the Major was hiding behind. The group suddenly became agitated and began to break apart. They had detected the Major and his men.

Before the zombies could attack, the Major gave the signal to open fire on them. He grabbed Dr. Sanderson and moved him out of harm's way as the sound of gunfire enveloped them.

There was little the zombies could do. They had spread out and were in an open field. It only took a minute or so and the Major and his men had half of them eliminated.

The Major had run out of ammo and had to replace his clip; he only had two left. His next shot dropped a young woman wearing a pretty blue summer dress. She stumbled and fell on her back directly in front of him. Looking down, his attention was drawn to a small pin attached to the front of her dress. It was blue and white and read: *It's a boy.*

He was frozen for a moment. The image of this woman at a baby shower celebrating and opening gifts from friends and family only to have it interrupted by this madness hit a nerve with him. It made him angry. He wanted to help this woman but he knew, of course, it was too late for her. It was then he decided that he would help this doctor and if he was able to find a cure, he was damn sure going to get it into as many hands as possible.

Refocusing on the current problem, he saw Private Sinclair blow a hole through the last of the zombies. He quickly looked around and saw no further immediate danger. The second group of zombies was farther away now and had just about joined the larger group coming from the front of the hospital.

"Ammo check," the Major ordered.

"Three spares," said Sanchez.

"Two clips," said Diaz

"Two here as well," Sinclair added.

"One left," said Stevens.

The Doctor looked at Major Bradley with his palms up indicating he had no weapon to say nothing of ammunition.

"Not much," thought the Major. The sun had set and they had virtually no light left. He had to assume Gunner was already on the roof, perhaps on his way down. He decided they needed to move. He saw another group of trees on the other side of the field

in front of him. It was much closer to the emergency entrance and away from the approaching horde of zombies.

The new location would make it easier to see and dispatch any zombies in front of the entrance. It would be problematic, however, it the large mass of infected coming around from the front of the hospital decided to follow them.

He decided it was worth the risk.

Gunner and his men were standing at the end of a long hallway. In-patient rooms lined both sides of the corridor. From what he could see most of the doors were closed. He motioned for his men to follow him.

As he walked down the hall he noticed the usual sterile hospital smell. The odd thing was it was how hospitals were supposed to smell. The infected had an odor. He had grown so used to the smell that the lack of odor stood out. It could mean that this floor was clear of infected.

He moved cautiously, however, looking for any indication of a maintenance closet or supply room. Looking in each room as he passed, his original assessment appeared to be correct; no infected in this wing.

They arrived at the end of the hallway and could go left or right. He decided to take a right because the hallway in that direction was significantly shorter. Moving together they passed framed portraits of former department heads and other distinguished personnel mounted on both sides of the wall.

At the end of the hallway they came to a single door that appeared to lead into some administrative offices. He was about to look through the window in the door when he noticed the solid non-descript door to his right. It was slightly ajar with a dim ray of light shining through the crack.

Gunner spread his men apart and indicated he was going to kick the door all the way open. The doorway was narrow and would allow only one man at a time through. Mikael, Gunner decided, was going in first followed by Stefan.

Not wasting time they did not have, he kicked the door open and his men raced in. Once inside, Gunner immediately recognized it as the HVAC room where the heating and air conditioning units on the roof were controlled. It was also clear of infected. An overturned box of filters was strewn across the floor.

Looking straight ahead he saw a series of iron handles protruding out of the cement wall forming a makeshift ladder. The ladder led up to an open hatch that provided access to the roof through which the final bits of sunlight came streaming down into the room.

Gunner stood at the base of the ladder, adjusted the black bag on his shoulder, and started to climb up. Before sticking his head through the opening he stopped to listen. The wind had started to pick up a little bit. He heard the shuffling of feet on the roof but it sounded like it was coming from farther away.

He popped his head through the hatch and quickly scanned the rooftop. In the northwest corner he saw eight to ten infected wondering back and forth as if they were looking for a lost contact lens. Behind them was a zombie simply standing at the edge of the building. He was not moving and had its back to Gunner.

Lifting the bag off his shoulder he placed it on top of the roof and finished climbing the makeshift ladder. Once on the roof he signaled for his men to join him as he turned to see if they had been noticed yet. The infected continued about their business.

Gunner recognized the motionless zombie as their lost test subject, Number 5 as the Doctor referred to him. He was dressed in the familiar hospital scrubs he had seen on the other subjects. Gunner decided they would eliminate all other threats first, then attempt to surround Number 5 and capture him like they practiced the day before.

Stefan, Ludvig, and Mikael had finally made it onto the roof. Gunner spread them out as there were no other infected on the roof except for the ones in front of him. He grabbed the black bag and moved his men forward. As the first zombie turned its head and took notice of them, Gunner had already fired the first shot.

Major Bradley and Dr. Sanderson arrived at the group of trees just to the southeast of the entrance. *"These trees provided better cover than the ones they had just come from,"* thought the Major. He had finished positioning his men so that the entrance was covered and Sanchez was again guarding their rear.

He looked past the emergency entrance all the way to the other side of the hospital just in time to barely make out the large mass of zombies turn the corner and head out toward the open field, not far from where they were recently positioned. He was confident they did not see him and his men make their way over here. It was getting very difficult to see much of anything at all. The wind had started to pick up and clouds were starting to move into the area.

He took a knee and stared at the entrance when he heard gunfire explode from the hospital rooftop. Gunner was on the roof. As he listened carefully he noticed, for the first time, gunfire coming from some distance away. His training and time spent on the battlefield led him to believe it was originating northeast of his position.

The hospital must have been blocking the sound before. Now that the Major was on the other side, he could hear it more clearly. A quick examination of the area confirmed the direction of the sound; it was coming from the convoy.

As the gunfire from the roof continued, the Major's comm link came alive with static and the unmistakable voice of his executive officer, Captain Morris.

"Major Bradley, come in. Please acknowledge."

Chapter 33
Scarecrow

Nick made his way to the front Humvee where Lucy, Kim, and the kids were standing. He instinctively reached to open the door even though Lucy had already tried it.

"It's stuck," Lucy said again.

He nodded and stood there for a second thinking.

"I'll try the other door," he said.

Nick ran around the front of the Major's Humvee and saw for the first time the battle taking place on the other side. It stunned him. The sheer number of infected was alarming. The soldiers were holding their own it appeared based on the number of dead zombies that littered the field between the convoy and the large building on the other side.

The rest of the zombies, nearly one hundred by Nick's estimate, were about twenty-five yards from the line established by the soldiers. They would probably have to fall back in a minute or two and use the vehicles as high ground. He decided that even if the door to the Humvee was open, it was not going to be the safest place in a few minutes.

He ran back around to the other side of the Humvee and rejoined the girls and Jason.

"We can't stay here. There's a shitload of infected over there," he said pointing to the other side of the truck.

He looked around trying to find another safe location. He wanted to get back to help Stephen and the corporal but he felt finding a safe place for Lucy, Kim, and the kids was a priority.

"How about there!" Lucy shouted indicating the small building next to the checkpoint.

"I think that's the visitor's center," Kim added.

There did not seem to be any infected coming out of or heading into the building. It was not that far away and they had a clear path to get there.

"Let's go!" Nick said.

Stephen fired the last bullet from the MP's gun into a zombie wearing a green and yellow apron that read *SUBWAY*. He threw the gun to the ground and grabbed his axe again with both hands.

They had whittled the number of infected down to a few. Corporal Levine took several steps back to regroup as he changed out his last cartridge. Stephen followed dragging the axe behind him.

The Corporal also wanted to get a wider view of the building to see if there were any more problems coming from the either side. Fortunately, there was not. They only had to deal with the ones in front of them.

Stephen raised his axe one more time and waited for the next victim. Corporal Levine, however, never let another get close enough as he dispatched the remaining infected. The last one falling at his feet, its head detaching from its body as it landed.

They gave themselves a second to survey the situation; making sure all the zombies that were lying on the ground were indeed no longer a threat. Stephen stood over a man with a sport coat and dress slacks. He thought he had seen movement. Not wanting to get too close, he poked at it with the end of his axe.

It suddenly reached out its left hand and grabbed Stephen's right ankle. He reacted by chopping down hard with his axe on the left arm of the zombie and removing it at the elbow. He shook his leg vigorously trying to get the arm off his ankle. Finally, it came loose. Realizing his job was not finished; he gripped his axe and proceeded to remove the thing's head just above the shoulders.

"I think we got 'em all," said Corporal Levine.

Stephen said nothing. He was staring down at the stub of an arm lying on the ground next to him. His body ached. He had lost count of how many times he had swung the axe. Shaking off his fatigue, he thought of Nick and the girls; and then Dave, he wondered where the hell Dave was.

Nick and Lucy led the way with Kim and her kids just behind them. They passed the checkpoint and slowed down as they approached the visitor's center. It was located on the north side of Screaming Eagle Boulevard. There was a small employee parking just to the west that contained a few cars.

The building was a small one story structure with handicap parking in the front and regular parking to the east in a long but narrow lot. It had double glass and wood doors. Nick looked through them and saw no movement inside.

They approached slowly, Nick holding Kim's glock in his right hand. Pushing on the door to the right labeled ENTER, Nick entered first with Lucy right behind him. Kim followed holding Danielle's hand tightly as Jason walked in backwards, checking their rear and holding his club out in front of him.

Once inside, Lucy turned around and closed the door tightly behind them. Nick quickly scanned the room. There was an information counter directly in front of them. Brochures littered the countertop. The walls were decorated with murals of helicopters and soldiers. There was a Coke machine just to the left of the door and a snack machine to the right.

Benches lined the wall to the right. To the left was a small open gift shop. It was filled with t-shirts, coffee mugs, books, and other commemorative items. To the right there was a sign directing visitors to the restrooms. The far end of the counter to the left had a partition that could be raised in order for employees to move from behind the counter and onto the floor.

Nick moved to that hinged partition and lifted it up. He moved slowly behind the counter. Looking to the floor he spotted a body lying face down. Startled, he dropped the gun on the floor. The noise did not seem to bother the unidentified body in front of him.

"What is it?" asked Kim.

Nick did not answer immediately; he bent down and picked up the gun. He flipped the safety off and pointed it at the body. Taking a few steps closer, he kicked its feet and then stepped back. Nothing happened.

"Nick," Lucy said impatiently.

"There's a body here. I think it's dead," Nick finally said.

A closer look revealed the mystery guest to be a male; probably thirty-five or so. The darkness made it increasingly difficult to see. There was blood near the head but not a lot of it. Nick was not sure what to do. As he saw with Dave, this guy might suddenly sit up and look at him. He needed to be sure, especially if was leaving the girls here.

He was, however, concerned with the noise the gun would make. Looking over the counter he surveyed the visitor's center. He thought he spotted something that might work. Heading back through the partition and onto the floor he went into the gift shop.

He grabbed a commemorative pillow and accompanying blanket. Lucy watched him as he went back behind the counter. He placed the blanket on top on the counter and stepped to the front of the body near the head. Hunching down he placed the pillow just above the head. Placing the barrel of the gun up against the other side of the pillow he steadied himself. Counting to three he pulled the trigger. The pillow exploded but did muffle the sound quite a bit. It was still loud but probably would not have been heard outside of the building.

Standing back up he grabbed the blanket and covered the body. He shoved the gun back into his waist as he moved back to where the unfortunate man's feet were, lifted both up and began to drag him to the lobby floor. He lifted the partition and started to move when he stopped and turned to Kim.

"Um … Kim you might want to …" he said as he glanced down at the kids.

"Yes, thanks," she replied turning her kids away from the counter to look out into the night through the front doors.

Nick dragged the body around the front of the counter and headed toward the bathrooms. There was some blood but the blanket had caught most of it. He arrived at the bathrooms; the men's room to the left, ladies to the right. He dropped the corpse's feet and drew his gun again.

Remembering the rest area in Virginia and the frightening experience there, he entered the men's room carefully. It was a small one person and at the moment, Nick was the only one there. It was the same in the ladies room. He dragged the dead body into the men's room.

A check of the remaining areas found nothing of immediate concern. There was a back door near a small office. He found a maintenance closet where he stole a broom and headed back to the information counter where Lucy and Kim were still standing.

"This place is safe for the moment," Nick said. "Try to stay out of sight."

He turned to Jason.

"You're the man of the house; keep your mom and sister safe."

"Okay," Jason said looking up at his mom.

Nick handed the broom, an industrial style with a thick handle and a long rectangular bottom, to Lucy.

"Put this through the handles of the front doors when I leave. It may not keep them out but it'll slow them down. Oh, there's a back door that locks from the inside. If they're coming through the front door, use the back one to escape," Nick said.

"Thanks," Lucy said.

If he stayed another minute he might not have wanted to leave. So, with nothing else to really say he nodded nervously and headed for the front doors; he was about to open them when he turned back around.

"One last thing, if you need to use the bathroom, use the ladies room … that includes you Jason."

Without waiting for a response, he opened the door and went out into the twilight in search of Stephen.

Captain Morris stood in the gunner's cupola trying desperately to contact Major Bradley. He began to fear the worst after several attempts went unanswered.

He was staring out onto a large open field with bodies and body parts strewn about like so much trash. His men were doing a great job but were getting dangerously low on ammo. They would soon need to retreat back to the convoy and use it as defilade. He was also worried about the quickly fading daylight.

He was about to switch back to channel two and communicate his instructions to the men when he heard his comm link crackle. A second later, Major Bradley's voice was heard coming through a fair amount of static.

"Bradley, over."

"Major, we are currently engaging nearly a hundred infected and have killed as many, maybe more. Convoy secure for the moment, over," Captain Morris responded.

"Casualties? Over."

"None, over."

"Good work Captain. We are currently assisting the group we saw land that plane earlier. I will explain when I return, over."

"ETA, over."

"Unknown at this time, over."

"Copy, I will keep you posted, over and out."

Captain Morris switched his comm link back to channel two and spoke quickly.

"Listen up, I need all personnel to gear up and fall back to the convoy. Take elevated positions and prepare for hand to hand."

He looked down as the men began to retreat to the convoy opening up a wide berth for the Captain to unleash the fifty caliber.

Nick stood in front of the visitor's center, it was that time of the day after the sun goes down but the moon and stars have yet to achieve full luster. He looked back to the convoy and thought it now seemed awfully far away and where he last saw Stephen and the corporal was even farther.

He was suddenly exhausted. He was not in the physical shape that Stephen, as a football player, was. He was a history major, not a lot of call for physical activity.

Looking south just past the entrance, he noticed something for the first time. It was probably because it was now dark enough to more easily make out. He spotted headlights. The thought of driving back to Stephen was very appealing. He might even be able to take out a few of those things along the way.

Moving out of the parking lot he crossed the very eastern end of Screaming Eagle Boulevard and made his way to Route 41. Turning right he got a closer look at the headlights and more importantly the vehicle they were attached to. It was a very old red pick-up truck. The engine was still running which would mean the keys were in it. The driver's side door was also wide open.

Piled high in the truck bed were bales of hay. A few were spilled on to the road. It appeared that the truck had come to a sudden stop and the driver fled out of the driver's seat. Of which, there was no driver in sight.

Nick approached the truck moving to the driver's side. He peered around the open door as he reached into his waistband to remove the Glock. He jumped around the door and pointed the gun at the front seat which was empty. As was the passenger's seat.

He relaxed for a moment and looked behind the seats. There was nothing but an old rope and a red gas can. He started to get into the truck when he heard a rustling noise coming from the back of it. He hesitated and then backed away from the door and took a step toward the truck bed.

Emerging from the bales of hay were two infected. They were both dressed in overalls and a plaid shirt. A large floppy farmer's hat sat atop one of them. Hay protruded out from everywhere. They looked like two undead scarecrows. They were having trouble moving as it seemed their legs were stuck, sandwiched between bales of hay.

Nick raised his gun and aimed it at the zombie in the hat. He was startled when he heard a voice coming from behind him. Turning around he saw a figure coming into view out of a few trees that lined the side of the road.

"Don't waste your ammo, kid," said Chester Boone.

"Use this," he added.

Chester threw a red road flair at Nick. He reached for it instinctively and caught it.

"Take the top off, strike the flair with it, and toss it in the truck bed … then run like hell," Chester instructed.

Nick did as he was told. He removed the cap and struck the flair once, then twice. It finally lit on the third try. He reached back and threw the burning flair into the truck. The dry hay and the gentle breeze created a quick firestorm. The back of the truck was quickly ablaze.

The zombies succumbed to the flames rapidly as they flailed their arms violently but to no avail. The heat became unbearable, as Nick turned and ran.

He was right behind Chester as they bolted up Screaming Eagle Boulevard. Nick found his second wind as they crossed the median and passed by the checkpoint. He could not resist the urge to turn around and look back. He slowed down and looked just in time to see the truck explode into a giant fireball that illuminated the convoy and the field next to it along with the dead bodies of the infected.

Chapter 34
Finally

Gunner pulled the trigger on his Walther P99 only to hear the click of an empty chamber. He did not have time to replace it with another cartridge so he bent down and retrieved his throwing knife beneath his pant leg. With surprising speed and uncanny accuracy he flipped the knife underhand connecting with the approaching zombie's left eye. It fell to one knee then collapsed onto its back.

He moved forward a couple of steps and bent down. Grabbing hold of the handle he pushed the knife in a little further and twisted slightly before removing it. He wiped the blade clean using the dead zombie's own shirt before sheathing it in his ankle holster. He now had a second to replace the empty clip.

Gunner and his men were now alone on the roof with the Doctor's test subject. He dropped to a knee and placed the black bag on the ground. He unzipped it, removed the restraints and distributed them as before. He stood back up leaving the bag right where it was and extended the pole with the rope on the end.

Their quarry was still standing in virtually the same spot as when they had first arrived. He had turned around, however, when Gunner and his men started shooting and just stood and watched. He did not try to run or attack, he just stood there.

He was now about fifteen feet from Gunner and looking directly at him. Gunner thought he had an almost quizzical look on his face. As if he was surprised that the other infected on the roof had failed to halt Gunner and his men from advancing. Speaking of his face; it was subject to the typical deformities that he had seen on other zombies he had come in contact with, only not as severe. He retained and almost human appearance.

All of that was interesting but not relevant to why Gunner was standing on this roof. His job was to capture and bring this thing back in one piece and that was exactly what he was going to do.

He approached the test subject with the pole in his hands. Ludvig followed behind with the leg irons, Stefan with the hand cuffs, and Mikael with the muzzle. Number 5 began to move to his right, shuffling along the edge of the roof. Gunner instructed Mikael to move further to the left and cut off what appeared to be an escape attempt.

Number 5 noticed this and stopped in his tracks. Looking back toward where he had just come from he saw Stefan approaching. He gazed down at the roof for a second before raising his head and staring directly at Gunner who was now only six feet away. Turning his head he glanced down behind him, over the side of the roof and onto the ground below. Looking up again he offered what could practically be called a smile.

Gunner sensed trouble. He was less than five feet away when he charged forward, pole outstretched, just as Number 5 took one step off the roof. He began to fall backwards as Gunner loosened the noose and lowered it quickly over Number 5's head. Both feet were now off the ground as Number 5 began to tumble off the roof.

Gunner was able to apply the lasso and tighten it just as Number 5 started to free-fall off the rooftop. The weight of the test subject falling would have likely either pulled Gunner off the roof with him or separated the head from the rest of its body if not for Stefan arriving just in time.

Reaching down Stefan was able to stop him from falling by grabbing Number 5's left arm. This, combined with Gunner pulling him back up onto the roof, stabilized everyone for the moment. Gunner then used his considerable strength to pull his target back onto the roof. He tightened the lasso even more and pulled forward attempting to get Number 5 away from the edge once he had him back on the roof. Stefan moved behind the zombie as Gunner moved him forward. He reached for the left hand and applied the first hand cuff.

Number 5 seemed to regroup quickly as he suddenly swung his left hand violently, knocking Stefan off balance. As Gunner tried to regain control, Stefan's right foot slipped on the slick surface of the roof. He tumbled backwards, his momentum carrying him away from the zombie, as he went head over heels off the side of the roof.

The three story fall ended on a patch of grass on the northwest corner of the property. Stefan likely had broken a rib or an arm or worse, but unfortunately that would not matter. The front of the hospital was still full of infected despite the large group that had moved around to the rear. It was only a matter of seconds before they were on top of Stefan. He did not stand a chance.

Gunner pulled with all his might and hauled the test subject forward and finally down to the ground. It continued to thrash about and attempted to get back up. Ludvig came up from behind and plowed his left knee into the small of the zombie's back. Gunner moved forward a foot or two so he was directly on top of the zombie and pushed down hard on the pole trying to keep the creature as still as possible.

Ludvig, leaning down over the zombie's feet, applied the leg restraints; the left leg first then the right. He then stood up and turned around facing Gunner then reached down and grabbed the hand cuffs attached to the zombie's left hand. He found the right hand pinned under the zombie's body. He pulled it out and wrapped it behind its back locking the two wrists together.

With the patient secure, Mikael carefully lifted its head up by grabbing the hair and pulling. He placed the muzzle over the mouth and secured it by pulling the strap on the back of the head. He moved quickly away and let Gunner get the zombie to its feet.

It continued to struggle but with its hands bound and feet chained together it was useless. Gunner used the pole as leverage to push the zombie up. Once on its feet, Gunner moved behind it and pushed forward. There was enough slack in the chains so that the zombie could shuffle along.

Ludvig retrieved the black bag and grabbed the last of the ammo. He zipped it back up and threw it down the hole in the roof and then climbed down. Gunner and Mikael stayed on the roof.

Mikael lifted the zombie's feet and lowered it through the opening as Gunner steadied it. Ludvig grabbed the legs as Mikael fed Number 5 through the hole. Once through the hatch and on the ground, Ludvig moved the zombie out of the way so that Gunner and Mikael could come down.

The room was now in almost complete darkness. Moonlight provided the only illumination. Gunner was concerned about the hallways that did not have windows. It would be too dark to see where they were going to say nothing of additional zombies. The trip up was relatively free of trouble but he could not be certain about the trip down.

Gunner realized at that moment that he really did not have an exit strategy. When Mr. Worthington handed him this assignment he barely had enough time to gather weapons and the restraining gear. After getting his team together he met him at the plane and then they were in the air.

He handed Mikael the pole as he took point leaving the HVAC room. He grabbed the black bag and slung it over his shoulder. Just as he was about to open the door he noticed something in the corner of the room that had been behind the door when they originally entered. He moved closer and discovered a flashlight standing lens down on top of a small step stool.

He reached down and grabbed it. Flipping the switch and hoping for the best he was pleased to see the room light up. He instructed Ludvig to follow behind Mikael and the zombie as he reached again for the door handle.

Major Bradley clicked off his comm link and turned to his men.

"The convoy is under attack. Captain Morris said they are currently holding their own and reported no casualties," he said.

"As soon as Gunner comes out of the hospital with your patient, we're needed back with my unit ASAP," Major Bradley said to Dr. Sanderson.

"Understood," the Doctor replied; adding, "I appreciate your help."

The Major turned his attention back to the horde of zombies that had now reached the back side of the hospital. They had originally made their way to the trees that he and his men previously occupied. Finding nothing of interest there, they now were heading toward the emergency room entrance.

Major Bradley estimated the enemy number to be at about seventy-five. A quick mental inventory put their ammunition count at several hundred rounds and they still had to get back to the convoy. Gunner had better show himself soon or things were going to get interesting.

Gunner and what was now left of his team had reached the door to the stairs with no problems. The third floor still seemed to be empty. He reached for the handle and pulled it open directing Mikael to go through first who shoved the prisoner out in front just in case.

As before, the stairwell was clear except for the blood stained gurney containing the dead male with the rather large hole in its head courtesy of Gunner. He shone the flashlight down the stairs. There was nothing to see.

The stairwell echoed with their footsteps as they passed the second floor and ended up on the first floor landing again. Gunner looked through the rectangular window out into the hallway. Shining the flashlight did not help much as he could see very little.

He opened the door, held it with his foot as he reached for his sidearm. Mikael again was first with Number 5 out in front. With everyone through the door, they turned left and headed down the dark hallway toward the labs.

Gunner stopped suddenly as he saw a glare bounce back at him like a deer's eyes in headlights. He saw another pair of eyes and then another. Moving the flashlight back and forth he saw four pair of eyes staring back at him. They were coming out of the labs. He became more aware of the shuffling feet and low moans of the infected. Number 5 became more agitated.

It actually sounded like more than four but that was all he could see at the moment. He leveled his pistol at the nearest zombie and pulled the trigger. The muzzle flash further illuminated the area for a split second. Long enough for Gunner to see that his suspicions were correct; there was more than four infected here. He could not be sure how many but he knew they had to get out of there immediately.

Taking the lead, he moved quickly past the labs with Mikael and Number 5 in the middle and Ludvig covering the rear. Ludvig began to open fire as well and took down several zombies of his own. Gunner fired once more clearing a path to the small double doors that led to triage.

He pushed through the doors with the flashlight in his left hand, gun in his right. Once in triage, the flashlight revealed a man in hospital scrubs staring back at him. Only he was no longer a man and was no longer lying on the floor where Gunner had left him twenty minutes ago.

He cursed himself for being sloppy. He had been so distracted earlier by the female zombie that lunged at him that he ignored the threat lying on the floor in front of him. He was not about to make the same mistake twice. Leveling the gun at the zombie's head he put a bullet in its left eye. He stepped over the body as he headed for the larger double doors.

The zombies in the lab were following them into triage. Gunner looked briefly behind him to ensure Mikael and Ludvig were with him. They were.

The large double doors were still open from when they had come through earlier. He moved into the reception area where it was not quite as dark. He could see well enough without the aid of the flashlight. Mikael followed with Number 5.

"Stänga dessa dörrar!" Gunner screamed at Ludvig.

Ludvig slung his semi-automatic over his shoulder as he reached out and began pulling the doors closed. The first of the infected had already pushed their way through the small double doors and were in the connecting hallway.

He struggled at first but it soon became easier as he pulled them shut. He managed to get the doors closed just as the zombies were about an arm's length from Ludvig. He felt them barrel into the door pushing hard. Fortunately, the zombies were not intelligent enough to try and pull the doors open.

Gunner stood in the middle of the reception area and turned around.

"Hålla dem utanför här!" he said to Ludvig.

Ludvig turned and braced himself against the door removing his weapon and holding it in front of him. He was pushing back with his lower body as his feet tried to gain traction. He could feel their numbers growing on the other side.

Gunner had to think and think fast. He needed to get his team out of there and Number 5 to the plane. An idea formed rapidly in his head. He charged forward heading to the sliding glass doors. He put his fingers between them and with a heave tried to pull them apart. He managed to separate them an inch and then two. Once he had them apart about two and a half feet he wedged his massive frame between the doors. With his back against one door and his feet against the other, he pushed. A few seconds later he had the doors open wide enough for his purposes and ran out into the night.

Gunner turned right and ran to the ambulance. He tried opening the driver's side door and to his surprise it opened. He felt for the ignition and found it empty. He flipped the visor down only to have several folded pieces of paper fall onto the driver's seat. Using the flashlight he searched the floor and the console but found no keys.

He ran around to the back of the ambulance but before he got there he noticed the dark shadows crossing the field in front of him heading in his direction. Infected; lots of them. He looked in the direction where he had left the Doctor and did not see him or the Major. It was dark so they may have been hiding behind the trees. He would deal with that later.

He opened the back of the ambulance and saw what it was he needed; the collapsible gurney. He grabbed it and lowered it onto the pavement extending the legs. He got behind one end and started pushing it into the reception area. It was then he noticed the Doctor along with the Major and his men. They were crouched behind some trees on the other side of the entrance. The Major and his men had their weapons trained on the approaching zombies. He nodded at the Doctor who responded the same.

Gunner pushed the gurney inside. He saw that Ludvig had managed to keep the zombies from coming through so far. Mikael had Number 5 under control. He stopped just in front of Mikael and lifted the zombie's feet up as Mikael grabbed it by the shoulders. Lifting up, they placed him on the gurney.

"Spänn fast honom i och ta sedan bort selen," Gunner said.

Before waiting for a response he went around the reception counter and began looking for a small box likely attached to the wall. He started searching at eye level and was unable to find what he was looking for. Lowering his sight line, he spotted a small square box tucked in the corner under the reception counter.

He reached for it and tried to open pull it open. It was locked by a small luggage style lock. He pulled his gun and fired shattering the lock and sending shards of plaster flying. He opened the box and saw a dozen or more keys. None of them were labeled. There was, however, a legend on the door. He scanned down the list until he reached key number seven which read *Ambulance.* He grabbed it but also looked to make sure there was not another ambulance key. There was another one labeled number eleven but it was missing. It must have been out on a job when all this shit went down.

Moving back around to lobby, he saw that Mikael had finished strapping Number 5 onto the gurney and was removing the noose. Gunner ran back outside. Hopping into the ambulance's driver's seat and shutting the door, he put the key into the ignition and turned. He could hotwire the ambulance if necessary but was fighting the clock. The engine roared to life.

Gunner put it in reverse and backed up to the sliding glass doors leaving enough room to close the doors in the back of the ambulance. He shifted into park and flew out of the driver's seat. As he ran in the building, he yelled over to the Doctor.

"Doctor, please get in the back with your patient!"

Dr. Sanderson stood up but was confused as he had not yet seen his patient being loaded into the ambulance but did as he was told again thanking the Major and his men and reminding him that he still might need his help. He moved from behind the trees and made his way to the rear of the vehicle.

Gunner grabbed the front of the gurney and lifted it up at the same time collapsing the wheels. Mikael lifted up from behind as they shoved the gurney into the back of the ambulance. Dr. Sanderson squeezed between the open ambulance door and the sliding glass door.

"We need to hurry, there's infected on the way," Dr. Sanderson stated.

Ignoring him, Gunner turned to Mikael and told him to get in the passenger's side. The Doctor climbed into the patient compartment as Gunner slammed the doors behind him. He made sure the latch was secure as he turned around just in time to see the large double doors Ludvig was pressed up against give way. The doors fell on top of him as dozens or more zombies poured into the reception area.

There was nothing Gunner could do. Ludvig was as good as dead. The infected headed straight for the ambulance.

Gunner turned and ran for the driver's side and jumped in, closing the door tightly. He pulled the gearshift down into drive and hit the accelerator. He peeled out traveling along the service road towards Indiana Avenue. He soon realized the ambulance's headlights were not on. Finding the knob, he turned them on revealing more clearly the mass of zombies converging on them.

Most were on either side of the road but a few had ventured onto the pavement. Gunner tried to avoid them but as he was in no mood, he clipped a couple, but was soon turning right onto Indiana Avenue heading back to the plane.

Major Bradley thought about taking out a few of the zombies in the ambulance's path until he saw the pack of infected emerging from the emergency room entrance. No sense drawing unwanted attention. He retreated back to the cover of the trees.

He turned to look behind them and saw they were all clear. They had to get back to the convoy as soon as possible.

"We are heading back to the convoy double time. Don't stop for anything. Avoid them if possible; blast your way through if necessary," he said to his men.

Major Bradley changed the channel on his comm link.

"Captain Morris, we're en-route to your position."

Dr. Sanderson sat on one on the cushioned benches that ran along either side of the cab. He looked down at his patient. Test subject Number 5. The last time he was this close to him he looked much different. The former Richard Kimbro's family had entrusted Dr. Sanderson to help him.

As he sat there now, contemplating what could have been, he noticed the calm that that had taken over his former patient. He just lay there in a peaceful state. If one did not know better one would assume he was sleeping. That is until he abruptly opened his eyes and stared menacingly at the Doctor.

Chapter 35
Next

Major Bradley led his men down a stone pathway that ended at the southeast side of the building. They were now on the other side of the same group of trees they had cleared of infected nearly a half an hour ago. Just ahead was the main parking lot on the east side of the building.

There was a few infected roaming the mostly empty lot but they would be able to avoid them easily enough. They traversed the parking lot and crossed the eastern spike of Joel Drive. Running across a small grass partition they ended up on Bastogne Ave.

It was now dark and their only light source was the moon and the few stars poking through the increasing clouds. The Major was not exactly sure the fastest way back but he knew they were close. The sound of gunfire was getting louder. They had definitely taken a shorter path back.

He decided to take a left and then a right cutting through a large asphalt lot that until recently held older Blackhawk helicopters used for training. The pads were currently empty. Moving quickly, they came to South Carolina Avenue. Looking to his left the Major could make out the rear of the army training center. His convoy was on the other side.

"We're going to head north along this road," the Major said to his men.

"Try not to cross over to the other side. When we get past the training center, we don't want to be in way of possible friendly fire," he added.

His men nodded and they took off down the avenue. The gunfire had become louder but also less frequent. That meant that Captain Morris had either eliminated the threat or they were running out of ammo. It was, however, the explosion they heard coming from that direction that quickened their pace even more.

Captain Morris had emptied the big gun and concluded his efforts had mixed results. The fifty-caliber had ripped through most of the remaining zombies but many were still crawling around because he did not hit them in the head. The infected that remained standing were nearly upon the convoy.

His men had retreated to the trucks as ordered and were now standing on top of the vehicles or the running boards to gain a tactical advantage. Some had run out of ammo; those that still were packing used what they had left sparingly.

He climbed down out of the gunner's cupola and moved to the backside of the convoy just in time to see Corporal Levine and Stephen run up alongside the Humvee. They both stopped in front the Captain. The first thing Morris noticed was that Stephen was drenched in sweat, his shirt and jeans were covered in what he assumed was zombie blood. The axe, hanging limply by his side, was dripping with blood and zombie parts.

"The lodge is clear for the moment Captain," Corporal Levine said.

"Well done Corporal … and you as well young man," Morris replied.

"Get yourselves on top of that Humvee and if you have any ammo left, take out the rest of these bastards. Major Bradley is en-route."

Their attention was suddenly shifted to the eastern end of Screaming Eagle Boulevard as a large explosion lit up the night sky. Stephen noticed two people running as fast as they could heading west up the road toward the convoy. He immediately recognized his good friend Nick but had trouble making out the other person.

Captain Morris had no such problem.

"Looks like we've located Mr. Boone," Morris said adding, "why is it every time I see this man something blows up?"

Stephen thought about heading to the cargo truck and see about Dave but decided to head toward Nick and Chester while Corporal Levine followed the Captain's orders and began climbing onto the Humvee. As Stephen closed the distance he wondered where Lucy was.

Captain Morris ran along the backside of the convoy checking the deployment of the men and assessing the ammo situation. It seemed that about half were out. He could hear the other half taking pot shots at the remaining zombies.

Specialist Sinclair had jumped onto the wheel well of the fuel truck and was busy plunging his combat knife into the skull of a zombie. It appeared they had reached the convoy. There was only a dozen or so still standing. The Captain felt pretty good about getting out of this mess with no casualties.

As he turned and headed back the other way his head was down and he noticed the dead bodies strewn about behind the cargo truck. He instinctively pulled his weapon and aimed it at the pile of flesh on the ground. There was no movement from the zombies. He relaxed and took a step forward.

The one on top, lying on its side, looked familiar. It was dark out and difficult to see but he moved a little closer to get a better look. It was one of those kids.

"Dave, I think. Where the hell did these infected come from?"

Lucy, Kim, Danielle, and Jason were hunched down behind the information counter, not far from where Nick shot the zombie and then dragged it to the men's room. They could hear the gunfire outside but it was unsettlingly quiet in the visitor's center.

Lucy poked her head up every few minutes to look at the door to see if anyone, or anything, was there; nothing yet. Jason stood ready with his club, just in case.

Lucy looked over at Kim and thought she noticed a single tear roll down her cheek. It was dark and difficult to see but she was sure of what she saw. Kim glanced over and caught Lucy looking at her.

"You alright?" Lucy asked.

Kim raised her right hand and wiped away the tear. She was hoping her kids did not notice her crying.

"Yea, I'm fine," she said. "I was just thinking that today is … or would have been … Marcus and I's anniversary. At least I'm pretty sure it's today. With all that's happened I've kind of lost track."

"How many years?" Lucy asked.

"Would have been twelve this year," Kim answered.

"A June bride, huh," Lucy said.

"It was actually the only thing I insisted on. My mom was married in June, as was my grandmother. At the time, it seemed very important to me …" Kim said, her voice trailing off.

They were all startled by the big explosion. It sounded like it came from the parking lot. Lucy looked up one more time but could see nothing. She moved out from behind the counter and headed toward the door.

"Be careful," Kim warned.

Lucy nodded and continued on to the door. She looked out and saw red and yellow flames shooting up in the sky from the road just outside the base. She could not see exactly what was on fire. She hoped Nick was okay but deep inside she knew he was somehow involved.

She started to move back to the counter when she caught movement out of the corner of her eye. Someone was moving around the corner of the building making its way to front doors. Lucy could tell it was an infected person.

She did not want to risk being seen heading back to the others. She quickly moved behind the Coke machine, making herself as thin as possible. Kim popped her head up from behind the counter and saw the panic in Lucy's eyes.

Lucy put her index finger to her lips with one hand and motioned her to get down with the other. The zombie moved slowly, dragging one of its feet behind the other. She hoped it would just move past the entrance and keep going.

Unfortunately, it stopped in front of the doors. It began to jerk its head back and forth and stare through the glass. It staggered forward only to be stopped by the door. More specifically, the broom handle in the door.

Lucy looked around for anything she might be able to use as a weapon. She saw nothing useful within her immediate grasp. She really wished she had Jason's golf club. The zombie was getting agitated, if that was possible. It kept hurling itself at the door. The broom handle held each time.

She knew, however, it was only a matter of time, especially if any of its friends showed up. She also realized that hiding behind the Coke machine was not doing any good because it obviously sensed they were inside. She decided to head back behind the counter and get Jason's club. They were not going to have time to use the back door. Who knew what would be waiting for them on the other side anyway?

She left the concealment of the Coke machine and made it to the counter just as the sound of the broom handle cracking echoed throughout the visitor's center.

Major Bradley and his men followed South Carolina Avenue past the army training center. Up ahead, to the right, he could see the convoy and was greatly relieved to discover it was not the source of the explosion. Turning right he cut across the northwest corner of the open field now covered with dead zombies.

He stopped and briefly surveyed the situation he saw before him. The rest of his men appeared to have fallen back and were using the convoy as cover. There had to be over two hundred zombies scattered across an otherwise beautiful grass field. Most were still but several were moving; crawling around on the ground. A few stragglers were approaching the trucks.

He pressed his comm link.

"Captain Morris, your location?" he said.

Stephen met Nick and Chester about halfway between the convoy and Route 41. Nick was out of breath and had slouched over putting his hands on his knees. Chester stood there with his backpack on his shoulder and his shotgun in his right hand.

"What the hell happened to you?" Nick asked, staring at the zombie blood covering most of Stephen's clothing.

"Infected don't kill themselves," Stephen said.

Turning to Chester he said, "Mr. Boone."

Chester nodded but seemed preoccupied.

"Captain said the Major is on his way back, we may be getting outta here soon," Stephen said.

Upon hearing that news Chester mumbled he had something to take care of and he would meet them back at the convoy then took off.

"Doesn't like to stick around much that one," Nick said.

"Where is Lucy?" Stephen asked.

"The convoy wasn't safe so I sequestered them in the visitor's center over there," Nick answered, pointing.

"Kim and the kids?"

"Also there."

"I'm pretty sure I saw infected coming out of there earlier," Stephen said. "It looked like they were headed toward the convoy."

"That must be where they came from," Nick muttered to himself.

"What?"

"Dave," Nick said, "he didn't make it. I found him … he was one of those things … I had no choice."

Stephen took a second to absorb what Nick was telling him. He should have been shocked and paralyzed with grief but after what he and the rest of them had been through this last week, he moved quickly to acceptance. It was a byproduct of the new world they found themselves in.

"The girls," he said and took off for the visitor's center.

Lucy grabbed the golf club from Jason.

"I'll give it back," she said.

She stood back up just as the broom handle gave way and the zombie nearly fell forward as it charged into the room. She cocked the club behind her ear and waited for it to come close enough to whack it on the side of the head.

It regained its balance, sort of, and started moving forward again. It quickly spotted Lucy standing behind the counter. She stayed there to provide herself some protection.

When the zombie arrived at the counter it reached over, attempting to grab Lucy. With all her might she whipped the club around and landed a serious blow to the side of its head. It staggered back but came forward a second later. A second and a third blow to the head landed the zombie on the ground.

Lucy came around the counter and told Kim to grab her children. They were about to turn the corner and run out the door when Stephen and Nick came bursting into the room.

"Come here!" Stephen yelled to Kim.

She corralled her kids and ushered them forward, meeting Stephen at the door.

Nick saw the sprawled out zombie on the floor trying to get back up. Lucy stood there hovering over it, holding Jason's club ready to take another whack.

Nick grabbed the Glock out of his waistband and without hesitation blew the zombie's head clean off. Lucy had mashed it pretty good, Nick just finished the job.

"Let's go," Nick said.

They ran out of the visitor's center meeting up with Stephen and Kim in the parking lot. Looking around Nick saw no other zombie's. They stopped for a second to regroup.

"The Major should be back by now, we need to get back to the convoy," Stephen said.

They all nodded and started off in that direction. Lucy wiped the golf club clean on a nearby patch of grass and handed the club back to Jason.

"There you go, as promised," she said trying to muster a smile.

The Major had found Captain Morris next to the cargo truck. The rest of the zombies had been neutralized. There was no more immediate threat and the Captain had ordered Privates Benson and Adams to move infected blocking any of the vehicles.

"Captain, we are very low on ammo. Have the men quickly search the zombies for any military personnel. Remove any weapons or ammo they find and bring it to the cargo truck. I noticed some of them are still moving, so make sure they're dead before you search 'em," the Major said.

"Yes sir."

Fifteen minutes later they had rounded up twelve handguns and a few extra rounds of ammo but overall it was a disappointing haul. Stephen, Nick, Lucy, and Kim had crawled back into the cargo truck. It seemed a little larger without Dave. Everyone was quiet as Sergeant Sanchez hopped into the back with them.

Major Bradley and Captain Morris stood in front of the Major's Humvee. Some more infected had started wondering into the area drawn by the gunfire or the explosion or both. It was time to head out.

"All personnel accounted for Major, we're ready to move out," Morris said.

Major Bradley took a deep breath and exhaled. He would tell Captain Morris about his conversation with the doctor later. Right now he needed to get his men away from here.

"Where to next?" Captain Morris asked.

"Where to next indeed, Captain."

As the Cargo truck lurched forward everyone was sitting quietly, immersed in their own thoughts. They were startled when Chester jumped into the moving vehicle and was almost shot by Sergeant Sanchez.

The ambulance weaved between zombies as it traveled down Indiana Avenue. Gunner had no interest in hitting any of them as it would only slow him down. He was using both lanes and traveling much faster than he probably should be.

As he neared the end of the road he grabbed his walkie and pushed the button.

"Come in Captain, over."

"Bannon, over."

"We're three minutes out. Will be arriving in an ambulance. Is the coast clear? Over," Gunner asked.

"Area is free of infected, plane is ready for takeoff, over."

"Copy, over and out."

Number 5 had been staring at the Doctor since leaving the hospital but had not moved or tried to get up. Not that he would have been able to anyway, he was handcuffed and strapped down tight to the gurney. It seemed to Dr. Sanderson that Number 5 *knew* that it was useless to struggle; but that was not possible, was it?

Gunner pulled the ambulance alongside the Gulfstream with a screeching halt. He and Mikael hopped out of the cab and met at the back door. Opening the latch, they helped the Doctor out of the back and grabbed the gurney.

Gunner had been thinking of how they would transport the prisoner once they got to the plane. About halfway there, it came to him. They extended the legs and rolled him to the cargo hold. Opening it up, they lifted Number 5, gurney and all, and slid it into the hold. A perfect fit.

Captain Bannon watched from the top of the stairs. The first thing he noticed after the zombie was loaded into the cargo hold, was that they were two people short.

"This business has gotten very dangerous," he thought to himself.

Dr. Sanderson walked up the stairs and passed the Captain offering only a nod. He slipped off his knapsack and settled into his seat, buckling up as usual. A minute later Gunner came up the stairs followed by the only remaining member of his team. He spoke quietly to Captain Bannon for a few seconds and then headed to the rear of the cabin.

The Doctor leaned his head back and stared at the cabin ceiling. He figured Gunner would think of this as the end of a long, dangerous mission. To the Doctor, however, it was actually just the beginning.

23 Days Later

Chapter 36
A Safe Place

Nick set his meal tray down on the table with a thud and then pulled his chair out, landing heavily into it next to Stephen. The others at the table looked up from their conversations. Stephen and Lucy sat on one side of the table while Kim and her kids were seated on the other.

"Seconds, Nick? You know they have a strict food rationing rule here. You are gonna get in trouble if you keep doing this," said Stephen shaking his head.

"What? I can't help it that the blonde behind the serving line has a thing for me," replied Nick with a mischievous grin.

"Well a little self-control wouldn't hurt," said Stephen.

"Self-control? Self-control is for the weak," replied Nick with a smirk as he shoved a fork full of mashed potatoes into his mouth.

"Eating is all you've done since we got here," Kim chimed in. "You would think with everything going on you would lose some of that appetite."

It had taken five days to reach Fort Carson, Colorado from Fort Campbell, Kentucky. Fort Carson lay just south of Colorado Springs and in the shadow of Cheyenne Mountain; home of the famed NORAD Headquarters. Major Bradley knew that the East

Coast had been completely evacuated. The military, and what was left of the United States government, was displaced to the area surrounding NORAD which contains Fort Carson as well as Peterson Air Force Base. For years NORAD had been running its operations from Peterson AFB with the Cheyenne Mountain Complex on standby in case of emergency. The Major hoped that the area had been secured and made safe from the hell that was unfolding in the rest of the country.

The trip from Fort Campbell would normally only have taken about 18 hours. However, these were anything but normal times. Several detours, namely around St. Louis and Kansas City, had added to their time. The convoy had also come across several civilian survivors traveling west. Those who were willing added their cars to the convoy and followed the Major to Fort Carson. The insistence of the Major to refill the tanker truck whenever possible slowed them down considerably but did ensure that plenty of fuel was on hand. Several nights were spent scavenging for food before holing up in abandoned houses. Finally, as the group's nerves were beginning to fray, they reached the outskirts of Colorado Springs only to find the once thriving town in almost complete ruin.

From the looks of it the Major believed the majority of the city had been wiped out by airstrikes and seemed at a loss about what to do next. It was then Specialist Simmons reported he had contacted someone on the radio. Shortly thereafter the convoy was welcomed in to a highly secured Fort Carson, the new home of the government and military of the United States of America.

The following few days were a blur as the group acclimated themselves to the Fort Carson community and settled into their quarters. It was hard to get an accurate count but everyone agreed there were nearly 1,000 civilian refugees alongside a large cadre of military personal. With more arriving every day. They all had many questions that went unanswered save for what the Major and Captain Morris shared. It had been a little more than three weeks since the civilians and soldiers met but the harrowing ordeals they had shared had helped developed a strong bond.

Major Bradley and Captain Morris would stop by the house being shared by the civilians in the evenings whenever their duties allowed, checking in on the group. From these meetings they all learned that this infection had spread rapidly throughout the Eastern United States in the first few days following the outbreak. By now the infection had spread through most of the United States decimating all the major cities and towns. There were even reports of outbreaks in Europe and South America.

Major Bradley also informed everyone that what was left of the United States government was assembled at the base, trying to establish some semblance of structure. The president and most of his cabinet had arrived safely but the vice-president had not been heard from in weeks. Almost half the members of Congress had made it to the Fort, including Nick's father, when Washington was evacuated. The cold hard fact, however, was that the military was running the show at Fort Carson, with strict martial law in place in order to keep those survivors gathered safe.

After the convoy arrived they were processed by the military personnel there. This consisted of a full medical exam to ensure no one was bitten or carrying any other infectious diseases. The military members of the convoy were then assigned barracks and duty stations while the civilians completed an ad hoc orientation session about their new lives at Fort Carson. In this session they learned the rules for living on the base which included the rationing of water, food, and electricity. Following the orientation they were given the option of a random housing assignment that would split them up or being assigned a house on base for all of them to share. They choose the latter and were quickly assigned a small two bedroom house. Lucy, Kim and her kids took the master bedroom while Nick and Stephen took the smaller one. Chester took the couch in the living room, but complaining of being cooped up behind the Fort's fences, was rarely there at night.

The morning following their arrival, after a short breakfast in a large dining hall, the group was met by Major Bradley and Captain Morris and led into a classroom were several military logistics officers had set up their office. Each member of the group was logged in to a roll book by name, social security number, and a physical description. Then each person was asked a list of questions to help find out where their talents and skills could be best used at Fort Carson.

Kim was assigned to the medical staff due to her experience as a dental hygienist. Jason and Danielle were both assigned to the small school that had been started on base for the refugees' kids. Nick was assigned as history teacher at the school for the morning session and in the afternoon was assigned to the work detail, which was currently working feverishly to reinforce the fence around the base. Stephen, on the recommendation of the Major and Captain, was assigned to military training for those civilians with real world experience in dealing with zombies. Stephen was also assigned to the work detail when he was not in training. Chester was assigned to the same unit as Stephen as well as being assigned to the hunting detail. Lucy's schooling as a business major made her a good fit for the civilian staff of the military's logistics unit. Everyone, including the soldiers, were assigned kitchen duty at least once a week. They were also responsible for washing their own clothes and the up keep of the house they were staying in.

They were then each given a ticket and told after the meeting to proceed to the commissary to pick up two sets of clothes for themselves. Afterwards they were afforded the rest of the day and the following day to settle in but were instructed to report to breakfast at 0700 hours each day and be at their assigned duty stations on the third day at 0800. There was some grumbling about being put to work but after the second day at their assigned jobs each of the group was happy for some sense of structure and normalcy.

Ignoring the other's remark Nick turned to Jason and Danielle and asked, "Did you guys finish your homework last night?"

"Yeah, I finished it before it got dark so I could play outside," said Jason.

"I had to wait for mommy to help me so I had to do mine with the candles on," said Danielle sheepishly.

"That's alright as long as you got it done," said Nick with a smile.

"Today I'll be teaching your class Jason, we are learning about World War II," he continued.

"Cool," replied Jason with a big smile.

"I can't believe they are letting you teach these young impressionable kids," said Lucy.

"History according to Nick, what could possibly go wrong," Stephen asked with a big grin.

"You guys are real comedians," said Nick finishing up the last of his food.

"Well as long as you aren't brainwashing my kids, I'm ok with you teaching," Kim chimed in.

"See, this is why I like Kim, she's the reasonable one, unlike you two love birds," replied Nick.

"Wha ... what are you talking about," Stephen asked incredulously quickly letting go of Lucy's hand under the table.

"Really, you guys think we hadn't noticed. Come on Kim, back me up here."

"It's true. You guys are like two love struck puppies," Kim said to the giggles of her kids. "Even the kids noticed."

"Umm well ... it just kind of happened," stammered a blushing Lucy.

"Oh, we aren't judging. You've had a thing for Stephen for a while. It just took a zombie apocalypse for Stephen to realize it," Nick said slugging his friend in the arm.

"What can I say, I am a bit dense sometimes," said Stephen putting his arm around Lucy.

"See there you go, no need to hide this budding romance," said Kim with an approving smile.

"Are you gonna kiss her?" Danielle piped up.

"Ewww ... that's gross," said Jason contorting his face to show his full disgust.

"Yeah, I'm with Jason, nobody needs to see that," said Nick.

"Alright, I think we've embarrassed them enough," said Kim trying hard to hide her smile. "Don't we all need to get to work soon?"

"Yeah, we should probably leave in a bit. I'm still not used to the military time they use around here. I'm fine in the mornings but once noon rolls around it takes me a minute to figure out what time they mean. I keep being late to things in the afternoon," Stephen said.

The others nodded in agreement and finished up the rest of their food. Just as they were about to get up Major Bradley and Captain Morris strolled up to their table.

"Morning folks, how is everyone doing today?" asked Major Bradley as he shook Stephen's hand.

"We are doing well all things considered," replied Kim.

"How are you and the Captain?" asked Lucy.

"We are busy, but good," replied the Major.

"How are the rest of the men from your unit? We haven't seen Simmons, Sinclair, or Sanchez lately," asked Stephen.

"They are good. Simmons is doing great work in the communications unit and Sanchez is in charge of a unit patrolling the fence line. Sinclair was promoted and is working in the motor pool," said Major Bradley looking around. "Is Chester here this morning?"

"Nope, haven't seen him since yesterday morning," said Nick. "He comes and goes as he pleases; you know Chester, he really feels cooped up here."

"Yes I do, and while he is a fine fellow he needs to follow the rules. He keeps slipping away from the hunting parties only to return with several deer as they are arriving back at the base."

"He also has a knack for finding weak spots in the perimeter fence and heading out on his own," said Captain Morris. "Although, this has been helping us find where we need to fix the fence."

"Either way, when you see him again please let him know I would like to speak with him. He is drawing some unwanted attention from my superiors," Major Bradley said.

"We'll let him know, not that he'll listen," said Kim. "Maybe I'll have Danielle tell him, he seems to have developed a soft spot for her. She could have him eating out of her hand if she wanted."

That brought laughs from everyone, except Danielle who looked confused by the comment.

"What does that mean Mommy?" she asked.

"Don't worry about it dear, it just means he likes you is all."

"One more thing before you all head off to work," Major Bradley said looking at his watch. "You all remember us telling you about that doctor we met at Fort Campbell; the one who might have a way to fix this whole mess at his lab."

"Sure, Dr. Sandersomthing," said Nick as the other's nodded.

"Well, I told my superiors about it and while skeptical, they want me to check it out. So Captain Morris and I are putting together a small unit to try and find the lab he was going to be working at."

"That's good news right?" asked Lucy.

"Yes it is, especially considering the reluctance of my superiors after hearing the story."

Turning to Stephen he continued, "We asked that you and Chester be assigned to our unit."

"Me, really?" asked Stephen in surprise.

"That's correct; we've gotten good reports from your training officer. We'll need good scouts like you and Chester if we're going to find him in time," replied Captain Morris.

"Does he really have to go?" asked Lucy.

"We can't force him to go, but as we can't spare many soldiers we could really use his help," said Major Bradley.

"It's ok Lucy, I should do this … for Dave … and … Emma," Stephen replied. "Plus I have been training as a scout not a fighter."

"That's right, he will quietly find the infected for us and then the soldiers will do any fighting," Captain Morris said trying to be reassuring.

As Stephen put his arm around her he said, "It's gonna be ok Lucy, I'll be safe I promise."

"I just don't want to lose anyone else."

"I know it's hard on us all but I need to do this."

"I know you do."

Turning from Lucy to the Major, Stephen asked, "When do we leave?"

"Tomorrow morning after breakfast at 0800 hours; you have the rest of the day off from your duties to get ready. But meet us at the armory at 1800 hours to get your gear together and for a briefing," replied Major Bradley.

"Yes sir, I'll be there."

"Don't worry Lucy, we'll take care of him," Captain Morris said gesturing to Stephen.

"Thanks," said Lucy. "I know you will."

"Alright folks I'll let you get to work. Remember, if any of you need anything just let us know. We'll stop by tomorrow at breakfast to say goodbye," said Major Bradley as he patted Jason on the head.

The Major and Captain turned and headed out of the dining hall. The group sat in silence for a minute before Jason spoke up. "Mom we need to go to school, I don't want to be late."

"Alright honey lets clean up and then we'll head over there."

"I can walk the kids to school so you aren't late, I am heading there anyway," said Nick.

"Thanks, I'd appreciate that," said Kim. Turning to her kids she continued, "Nick's gonna take you to school, I'll see you at lunch. I love you both."

Kim gathered the trash and trays off the table and emptied them into the proper containers before leaving the dining hall.

Nick helped Jason and Danielle gather up their school things and then, holding Danielle's hand, walked with both kids out the door towards the school building.

Stephen and Lucy sat there a while longer without saying a word. Stephen was about to say something when Chester appeared in front of them and sat down with a tray of breakfast. He leaned his gun against the table and began to eat as people around them gave him worried looks.

"Where have you been? The Major was just looking for you," asked Lucy.

Chester gave a grunt as his mouth was full of food.

"The Major has a mission for us. He wants to find that doctor from Fort Campbell," said Stephen.

Chester finished chewing and said, "I know, I saw him in the hall. I'll be ready tomorrow. And don't worry Miss Lucy I won't let your boyfriend out of my sight."

"Thanks," said Lucy sheepishly, starting to blush again.

"Don't mention it, now you two better get to work before one of those logistics officers gets their panties in a wad."

Lucy and Stephen got up from the table and after a quick hug Lucy headed out while Stephen hung back.

"Thanks Chester, it will help Lucy sleep better knowing you've got my back."

Chester let out another grunt and turned his focus back to his food as Stephen headed out the door to prepare for his first mission outside of the safety of Fort Carson's fences.

Chapter 37
The Man Behind the Curtain

Dr. Sanderson was sitting on a stool next to a small workbench in the corner of an elaborate laboratory. It was much larger than the one in Florida and contained the most up to date equipment available. The only problem was he did not know exactly where he was.

The return flight from Fort Campbell had taken a little longer than the Doctor expected and used up most of the Gulfstream's fuel; at least according to Captain Bannon. When he embarked from the plane the Doctor had expected to see snowcapped mountains, instead he was looking at a flat expanse of land that appeared to be a desert.

When he inquired as to where they were he received no answer. When he pressed the issue, all Gunner would say was that Mr. Worthington would explain. The drive to the laboratory through the barren wasteland was a short one. The Doctor noticed that there did not seem to be any infected in the area. They passed a few deserted buildings and drove down a long road that ended in front of a large stucco house. It appeared to be the only functional building for miles.

The inside was spacious but sparsely decorated. It did not appear to have been lived in; at least not on any kind of regular basis. The bottom floor contained a moderately sized kitchen, a living room, bathroom, and a den. The upstairs had four bedrooms and another bathroom along with a small reading area.

The real gem was the basement. It was as close to the floor of a modern hospital in size and scope as you could get without actually being in a hospital. There was an office, three examination rooms, an operating room, and a large laboratory that the Doctor was currently sitting in. Mr. Worthington soon explained that the change in venue had been necessary because the laboratory here was the best he had and also the most remote.

Dr. Sanderson had spent the last three weeks working fifteen hours a day in the lab only taking time out to sleep, eat, or step outside for a breath of fresh air. Except that the air was dry and hot and not overly refreshing. The only people he saw were Benton, Gunner, and a staff member whose name he had unfortunately forgotten.

Down the hall from the laboratory, to the right, was examination room three. Locked inside, strapped to a hospital bed, was test subject Number 5. He had been removed from the cargo hold of the plane and immediately transferred to the examination room.

Dr. Sanderson had been there countless times over the last several weeks extracting samples from Number 5. Blood samples, spinal fluid, and skin grafts. He had introduced human cells into the samples in order to see how they reacted. In each case, the infected cells consumed the human cells. He tried similar tests at different temperatures and in different quantities with the same results.

As in Florida, he could not figure out how The Principle worked. It essentially destroyed the living human cells and subsequently shut down the organs but allowed minimal brain activity that did not even register on most machines. There, of course, was no way this should be happening. Everything Dr. Sanderson knew about medicine and more specifically the brain, worked against what he was seeing with his own eyes.

Another thing he did not know was what would happen if the infected were deprived of food; in this case human or animal flesh. So, at the insistence of the Doctor, Mr. Worthington agreed to bring in fresh meat periodically for Number 5 to feast on. He had no idea if this kept his former patient functioning or not but he did not want to take any chances. He did not ask, nor did he want to know, where Benton was getting the meat from.

There did not seem to be any threat from infected. He had not been informed of a single incident since he had arrived. As he spent most of his time in the basement and in the lab, he doubted he would hear anything anyway. He was sure Mr. Worthington did not want him distracted and would keep such information to himself.

So there he was, in the middle of a desert, staring at the most recent results from yet another test. Unfortunately, they yielded the same information as all the others. He was starting to think he was not going to be able to figure this thing out.

He was saving Number 5's brain tissue for last. He was aware that destroying the brain was the only way to kill these things for good. Since he did not know what part of the brain in particular was vulnerable, he wanted to proceed with caution. However, it was looking like he was going to have no choice. Nothing else seemed to be working.

As he was about to file the test results in a binder and consider what part of the brain he was going to experiment on first, the door to the lab opened. Standing in front of the Doctor was a small dark skinned man of probable Hispanic descent wearing black pants, a black vest over a white dress shirt. He was the only other person besides Gunner and Benton with which the Doctor had contact with.

"Mr. Worthington asked me to see if you were hungry Doctor," he said.

As usual, Dr. Sanderson had been working straight through and had not even considered lunch; or would it be dinner? He had no idea anymore whether it was day or night. It all ran together. He kept a small refrigerator in the lab with cold drinks but needed to go to the kitchen if he required food.

Benton must have had some kind of generator powering the building because he did not see any cables connected to it. Although, with all the sun the place got, it could be solar powered.

"Is it day or night?" the Doctor countered.

"Late afternoon I would say, sir," he said.

"I'm sorry but I have forgotten your name."

"My name is Manuel, sir," he answered.

"Well Manuel, I think I am a little hungry. What's on the menu?"

"What would you like, sir?" he asked.

"Let's see … how about a chicken salad sandwich?" the Doctor inquired.

Dr. Sanderson noticed Manuel looking at the large binder in front of him with all the reports and test results.

"Everything okay Manuel?" he asked.

The question seemed to snap Manuel out of his trance.

"Fine, sir. What type of bread would you like your chicken salad on?" he asked.

"Surprise me," the Doctor said.

"Very well, sir," Manuel said as he continued to stand in front of the door.

"Something on your mind?" Dr. Sanderson asked.

"What kind of doctor are you?" he asked, this time without the sir attached.

"I am a Neurologist," the Doctor answered.

The blank stare told him Manuel had no idea what that meant.

"I study the human brain and try to figure out how it works and how to prevent or cure diseases that affect the brain," he clarified for Manuel.

"Oh. Is that's what is wrong with the person in the room down the hall," he asked.

"That's what I'm trying to find out," the Doctor answered.

"My Uncle Hector died a few years ago of some brain thing. He couldn't move his arms and then his legs and then he just stopped breathing. It was a terrible thing to see. He had some disease with a bunch a letters in it," Manuel said.

"Was it ALS … also known as Lou Gerhig's Disease?" the Doctor asked.

"Yeah … ALS … that was it. Who's Lou Gerhig?" he asked.

"He was a famous baseball player many years ago who died of ALS."

"Oh. Well good luck. I'll go get your sandwich now, sir."

"Thanks, Manuel. And I'm sorry about your Uncle."

Manuel nodded, turned around, and headed out the lab door and down the hall heading toward the stairs.

Dr. Sanderson closed the binder and placed it on a small shelf above the workbench. He would try to remember to ask Manuel when he returned, now that they are on a first name basis, where the hell they were.

Twenty minutes later Dr. Sanderson was carefully examining several MRI images of Number 5's brain taken here in the desert lab and also in the Florida lab. He was comparing them to see how its brain had changed over time and what area seemed a likely candidate for experimentation.

He had nearly forgotten about his sandwich when the door to the lab opened again. The Doctor turned and was surprised to see Benton Worthington III standing in front of him holding a white ceramic plate containing a chicken salad sandwich on wheat bread accompanied by a generous pile of potato chips.

"Good afternoon Doctor, just wanted to see how your experiments were progressing," Benton said.

"What happened to Manuel?" Dr. Sanderson asked.

"I had another errand for him, besides like I said, I was understandably curious about your progress," Benton answered.

"Your sandwich," he said extending his arm holding the ceramic plate.

"Thanks."

The Doctor grabbed the plate from Benton and placed it down on the workbench in front of him. Removing the sandwich, he took a big bite of it.

"Not bad, given the circumstances," he thought.

Benton looked around the lab for a second giving the Doctor a second to chew his food. He was very proud of the medical facility he had created here. It was state of the art, self-sufficient, and most importantly, isolated.

"So … how is it going?" he finally asked.

"I wish I had better news to report Mr. Worthington. I have performed a myriad of tests and still am no closer to a solution. The bacterium destroys the living human tissue and nothing seems to stop it. I have decided to remove some peripheral brain tissue and initiate experiments on that. If you'd like, I can show you where I plan to begin," Dr. Sanderson answered.

"That won't be necessary Doctor," Benton said. "I will leave you to your lunch."

"And don't hesitate to let me know if you need anything," he added.

"Thanks again, Mr. Worthington. Hopefully the brain tissue samples will yield some answers," Dr. Sanderson said.

Benton nodded and headed for the door.

Dr. Sanderson turned his attention back to the sandwich. He reached down under the workbench, just to the left, and opened the refrigerator removing a Sprite. He popped the top and took a swig.

Enjoying his lunch, his thoughts turned to his family. He had asked Benton shortly after his arrival if he had been able to locate his wife and daughter. Benton said not yet, but they were working on a couple of leads but he would not go into detail. He would have to ask Benton again, maybe when he had something positive to report.

Putting a potato chip in his mouth he thought about, surprisingly, Manuel's Uncle. ALS was a dreadful disease. There had been some significant advances over the last few years but its causes were still largely unknown. A defect in Chromosome 21 has been linked to many cases worldwide, specifically those involving heredity.

It had been a significant part of his research over the years and he had treated many patients suffering from ALS. He even had a couple of patients down in the Florida lab who had suffered from the disease.

"It was unusual that ..."

Dr. Sanderson stopped his thought in mid-sentence and bolted upright, knocking his stool to the ground. He raced to the door and opened it in a hurry. Stepping into the hallway he looked in both directions. No sign of Mr. Worthington. He was going to need him for what he had in mind.

Moving to the end of the hall the Doctor was about to turn left and head upstairs until he heard voices coming from the office to his right.

At first he couldn't make them out. He turned and slowly moved toward the office door. As he got closer he recognized Benton's voice and noticed the door was slightly ajar. The other voice had a definite German accent.

He peeked through the crack in the door and listened.

"Dr. Sanderson has not made a great deal of progress but I feel confident he will have a breakthrough soon," Benton said.

"When he does, I will need you to be able to duplicate and reproduce what he discovers," he said to the other man in the room.

"That shouldn't be a problem," said the man with the accent.

Dr. Sanderson shifted slightly to get a better look without being seen.

"Unfortunately Dr. Ehrlich, Dr. Sanderson will want to distribute the vaccine to the masses for free. I didn't become one of the wealthiest men in the world by giving away what I have rightfully paid for," Benton stated.

"Ehrlich," Dr. Sanderson thought.

Dr. Werner Ehrlich was a neurologist such as himself but with a somewhat shady past. He had been working on a drug that significantly improved the cognitive ability of Alzheimer's patients a few years ago. Unfortunately, he manipulated much of the test results in order to get it approved by the FDA. His malpractice was discovered just before the drug was set for approval. He was disgraced and cast out of the medical community.

By most accounts, however, he was a brilliant man, who just lacked a certain moral compass. It looked to Dr. Sanderson that Benton had brought Ehrlich in to take over for him after he found an antidote. Ehrlich would have little pause in selling whatever he came up with for a profit.

He heard shuffling in the room and it looked like they were heading toward the door. Dr. Sanderson turned the corner heading back down the hall and ducked into the bathroom.

He stood there and tried to digest what he had just heard. He could not let Benton sell, or whatever he planned to do with it, anything he was able to produce. It had to be made available, free of charge, to everyone who was still … human. Also of grave concern was what Benton was planning to do with him when he was finished with him.

Unfortunately, he needed Benton and his lab to complete his work. What happened afterward, the Doctor would have to deal with then. It would not be too much longer anyway, he was confident he had figured it out.

Chapter 38
Breakthrough

Dr. Sanderson spent the next several days putting together what he needed for his experiment. He went about his business as usual, not letting on that he overheard Benton and Dr. Ehrlich in the office. Benton was very helpful in getting everything he required and was nearly as excited at the possibility of a breakthrough as the Doctor was; but for very different reasons.

As with most revelations, once one is undergone, you spend time trying to figure out how it had not occurred to you earlier. Dr. Sanderson was currently wrestling with that very problem. The experiments in Florida had produced some amazing results before The Principle had taken over and shut down the host organisms. One of the most intriguing aspects of his research was the few ALS patients that he had brought down to Florida, showed no effects from the bacterium.

He was so absorbed with the others, such as Number 5, who were making great strides at first that he completely disregarded what was not happening with the ALS patients. Going back over his notes from the Florida lab, he remembered that the ALS test subjects not only failed to show any progress, they did not show any accelerated regression either. In other words, The Principle was ineffective when administered to humans with ALS.

Recent advancements in ALS research have pointed to mutations in the enzyme superoxide dismutase, or SOD1, as a probable cause in a number of cases. Over one hundred different mutations have been discovered already with more probably waiting to be discovered. Unfortunately, the ALS test subjects in Florida did not have the same exact genetic mutation but did have one thing in common; their bodies were producing excess amounts of SOD1.

SOD1, simply stated, protects cells from superoxide toxicity. It is an anti-oxidant. The mutations occur in the form overproduction, underproduction, or a lack of production.

One of the great things about enzymes are they can be artificially created; simulating what the human body naturally produces. People had ingested synthetic enzymes every day; most commonly in over the counter multi-vitamins.

The Doctor believed that introducing excess SOD1 into living human cells would prevent the bacterium from taking over and infecting its host. Unfortunately, the choice of dying from ALS or a bite from an infected person was not much of a choice. He was betting, however, that by creating temporary elevated levels and the fact that the body itself was not generating the excess enzyme, the probability of contracting ALS would be slight; if at all.

Creating the enzyme would be the easy part. All he had to do was mix the active ingredients with some kind of excipient like glucose. The difficulty would be determining dosage and frequency. The Doctor envisioned it in pill form, taken as a supplement. Determining how much to take and how often would be problematic. Too much and you increase the risk of disease; too little and you risk infection.

"These are all interesting questions," thought the Doctor, *"but irrelevant if it didn't work."*

He started by using small amounts of SOD1, not much more than the human body produces on its own. He introduced the bacterium onto slides that contained human cells. The Principle made quick work of these cells, killing them instantly. He gradually increased the dosage a little each time.

The first dozen trials ended with the same result; the bacterium overpowering the human cells and killing them. It was not until he had reached roughly double the usual level of SOD1 in the human body that he saw some changes.

The Principle was having a much more difficult time achieving victory over the human cells. It eventually won the battle but it took much longer than before. He continued to increase the levels.

Almost a week after Manuel's story about his poor Uncle Hector, Dr. Sanderson stared intently into his electron microscope. He had just introduced the Principle into cells with nearly three times the normal level of SOD1. Small beads of sweat had begun to form on his forehead. He had spent every waking hour during the past week under hot fluorescent lights staring into microscopes.

He watched and waited as the foreign invaders sought out the human cells. They attacked and then attacked again but nothing happened. Dr. Sanderson pulled his head away from the lens and grabbed a paper towel to wipe the perspiration from his brow. He removed his glasses and rubbed the corners of his eyes with his thumb and forefinger. Putting his glasses back on, he looked into the microscope.

He was surprised to see the human cells still intact. As a matter of fact, it appeared that the Principle had been surrounded by the human cells; quarantined if you will. He watched for several more minutes as the human cells closed ranks and slowly destroyed the invading bacteria.

There was an overwhelming sense of relief followed by a feeling of accomplishment. It had been almost two months since test subject Number 5 walked out of the lab in Florida. A lot of people had died and life as he knew it had been altered forever. There was also a feeling of redemption. He felt responsible for the hell that had been unleashed on humanity. Now he believed he had a chance to right a terrible wrong.

Benton checked in from time to time looking for updates from Dr. Sanderson. He obliged with vague information and simply indicated they were moving in the right direction. When Benton asked for more details, the Doctor spewed technical data that was impossible for the lay man to comprehend in the hopes Benton would stop asking and leave.

He was purposely keeping certain pieces of information from Benton, feeling he needed to buy himself some time. The Doctor had not seen or overheard him speaking with Dr. Ehrlich again but knew that he must be nearby.

The plan he was hatching in his head was risky but necessary. Benton had obviously enlisted the German to take over for him when he produced the antidote. They planned on selling the pills to the remaining human population. Paper currency probably had no value now so he would most likely ask for food, or weapons, or knowing Benton … allegiance.

Unfortunately, the SOD1 was only a temporary solution. It would eventually work its way out of the body and one would need another dose. It would make the person with the antidote the most powerful and important human alive. Perhaps, one day, he would find a more permanent solution. Until then, Dr. Sanderson would try to get the SOD1 to as many people as possible.

His idea involved making and storing as many pills as feasible, giving Benton just enough to wet his appetite. Benton would, of course, turn the supply over to Dr. Ehrlich and have him finish production. By then, the Doctor had hoped he would have successfully bargained with Benton to let him go, now that his job was done. He considered simply trying to sneak out at night but he had no idea where he was or how far he might be from another human being; not to mention the infected. The pills might have protected him from the bite of one or two of them but not from an advancing horde intent on having him for dinner.

He would bring the extra supply of pills with him and try to reconnect with the Major. It was a long shot, all of it; Benton letting him go, escaping with the antidote, finding the Major. He figured that Benton probably had cameras in the lab watching his every move. Unfortunately, he did not see too many other options at the moment.

The next few days were spent narrowing down the dosage and trying to figure out the SOD1's disposition curve. After a couple dozen trials he was confident he had determined the optimal dosage; one that was safe and provided some lasting protection. He estimated that an individual pill would be good for about two weeks minimum; perhaps more for some. He was not nearly as confident about this projection as he was the dosage but figured about twenty-five pills would last any one person an entire year.

He started making the pills in the far corner of the lab, away from any possible cameras Benton may have hidden. If Benton asked, he would say they were placebos or that they were the wrong dosage. He would sneak a small amount of pills up into his room daily using the excuse he needed something from there or he was going to take a quick nap to clear his head.

He tried to act nonchalant and not do anything to arouse suspicion. Benton could have this entire house wired, even the bathrooms. He continued to make additional pills over the next few days but it was getting increasingly difficult to keep Benton at bay. His trips to the lab were becoming more frequent. He was obviously becoming impatient.

The Doctor had filled his backpack upstairs with pills and had created a small cache to give to Benton. He reckoned he had stalled long enough and Benton or no Benton, he had discovered an antidote and world should know about it. He just hoped they would not have to pay dearly for it.

He was about to leave the lab and head upstairs to make the official announcement that he had found an antidote when the door to the lab opened and Benton poked his head inside.

"Doctor, could you join me in examination room number three, I have something I need to show you," he said.

Chapter 39
Wild Goose

Major Bradley watched as the trees zipped past his Humvee. Everything looked so peaceful, so normal, but the reality of his current mission kept him from being lost in the serenity around him. It had taken Major Bradley nearly four weeks of constant petitioning before he had convinced his commanding officer, Colonel Jepson, to authorize the mission.

The story Major Bradley conveyed about the conversation with Dr. Sanderson at Fort Campbell and the possibility of a cure had been compelling, until the involvement of Benton Worthington III was mentioned. Unfortunately for the Major, Colonel Jepson had his own run-ins with Worthington on Capitol Hill and none of them were pleasant.

For the next three weeks Major Bradley laid out a case for his mission. At every juncture he had been met with an excuse. First it was Worthington's involvement, and then it was the lack of concrete proof that this Doctor was actually close to developing anything. Limited resources and a shortage of manpower had been the biggest obstacles for the Major to overcome.

Finally a breakthrough occurred when, using help from Nick's father, the Major was able to garner enough support for his plan. In the end, the mission was given the green light but not after severely cutting the number of men the Major had requested. Thankfully he had been able to bolster his numbers slightly with the addition of civilian scouts. Even better, the civilian scouts were Chester and Stephen, two of the civilians Major Bradley and his men had seen in action and grown close to on the trip to Fort Carson. Also along on this mission were Cpt. Morris, Sgt. Sanchez, Spc. Simmons, and Cpl. Sinclair.

The group was traveling in two Humvees, each with its own mounted weapon. With the exception of Chester, who carried his own rifle and shotgun, the men each carried silenced weapons recently obtained from Fort Carson's arsenal. The Major and his men had learned from their time on the road that gunfire only attracted more of the infected. Each man was also armed with a close combat weapon; Chester with his machete, Stephen with his axe, and the soldiers each carrying a combat knife that could be used as a bayonet on the end of their rifles.

The mission was simple in concept; find the Worthington Estate and extract Dr. Sanderson and any work on a cure. As is the case with most things, it would likely be easier said than done. Major Bradley knew that Benton would not simply hand over the doctor. Even though the Major carried an executive order from the President of the United States, he knew this would not hold much weight in the eyes of Worthington.

The Major was hoping he could strike some kind of deal with Benton but held little hope that a compromise would be easily reached. As long as the doctor was not being held against his will, Major Bradley hoped he could convince him to come with them of his own accord. He wanted, above all else to avoid any kind of violence, but was well aware of the armed security that Benton usually employed; like the mercenaries he had seen protecting the doctor at Fort Campbell.

The trip to The Worthington Estate went by quicker than the team expected, primarily as a result of their ability to ignore the posted speed limits. Dr. Sanderson had given Major Bradley an exact address of the estate so it was not difficult to find.

As the convoy rolled to a stop in front of the estate's entrance, Major Bradley was surprised to see no one guarding the gates. Getting out of the Humvee, the Major punched the buzzer on the intercom box hanging on the wall of the guard house. Several seconds passed with no response. He looked around locating the camera pointed in his direction. Waving his hand over his head he pressed the buzzer again. Again nothing emanated from the intercom. Growing frustrated Major Bradley moved to the gate itself and found it locked.

Realizing nothing short of running through the gate with the Humvees would open it, Major Bradley moved to the guard house door. Trying the nob he unsurprisingly found it locked. This was, however, quickly rectified by several heavy boot strikes to the door. With a crack the door bolt dislodged from the frame and the door swung open. Inside the Major found a desk with several security monitors and a switch board. Everything seemed to have power and the Major searched the switch board until he found a button for the front gate. Pressing the button Major Bradley was rewarded with the sound of the gate unlocking and swinging open.

Stepping out of the guard house and closing the mangled door behind him, he motioned for the two Humvees to move through. Once they had cleared the gate, the Major followed, closing the gate via the control panel inside the perimeter. He jumped back into the Humvee and directed Corporeal Sinclair to continue on to the main house.

The Worthington Estate was, as one would expect, opulence embodied. The mile and a half drive from the entrance to the main house was nothing short of breathtaking. Even in the midst of the current crises the grounds were perfectly manicured. Large trees like pillars towered over the wide driveway. Beyond the tree lined drive stood magnificent gardens and lawns. As the Humvees crested a final hill the trees parted and the main house came into view.

The house, more like a mansion really, was enormous. The stone work was immaculate and a massive porch wrapped itself around the length of the mansion. The Humvees pulled up in front on what was now a brick laid driveway circling a large fountain. Major Bradley and Captain Morris exited their vehicles signaling to the others to keep their eyes opened. Chester, with Stephen in tow, stepped out of their vehicle as well and quickly disappeared around the side of the mansion.

Major Bradley and Captain Morris quickly ascended a wide flight of stairs under an archway arriving in front of two heavy wooden doors. A large burnished knocker hung from each door, Major Bradley grabbed the one to the left and knocked three times rapidly. As they waited, both officers looked into the floor to ceiling windows on either side of the door but saw nothing as the curtains were drawn tightly across both. Finally, as Major Bradley prepared to knock again, he heard the sound of someone unlocking the door. With a groan the doors opened inward and revealed a short stout man with a grey beard and white hair dressed in a dark suit. Slightly taken aback by the two military men standing on the porch, the man took a minute to collect himself while looking the Major and the Captain over.

"Welcome to the Worthington residence, my name is Winston, how may I be of service?"

Extending his hand Major Bradley replied, "I am Major Charles Bradley of the United States Army and this is my senior officer Captain Morris."

"Pleasure to meet you gentlemen," replied Winston, shaking each man's hand.

"We were hoping to meet with Mr. Worthington," continued Major Bradley.

"Ahh, Mr. Worthington. Well I am afraid to tell you that Mr. Worthington is out of town currently. He has been for several weeks now and we are not sure when to expect him back."

"Of course he is," Major Bradley replied with a chuckle.

"Do you have any way we can contact him?" asked Captain Morris.

"I am afraid not, I am sure you can appreciate Mr. Worthington's need for privacy."

"Well if Mr. Worthington is not available, perhaps we can speak with Dr. Sanderson," said Major Bradley looking straight into Winston's eyes.

A hint of recognition and then surprise crossed Winston's face before he could compose himself and answer the Major.

"Dr … Dr. Sanderson did you say? No, I am not familiar with that name. I know all the staff and guests who live and work here and there is certainly no one by that name here."

"I see," replied Major Bradley.

"I am sorry I could not be of more help to you gentlemen."

"Yes, so are we," answered Major Bradley. "Perhaps we can leave a message and our radio contact information so that when Mr. Worthington does arrive we can speak with him?"

"Ah yes, that will do just fine."

"Let me go speak to our radio Specialist to get the frequency we are using."

"That won't be necessary Major. I can assure you that Mr. Worthington will gladly contact you at Fort Carson once he has returned."

"How did you know we came from Fort Carson?" Captain Morris inquired.

"The patch on your shoulder Captain, of course," Winston answered.

Captain Morris glanced down and looked at his uniform.

"If that is all gentlemen, I bid you a good afternoon," Winston said as he turned and slowly closed the doors behind him.

Major Bradley and Captain Morris moved down the stairs back to the Humvees silently. Reaching the first Humvee both men turn back around and stared at the mansion.

"Think he is telling the truth about any of that, sir?" asked Captain Morris.

"I doubt it Captain. When it comes to situations involving Worthington it's hard to know who to trust or what to believe."

Just then, coming out at a jog from around the house was Chester. He slowed to a walk and approached the two men at the Humvees.

"Ah … Mr. Boone I see we are still up to our old tricks," said Major Bradley with a half-smile.

"Some habits die hard Major," Chester said gruffly.

"So, did you find anything of note?" asked Captain Morris.

"The place seems to be free of infected and locked up tighter than a drum. I don't think he is here."

Just then Stephen appeared from behind one of the large topiaries.

"I see hanging about with Mr. Boone has rubbed off on you son," said Major Bradley.

"I guess so sir."

"What do you have for me?"

"Well, Major I found what looked like an extravagant garage. Two vehicles appear to be missing," replied Stephen.

"I guess it is safe to say they aren't here," said Major Bradley.

"I guess there is no need to storm the mansion then," said a somewhat disappointed Captain Morris.

"Yes, no need. Let's mount up and get back to Fort Carson and report our findings. My bosses aren't going to be very pleased with this after all the strings I had to pull," said Major Bradley as he climbed back into his Humvee.

"I believe this is where I say I told you so Butch," said Colonel Jepson after hearing Major Bradley's mission report.

The Colonel and Major Bradley stood in a large command and control room in NORAD, underground in the Cheyenne Mountain complex. The hum of the generators powering the complex could be heard in the silence as Major Bradley waited for the Colonel to continue.

"The president is not going to like hearing this. And you are sure he wasn't there."

"As sure as we could be sir; short of searching the mansion. We drove past his private airstrip on the way back and checked it out. His private jet wasn't there so it's a safe bet he is somewhere else; and he probably has the doctor with him."

"Well if this doctor has found some kind of cure it's almost a certainty that Worthington has it hidden somewhere with him."

"I agree sir."

"The question is how in the world how are we going to find him. Any thoughts Major?"

"Yes sir, on the trip back here I was discussing the problem with my men. Spc. Simmons wondered if this installation had the ability to track the movements of Worthington's plane."

"We have had the radar up and running for just over a month now hoping to contact anyone who flies into our airspace from another country."

"Well if your radar technicians are keeping logs we should be able to track his plane or at least the one being used by the doctor we met at Fort Campbell."

"Good thinking Major," Colonel Jepson said turning to look around the room.

"Jackson, bring the radar logs for the past couple of months up here on the double," Colonel Jepson yelled.

"Yes sir," came the reply as Pvt. Jackson scrambled to gather the requested charts and paper work.

Taking the logs from Pvt. Jackson, Colonel Jepson and Major Bradley quickly laid them out on the table.

"What are we looking at here son?" Colonel Jepson said gesturing to the maps.

"Well sir, whenever we have a radar contact we record the date, time, and location and then plot its movements on this map overlay. We also record any contact we have with them and the outcome," Jackson said.

"Alright then, all you need to do is find the entries for when my men and I left Fort Campbell four weeks ago. You should have a radar contact flying into and out of Fort Campbell's airfield. That is the one the doctor was on," said Major Bradley emphatically.

The three men started sorting through the log papers looking for the date in question. Jackson found the prize and laid it out before the Colonel and Major.

"Sirs, this looks to be the contact coming out of Fort Campbell at 8 p.m. on Monday the 2nd. It flew into the airfield earlier that evening," said Pvt. Jackson.

He continued, "Funny thing is we had been tracking that same plane up and down the East Coast for a few days but never made a successful contact."

"So where did it go after leaving Fort Campbell?" asked Colonel Jepson impatiently.

"Let's see. Looks like it flew to Colorado but the abruptly changed course and headed south through New Mexico," replied Jackson.

"And?" said the Colonel.

"And then it disappeared from our radar shortly after it crossed into Mexican airspace."

"So what does that mean?" asked Major Bradley.

"It looks like they were descending, probably to either land or avoid further radar contact," replied Jackson.

"Well it looks like Worthington is on the run with something. Maybe this doctor of yours was on to something," said Colonel Jepson.

"So what do we do now sir?" asked Major Bradley.

"We survive, Major. That is all that there is left to do."

"Survive without a cure ... unlikely," thought the Major.

Chapter 40
Reunion

Dr. Sanderson followed Benton out the lab door and turned right down the hall. Benton remained a few steps ahead as they passed the first two examination rooms. Benton arrived first and opened the door to examination room three. Without a word he motioned for the Doctor to enter as Benton followed behind.

The Doctor moved inside as Benton closed the door behind them. He saw Number 5 lying on a hospital bed in the middle of the room. He was still strapped down and appeared unconscious. No real change from the last time the Doctor was here. The room had a small sink along the far wall encased in a vanity with cabinet doors. A silver tray and a stand that held a variety of medical instruments stood off to the right side of the bed. The major addition to the room was Dr. Werner Ehrlich, who was standing just off to the left side of the bed.

Dr. Sanderson looked at Dr. Ehrlich and then back to Benton. He was about to speak when Benton beat him to it.

"Have you met Dr. Werner Ehrlich, Doctor?" Benton asked.

"What the hell is going on here?" Dr. Sanderson demanded even though he already knew the answer. He ignored Dr. Ehrlich.

Dr. Ehrlich extended his right hand.

"Doctor," he said.

Dr. Sanderson continued to glare at Benton pretending he did not even see Dr. Ehrlich.

The half-smile that Benton had on his face when they entered the room was now gone. It had been replaced with a serious demeanor.

"Please tell us about this," he said raising his right hand holding one of the SOD1 pills between his thumb and index finger.

"Where did you get that?" Dr. Sanderson inquired.

"From your knapsack upstairs, of course," Benton answered.

Dr. Sanderson was stunned. He thought he had been so careful. He immediately saw his plan beginning to unravel before his eyes. His mouth opened but nothing came out. His mind began to race. He needed a plan B and quick.

Benton saw the look on Dr. Sanderson's face and knew he was thinking of a way out of this room but was not concerned. He was not a man who left a lot to chance.

"I have paid you the courtesy of not underestimating you Doctor but I fear you may have underestimated me," Benton said.

"Overestimated I would say," Dr. Sanderson replied.

"There are people dying out there Doctor so I will ask one more time; tell me about the pill."

"It still needs more testing," the Doctor said. Which was true; he felt confident that it would work but the side effects, if any, were still unknown.

"Perhaps you're right. The only problem is where to find a suitable test subject," Benton said looking in the direction of Number 5.

Dr. Sanderson realized immediately what Benton was thinking. He was not entirely sure what would happen if SOD1 was introduced into an infected organism. He had trialed with only a few cells at a time. The experiments concluded absolutely that the SOD1 cells destroyed the infected cells; they did not heal them. But how a larger system, like Number 5, would react as the SOD1 slowly made its way through the body, was an unknown. It could be very dangerous.

"It's an antidote, not a cure," he said.

Benton looked over at Dr. Ehrlich as he nodded in agreement to what Dr. Sanderson was saying. It was now clear to the Doctor what Dr. Ehrlich's purpose here was. He was here to ensure the Doctor did not lie to Benton.

"How long, once ingested, does it take to circulate through the body," Dr. Ehrlich asked, speaking for the first time since he attempted to introduce himself.

"I estimate about twenty minutes," Dr. Sanderson answered.

Benton extended his hand holding the pill in the Doctor's direction.

"Do you require a glass of water," he asked.

"What?"

"I see no better test subject than the person who created it," Benton said.

Dr. Sanderson did not know how to respond. He instinctively reached out and took the pill from Benton. He thought about bolting for the door. It was not far away but Benton had strategically placed himself between the Doctor and the door. It would be two against one and the two were both younger and stronger than him. Not to mention they could be concealing weapons. He pleaded with himself to come up with a plan B. Nothing came.

"Not necessary," he said as he swallowed the pill. If nothing else it would buy him some time.

Benton looked at his watch.

"We'll give it twenty-one minutes, just to be safe."

"So," Dr. Sanderson said "how much will you be charging for the antidote. How much exactly is a life worth, Benton?"

"We will let the market determine the price … I'm nothing if not a capitalist," Benton said.

"You're a sick, greedy, bastard."

"I was hoping we wouldn't resort to name calling Doctor. I think we're above that."

"You can't get rich if there's no one left to get rich off of," the Doctor said. "How much is enough?"

"Wealth will be defined in a different way going forward. Currency will no longer be the standard. Power and influence will rest with those who have what people want. I intend for that to be me."

Dr. Sanderson said nothing. He was reassessing the man in front of him. It appeared that Captain Bannon and the Major were right after all. This was a megalomaniac who cared for nothing and nobody but himself. Dr. Sanderson was fooled into thinking that simply because the man funded countless types of medical research he was trying to help mankind. He may have been, but for a price.

"Was this the plan all along?" Dr. Sanderson asked.

"The plan, as you refer to it, has taken many forms over the last month," Benton answered, "but you have been at the center of it from the beginning."

The Doctor felt an anger rise in him that he had not felt for a long time. No one liked the feeling of being used, he was no different. It was especially galling given that so much was at stake.

"You think this is some kind a game, Benton?" the Doctor asked.

"On the contrary Doctor, it's deadly serious," Benton responded with a steely gaze.

Several more minutes passed as no one said a word. Dr. Sanderson evaluated his situation. It was not looking good. Maybe he could make his way over to the surgical tray and pick up a scalpel. Dr. Ehrlich, however, was unfortunately blocking his way. He tried to figure out exactly what this crazy billionaire had in mind. Benton checked his watch for a third time.

"So what happens in seven minutes," the Doctor finally asked. "Do you give me a physical; run a battery of tests; have me pee in a cup."

"Of course not Doctor, we don't have time for that. I have spent the last month setting up a distribution chain that will get this to the most amount of people possible," Benton said.

"Yes, but for a price."

"To answer your previous question Doctor, in approximately five minutes we will test the effectiveness of your antidote," Benton said.

"How exactly do you plan on doing that?" Dr. Sanderson asked.

The half-smile returned to Benton's face. He looked directly into the Doctor's eyes causing a shiver to travel the length of Dr. Sanderson's spine. He paused a moment and then looked over to the hospital bed.

The full horror of what Benton had in mind was now apparent. Dr. Sanderson felt his face blanch. His knees started to buckle and he felt faint.

"I ... won't ... do it," the Doctor managed to stammer.

"I don't see how you have much of a choice Doctor. Where is the courage of your convictions?" Benton replied.

"You can't be serious," the Doctor said with a little more confidence this time.

"Perhaps with the proper motivation, you'll see things differently," Benton said.

He took a few steps toward the door and knocked twice sharply on its surface. A few seconds later the door opened. Gunner walked into the room; his huge frame barely fitting through the opening. It was, however, the two people he brought into the room with him that shocked Dr. Sanderson.

He watched as his daughter Zoe somehow broke free of Gunner's grip and ran full speed toward him. Gunner quickly moved forward attempting to grab her when Benton raised his right hand signaling Gunner that is was alright to let her go.

"Dad!" she screamed.

The Doctor opened his arms as Zoe leapt into them. He wrapped them up pulling her tight against his chest. She began to sob tears of joy. As he held his daughter he looked over at his wife Holly, standing in Gunner's shadow. Her eyes were moist and her lower lip was quivering slightly.

Looking down his eyes met his daughter's.

"Are you ok?" he asked.

"Yea, we're … fine," she managed to get out.

"Where have you been?"

"We were in Vancouver when they started evacuating," she said. "They moved us to some military base near Brackendale. We were there for a week or so when they were about to move us again. Mr. Worthington showed up and told us he could bring us to you. So Mom and I left with him."

Dr. Sanderson glared at Benton and then looked at his wife. Benton turned around and nodded at Gunner who let Holly Sanderson go. She walked quickly toward him. A second later all three were in an embrace in the middle of examination room three.

"I love you," she whispered.

"I love you, too," he said.

"We've been staying at someplace in the mountains for the last three weeks," Zoe continued. "He kept saying you were on your way and would be here soon. Then two days ago he picked us up and said he was bringing us to you."

"Well, we're together now, that's all that matters," Dr. Sanderson said.

They embraced again as Dr. Sanderson gently kissed his wife for the first time in over two months.

"I'm all for reunions but I'm afraid time is up Doctor," Benton said tapping his wristwatch.

"Time's up?" Holly asked.

The Doctor looked at his wife and then his daughter but said nothing.

"What does he mean by that Dad?" Zoe asked.

Before he could respond Gunner had moved over to the Doctor and his family. He pulled Holly then Zoe away from him and moved them back near the door again. They both looked around the room desperately hoping someone would tell them what was going on.

"Now Doctor, are we in need of a new test subject? I have brought more pills with me if necessary," Benton said.

He knew now that Benton would make good on his threat. If he did not go through with it, he would make either his wife or daughter do it. He was out of options. Benton held all the cards. He had no other choice.

"Ok Benton, you win," Dr. Sanderson said.

"Let's hope you're as smart as we all think you are Doctor, then we all win," Benton said.

He motioned for the Doctor to move alongside the hospital bed where Number 5 had begun to stir.

"I have deprived him of sustenance the last couple of days," Benton said. "He should be ready to feed."

The Doctor looked down at his former patient. Number 5's head began to twitch as he sensed fresh meat. Dr. Sanderson rolled up his sleeve exposing his bare forearm.

He looked across the room at his wife and daughter. They stood frozen under the fluorescent lights of the examination room. He mouthed 'I love you' to both of them.

Number 5's head restraint was removed by Dr. Ehrlich. The zombie's head popped up searching for the human flesh it smelled. Dr. Sanderson moved his arm closer to Number 5's mouth. He had his hand clenched in a fist and his brow was wet with sweat.

The last thing Dr. Sanderson heard before Number 5's teeth ripped through his flesh was his wife's blood curdling scream.

Epilogue

Dr. Lemuel Sanderson was laying on his back on a hospital bed in the middle of a starch white room. His torso was tucked tightly under bright white bed sheets up to his armpits. His head propped up slightly by a large king size pillow. If his eyes had been open he would have been staring at a row of fluorescent lights.

Both of his arms were exposed. The left one hung limply at his side. The right one sported a field style dressing covering a large bite mark. Each was secured to the bed at the wrists with thick leather straps. His legs were also strapped to the bed beneath the sheets.

A small table sat next to the bed. On top of it was a pitcher of water and two glasses. Some of the Doctor's personal effects were on the table as well; his wallet, eyeglasses, and a pen. On the other side of the bed was a chrome plated medical drip holder which was currently empty.

A door at the far end of the room opened and Benton Worthington III entered. He carefully closed the door behind him and walked toward the bed, stopping just short he looked down at the Doctor. His head tilted slightly to the left, as he put his hands on the raised metal bar at the foot of the bed. He stood there for a minute or two before turning around.

He grabbed an aluminum chair from the corner and put it down a few feet from side of the bed. Lifting his pant leg slightly he sat on the chair and crossed his legs.

"Can you hear me Doctor?" he finally asked.

There was no response from the bed.

"If you can hear me please nod."

Nothing.

"It's been nearly two days. We need you to wake up Doctor," he said.

Still no response.

"It would appear that you hold one final card Lemuel. We can't proceed with the distribution of the antidote until we know for sure if it works."

Dr. Sanderson remained unresponsive. He had been this way since he had been strapped into the bed. Benton sat silently for another few minutes before getting back up and returning the chair to its proper place in the corner. He turned once more to face the bed.

"Dr. Ehrlich will be in shortly to check on you," Benton said.

Giving the Doctor one last chance to acknowledge his presence, Benton stood with his arms folded at the end of the bed. When it was clear Dr. Sanderson was still unconscious and not going to respond, he turned and opened the door. The sound of the heavy door closing behind him echoed loudly in the examination room. His footsteps could be heard fading down the hallway.

As quiet once again enveloped the room, Dr. Sanderson's left arm twitched almost unperceptively; and then it did so again. A second passed, then another. His right arm followed suit, twitching even more obviously than the left.

Then his eyes opened. They were bloodshot with the pupils rapidly darting back and forth. He stared up at the ceiling as he tried to lift his arms but was unable to because of the restraints.

The look on his face was one of confusion mixed with fear. He was not sure where he was or what had happened to him. The only thing he was sure of; the only thing he was certain of was that he was very, very … hungry.

Look for The Zombie Principle II

Coming soon

About the authors

David R Vosburgh

He was born in Upstate New York and attended SUNY Geneseo where he was class fencing champion. He figured it was a skill that might come in handy one day. He currently lives in Northeast Pennsylvania with his wife Karen and a seven year old yellow Lab named Lucy.

Daniel J Pinkham

He was born in Africa, raised in North Carolina, attended college in Ohio, and currently resides in Northern New Jersey with his wife Laura. You could say he gets around.

This is the first published work for both of them.

www.ingramcontent.com/pod-product-compliance
Lightning Source LLC
Chambersburg PA
CBHW070404260626
47161CB00001B/274